AF373953

# leaf well enough alone

KIRBY FALLS

BOOK 5

LANEY HATCHER

Developmental Edits: Nicole McCurdy, Emerald Edits
Editing: Ozor Edits
Proofreading: Judy's Proofreading
Cover Design: Blythe Russo

Print ISBN: 979-8-9959490-0-8

*For Jeff*

*If home is where the heart is, then you're mine.*

# *one*

IAN

"Are you alive down there?"

I blinked my eyes open at the sound of the woman's voice.

A pair of long, tanned, toned legs came into view. My gaze took a leisurely path up her body, past thin-fabric running shorts, a gray V-neck tee shirt, across collarbones shiny with perspiration, before finally reaching a pretty intimidating scowl beneath a maroon baseball cap.

I'd expected to see concern or confusion at the very least. But the face of the woman staring back at me was creased in disapproval, or maybe suspicion.

I suppose I was a stranger on land that wasn't mine. A weirdo laid out on the edge of a dirt path like a chalk-outlined victim on an episode of *Law and Order*. I'd played that role once, back when I was just getting started. Mob Corpse #3. It was surprisingly difficult to hold your breath.

I definitely wasn't holding it now as I struggled to inflate my lungs.

Admittedly, I probably looked a little suspect lying here in my incognito attire—workout clothes, sunglasses, and a Columbus Blue Jackets hat.

Maybe this grumpy mystery woman wasn't a hockey fan.

I worked to even out my breathing. I no longer sounded like someone with a severe peanut allergy suffering from asphyxiation.

"I'm okay," I barely wheezed, forcing my upper half into a sitting position.

The woman took a step back. Her stern expression went nowhere, and she radiated distrust.

"Did you hurt yourself somehow?" she asked, voice low and accusatory.

I smiled. I couldn't help it. She just sounded so damn ornery.

Squinting against the bright sunlight, I tried to make out her features, but the hat covered a lot. She'd clearly been out for a run, and from her lean, lithe form, *she* didn't have any trouble jogging across North Carolina farmland.

"I'm fine," I told her. "Not hurt. Just out of practice."

That was a lie. I'd never been good at cardio. I could bench-press over three hundred pounds and do squats and lunges all day long—or until my trainer, Maurice, told me to stop. I'd been blessed with a good metabolism, and I hated cardio, always had.

But there'd just been something invigorating about the sunshine on this mild November day. The rolling hills of the farm had called to me. As had the mountains in the distance. Apple trees formed orderly lines all over. Even though the leaves were brown and in the process of falling, the landscape was still undeniably beautiful. I knew a field of dead and dying wildflowers spread out behind me. I'd admired it briefly before I'd collapsed in a heap from exhaustion on the grass this side of the wooden fence.

We had sunshine and scenery in Los Angeles—an abundance of it. But we also had smog and people and traffic and paparazzi.

When I'd stepped out onto the porch of my rental house over at Grandpappy's this morning, I'd sucked in a lungful of crisp mountain air and been transported. Totally charmed. Utterly gobsmacked by the urge to touch some grass and maybe even an apple tree.

Exploring the property that would be our film set in a few weeks had sounded refreshing. Until I remembered that I wasn't a runner, and what the hell had I been thinking, going out for a leisurely jog without my phone?

Air was definitely easier to pull in now. There were no longer black spots crowding the edges of my vision.

Still, the woman stared like I was an inconvenient trespasser.

"Can I get you some help? Call someone for you?" She looked around like maybe my keeper was nearby, since I obviously couldn't take care of myself.

I noticed the end of a stubby brown ponytail sticking out of her ball cap before she turned back to me.

"I was just resting here a minute to catch my breath," I said simply, adding a smile to see if that might put her at ease. I had a great smile. It had been voted the best one in Hollywood by *People* magazine three months ago. Reigning male champ. No big.

But my "sparkling visage of masculine charm"—*People*'s words, not mine —didn't seem to have any effect. If anything, she scowled harder, creases bracketing a wide mouth with surprisingly full lips. This woman was all long, lean lines, but those lips were lush, maybe the softest thing about her.

Thank God I had sunglasses on, or she'd undoubtedly gut me with a Swiss Army knife for checking her out. These rural types were resourceful like that.

Despite the cover, I still made a point to look away from her mouth.

"What are you doing on my family's land?" she snapped, and I could tell now *that* was what she'd wanted to know all along. She'd determined that I wasn't dying or in need of medical attention before she brought it back around to what she'd intended to ask in the first place.

I wondered if she thought she'd actually pulled off the caring, concerned routine.

She hadn't. Nothing about this woman screamed warm or nurturing, not even when she'd asked after my health or offered to call someone for me.

That made me want to smile again, but I resisted. I had a feeling grumpy-pants wouldn't like it.

"Right." I nodded. "Your land. You must be one of the Judds."

I'd seen the sign by the road advertising wholesome family fun—apple orchards, pumpkin patches, farm stand, concessions, the whole small-town shtick for tourists. And I was sure there were production notes in an email somewhere telling me exactly whose property I was trespassing on.

"I am," she agreed, but didn't offer a first name.

Unbothered, I slowly gained my feet and held out a hand. "I'm Ian Wells. I'm with the film."

She hesitated just a beat before giving me a surprisingly firm shake. Her hand was a little rough. I could feel callouses sliding across my palm that made me even more curious about her.

Despite the handshake, she still didn't offer her name. "So you're with the production crew?"

"Yep." That was technically true. I'd had my agent negotiate for a producer credit—my first one.

"Then you should know that all the trailers and equipment aren't coming for another week."

I nodded again. I did know that. I'd come to town early to get settled with Georgie and my staff. Plus, I'd wanted a break before we hit the ground running. There was no easing into film production. Once we started, it would be full throttle until the holiday break, and then we'd be back at it again until early spring, when we'd return to LA to film a few scenes in the studio. The timeline took place over several months, and we'd need to shoot in various settings, but most of them centered on the mountains of Western North Carolina.

"I was just out for a little stroll to check things out." I busted out the "megawatt panty-dropper." Again, *People*'s words, not mine. "Sorry if I overstepped. I just love it out here, and I was eager to see your home."

Her eyes narrowed, and I played back my words.

"Not *your* home specifically. I just meant the land—Kirby Falls—in general." I laughed good-naturedly. She did not partake. "I wasn't planning on peeking in any windows or anything," I joked.

She stared at me like I was a lunatic. This wasn't going how I'd hoped. I hadn't met many locals yet, but I'd been looking forward to charming them.

This woman did not look particularly charmed. What happened to Southern hospitality? Her face looked like where it went to die.

Better to get out before she pulled her Swiss Army knife on me. "Welp, I'll let you get back to your run. Thanks for checking on me. I'll head back across the road now. I'm sure we'll be seeing each other arou—"

"Back across the road?" she interrupted. "You're not staying in town?"

I smiled again, pleased that she was finally curious about something. "Nope. I'm over at the Clarks'."

The woman put her hands on her hips and grumbled something under her breath. I only caught "Maggie," and "meddling," and "dammit."

Huh. I guess she knew Maggie, too.

I'd run into Maggie Clark, the head baker for Grandpappy's—the tourist farm across the highway from Judd's—on my second day in town. We'd struck up a friendly conversation, like normal people, after she'd asked for a selfie. Then, she'd ended up offering me a place to stay long-term for the shoot.

Initially, she'd mentioned a tiny house—a rental they had available—but with Georgie and the rest of my team, I'd needed a bigger space. So we'd worked it out that I'd rent her mother- and father-in-law's home. They were apparently snowbirds who lived in Florida and traveled in their RV the majority of the year.

After nearly a week in the big house by the pond, I was extremely grateful for that charming grocery store run-in with Ms. Maggie. It had been the perfect solution. My little entourage had plenty of space to spread out, and it had gotten us away from that bed-and-breakfast downtown with the nosy and handsy owner.

Serendipitous, if I did say so myself.

But judging by the muttered curse words from the woman in front of me, maybe it wasn't such good news.

"Is there a problem?" I asked politely.

"Nothing we didn't ask for," she grumbled.

She took another two steps back, and I could tell she was preparing to leave, feet bouncing slightly with unspent energy.

"I didn't catch your name," I said just as she started to move.

Her feet picked up the pace, and she took off down the dusty path in a relaxed, effortless stride that spoke of years of experience and athletic prowess.

I watched, trancelike, as her body moved. The calm, cool efficiency, something to behold. Her tiny ponytail was actually pretty cute as it bounced. And her backside was—

"I didn't throw it," she called over her shoulder.

I felt my lips part around my grin. "I'm Ian, by the way."

"So you said," she hollered without turning.

I chuckled and could not help the absolute delight I felt at being so instantly disliked and disregarded by this mystery woman. She'd been surly and unfriendly, and that only made me more determined to win her over.

It had been a minute since someone overlooked my fame and stardom. Then again, the hat and sunglasses did cover most of my face. And I'd introduced myself as Ian instead of the name everyone knew me by.

Dorian Masters was the action hero. Dorian Masters had the best smile in Hollywood. Dorian Masters was the man everyone wanted to know.

Ian Wells was just a kid from Ohio who'd made it to LA. In a place where personal training and modeling and waiting tables could land you a chance encounter, I'd been one of the lucky ones, in the end. I'd met my agent, gotten auditions, and after years of commercials, voiceovers, and even that one romance audiobook I'd narrated, I'd landed my big break.

Now I was a "fan favorite" with "staying power" in an industry that could change overnight. I knew celebrity status was an illusion. I was one bad decision or social media mishap away from being a has-been or a never-was. But right now, I was on top of the world.

And that farm girl with the great ass in running shorts and a ball cap hadn't given me the time of day.

My face could barely contain my award-winning grin.

"Nice to meet you!" I shouted at her rapidly retreating form.

She tossed up a hand that would have won an Academy Award for the most impatient and halfhearted farewell of all time.

This little town was getting more interesting by the second.

I stood there like an idiot, luxuriating in my own hubris and the midmorning sunshine, before I remembered I still had a one-mile trek back to the rental house.

"Shit," I huffed.

Then I reached down to touch my toes in an attempt to stretch and heard my spine crack in three places. Alright, never mind. I'd just walk it.

My sneakers scuffed along the dirt of the tractor path and dislodged tiny pebbles as I began the long trudge back to the main road.

I'd work up to running, I decided. Maybe I could even find a workout partner to teach me their ways. Someone with a penetrating stare and an uncompromising scowl.

And I knew just where to look.

## JOAN

There was a kid standing over my shoulder.

I wasn't sure when he'd arrived or how long he'd been there, but he stood quietly, about six feet away, watching as I worked on the conveyor belt.

The machinery had been acting up, sensitive to too much weight on the ramp. I'd been waiting for some downtime to take a look inside and tune up the conveyor that delivered the apples to the press. Today had been good enough.

It was early November. The u-pick apple season was over, and we had another week before the Christmas tree lot went up. So there was a bit of a lull in tourist traffic.

The kid shuffled more to the right to see around my elbow as I worked the crescent wrench around a stubborn bolt.

I hadn't been in the presence of many children, save for the ones who visited the orchard. Those interactions were often entertaining—you never knew what a kid was going to say—but they were typically fleeting. I remembered the locals and regulars who frequented my family's farm. Connie Hixson brought her granddaughter every year to pick apples the last weekend in September. I'd seen little Darla grow from a chubby-cheeked toddler to a surly preteen. There were a few others who'd crossed my path regularly, too. Amos Coates was a teenager who worked part-time at the orchard, and I liked him well enough.

But despite my inexperience with small children, even I could tell the kid lurking behind me was young. Not *too* young, though. He didn't need diapers or anything. But he probably shouldn't have been off on his own. He was, maybe, six or seven years old.

The bolt came loose so suddenly that it ricocheted out of the underbelly of the conveyor onto the dusty wooden planks beneath my feet. At the same time, the wrench slipped, causing my knuckle to bang painfully on the gears nearby.

I let out a sharp hiss rather than the curse word that had been ready under my tongue.

Instinctively, I clenched my fist, eyeing the bright crimson droplet welling on the knuckle of my right index finger.

The troublemaking bolt entered my periphery, held in a tiny, dirt-streaked palm like a silent offering. And maybe that's what it was about this kid . . . I'd never been around one so quiet. Kids at the orchard were always wild and rambunctious, dashing through rows of apple trees and tumbling across the giant bounce pillow, volume ranging from earsplitting to migraine-inducing.

"Thanks," I murmured, accepting the round piece of metal and placing it atop the unmoving belt.

"I can get a Band-Aid from my emergency kit, if you need one." The voice was high and sweet, but oddly solemn for someone so small.

I didn't know what an emergency kit was, but I was pretty sure adults were supposed to be the responsible ones. It had been a long time since anyone took care of me but me.

"Thanks," I repeated, finally turning to face the boy. He was staring at the little bead of red on my finger, face pale. "But I can get a bandage from the office." Instead of doing that, I pulled a handkerchief out of my pants pocket and wiped the blood away.

He blinked big blue eyes as if coming back to himself from a short mental vacation. Then he focused on my face.

"What's your name?" I asked.

"George," he replied, gaze flicking toward my injury briefly.

"I'm Joan," I offered.

George was motionless—another deviation from the children I typically saw. He wasn't fidgeting or squirming. He was as still as a little statue. Maybe it had been the blood that had him rooted in place. He was free from the spell now, and yet he still wasn't wiggling around.

He looked clean—for a kid—and healthy, a slight roundness in his face and limbs that I associated with youth and innocent indulgence. Regular desserts after dinner and snacks on demand. I wondered if George and his family had visited Knottsford Creamery downtown.

Speaking of family, my gaze strayed over the boy's head, beyond the shaded roof of the open-air Apple House, to the berry patches and fields in the distance. I didn't see any adults wandering around, looking for lost little boys.

"You're a farmer," he said suddenly, drawing my attention once more.

It wasn't a question, but I answered anyway. "I am. What are you?"

"An inconvenience," he muttered.

I frowned. "Did someone call you that?"

"Gloria," he replied offhandedly, with an accompanying eye roll that made him look like a tiny teenager.

I wondered if he even knew what the word meant. And why the hell someone had called a kid an inconvenience? *Christ.*

"Did you go to school to be a farmer?" George asked in his next breath.

"No, I didn't. I learned from my father and my grandfather. We're all farmers."

The boy seemed to chew that over as I wondered how I was going to find his parents and considered what I'd do if I found out his mother's name was Gloria.

"Do you think I could be a farmer?" The soft question drew me away from my fierce thoughts, a fictional argument already half formed in my mind with a hypothetical Gloria somewhere.

With slow movements, I shifted my body on the step stool to face the boy more fully. A serious question deserved serious consideration. I didn't really know how to talk to kids, but this was how I'd want somebody to talk to me.

I held his gaze. "Well, do you like being outside?"

George nodded eagerly.

"Even when it's rainy and muddy," I pressed.

He kept right on nodding.

"Do you like working with your hands? Getting a little dirty, if need be?"

The boy's eyes brightened, as if the idea that there could be a job where you were allowed to get dirty had never occurred to him, and he liked it. But he wasn't smiling. In fact, I hadn't seen a smile cross his stoic little face even once. But I hadn't smiled either, so who was I to judge?

"Then I think you'd make a mighty fine farmer," I told him.

In my limited experience with children, I assumed this pronouncement might get a grin out of him. Both kids and adults liked it when you said what they wanted to hear. It was a universal trait. And it was obvious, even to me—someone who was better with plants than I could ever be with people—that George wanted me to agree, to say he could be a farmer, too.

But the boy still didn't smile. He did something better. He straightened and took a deep breath, like confidence was filling him up from the inside. Then he nodded once. "Okay."

I waited, but he didn't say more. My eyes, again, drifted over his shoulder in an effort to locate his family. But before I could push to stand and get the search underway, George's watch beeped.

He sighed, eyes dropping to the little device on his wrist. I couldn't tell if it was a fancy watch that received text messages or just an alarm that had gone off. However, I did notice that he wasn't wearing one of the bounce pillow bracelets that acted like an entry ticket for the most popular children's attraction on the farm.

"Better go," he muttered, clearly reluctant.

Concern had me frowning. "Do you need help finding your parents?"

He shook his head, dark hair swinging into his blue eyes briefly before he shoved it away. "Nope. Bye, Joan. Have a nice day."

I stood as he trotted back out into the sunlight. He didn't circle back to the front of the Apple House, where most orchard visitors would be, gathered near the picnic tables, enjoying a freshly pressed cider or an apple hand pie. George didn't head in the direction of the giant bounce pillow either. He crossed the grass all the way to the tractor path that led to my parents' house.

I was willing to bet that if the little boy was walking that way, he was going to the rear of the property, where the trailers and production teams were setting up.

Sighing, I turned back to the conveyor belt.

He was probably with the movie people. It seemed about right that one of those Hollywood types would just let their child roam free, where he could get hurt or lost on someone else's land.

Still, I hesitated, half tempted to go after the quiet little boy and make sure he found his way back safely. But soon, he was out of sight, and I was still very much a stranger.

I could feel myself frowning at the thought of what was to come. For the majority of the next five months, there would be a film crew at the orchard. Well, parts of the orchard. There were limitations and boundaries, minimal as they were. But for the next few months, our land would host bigwigs from Hollywood as they filmed a major motion picture.

And wasn't that just dandy?

Apparently, some hotshot director had visited our orchard a few years ago. She'd become enamored with Kirby Falls and the surrounding area and had written a script set right here in Western North Carolina.

On that front, I couldn't really blame her. The land was beautiful, and our town was friendly—practically designed to lure in helpless leafers who sought out tourist activities and beautiful autumn foliage. I'd met more than a few new arrivals and retirees who'd settled here after a vacation or two.

But this was the first time a newcomer had brought their work with them.

Once the director, Della Stewart, had found someone willing to fund and produce her film, they'd approached us with an offer. It had been generous enough to seriously consider. In fact, it would allow my parents to retire a few years early. And it more than made up for the business we'd lose out on by only opening to the public two days a week instead of four.

On Monday through Friday, the production crew would have free rein of Judd's Family Orchard—except my parents' home, as well as my cabin on the opposite side of the property. We had a contract and everything. They wouldn't damage our crops or equipment or outbuildings, and they had to provide a shooting schedule in advance. There would be no impacting our weekend business or impeding upon our private spaces.

We had a film liaison who kept us apprised of any updates or pertinent information, but I was making Candace deal with all that. Quite frankly, I didn't want to see or manage any part of this. I needed to tend to my duties, keep my apple trees healthy, and protect our legacy from whatever hell we'd wrought by making a very lucrative deal with the devil.

But already the lines were getting blurred. First, there had been that production crew guy poking around the property a few days ago, and now I was somehow playing tour guide for one of their kids.

I shook my head, swiping at the blood on my knuckle one last time before getting back to work.

The following morning left me chilled as I jogged the familiar path between my small cabin and my parents' house. I generally ran every morning, then joined my dad for coffee before showering and changing to start my workday on the farm. My sister, Candace, jogged with me a few days a week for at least part of my run, but I knew she was busy this morning with wedding plans.

Candace ran our social media, public outreach, and education program. She scheduled events, gave presentations, and handled the tour groups. It was the perfect role for her since she was friendly and personable. Unlike me, Candace genuinely enjoyed working with the public. After returning to Kirby Falls two summers ago, she had decided to stay for good.

A big part of her decision to remain in our hometown was Mark Mercer, my longtime co-worker and friend. The two had fallen in love, and now Candace finally felt like she had a place where she belonged.

They were getting married next month, and I couldn't be happier for them. They made a good match—balanced each other out in a way I never would have expected. I could see how love and romance worked for some people, but I'd never experienced it personally.

I was glad my little sister was back, but our relationship was a work in progress. We had nine years separating us, and our personalities hadn't always meshed. Actually, that wasn't true. It was *my* personality that was the problem.

I was often too severe and exacting. The term "ballbuster" had been bandied about. I didn't care much about people pleasing, and I had no problem saying exactly what I meant. That didn't always make for good relationships or easy connections. I wasn't friendly, but I was trying where Candace was concerned. I hadn't always made her feel welcome here on the farm; however, I was working hard to correct that mistake.

She was my sister, and familial loyalty *was* in my wheelhouse. I would do anything for Candace—and Brady too. My siblings, my parents, and this farm were the most important things in the world to me. But I was the sort of person who didn't leave a lot of space for anything else. I had my priorities and my responsibilities, and if you weren't on the list, then my energy rarely extended far enough to reach you.

I had friends who'd mostly elbowed their way in as Candace's and Brady's spheres had grown to encompass significant others and their families. I was grateful for those relationships, too. People were patient with me. They accepted that I didn't talk much, and when I did, I wasn't subtle. They accepted me, full stop.

Maybe that's what friendship really was. When you stopped trying to find a place for someone in your life and just let them take up the space they occupied.

I breathed out a plume of warm air into the chilly expanse as I fought to clear my mind. Typically, I used my run as a time to reset and center myself, to focus on the day ahead. I was distracted, though. The farm had always been the one constant in my life, but so many things were changing.

While I still worked with Mercer and Brady and Candace and my parents most days, this next season would be a difficult adjustment. The whole movie thing was a disruption, and I wanted it to be over and done with.

Yes, I'd agreed to it when my family had put the decision to a vote months ago. But that didn't mean I had to like the interruption to my daily life, the noise, or the new people coming and going.

Speaking of new people coming my way. I squinted into the foggy November morning as a hulking form materialized. My brows pulled together in annoyance as the man smiled cheerfully and waved.

"Hello again," he called.

It was the lurker from the other day. Whatever-his-name-was with the stamina problem. He was wearing his sunglasses again, but he'd substituted the ball cap for a toboggan. The gray knitted fabric covered his ears and all of his dark hair.

I had every intention of running right by him, but he turned and fell into step next to me on the dirt path.

"Mind if I join you?" he asked. I could feel him watching me, even with the shades over his eyes.

I kept my gaze forward, but noted that he left a respectable distance between us, which I appreciated. "Would it matter if I said yes?"

He chuckled like I'd told a funny joke. "So, we're neighbors," he managed, clearly struggling for breath as he both ran and spoke. "Isn't that great? I just love small towns. Everyone is so friendly."

That earned him some side-eye. He was either oblivious or trying to get a reaction out of me. While the majority of Kirby Falls was mighty neighborly, no one had ever accused me of it.

I made a sound that was a cross between a hum and a grunt of agreement.

The stranger continued, undaunted by my lack of participation. "I love it out here. The mountains, the quiet. We don't have air like this in LA." As if to demonstrate or maybe to simply remain conscious, he struggled through a large inhale. "Makes me want to grow a beard."

My eyes slid in his direction again. *Be a shame to cover up that Dudley Do-Right jawline*, I thought to myself.

"I'm Ian, by the way," he panted happily, calling to mind an eager golden retriever puppy.

"So you keep reminding me."

I could feel the power of his grin directed toward the side of my face.

But I didn't owe this man anything, least of all my name. No matter what he said, we weren't neighbors. He was here temporarily, an inconvenience and a minor blip in my small-town life. Like he was trying on someone else's shoes and attempting to run a mile in them. Although if he struggled with small-town living as much as he was struggling through this morning's workout, he might be headed back to Hollywood sooner rather than later.

Seriously, what was this guy's deal? He was absurdly fit. Even I, a perpetually single woman who was uninterested in dating, could appreciate the wide assortment of muscles bulging beneath his workout pants and long-sleeved pullover. His biceps bunched, and his calves strained the seams of the fabric. He had to be at least six foot three and built like Superman.

I couldn't understand how a man with a body sculpted from hours upon hours in a fancy gym somewhere could be so bad at jogging down a dirt path.

"Do you run here every day, or are you just stalking me?" he asked suddenly.

I turned my head sharply to glare, but he was already smiling—or maybe he was still smiling. Did he ever turn that thing off?

"Not that I'm complaining," he added hurriedly, undeterred by my obvious annoyance. "I read a romance novel that started with well-meaning stalking. Lots of obsessive pining. I was into it."

I blinked, thinking my book club had read that one too, and I hadn't hated it.

"I'm not stalking you. I work here," I grumbled.

"Me too," he replied brightly. "We have so much in common."

"You work *nearby.* Temporarily. It's not the same."

"Ah." He sucked in another fast breath. "You're a stickler. I might have known."

I fought the urge to up my pace and leave this joker in the dust. Maybe that was why I wasn't intimidated by his size or presence. He was bigger and stronger, sure. But I could easily outrun him.

Instead of hightailing it out of there, I found myself saying, "You know, it might be easier to breathe if you weren't constantly talking."

As if on cue, his grin went supernova. Straight white teeth practically blinded me. "Sorry." He didn't sound sorry at all. "I like to yap. I am a certified yapper."

"Great," I replied flatly.

Ian chuckled again.

After a few blessed minutes of silence, the only sounds the scuff of our sneakers, morning birdcall, and his labored breathing, Ian spoke up. "I was actually wondering if you wouldn't mind having a running partner. I'd like to work some cardio into my routine while I'm here, and get better at this. You obviously know what you're doing. I'm a fast learner, and I can try to keep my yapping to a minimum."

"You want to run with me?"

"Well, sure," he said, like it was obvious.

But I wasn't getting it.

"Why?" I asked, incredulously. "You don't even know me."

"Not yet, at least."

I watched his face for a moment, trying to make sense of his request. A bead of sweat made its way down his temple and cheek before dripping off that blade of a jawline. This guy was young—had to be in his twenties. He was objectively attractive. Was he a serial killer? A cult leader? Or worse, trying to sell me supplements?

I didn't trust what I couldn't understand, and the motivations of this outsider were a total mystery to me.

"You training for a 5K or something?"

"Nah," he said, then quickly corrected, "I don't know, maybe? Y'all have a Turkey Trot? I could probably give that a try in a couple of weeks."

Kirby Falls did indeed have a Thanksgiving Day 5K. I didn't think you could claim small-town Hallmark status without one.

"You want me to train you for the Turkey Trot?" I sought to clarify.

"Yes, that would be great." Christ, he was still smiling. Did his cheek muscles ache? Mine did, just from looking at him.

Would he keep showing up to pester me if I didn't agree to this? I didn't have a problem telling someone to fuck off. But this guy seemed so earnest and friendly. It was a little like kicking a puppy, and I'd been pretty rude to him already.

I thought briefly about my vow to be more welcoming to Candace—to be better, in general. I didn't hate that this guy had a goal he was striving for. And as I listened to him wheeze and struggle, I realized I could actually help him. Running was something I enjoyed. I'd been doing it regularly since high school.

I sighed. "Fine. Two days a week."

"How about three? I'm in terrible shape."

My eyes dipped to his muscular chest, then down to where his black pullover hid a flat stomach that I'd bet my favorite forklift contained six-pack abs. When I wrangled control of my wayward gaze, I found Ian wearing an annoyingly pleased expression.

I rolled my eyes and faced forward once more. My parents' house was just coming into view. The white, two-story farmhouse emerged from the fog slowly, so familiar that my feet could find their way with my eyes closed.

"Fine," I repeated. "I'll meet you at the gate to the orchard in the morning. Six a.m. Don't be late."

"Bright and early. I can't wait."

I could see the light on in the kitchen and a dark shape moving in the window. I hoped it was my dad making coffee and not my mother being nosy.

"I'm going in to have some coffee. I'll see you tomorrow morning," I told him, still unsure why I'd agreed to run with him.

"Coffee?" he asked, completely out of breath now. "I happen to love coffee."

"Really?"

"Yeah." He brightened.

I almost felt sorry for him. *Almost.* "Well, Cubhouse Coffee on Main Street makes a mean latte. They probably even have matcha or oat milk—whatever you city folks are into. You should try it."

Then I accelerated to my normal speed and took off toward the back porch.

"I'll do that!" he called happily, just as the screen door snapped closed behind me.

I made sure to wipe the smile off my face before I entered the kitchen.

———

Ian was waiting for me the following morning just off the highway, next to the chain strung across the tourist entrance to the orchard.

I'd half expected him not to show, and felt slightly annoyed that I'd been proven wrong.

He was still sporting his sunglasses, even in the near darkness at 6:00 a.m. With the toboggan missing, his dark hair was on display, the glossy strands swooping back dramatically in an obviously expensive cut. Despite the threat to grow a beard, his jaw appeared freshly shaved.

I caught a whiff of something clean smelling as I approached, like expensive bodywash that reminded me of warm spice and spruce boughs at Christmastime.

"Good morning." He smiled in greeting.

"Mornin'," I offered warily.

All day yesterday, I'd wondered why I'd agreed to this and regretted my decision. In fact, I'd had half a mind to just not show up this morning. But that wasn't who I was. I couldn't purposely break my word and leave someone waiting. I didn't particularly care what this outsider thought of me, but I didn't want *anyone* thinking Joan Judd was unreliable. Apparently, being a pampered Californian didn't exclude him from that.

"We'll do a two-mile loop today. Nice and easy. Practice keeping your pace even with your breaths. You ready?"

He nodded. "Yes, ma'am."

True to his word, Ian kept his yapping to a minimum. It was only after we'd warmed up for about a quarter of a mile that I told him to stop swinging his arms so much and conserve his energy. He listened, and on we went.

I kept our pace slow. He could work on getting faster later, if he wanted. Our current goals were distance and improving his stamina.

Twenty-six minutes later, we returned to where we'd started. I planned on getting in another four miles after I got rid of my giant pine-scented burden.

"Now that you're warmed up," I told him, "sprint the length of the Clarks' driveway up to the General Store. Then take tomorrow off. I'll see you back here on Thursday. Same time."

"Sure. I can do that," he replied, but I'd already turned back down the path toward the orchard.

"Do I get to know your name yet?" he hollered. "What do I even call you?"

"'Hey, you' works just fine." Then I threw my hand up in farewell and used the next forty minutes to review my upcoming tasks for the day. More movie equipment had arrived in the south field, and I had pruning to do on the rows of Honeycrisps nearby. We'd be wrapping up the last of the pressing this season and freezing the remaining apples we'd managed to pick before the first frost.

Thursday morning's run with Ian went much the same. He didn't talk a lot, and for that I was grateful. He even managed to shave two minutes off his time. It wasn't uncomfortable to run with him, exactly, but I was aware of his big body next to mine. That evergreen scent lingered, and his steady footfalls didn't ever let me forget he was there.

But I still had that nagging feeling that I couldn't figure out his angle. The reason why he'd wanted to run with me hadn't revealed itself yet, so I was distrustful. I continued withholding my name, which at this point, was more of a game than a battle of wills.

Candace, Mercer, Brady, and I got the Christmas tree lot set up on Friday in time to welcome orchard visitors for the weekend. I briefly helped out in the refreshment stand selling hot chocolate and homemade marshmallows with my mother, but mostly, Mercer and I handled wrapping and hauling trees for locals and leafers to take home.

On Sunday, I ate dinner with my family, as usual. Brady's girlfriend and my friend, MacKenzie Clark, joined us, and Candace gave her the update on the movie. Filming was set to begin on Wednesday. I had the schedule and reminder in my email, and I knew which areas of the farm to avoid. There was plenty to keep me busy without running into the camera crew.

Everyone in town seemed pretty excited about the prospect of seeing a movie star. I'd heard reports in the Kirby Falls Facebook group about a few sightings. I'd helped some clueless assistant with his flat tire the other day on my way into town. He'd been nice enough, I supposed.

But I just didn't see why all this mattered. I didn't have Mac's curiosity or wonder over the whole thing. Nor did I have Candace's optimistic certainty that a film set at our orchard would mean more tourists and increased sales in the coming months and years. My brother, Brady, was chomping at the bit to watch them film and meet the actors. I did not share his enthusiasm. I hadn't even asked Candace who was starring in the movie. I'd met the writer/director months ago when she'd set up a meeting to propose this whole ridiculous thing, but that was it.

I mostly felt out of sorts at how disordered everything was. I hated knowing there were places we couldn't tread on our own property. I'd never been very good at sharing. This was just one more example.

I kept my opinions to myself, however. There was no point in raining on anyone's parade or dimming local excitement. This was all temporary, and that was the comfort I would cling to.

Ian and I ran again on Monday morning. We made it three miles that day, and I'd rewarded him by answering his questions about some of my favorite restaurants in town. There was no way I was telling him about Mattie B's—our local watering hole. He and the rest of the production crew could keep visiting the leafer bar on Main Street called Magnolia. But I did clue him in to Apollo's and the best pizza in the county.

"Does your name start with a C?" he'd asked after we'd finished up, sweat still glistening on his muscular neck.

I'd blinked and cleared my throat, tugging my foot up into a standing quad stretch. "Nope, not a C."

"What about an L? Are you a Laura?"

I'd straightened and shook my head, amusement tugging at the corners of my lips. "Sorry, not a Laura. That's enough guesses for today."

His grin had said he didn't mind too much.

My amusement had faded by degrees. It had been over a week of this. Ian was still friendly and unfazed by my standoffishness. He listened when I offered advice about his form and technique. Occasionally, he asked questions, but he didn't press. I could feel his charm hovering beneath the surface, waiting to pounce, determined to win me over. But he kept it in check.

I hated that, for the most part, I was wondering why he was buttering me up, why he was trying so hard. Surely there were easier, friendlier marks out there. My theories ranged from him trying to get access to more land than what the film had negotiated to thinking I would be an easy lay for the duration of his time here.

I'd mostly crossed that last one off the list. The guy was a looker—even with his ever-present sunglasses and unrelenting smile. He could go down to Magnolia any night of the week and pick up a willing bedmate.

I, on the other hand, was more trouble than I was worth. Plus, I was pretty sure he was much younger than me. His hot body and youthful, action-hero profile suggested someone in their early to mid-twenties. I was thirty-six. Not dead yet, but not really someone he might go for.

My short brown hair was liberally shot through with gray, something I'd made my peace with a decade ago. And while I was in good shape, strong and healthy, my body was lean with few curves to speak of. I wasn't the sort of woman men went out of their way to land. I was too honest, too rough around the edges. This guy would get his feelings hurt without me even trying.

Maybe it was shitty to make so many assumptions about someone I barely knew. Something in my gut told me that this man was not trying to get into my pants.

But that didn't mean I wasn't suspicious. He definitely had to want *something* to keep coming out here in the cold, at the ass crack of dawn, while I tortured him with cardio and refused to tell him my name.

I felt like I was waiting for the other shoe to drop. Or maybe, all of my wonderings wouldn't matter in the end. Because a big part of me thought all of this would be over just as suddenly as it had started. People weren't typically very dependable. Perhaps Ian would simply stop showing up. Maybe the mornings would get too cold and his bed a bit too warm. It wasn't uncommon for folks to slack off on their goals. There was every chance that this man would turn out to be exactly what I thought he was . . . a disappointment waiting to happen.

I could admit, at least to myself, that it might be nice to be proven wrong for once.

## JOAN

On Tuesday morning, I skipped my solo run in order to drop off some donations to the local food bank. I planned on stopping by the farmhouse afterward and having breakfast with my parents and whoever else was hanging around the kitchen—usually my little brother acting malnourished and begging for scraps.

I'd just returned to the farm when a sound had me freezing with my body halfway out of the cab of the orchard's small box truck.

It was nearly 9:00 a.m., and the autumn sunshine had burned away the morning dew. It was unseasonably warm, and the projected high for the day would likely see me in short sleeves by lunchtime.

No matter the season, when the weather was mild, it wasn't unusual to hear my family on the screened porch at the back of the house. My mother spent a lot of time out there reading and sewing, and I knew that Candace liked to join her for tea in the cozy space.

So it wasn't the sound of their familiar laughter drifting through the mountain air that stopped me in my tracks; it was the stranger in their midst.

Before I'd even rounded the corner of the house, I could hear Ian's voice, bright with amusement as my family joined in.

What was that guy doing here? Was this part of his plan—to worm his way in? Nowhere in that thick stack of contract papers had it said that we'd be interacting with any of the production crew. That was what the liaison was for. What was Ian's angle, and why was I so irritated that he'd gone behind my back to seek out my family?

In my frustration, I opened the ancient screened door harder than I should have. The hinges snapped in protest, and every head in the room turned to look at my sudden appearance.

"Joan!" my mom called in happy surprise. "Come meet Dorian Masters."

My eyes found my mother. Amy Judd was bright-eyed on the wicker love seat next to my sister, Candace. When the two were together, all their similarities stood out like a genetics billboard, loudly proclaiming them mother and daughter. I looked more like my dad, and Brady was a pretty even mix of both our parents.

Speaking of my brother, his tall frame was sprawled in a chair he'd clearly dragged out from the kitchen because the only other available seat was occupied by Dorian Masters.

Dorian Masters . . . who sounded like Ian Wells.

Ian, the lurker. Ian, the sunglasses-wearing out-of-towner. Ian, the guy who could barely run a mile without wheezing like an asthma sufferer. Ian, the man who'd told me he was part of the production crew.

"Amy, please call me Ian."

My attention sharpened on the figure folded into my mother's wicker rocking chair. The piece of furniture gave an admirable attempt to contain his godlike proportions, but the man hardly fit. He overwhelmed the delicate seat, and I found myself pleased that this scheming interloper might be uncomfortable.

He'd had a haircut since our run yesterday; the dark mop was now buzzed down close to his head. And the ever-present sunglasses were nowhere to be found. Dorian gazed at me with blue eyes so crystal clear that there might have been a sandy ocean floor somewhere at the bottom. His eyelashes were ridiculous. Long and luxurious as a Maybelline ad. Jesus, did he curl them?

The man was, of course, smiling. I could feel my molars grinding together as a result.

"Joanie, aren't you going to say hi?" my sister said, nervous laughter accompanying her question.

"Oh, we've met," Dorian—Ian, whoever he was—offered. "Well, half met. Joan, is it?" He raised one dark, perfectly-sculpted-by-some-high-priced-salon eyebrow. "Nice to officially make your acquaintance."

"Yeah. Same." My voice was gravelly, the words might as well have been made of dust, dry as they were.

I could feel my pulse hammering in my neck. Anger kept my body rigid and immobile by the entrance to the screened porch. I knew my family was staring at me. But the weight of their attention and confusion wasn't nearly enough to distract me from the trespasser.

Looking at Dorian, sitting happily in my childhood home, I could see it now, what I'd missed before. The shiny veneer, the polished edge. How he was perfectly content to have all the attention focused on him. The way he absorbed it like a sponge. This man looked like he was a guest on a late-night show, entertaining his audience and adoring fans.

His face, his body, his easy manner. It all practically shouted, "I'm not from around here," or "I have people for that."

The Ian I'd met on the tractor path last week had been playing a role, giving me a private performance, and I felt like an idiot. But I'd had an inkling, hadn't I? Something had been off. I'd known there was an angle, a grift . . . *something.*

And here it was. Dorian Masters—international celebrity, beloved movie star, and fame incarnate—was having a little fun with the backwoods locals. I could see from the grin that he'd been doing a little teasing at my expense. Maybe he'd thought he was funny. Maybe he'd just been bored.

But I was nobody's fool.

While I didn't keep up with Hollywood gossip the way my mother and siblings did, I wasn't living under a rock. I knew who Dorian Masters was. For the last two or three years, it had been nearly impossible to wait in the checkout line at the Winn-Dixie without seeing his beaming face plastered all over the magazines.

What movies he made. His workout routine. Who he was dating. It was all up for public consumption. I'd never really paid it much mind.

That was, until earlier this year, when he'd starred in a film adaptation of one of my favorite books. We'd gone to see it—my friends and I—as a book club. Fully prepared to be disappointed, we'd bought popcorn and candy and sat in a dark theater. I'd been ready to pick apart the dialogue, to scowl at the important moments that wouldn't get translated to the big screen. And most of all, I'd been eager for the chance to judge Dorian Masters in his role as my favorite romance hero of all time.

But during his first scene, Dorian—clad in tight breeches and an intricately knotted cravat—had done nothing but capture my attention.

Our row of whispering, popcorn-chewing women had gone completely silent as we'd watched Dorian Masters blow every single expectation out of the water. The adaptation had been skillful and bold. It had stuck closely to the original novel and honored it in such a way that we'd all sat in stunned silence afterward before bursting into a flurry of excited chatter.

I hadn't squealed with delight. I hadn't turned to Candace in her oversized theater recliner at my side. I'd simply sat and stared at the rolling credits and felt an odd sense of disappointment. I'd been ready to hate the film and nitpick the performance. This young, hotshot actor with his annoyingly good looks and bright white teeth had taken my expectations and dismantled them.

It seemed that was one thing Dorian Masters had in common with whatever version was sitting on my mother's screened porch.

I wasn't about to mention my book club or the film now, though. I sure as shit wasn't going to admit having seen it or the DVD on my shelf at home that featured heavily in the rotation.

So it was, of course, then that my sister opened her big mouth and said, "Joan loved *The Tycoon and the Aristocrat*."

I resisted the urge to sigh.

"Is that right?" Ian looked absolutely delighted, like someone had dropped a present in his lap. A big one.

I was going to strangle my sister.

Candace met my gaze, and whatever she saw there had her eyes widening as she abruptly backtracked. "Well, we all loved it. Our book club went to see it. You know, I was probably thinking of my friend Bonnie. Joan doesn't even watch movies. Or read books." Candace winced. "I mean, she *can* read, of course. She's just so busy. With the farm."

Ian, unfazed by my sister's nervous word vomit, smiled graciously. "So your book club enjoyed the film?"

Candace nodded eagerly, obviously grateful for the lifeline he'd just hit her over the head with. "The whole adaptation was amazing. The music, the costumes." She paused to smile dreamily. "And, of course, the performances. It was a book lover's dream."

"High praise," Ian said softly to Candace, but he was looking right at me. "I'm so happy you enjoyed it."

"I'm going to grab some coffee," I said flatly, with all the grace of an air horn, effectively ending the conversation and glowing five-star review.

Candace glanced at me worriedly.

I shot her a look that was probably none too friendly before making my way inside the house.

Conversation resumed beyond the sliding glass doors. I could hear the muffled sounds of Brady's and Ian's voices coming from outside my parents' warm kitchen.

A moment later, as I was adding a splash of milk to my mug, the door slid open quietly, and Candace stepped inside.

She winced and joined me at the breakfast nook.

"I'm sorry I told him you loved the movie," Candace offered, fidgeting with the shiny engagement ring on her finger. "I just thought you'd be excited."

"What about me makes you think I'd be excited to meet some actor from Hollywood?"

"That's fair," she admitted. "You didn't even want to know who was starring in the movie being filmed at our farm."

That was true. Every time Candace had brought it up, I'd told her it didn't matter. This whole thing was an inconvenience, and I didn't want to know any more about it than I needed to in order to get by. It was just five months out of our lives, and then everything could get back to normal.

Furthermore, I wasn't interested in famous people or their lives. That was like caring about what aliens did on their home planet. It was so foreign to me, I couldn't even bring myself to consider it. So, no. I hadn't wanted to gossip with my mom and sister about the bright, shiny movie people taking over our property and our town.

"But if not excited," she wondered, "I thought you'd at least be polite to your favorite movie star."

"He is not my favorite movie star," I argued. "I don't *have* a favorite movie star. That would be like picking a favorite zoo animal."

"Most people have a favorite zoo animal, Joanie. And a favorite movie star."

Frowning, I said, "Well, I don't."

"Okay. But why were you looking at Dorian Masters like he started a forest fire or bad-mouthed Dolly Parton? What could have possibly happened in the few days he's been here?"

"It hasn't been just a few days. He's been here over a week. He showed up before the trailers and the equipment. I ran into him on the tractor path, and we've been . . ."

Candace leaned forward in her seat, interest doubling at my hesitation.

I swallowed uncomfortably and finished, "Running together in the mornings."

My sister's lips parted in surprise.

"I didn't know who he was," I said, slightly defensively, before she could ask. "He wore sunglasses and hats. Introduced himself as Ian. Said he was part of the production crew. I didn't recognize him."

"Oh."

We were both quiet for several moments. I could still hear Ian and Brady bro-ing it up out there.

As irritated as I was at the surprise of it all, I was equally annoyed with myself for failing to recognize Ian for who he was.

"You think he was messing with you. Hiding who he was intentionally?" Candace asked quietly.

"Maybe. I don't know. Feels that way though."

I was both relieved and disappointed that my sister's thoughts had traveled the same suspicious path as my own. I felt a little less cynical, but once again annoyed that I'd been taken in—no matter how briefly—with Ian's good-ol'-boy routine.

I sighed, angry with myself for ignoring my instincts. The irritation I felt right now was my own damn fault. Actually, no. Ian probably did this on purpose. Probably as payback for me not telling him my name.

After a while, I'd enjoyed keeping it from him, teasing him with it. It had been dumb to act that way   juvenile even, like I was some silly teenager, flirting.

I paused with my mug halfway to my mouth as a thought struck. Had all of it been a lie? Even the running?

Sure, we hadn't formed some everlasting bond by exercising together a few times. But he'd been friendly and eager to learn. Or so I'd thought. Jesus, was he faking being terrible at cardio?

I considered that and then shook it off. While he'd improved over the last week, he was still struggling. He'd never be able to maintain my normal pace or distance, not without a lot of training. I didn't think he could fake his ragged gasping or visible relief when we reached a stopping point.

Although my suspicious mind whispered something I'd never admit out loud: He *was* a damn good actor.

"Maybe you should talk to him," Candace offered, tucking a long strand of brown hair behind one ear. "He's been nothing but polite. He helped Mom fill the birdfeeders this morning. That's how they met. He was jogging and rushed over to hold the giant bag of seed for her. Then Mom invited him in for coffee. I got here just in time to watch him agree to be a groomsman in Brady and Mac's future wedding and Mom's spades partner for card night over at Lonely Mountain Winery."

"Jesus," I groaned.

But something about my sister's words made me want to believe Ian wasn't some attention-seeking manipulator. It had been nice of him to hurry over and help my mother. And part of me liked that he'd been practicing and making an effort to run on his own today.

"Obviously, I don't know him," Candace began gently. "But he seems so nice and friendly. Genuine, even. Anyone else would have been dying to get away at the first opportunity. But he's been out there for nearly two hours chatting. He's had three coffee refills, multiple slices of Brady's banana bread, and he was devastated that he missed meeting Dad."

My doubts didn't go away entirely, because why would someone want to hang out with a random family they didn't even know? Did the mega star need attention that badly that he'd let small-town strangers fawn all over him in exchange for some admittedly delicious banana bread?

"Maybe I'll give him a chance to explain," I agreed reluctantly. I could feel the tightness in my forehead, the way my brows were drawn together in a scowl, so I worked to soften them before I glanced up at Candace.

She beamed, and I felt like I'd said the right thing, given the correct answer on a test, or proven I was more human than robot, for once.

"But not today," I added. "I'll see him tomorrow for our workout."

Her smile dimmed, but she nodded. "Are you going to be weird around him now?"

"Weird?"

"Yeah. Nervous because you know he's a big movie star."

I snorted a laugh. Sure, I'd watched Ian on the big screen, but I'd also watched him pant like an old Labrador when I'd made him sprint up the hill near the pond.

"No, Candace. He's just a person. He puts his sneakers on one shoe at a time."

She smiled and shook her head. "Actually, he probably has someone who does that for him."

I grinned. "Yeah, I bet some poor assistant has to sort all his M&M's out by color."

Candace chuckled. "And then feed them to him so he doesn't get chocolate fingers."

Laughing, I agreed, "You're probably right."

It was good to keep things in perspective, to remind myself just who Ian was. My sister and I were poking fun right now, but the life of Dorian Masters was undoubtedly very different than our own. Maybe he didn't have a designated candy sorter, but he likely led a life of wealth and privilege. He wasn't better than me or anyone in this town, but he would be getting a lot of attention from the people who lived here. People who hero-worshipped celebrities, who thought they were something special.

I needed to remind myself that Ian was only a person. The man from my favorite movie was just a man on a screen. And before that, a character on the page. This changed nothing.

And like I'd said, it would all be over in five months. The movie would wrap, and the trailers would roll out of town. Dorian would go back to his penthouse or beach house or wherever he lived. And I would get back to my regularly scheduled programming.

Nothing about this situation was worth getting all bent out of shape over.

"Where's Mercer?" I asked my sister. If there was one other person who'd be just as unaffected by Dorian Masters's charm, it was Mark Mercer. There was no way he'd be outside swooning over the movie star the way my brother was right this very moment.

"Out in the Dandee Reds, pruning."

I finished the last of my coffee. "Great. I'll grab my gear and join him."

"See you for lunch?" Candace asked. "Becca's bringing chicken salad."

I didn't stop to think about how coming back to the Apple House in a few hours would be a waste of time, or how I'd rather grab a protein bar and work through lunch. I didn't pause to consider if I would be a third or fourth or fifth wheel, depending on who else would be attending. I just nodded as I stood to wash my mug and said, "Yeah, that sounds good."

My sister smiled, and I felt like I'd, once again, provided the right answer . . . the one a good sister would give. If it made her happy, I'd agree to chicken salad around a picnic table whenever she wanted. That was compromise. That was maintaining a relationship.

On my way to the sink, I peeked out onto the screened porch. Ian was facing away, but I could see the way his head was thrown back in laughter over something my brother had said. His massive shoulders shook, the muscles visible beneath his pullover.

Swallowing hard, I looked away, right into the grinning face of my mother. She gave me a little wink.

I waved, ignoring the heat climbing my cheeks, and threw a thumb over my shoulder, indicating I was taking off.

After all, I had work to do. I couldn't just sit around all day, waiting for someone to sort my yellow M&M's and then feed them to me.

IAN

"Hey, Georgie. What would you like for breakfast?"

My nephew regarded me, but didn't speak.

"Do you want pancakes? Maybe some cereal?" I opened the fridge and peered inside. "There's probably some eggs and bacon in here, but if not, I can have Sophia or Darren run to the store."

"I don't eat animals," he said softly.

I glanced over my shoulder. "Since when?"

"Since I was six."

Frowning, I shut the refrigerator door. My nephew had been a vegetarian for nearly a year? Had I really not realized that? Granted, we'd been busy getting acclimated to one another for the last eight months, and Georgie had been a little reserved with me, but I couldn't imagine missing something so important.

When my older sister, Dawn, passed away a year ago after a car accident, Georgie had gone to live with my parents. But it hadn't taken long for them to contact me about taking over their grandson's care. There were several factors, namely my parents' advanced age, but they feared they wouldn't be able to give Georgie the sort of life he deserved.

My sister and I hadn't been very close. A fourteen-year age gap made things difficult even before I'd put physical distance between us and moved to LA at eighteen. Dawn had had her life, and I'd had mine. And the sad truth was, we'd never bothered to make space for one another. I had a lot of regrets, but not making an effort with my only sibling was something that would haunt me for the rest of my life.

"You had chicken nuggets three nights ago, little dude," Sophia called, sweeping into the kitchen out of nowhere, long, dark hair trailing in her wake. Sophia was a combination live-in nanny and tutor, and she handled child care and education for my nephew like a pro. Maybe it was her youthfulness and age—early twenties—or her laid-back, free-spirited approachability, but Georgie adored her.

We'd tried a private school back in LA, but that hadn't gone very well. Georgie was . . . mature for his age in a lot of ways. Very smart, but also a bit behind socially. Kids could be cruel, and I wasn't subjecting him to that. Plus, I traveled a lot and didn't want him to grow up in a boarding school somewhere. I'd rather he stay with me, with his family.

This would be my first time having Georgie on set, and Sophia had been on board with joining us in North Carolina for filming. She planned to head back to California for a few days around the holidays, but otherwise, she was taking point on all things Georgie for the time being.

I had production and planning meetings today, as well as a final table read before shooting began in a few days. But I'd wanted to make sure I saw Georgie this morning before I left for work.

"Well, I don't eat animals anymore," my nephew informed us.

Sophia shot me a knowing grin. "I'll handle breakfast, Ian. I know you have a busy morning."

She knew because my assistant, Eddie J, had emailed out my weekly schedule to all members of my team. He might not be physically present here in Kirby Falls, but Eddie J was still frighteningly capable of running my life from his couch in Silver Lake, California.

Aside from Eddie J, the team included my agent, Jocelyn; Georgie's nanny, Sophia; my longtime bodyguard, Darren; my manager, Gloria; and

Baxter, the on-site production assistant specific for this film. They were the people who kept me organized and focused, or tried to, at least.

It had taken some time, but Georgie was finally a little more comfortable with me. Prior to my sister's death, I'd only seen the kid twice. I was sure, to him, coming to live with me had been like getting shipped off to a stranger.

Not that living with my parents had been much better for him. Newel and Ellen Wells were good people, and they meant well. They just didn't have a lot of patience for children. They'd been in their mid-forties when I came along, a surprise baby who grew into a hyperactive, mischievous kid.

As a child, I hadn't understood that my parents had already raised the kid they'd planned for. They'd scrapbooked milestones and planned Disney vacations. They'd made Halloween costumes and attended parent-teacher conferences. I'd been a wrench in their retirement plans.

My parents loved me, but they didn't have a lot of energy for another kid. Starting over again with a newborn had been a struggle. Plus, I'd been a handful as a child and adolescent. I'd tried out for school plays and helped out behind the scenes of local productions. They didn't understand why I wanted to be a performer or why I was so loud or up so late. Or a hundred other things that made up this person they'd been saddled with.

I'd been safe and warm and fed, which was a lot more than some kids could say, but my childhood had been lonely and devoid of a family who really understood and accepted me.

There was a thin line between well-meaning and someone who thought they knew best. My parents typically overshot the former and ended up firmly in the latter.

Dawn had been the overachiever, the valedictorian, the responsible adult they could be proud of. Even when she'd decided to go the nontraditional route in her thirties and had a baby on her own, they'd never been happier.

Now, at over seventy, my parents didn't have the capacity to raise Georgie, starting all over once again. It wasn't their fault that their grandson was a painful reminder of the daughter they'd lost. None of this was fair. But I couldn't make them see that Georgie was a beautiful part of Dawn, one that they should be grateful for.

As frustrating as the situation was, I understood and wanted to help. I would do everything I could to make sure my nephew felt supported in the things he loved—in the person he'd become.

Georgie was a good kid—a great kid—and he deserved better than a part-time uncle to stand in for an amazing mother who'd been taken too soon. But I was doing my best, and that had to count for something.

I wanted my nephew to have a support system he could rely on. It was about more than ensuring he was safe and warm and fed. I needed Georgie to know that he could always count on me.

Adjusting to life with a small child hadn't been easy, but the love and protectiveness had been there from the beginning. The desire to do right by Georgie had me rethinking the future of Dorian Masters and re-evaluating all aspects of my life. Did I really want my nephew growing up in Hollywood? I wasn't sure how to rectify the public demands of my career with my need to maintain a safe environment for Georgie. But it was something I was actively trying to figure out.

"Thanks for managing breakfast, Soph," I told the young woman.

She nodded, dark eyes patient and understanding. "No problem, boss."

I stepped around the kitchen island to where Georgie sat on a high-backed leather stool. He was missing a sock and still had pillow creases on his cheek.

"You have a good day, buddy. Listen to Miss Sophia and remember to stay close to the house. You scared us the other day when you wandered off."

Georgie's little brows furrowed. "You said I could see the apple trees, Uncle Ian."

I ruffled his hair. "I know. But I meant the ones on *this* farm. Crossing the highway on your own is very dangerous."

He appeared betrayed that I could find him so incapable. "I looked *both* ways."

Sophia snickered from behind me, where she was digging around in the pantry. Georgie was big on following the rules, but he was also a proponent of technicalities. He was a very literal kid. You had to spell things out for him explicitly.

"I'm sure you did. But it's still dangerous. Plus, they have bears here. So stay close, yeah?"

"Okay, Uncle Ian."

"Thanks, Georgie." I smiled and gave him a big hug. He was stiff in my arms and gave my back an awkward pat.

Ah, well. We were getting there.

The production meeting was being held downtown at the Sterling House Bed and Breakfast, where our director, Della Stewart, was staying for the duration of filming. They had a meeting room on-site, and the owner had put out a nice breakfast spread and fresh coffee for everyone.

If you ignored all the lace doilies, inspirational wall art, and the handsiness of Vera Sterling, then maybe this little trip into town wouldn't be so bad.

Della and a few of the other assistant directors and executive producers had yet to arrive to the meeting. I was pouring coffee into a mug as several of the production assistants argued on the other side of the room.

"Can't we just talk to Candace about clearing that part of the property to build the set? It's only ten yards more than what we originally discussed," Zoe whined.

Archer snorted. "You know Joan handles equipment, and we're going to need her help to do it."

"But Candace is the nice one," Zoe argued. She was only a few years younger than me, but she sounded like a teenager being forced to clean her room.

"Too bad," Angelo added before taking a big bite of cheese Danish and licking his thumb. "Someone is going to have to bring it up with Joan."

The production assistants all groaned in unison, and I resisted the urge to laugh out loud. Of course, the woman had a reputation on set, and we hadn't even started filming.

"Let's just draw straws," Zoe suggested.

I drifted closer and took a seat next to Baxter, content to watch this play out. My assistant was quiet, reviewing something on the tablet in front of him.

"I'm not doing it," Archer argued. "I refuse."

We all turned to look at the young man. His cheeks were flushed beneath his pale complexion. He looked very uncomfortable.

"Joan made him cry," Angelo offered up with a devious grin.

"I did not cry," Archer squawked, the tips of his ears violently red.

"Yes, you did." Angelo rolled his eyes. "And you deserved it."

"What happened?" Zoe asked, breathless.

"Archer made some sexist remark about women farmers," Angelo explained. "Joan overheard and laid into him. Not only that, but she treated him to a lengthy lecture about power dynamics and stereotypes in traditional occupations as well as modern farming families. Pretty sure Archer donated to about six different charities to atone for his ignorance. So, yeah, I imagine he *really* doesn't want to be the one to touch base with Joan about a favor."

"What about Della's new intern?" Archer asked hopefully.

"I'll do it," Baxter said suddenly, from my side.

Everyone swiveled to peer at him.

He turned his focus away from his tablet and pushed his glasses up his nose, obviously uncomfortable with the attention. "She, uh, helped me change a tire on my rental car the other day. I'm pretty sure she thinks I'm an idiot, but I don't mind asking her about clearing the land next to the lavender field for the set."

"She changed your tire for you?" I asked.

Baxter glanced at me briefly before nodding. "Yeah. She actually had me help her so I could learn how to do it. I think I could probably manage it without a YouTube video now."

I brought my coffee mug to my lips to hide my smile.

In truth, I didn't know Joan all that well, but that sounded like something she'd do. Confidently delivering lengthy lectures to ignorant outsiders, but wholly incapable of ignoring someone in need, even a stranger. That was how I'd wormed my way into her good graces, after all.

Thinking back to the other morning on the Judds' screened porch, I wasn't so sure that grace extended to me anymore. Joan had obviously been surprised by my presence there. She'd been closed off, and if I wasn't mistaken, she'd looked almost betrayed. The chill around her had rivaled the brisk mountain air. She hadn't been happy to find me with her family members, and I could understand that. I was protective about Georgie, after all.

But it truly hadn't been my intent to impose upon her family. I simply hadn't been able to ignore Amy Judd struggling under the weight of that birdseed. And then it had seemed impolite to turn down her invitation to coffee. Before I'd known it, I'd been surrounded by Judds and genuinely enjoying myself.

Joan's appearance had changed the atmosphere. Her reaction to my presence hinted at more than passing annoyance, though. And, maybe, I'd handled it all wrong, being flippant and teasing.

I supposed I'd find out just how upset she truly was tomorrow morning. We had another run scheduled.

I imagined she'd still show. That was another tidbit I'd picked up about Joan in our brief acquaintance—she was dependable, true to her word. Even something as casual as an early-morning workout wouldn't be overlooked by the stalwart farmer.

I was relatively certain that if Joan Judd made plans, she stuck to them. I liked that about her. She was an original—a grumpy, principled original.

And I couldn't wait to see what happened tomorrow. If she was actually angry over the way I'd butted in with her family, I'd let her take it out on me. Part of me thought I wouldn't even mind a little punishment.

Archer frowned at Baxter. "Why didn't you just call roadside assistance?"

"I was going to," Baxter admitted. "But she just pulled over and started getting tools out. I wasn't going to argue with her. You've met her."

I just barely caught my snort of amusement before it could escape.

Archer opened his mouth to say something else, but Della swept into the room with the aforementioned intern trailing her, stacks of papers in hand.

"Good morning, friends," Della called, in that way of hers. She was the writer and director for the film, and she wasn't like anyone I'd ever worked with before. After meeting her and auditioning, I'd known immediately that I wanted to be a part of this project. It was outside my typical roles, but I could tell it would challenge me in new and exciting ways. Plus, I liked her vision for the project.

Della was probably in her early fifties, and she didn't seem to have any fucks left to give, but I meant that as a compliment. She wasn't concerned with how everyone else did things. Della wanted them done right, and to her, the right way was with kindness, respect, and consideration.

She was insightful and observant—probably a hippie in another timeline, judging by her long, graying braid and the colorful skirts she always wore.

Whenever we spoke, she always asked about my well-being. Most people said, "How are you?" But Della Stewart asked if all was well within your heart.

She was weird, in a good way. I liked her a lot, and I was excited to make this movie together.

"Is everyone feeling nourished?" Della asked, gesturing to the pastries and coffee.

A chorus of yesses rose from the assistants and the other producers who'd filtered in.

Our director grinned and clapped her hands together. "Fantastic. Then let's begin."

I'd bet myself five bucks that Joan would be waiting by the entrance to the orchard the following morning, and, wouldn't you know it? I was right.

Being able to accurately predict her motivations didn't really account for the relief I felt at seeing her, though. It couldn't explain the sudden nervous energy buzzing beneath my skin either.

"Good morning," I called as I approached.

She eyed me cautiously, like I might pull a knife on her instead of the smile I was already wearing. I hadn't bothered with the sunglasses, but the beanie was necessary. It was cold this morning on my newly shorn scalp.

Joan grunted something that might have been "good morning" or "hurry up." I wasn't sure, but when she took off down the gravel path at a brisk jog, I moved to keep up.

I fought against my amusement at her surliness as I forced myself to focus on my pace and breathing—like she'd taught me. But after a few minutes, I couldn't take it.

"So, you're mad," I said.

"Nope." The word snapped out and landed with the subtlety of a live grenade.

Well, at least she wasn't starstruck. If she'd shown up this morning a staring, bumbling mess, I would have been strangely disappointed. Impressing Joan was one thing; using my celebrity status to do it was something else entirely.

But we were obviously back to square one. She was spooked and distrustful, and had basically reverted to ignoring me and giving one-word responses.

"Listen, I won't bother your family anymore if you don't want me to," I told her, not entirely sure how to keep that promise should she demand it. I already had plans with her brother and a group chat with her mom and dad.

"None of my business," Joan bit out before picking up the pace a little. It was her way of shutting me up. If I couldn't breathe, then I couldn't yap.

Unfortunately, I was persistent, often to my own detriment. Who needed oxygen anyway?

"You seem like a private person, and I get that. I really do," I said, panting a little. Okay, a lot. "But we're neighbors for the time being and I don't mean any harm. I want to be on good terms with you and your family. Friends, you know?"

She didn't answer.

"So how long do you think you'll be mad at me? You're not breaking up Team Turkey Trot, are you? Because I already registered us, and I think we can easily place in our age groups."

Joan cut me a look sharp enough to impale before facing forward and rolling her eyes.

That was progress.

I needed to get this next part out. There was a hill coming up, and I'd be fighting for my life just to make it to the top. "Feel free to punish me for encroaching on your home life. You can make me do sprints after our run, or, hey, you could spank me, if you wanted."

She stopped so abruptly that I nearly stumbled before turning to face her.

Joan's glare was worse than incendiary; it was stone-cold.

I raised my hands in surrender. "You're right. That was inappropriate."

"Do you think this is funny?" she gritted out.

"No?" I replied warily. It was clear from her tone that the question had been rhetorical.

"All some big joke? Tricking me into thinking you were just some *regular guy*?"

"Oh, that." I chuckled. "I mean, yeah. It's a little funny. No one actually thinks that you can hide Superman with a pair of Clark Kent glasses, but it actually happened. You didn't recognize me with my sunglasses on." I laughed again, but Joan didn't.

"You cut your hair," she accused.

"Superman uses gel, and Clark is all disheveled, but same difference."

"I'm *not* an idiot," she said, and I sobered immediately.

"I never said you were," I replied slowly.

"Well, you must have assumed it when you pulled a fast one on me." Her blue eyes were angry—legitimately furious.

Confusion had me shaking my head. I fought to catch my breath. "Hold on a sec. I think—"

But she didn't let me finish. "And you're different when you're—you're—"

"When I'm what?" I wondered, genuinely curious.

"Performing." She practically spat the word. "Putting on a big act, making my mother laugh, charming the pants off my siblings. Acting like you're chummy with the country mice."

I frowned, feeling suddenly cold, and not from the sweat drying on my skin. "Is that what you think? That I was . . . acting?"

"I don't know," she admitted. "One minute I thought you were a cameraman or—or a lighting specialist, or one of the guys with the big sticks with the microphones on the end."

"Boom operator," I supplied automatically, wincing as I realized I wasn't helping.

Joan glared and put her hands on her hips. "I thought you were a normal guy who was bad at cardio and needed a running partner. Then I get ambushed in my own home. And I felt so st—" She cut herself off, but I heard what she hadn't said, loud and clear.

*Stupid.* I'd made her feel stupid, and she was angry at herself for trusting me.

Throat dry, I swallowed uncomfortably. A painful combination of guilt and awkwardness tightened my chest. "I'm sorry I didn't tell you who I was, right off the bat. That was wrong of me. There was honestly no premeditation on my part."

"Wasn't there? Were you, maybe, having a little fun with the locals? Playing games to amuse yourself?"

I shook my head. Part of me *had* really liked the fact that Joan didn't know who I was. I'd wanted to be Ian Wells a little longer. But I'd never meant to deceive or hurt her. And I hated that she'd assumed I'd do something like that.

"No," I insisted, taking a step closer. "I apologize for making you feel that way. It was not my intent to be malicious or withholding. At first, it was nice to just be Ian—that's my real name, by the way—just a guy who sucked at running. Then you wouldn't tell me your name, and it was fun. Like we had an inside joke. I got to be myself without any expectation. I thought, maybe, you didn't know who I was. Believe it or not, I'm not some egotistical asshole who assumes everyone knows the great Dorian Masters."

Joan snorted an incredulous laugh, but her eyes had gone from hard blue daggers to something a little softer—possibly butter knives. Still sharp enough to carve out my heart, though, if she put time and energy into it. But something about her expression made me think she was actually hearing me.

"I never meant to make you feel like I was teasing you or enjoying myself at your expense," I explained. "You've been kind." Her look was disbelieving, so I amended, "Kind of tolerant of me."

One side of her mouth quirked, like she was fighting a smile.

I didn't let the sight affect me, though, and continued earnestly, "And your family was very welcoming. I wasn't pretending anything, with any of you."

Joan let out a breath—part aggrieved, part resigned. She moved to gather her chin-length hair into a short ponytail, but the black hair band snapped away in the process.

I leaned down to pick it up off the ground.

"Well, don't expect any special treatment," she said, already pulling a different elastic from her wrist. She wound it around the brown strands that were shot through with gray.

I knew from my conversation with her family the other morning that Joan was thirty-six—young to be going gray. And knowing what little I did about her, I could easily see her being the sort of person who didn't give a fuck if her hair was gray or brown or polka dot. Of course, she wouldn't dye it regularly or care what people thought about her age or her looks. But it suited her. All her features, from her sharp cheekbones to her lithe, strong body to her brilliant blue eyes, were striking. Her hair was just another memorable piece of her. Something that set her apart, made her who she was.

She ignored the hair tie I held out to her and skewered me with a severe frown. "Just because you're some big movie star, doesn't mean you're better than anyone else. Your wants and desires aren't any more important than mine. And all that fame won't change the fact that I don't plan on going easy on you. If you still want to get in shape for your run—"

"I do," I rushed out eagerly—embarrassingly so. Truth be told, I was relieved she was still giving me the time of day. Once I realized how truly angry she'd been—how much I'd hurt her with my carelessness—I'd fully expected her to write me off as more trouble than I was worth. I couldn't pinpoint why that made me feel so awful. Like, if Joan Judd thought I was an insignificant waste of space, then maybe I really was.

"Then you're going to have to work," she said finally. She'd missed a piece of hair, and it clung to the side of her long, graceful neck. I told myself not to stare at her smooth skin. "I'm not some fancy personal trainer out in Hollywood."

I slipped the hair band she wouldn't take into my pocket. It was all stretched out anyway, with part of the white elastic showing beneath the black fabric. "I would never dream of comparing you to Maurice."

She shook her head, but reached her arms up to stretch, like maybe she wasn't done with our workout yet. "See, I knew you had people for that." She said *people* like they were the worst, most ridiculous thing she could think of. Someone who wore berets or didn't return shopping carts to the corral or was Creed's biggest fan.

"I actually think you'd love Maurice. He takes great pleasure in kicking my ass."

Her brows went high, obviously impressed. I guess the thought of me in pain was doing it for her. "Oh yeah?"

I nodded eagerly, playing it up a little for her benefit. "Definitely. I've been doing virtual workouts with him since I've been in North Carolina, but I'm going to meet your brother and someone named Abby at the gym tomorrow morning."

Joan shook out her arms. "Jesus. So it begins."

"So what begins?"

She motioned for me to follow her, then resumed her jog. "Your indoctrination into this town. Before you know it, you'll even be in the fucking Facebook group, arguing with the lunatics who live here." Her words were a little harsh, but there was fondness in her tone, a softness around her mouth, like maybe they *were* lunatics, but they were *her* lunatics.

"There's a Kirby Falls Facebook group?" I pulled out my phone. "I want in. Send me an invite."

She rolled her eyes once more, but she kept our pace slow and steady as we made our way up the hill where the Cosmic Crisps grew.

It felt like a gift.

From someone who didn't hand them out very often.

JOAN

Filming started this week.

There was more traffic on the highway, new people crowded around brewery tables in the evenings, and if I listened hard from the fields, I could hear people shouting orders and equipment moving around.

Ian's schedule was now unpredictable. Some days he had early call times, so he joined me for runs when he was able. I made sure to keep my route the same in case he needed to find me. It was easy enough to manage, on my part. But it felt like a concession, a little like weakness where he was concerned.

My little visitor returned two days ago to watch me work on the tractor. George stayed for forty minutes and only asked two questions, but he watched and listened as I showed him what I was doing to the engine. I managed to confirm that he was in town with the movie people and was seven years old.

Similar to the first time I'd seen him, his watch buzzed after a while, and he told me to have a nice day before hurrying off in the direction of the set.

Now, he was standing on the step stool to my right, watching me prune some of the early varieties.

"How old is that tree?" George asked as he squinted into the early afternoon sunlight.

"Probably ten or twelve years old. I have records back in the office, but judging from the size, that's about right."

"Do the trees ever die?"

I glanced his way. His expression was a little more intense than the question warranted. I wondered for the umpteenth time what this kid's life was like and what had molded him into the quiet, thoughtful, curious boy at my side.

"Sometimes," I explained. "But that's why I'm pruning. When apple season is over, we try to keep the trees healthy and watch for any disease while they're dormant. But after a while, the older trees produce less and less fruit. So we rotate them out every five to ten years and plant saplings in their place."

"Oh."

I moved to the next tree, and George carefully shifted the step stool over. His watch buzzed for the second time in the last few minutes, but he ignored it.

"Do you need to go?"

He sighed. "Probably."

"Are you going to get in trouble?"

His brows furrowed. He looked deeply offended. "Of course not."

"So your mom doesn't mind you running off and hanging out in the fields?" I kept my tone casual. He usually clammed up when I asked about his parents.

George shook his head. His dark hair flopped into his eyes, and he pushed it back. "Oh, I made you something."

From the ground, beside the step stool, he produced a lunchbox he'd dropped there earlier. It was old-fashioned and metal with hinged latches. There was a race car on the front, but the paint was faded, and I couldn't read the number on the hood.

Then George's hand was in front of my face, dangling a bracelet. It was a circle of stretchy elastic with black-and-white letters and green, yellow, and red beads, like something a kid would make. Like a kid *had* made, apparently. For me.

I held the bracelet in the palm of my hand and flipped the round bubble letters until they were all lying flat. *Apple Lady*, it read.

Smiling, I met George's gaze. "You made this for me?"

"Yep," he replied easily, the *p* popping.

My smile widened as a strange, warm weight settled in my chest. *Apple Lady*. That might have been the nicest thing any kid had ever called me. His surprise was baffling, but also touching.

George was a mystery. And I still worried about him running all over the place by himself, but he was a sweet kid. Curious and smart, with amazing comedic timing. And I knew I was only seeing a small portion of who he was, but so far, he'd been very unexpected.

Most kids were silly and loud. Candace had been, when she was little. I could remember being fifteen or sixteen, and Candace wanting me to play circus or watch her dance and sing. But I'd been too old or uninterested in the games my baby sister had wanted to play, so I'd usually ignored her or foisted her off on Brady, who was only three years her senior. It was probably why we hadn't been close as kids.

I'd just never been the sort of person—even as a child—who wanted all the attention, who acted silly in order to get it. I'd been more like George. A little too serious. More introspective. It was like I could see the gears turning in his mind.

But I got the impression that George hadn't always been so solemn. That perhaps something had caused him to be more mindful and adult, still innocent but less childlike. Maybe it was having an absent parent who didn't care where he ran off to. I didn't know.

But I did wonder.

His watch picked that moment to buzz again.

George ignored it and sat down on the step stool to get his lunchbox back in order.

"Is that your kit? What did you call it?"

"My emergency kit," he replied without looking up.

Crouching down, I asked, "What's in it?"

He held out things as he explained, "Band-Aids, ChapStick, a compass, binoculars, two granola bars, a pencil, a ruler, dental floss, matches, chewing gum, a flashlight, a whistle, and a drawing pad."

I watched quietly as the boy carefully rearranged each item so it fit neatly into the metal box. And I wondered why a kid would have all that. Why would he be planning for emergencies?

Before I could figure out a way to ask, an engine sounded in the distance. As it grew closer, George and I both turned to see Ian on a baby-blue side-by-side driving down the tractor path before stopping beside us.

George sighed, latching the closure on the lunchbox.

He stood as Ian climbed out of the vehicle and said, "Georgie, can you please get in? It's time to go back to set. Miss Sophia has been looking all over for you. You didn't answer your watch. That's why we got it for you, bud."

"Well, she didn't look here, or she would have found me," the boy said. But instead of protesting, he walked right over to the side-by-side and climbed up.

What was going on? Was George Ian's son?

Rising to my feet, I tried to catch Ian's eye, but he wouldn't look at me. I'd never seen him like this—jaw tight, shoulders tense, and so closed off he may as well have had a sign swinging from his chest warning people away. For the first time in weeks, the man wasn't smiling.

Just before he slid behind the wheel, Ian's eyes—cagey and dark—met mine. He nodded stiffly and said, "Joan," before making a U-turn and heading back the way he'd come.

George raised a tiny hand and waved goodbye, and like an idiot, I stood there and waved back, the little beads on my wrist clicking together as I moved.

———

"So, he just took off with the kid and didn't say anything?" Mac, Brady's girlfriend, asked.

I nodded and grabbed another broccoli floret from the tray.

"He didn't explain?" Mac's sister, Bonnie, wondered.

"Nope," I replied. "He left without a word."

"That's so strange," Candace said as she chewed absently on a cheese straw.

We were gathered around the central island in Will and Becca's kitchen. Becca was hosting book club, like she did most months, at the Clark homestead halfway up the mountainside.

It was a small group this month, just me, Candace, Mac, Bonnie, and Becca.

Becca had started the book club after moving to Kirby Falls last year. She'd been visiting on an extended working vacation and happened to meet Will Clark, and fell in love. She'd shifted her life from Michigan to North Carolina and hadn't looked back. The town loved her, and she was a genuinely nice person. She'd been good for Will, too. Since we were neighbors, I'd known the Clarks most of my life. With both of our families being in the apple business, our circles overlapped quite a bit.

"Can you imagine? Dorian Masters, a single father," Bonnie said dreamily, like the prospect of having a child made the movie star even more desirable.

"Maybe the mother is an actress," Candace offered.

"Maybe she died tragically, and Dorian is just doing his best to keep it all together," Mac said dramatically.

I rolled my eyes. "Yeah, maybe Ian saved George from a burning building along with two dozen kittens. Y'all have been reading too many romance novels."

Mac booed and threw a cube of cheese at me. I caught it and popped it into my mouth.

"And he never mentioned having a kid?" Candace asked at the same moment Becca said, "What do you mean 'Ian'?"

My chewing slowed as I realized what I'd inadvertently admitted. I swallowed the glob of cheddar, and all eyes turned toward me, the romance-addicted book junkies suddenly very curious.

"Why would he have mentioned anything to you, Joanie?" Mac said, gaze narrowing. "Are y'all friends?"

Candace made a whoops face and put another cheese straw in her mouth.

Sighing, I reminded myself that these were my friends. My closest friends. And they didn't mean any harm. They were just nosy. And Ian wasn't simply some goofy, smiling bozo to them. He was Dorian Masters, international celebrity and mega movie star. They'd been buzzing with questions about the production as soon as Candace had told them about it at our previous book club meeting.

"We've been running together," I admitted, and then reached for more broccoli like it was no big deal. It wasn't a big deal, but I knew they wouldn't see it that way.

Rapid-fire questions exploded from Bonnie, Mac, and Becca. Candace shoveled more cheese straws into her big mouth.

I held up a hand, and they quieted immediately. "We met when he first came to town, by chance. He was roaming around the property, checking out where they'd be filming. I didn't recognize him because he introduced himself as Ian—his real name—and he was wearing sunglasses and a hat."

Becca choked.

Mac groaned. "God, only you, Joan. He pulled a damn Clark Kent, and you fell for it."

I glared, feeling my cheeks heat. But she merely clapped her hands impatiently and gestured for me to keep going.

"Then I ran into him again," I explained. "And he asked if we could run together. So, we have been. A few days a week. I realized who he was"—Candace carefully avoided eye contact—"and that's it. The kid has been over a handful of times, too. I had no idea they were connected until Ian showed up and carted him off."

I thought about the way Ian had looked earlier that afternoon. The complete one-eighty from the cheerful, easygoing guy I'd gotten used to. When he'd driven over the hill and spotted George, the relief on his face had been obvious. Maybe I hadn't registered it at the time, but Ian had been scared—worried about the kid—possibly *his* kid.

Then after, still unsmiling, he'd avoided my gaze, unwilling to address the elephant in the apple orchard. And it hadn't been embarrassment at being found out. It had been something else. More than secretive. He'd looked at me like he didn't trust me.

I didn't know how I felt about that. I was private, too, so I understood. But the twinge of discomfort in my belly wasn't anything I could explain.

The women surrounding me looked thoughtful. Well, Becca looked entirely too pleased. Her blue eyes were bright and manic with the possibility of a love story unfolding right across the highway. She was so obvious, bless her heart. I didn't have it in me to tell her *that* was the last thing that would ever happen between Ian and me, for a variety of reasons.

"Are you going to see him again?" Bonnie asked.

"Are you going to talk to him about the kid?" Mac spoke over her sister.

"Are you going to ask him out?" Becca added, and we all turned to look at her.

"What?" she said. "You're all thinking it."

Candace choked on yet another cheese straw.

I slapped my sister on the back and ignored the hopeful blond romantic at the end of the island. "I don't know when I'll see him. His schedule is all over the place, but he usually joins me on my morning run, if he has the time. If he wants to tell me about George, then he can. It's none of my business."

Mac frowned. "Ugh, why do you have to respect people's boundaries and be such a shining example of maturity?"

"Well, I am the oldest person here."

She threw another cheese cube at me, and I caught it in my mouth, smiling obnoxiously as I chewed.

"I don't know how you Clarks didn't already know about Ian," I told Bonnie and Mac. "He's renting your grandparents' house for the duration of filming."

"What?" the sisters practically shouted in unison.

"Maggie didn't tell you? Junior and Nola are renting their house to Ian and his entourage."

Mac was already typing on her phone, grumbling, "What if I'd gone over there to pick up something out of storage or grab my favorite spatula?" Mac and Brady had been living together for a couple of months. It wasn't official or anything, but no one was surprised when all of Mac's stuff had ended up at my brother's apartment.

The phone buzzed in her hand a moment later.

"Grandma Nola said she signed an NDA, so she couldn't tell us," Mac announced, reading from her screen. Then she squawked in disbelief. "And she changed the locks, so I wouldn't have been able to get my spatula, even if I wanted it."

Bonnie rolled her eyes. "You can barely cook. You don't have a favorite spatula. Brady makes all of your meals."

"Well, I would have liked to have had the option," Mac complained indignantly. "I can't believe they rented the house out from under me."

Junior and Nola Clark were snowbirds who usually only came back to Kirby Falls for the holidays and the summer months.

The phone buzzed again, and Mac recited in an even monotone, "'Why do you care anyway, MacKenzie Eloise? You're living in sin with that sweet Brady Judd. LOL.'"

The rest of us laughed.

Mac glared down at her phone. "Who taught her LOL anyway?"

Suddenly, she straightened, her perfectly lined eyes going wide and her affront forgotten. "Do you think Dorian Masters is staying in my room? Sleeping in my bed?" She seemed giddy at the prospect.

I shook my head at the display. "He is just a person, Mac. Just an overgrown man-baby who is bad at running."

"But he's a famous man-baby," she argued. "How can you be so lah-de-dah about all this? You've seen his face on a movie screen. There are fan clubs dedicated to his abs. He has a damn action figure and a car endorsement, cologne ads, and billboards in Times Square. Everyone and their brother knows who he is, but you're acting like he's just some guy you ran into down at the feed store."

Candace finally stopped stress eating and came up for air. "I'm actually a little curious about this, too. Are you unimpressed with all celebrities, or is it just him specifically?"

I thought about it and decided on the easiest answer. "Once you've seen someone flat on their back after trying to run half a mile . . . I don't know, some of the shine wears off."

"Huh," Mac mused. "You really are a robot."

Everyone laughed—myself included—because it *was* funny and I knew Mac meant it lovingly. But the joke also rubbed up against something I'd known my whole life. I wasn't as emotional or affected as everyone else, and when I did happen to be those things, I rarely showed it, even to the people who mattered.

I got home just after 8:00 p.m. It was cold and rainy, and as I stepped out of my car, my eyes immediately went to the property neighboring mine.

A decade ago, when I'd had this house built on Judd land, I'd been surrounded by forest on all sides. It had been peaceful, the perfect private sanctuary in the place I adored.

But then a few years ago, Buck Adams's wife finally kicked his ass to the curb, and he'd purchased the acreage next to ours. A few buddies had helped him down enough trees so he could plop a mobile home in the overgrown field bordering my solitude.

There was a hundred yards between our back doors, but this time of year, the leaves were off the trees, so I could see and hear more than I ever wanted to out of that pain in the ass.

And right now, I could tell his truck wasn't in the place he normally parked it. Even though he'd lost his license back in the spring for driving drunk and nearly killing my brother in a car accident.

Anger had my hand tightening on the doorknob as my gaze searched Buck's backyard. There was the goat, huddled beside the trunk of the big pine tree it was tied to.

I'd checked the weather earlier in the day, so I knew it wouldn't get cold enough to snow, but that didn't stop the irritation I felt. The goat occasionally chewed through its rope and ended up on my porch. I usually took it back and tied it up without being noticed. Talking to Buck didn't help. He didn't care about the thing. He only kept it out of spite, knowing how desperately his ex-wife, Jolly, wanted it.

The yard was littered with car parts and trash piles that Buck burned on the weekends. There were aluminum beer cans and amber bottles scattered from the back steps to the sheds and outbuildings where he stored his crap —all sorts of things that the goat tried to eat because it didn't know any better.

The fact that the animal didn't have shelter or regular feed made me mad enough to insert myself and try talking some sense into the old man, but it didn't do a damn bit of good. He'd threatened to call the sheriff if he found me on his property.

Buck was content to make everyone around him miserable—just ask the man's ex-wife, who'd suffered through forty years of living with an abusive drunk.

Sighing in disgust, I shook my head and went inside.

It was quiet. I'd left a small lamp burning on the kitchen counter, and it welcomed me with a circle of warm light. I took off my boots and hung my jacket on the back of a barstool to dry.

My coffee maker was scheduled for 5:04 a.m. I added a new filter and fresh grounds, then placed my favorite mug on the counter for the morning.

I was a creature of habit. My daily routine often stayed the same, with a few exceptions. I had a book club meeting once per month, and bowling league every other Wednesday, with the occasional trivia night thrown in. There were Sunday dinners with my parents and siblings over at the farmhouse, and various town activities and festivals to plan for. But for the most part, I lived the same life day in and day out—the life of a farmer. I went to bed early and ran in the mornings. I spent time with my family and let my life revolve around the orchard. I liked it that way.

So it was easy enough to pinpoint why I was feeling restless. Things were changing, and the film was a major distraction. There were new people in my life for the first time in quite a while. But that didn't explain why I lay in bed that night, thinking about Dorian Masters and Ian Wells, one man but two very different people in my head.

I'd told my sister and my friends that he was just a man—a normal person like anyone else. But that wasn't quite the truth. The fame, the celebrity status, and the larger-than-life persona weren't what made me uneasy. It would have been better if that was all Ian was. Just a social media presence, a walking hashtag, the glossy cover of a magazine.

But he'd been different today. More than the charm and sass I'd come to expect. What was keeping me up was the look on his face that afternoon when he'd spotted George in the field with me. The relief, the distrust, the vulnerability that had made him more real than any side of him I'd seen before.

Annoyed with myself, I rolled over and closed my eyes, forcing away thoughts that didn't fucking matter. Ian and George were strangers— temporary blips in my life. There was no mystery here or a place for me in whatever drama was unfolding. It was time for me to get back to my comfortable, small-town existence.

I was still in a shitty mood the following morning.

Before heading out for my run, I'd dropped off some carrots for the goat, who'd munched happily despite the cold.

Not that I'd expected him, but Ian hadn't shown up at any point during my six-mile route. He was busy with work, which was fine. Nothing wrong with dedicating yourself to your job. I could understand that. I'd known since I was a teenager that I'd be the one taking over the fields once my parents retired from the orchard. It was what I wanted. Some people were just born with different expectations.

I understood better than most about having responsibilities and obligations.

*Obligations.*

The word triggered my memory of George calling himself an inconvenience. I wondered again who Gloria was and why she'd ever been allowed within ten feet of the boy.

Maybe that was part of my disappointment around not seeing Ian this morning. Maybe I was curious about George and his well-being, and Ian was the one person who could provide the answers to my questions. I wanted to know why George wasn't in school and why he was allowed to wander around alone to fend for himself.

My gaze strayed briefly to the *Apple Lady* bracelet on my wrist, barely visible beneath the sleeve of my shirt.

I was curious who the kid was to Ian and why their exchange had been so strange. I thought I'd been content to let all this go, but nearly twenty-four hours after they'd taken off in that side-by-side, here I was, chewing on the inside of my cheek and glaring at the tree I was pruning.

Mercer was working beside me, but he was giving me some space. Not that Mark Mercer was one for small talk—thank Christ—but I could tell he was being quiet for my benefit. Maybe my thoughts were so loud, he was hesitant to get involved.

We both heard the sound of a low engine and turned. It was the same blue recreational vehicle, but the driver was a man I'd never seen before.

He stopped on the muddy tractor path and unfolded his large form. The guy had to be six five and built like a defensive end. He wore a wool hat and a heavy winter coat, as if he wasn't used to the weather in the mountains in mid-November. His skin was a warm dark brown, and he looked to be in his early thirties.

Unsmiling, he approached with a big manila envelope in his hands. "Joan Judd?"

I took off my work gloves and held out a hand. "That's me."

The man paused briefly as if surprised, but slid his large hand into mine and gave it a firm squeeze. "I'm Darren. I work for Mr. Masters. This is for you."

I could feel Mercer at my side, a question in his gaze, but he remained silent.

Frowning, I accepted the folder, sliding out a thin stack of papers. I shuffled through the pile, registering words like *scope* and *parties*, and *confidential, terms,* and *exclusions.*

"Why would this be for me?" I asked slowly.

"I'm not at liberty to discuss private matters," Darren replied. "If you could just please sign. You'll be mailed a copy for your records."

I forced myself to focus and turned back to the first page. A nondisclosure agreement. This was an NDA from Dorian Masters.

"What is it that he doesn't want me to run my mouth about?" I asked Darren, some venom in my words.

The big man looked pained. His dark eyes glanced briefly to Mercer at my side. "I'm sorry, I'm not at liberty—"

"To discuss private matters," I finished for him. "Yeah, alright."

"I'm not supposed to leave until you sign it."

My thoughts raced, and for some reason, I could feel my heart pounding out an angry beat in my bloodstream. I'd been right yesterday. Ian *hadn't* trusted me. And the result was clenched in my fist, big words and phrases crinkled around my fingers.

Ian had been the one to insert himself into my life, my home, my routine. He'd misrepresented himself and withheld all sorts of information, apparently. But now *I* was the one who couldn't be trusted, while having my morals and honor questioned? By some stranger from Hollywood, on my own damn farm? When I hadn't done anything but give this man the benefit of the doubt—multiple times.

I glanced up at Darren, who looked ridiculously uncomfortable.

And then I started to read. I read the paperwork front to back. It took ten minutes of mind-numbing legalese and a headache at the base of my skull. After understanding less than a third of what I'd just consumed, I decided I'd gotten the gist and accepted a pen from Darren.

He took the packet with a quiet nod before climbing back in the side-by-side and returning the way he'd come.

"What was that all about?" Mercer asked as we both stood staring after Darren.

"I don't know. But I'm going to find out."

## JOAN

After sifting through my rarely used email inbox, I found the shooting schedule for the week from the film liaison and made my way clear across the farm.

It was just after 4:00 p.m. when I approached the forest bordering the lavender field. I nearly did a double take at the sight. They'd transformed the land into something unrecognizable. A place I'd lived and explored and managed my whole life was suddenly foreign amid tents and lights and equipment I couldn't name. It was as if I'd stepped into an alternate reality.

It was unsettling how easily they'd taken something foundational to me and rewritten it for their purposes.

There were more people than I ever would have imagined on a movie set. What did all these people do? Tables of food were set up near a trailer. Beneath a white tent, folks in puffy jackets gathered around a woman with a headset as they reviewed something on a tiny screen. There were monitors and cameras and even a person operating *something* on a track system, like a little train car.

I spotted Ian right away. He wasn't hard to find. He was big and imposing, drew attention like a lighthouse.

As I stomped my way in his direction, I shook off the unease of what I was walking into. Was it unfamiliar? Yes. Was I intimidated? Fuck, no.

I didn't care who these people were or the fact that I was about to cause a scene. I wanted answers from the man who'd been too cowardly to confront me himself. He'd sent someone else to do his dirty work.

A young man in an absurdly furry trapper hat was the first to see me as I approached the set. He seemed vaguely familiar, but I wasn't in the mood for chitchat.

The man squeaked and nearly fumbled his clipboard before hustling out of my way.

"I'd like a word," I said to Ian when I reached the people gathered in a semicircle around the tiny screen.

They all turned, startled, and the woman seated in the middle of them pulled her headset off and eyed me curiously. If she was mad that I'd interrupted, she didn't show it; she merely gave me her attention and a surprised smile.

I knew she was the director—Della . . . something. She'd come to the house and introduced herself to my family. I knew this whole project was her idea. I'd known it even before I'd met her because she'd called and talked to my parents prior to them signing on with the production company and allowing the film to use our land. Her enthusiasm and love for the area were what convinced my family to say yes.

I ignored the fact that I actually liked this woman. She was different from what I'd expected. I'd assumed a Hollywood director would be more businesslike and professional. Della wore rings on every finger and flowy skirts. She talked about the spirit of the land and was obsessed with my mother's zucchini bread. I didn't know her well, obviously, but there was no artifice I could detect in her dealings with us.

But I wasn't here for a social call.

Ian frowned for maybe the first time in his entire life and looked around the set. I followed his gaze to where Darren sat near the trailer. The large man's eyes widened when they landed on me, and he stood.

Ian shook his head, and Darren stayed where he was.

"Excuse us a moment," Ian said smoothly with an artificial smile.

I hated that I knew him well enough by now to know that it was fake.

The puffy-jacket-wearing strangers watched us with interest, but it was Della who spoke. "Of course, Dorian. We make time for what's important in life."

She sounded like a television psychic mixed with a Magic 8 Ball, and I fought the urge to roll my eyes.

Ian led me away from the tent, past the hungry gazes of curious onlookers, to the back side of a small trailer. Secluded as we were and facing away from the set, the landscape looked familiar in this direction. Trees I recognized and a field I'd plowed back in the spring. Something settled into place, and I was finally able to take a deep breath.

But then Ian stepped in front of me, stealing my focus. "What did you need to discuss?"

"What was that all about? An NDA, Ian? What the hell?"

Ian swallowed visibly. "It's for—it's to keep him safe."

"Who?" I practically demanded.

There was no one nearby, no one to overhear, but Ian still lowered his voice. "Georgie."

Confusion must have shown on my face, because he sighed and admitted, "No one knows about my nephew, Joan. And I want to keep it that way. Just because he's saddled with me doesn't mean he should be subjected to the media and rumors. I want him to have a normal life." Then he winced, as if remembering he was, in fact, a fucking movie star who wouldn't know normal even if it hit him in the face. "Well, as normal a life as possible."

I felt the tension in my jaw loosen. "He's your nephew?"

Ian hesitated. "My sister died last year."

"I'm sorry," I said immediately, reflexive but sincere.

"And my parents aren't able to care for a little kid. So he's living with me. And we're making it work, even with . . ." He gestured with his hands, as if he could encompass the film and the set and the giant spectacle that was his life. "Everything. I didn't know he was with you until yesterday. He's been running off, leaving the house to go explore. Scared the shit out of Sophia—his nanny—when he ignored her and didn't come back yesterday."

Well, I'd wondered where George was coming from. Now I knew. Sadness and empathy welled within me for the quiet little boy.

"At first, I thought his family was visiting the orchard," I confessed. "But with the timing of the crew's arrival, I assumed he'd wandered away from the set."

Ian nodded like that made sense. "But I can't have anyone finding out about him. We'll never have any peace. Paparazzi will hound us, and they'll do their research. They'll track down my parents, looking for a story. Georgie is too—I don't want to make things worse. He's been uprooted enough as it is. This lifestyle . . . it's not for children. I'm trying to figure things out, but I can't—I don't want—"

"Hey, it's okay," I said quickly, placing a staying hand on his forearm and regretting it immediately. I'd never seen Ian like this, so unsure, so unsteady. I'd only ever witnessed the carefree flirt, the confident movie star, the charming figurehead. This, I realized, was the uncle who was very afraid of fucking it all up. "I won't say anything. I signed the form. I won't tell anyone about George."

I would need to tell my sister and my friends to keep their traps shut about what I'd already divulged, but they would.

Ian nodded, relief plain on his face.

"What about the film people here?" I asked. "Or your friends back home? Do they know about your nephew?"

But Ian was already shaking his head. "Della knows. That's it. And my team, of course—my assistant, my manager. I don't have anyone back—" He cut himself off abruptly and looked away.

I felt surprise slice through me, enough that I shifted on my feet. Was Dorian Masters about to admit he didn't have friends to confide in about George? Surely, that couldn't be right.

"There's no one else," he finally acknowledged.

Again, the urge was there to offer a comforting touch, a squeeze of my hand, but I resisted, and I said, instead, "Okay. Alright."

I understood the reason for the secrecy. I thought of the solemn little boy who was thoughtful and inquisitive but rarely smiled, and my heart squeezed. The honor-questioning, righteous indignation I'd marched over here with had fizzled out, a firework flaring bright before burning down to nothing.

My fury may have faded, but I still had more questions. Where was George's father? Why were Ian's parents unable to care for their grandson? Why was he running away from his nanny?

At least her name wasn't Gloria.

But perhaps this wasn't the time or the place for my curiosity.

"Thank you," Ian finally said. "For keeping this secret. For protecting Georgie. I'll make sure he stays away from the orchard. We'll make new rules and Sophia can—"

"You don't need to do that," I interrupted. "Now that you know where he's sneaking off to, you don't have to be worried. And I don't mind having him around. He's quiet and smart. He's not any trouble."

Ian's face did something funny. He was an actor and could probably pluck out any reaction and emote the hell out of it. But whatever he was feeling right now, I didn't have a name for.

I watched his bright blue eyes move between mine. Then, after another hard swallow, he nodded. "Maybe he can visit you a couple of afternoons a week. After he finishes his schoolwork."

"That's fine. I'm always at the farm on Wednesdays and Thursdays. I can meet him after lunch at the gate, walk him across the highway, so you don't have to worry. Probably be better if he avoids the weekends while we're open. Too many people—strangers who might talk to him."

"You're sure this is okay?" Ian looked conflicted.

I didn't understand it myself. This man was a glorified stranger, and so was George, but I liked the kid. And now I knew he was more alone than I ever could have imagined. His little voice calling himself an inconvenience flitted through my head and tightened my chest.

He'd sought me out—the Apple Lady—and for some inexplicable reason, that made me feel good, almost proud. For a kid who'd gone through so much, this was an easy wish to grant.

"I could pay you to watch him," Ian offered when I'd been quiet too long.

My frown was immediate, and I snapped, "I don't need your money. Not everything needs to be bought and paid for like a transaction."

Ian still eyed me warily but nodded. "Sorry. I didn't mean anything—"

"It's fine." I forced myself to take a breath and ignore the reminder he'd lobbed between us. As if I could forget he was rich and famous and used to buying loyalty and trusting no one.

I had him put Sophia the nanny's number in my phone, in case I needed to contact her. Then Ian and I agreed that George would come visit tomorrow afternoon, if the boy wanted to. He gave me the okay to be honest with my family, should they run into George around the farm, saying he didn't want me to be forced to lie to the people I cared about.

"I'll let you get back to work," I said, once the logistics were covered, and turned to walk away.

"I have an early call time in the morning, so I won't be able to join you for a workout."

I glanced over my shoulder. "That's fine. I realize that you're busy."

"What about Saturday's run? Can I see you then?" He put his hands in the pockets of his puffy coat and then took them out again.

The nervous gesture nearly made me smile, but I ignored the urge and battled back the inclination to read too much into Ian's desire to still spend time with me. "Sure," I said, keeping my tone unaffected.

"Bye, Joan," Ian called once I'd resumed walking.

I threw a halfhearted wave up in the air.

The sound of Ian's laughter faded as I crossed the threshold back into reality. My boots carried me over dead grass and muddy ground. I put distance between me and the movie star. Away from cameras and strangers and a whole other world that I'd never understand.

<hr>

## Ian

I found a parking spot for my rental car off Main Street and located the address Brady Judd had texted me easily enough.

He sat at a high-top table for six and waved me over as soon as my feet touched the sticky wooden floors. Candace was seated across from him with her fiancé, Mercer—a quiet, bearded man I'd met briefly in the fields during one of my solo runs. I didn't recognize the fourth member of their party. She had long, dark hair, and I assumed she was Brady's girlfriend, MacKenzie, from the picture I'd seen on the lock screen of his cell phone.

My eyes took in the comfortable and worn interior of the bar as the jukebox played an old George Jones song. This felt like a hometown watering hole—looked like one, too. The warm overhead lights gleamed, reflecting off a wall of liquor bottles behind a long wooden bar top that made up the whole left side of the establishment. The opposite wall was lined with booths, and there were dartboards and pool tables in the back.

I imagined those were regulars sitting at the bar, watching a college basketball game, and sipping whatever was on draft. High-top tables were scattered throughout, but only about half were occupied. Not bad for a Wednesday night, though.

A red-haired server was delivering a pitcher of beer as I approached the table.

Brady grinned. "Hey, man. Glad you could make it."

"Thanks for inviting me," I said, meaning it, as I slid off my jacket and draped it across the back of the empty chair next to Mercer. Some of the other cast members were having a late dinner delivered to the Sterling

House, but I didn't really want to talk about the film or whatever projects everyone else was working on. It would be a lot of gossip and posturing, and I wasn't in the mood.

I felt a bit guilty about being out instead of with Georgie, but he'd been watching his nightly episode of *Wheel of Fortune* with Sophia and Darren. I'd been banned from joining them because I shouted out the answers. Georgie said he'd think about removing the ban on Friday.

"This is Mattie," Brady said, indicating the server. "She owns the place and puts up with us."

The redhead gave Brady an indulgent grin before turning to me. "Nice to meet you. I brought you a glass, but let me know if you'd rather have something else. I can make just about anything from the bar. Might not be what you're used to, though."

Mattie seemed friendly enough, but I could tell she expected me to have a special request, something high-maintenance from the visiting celebrity.

So I smiled and said, "Beer's fine."

"I can't believe you introduced him to Mattie before you introduced him to me," came a hissed whisper from the brunette next to Brady.

"She was standing right there," he replied. "Did you want me to just ignore her? That wouldn't be very neighborly."

I faced MacKenzie and extended my hand. "You must be Mac. I've heard all about you."

Her bright blue eyes shot to her boyfriend as she straightened abruptly.

Brady chuckled and held up his hands in surrender. "Good things, I swear."

My grin widened. "Can confirm."

Mac slipped her hand into mine and gave it a firm shake. "It's nice to meet you, Dorian."

"Please. Call me Ian."

I'd been to the gym a few times with Brady and his best friend, Abby, short for Abernathy—as in Cole Abernathy, local business owner and restaurateur. The two men were fun and easy to be around. Good guys. And Brady talked about Mac nonstop. So I knew she could be very opinionated and sassy, and she was also a fan of my *Inferno Man* action films.

I could see it now in Mac's expression and the sudden quiet bashfulness that had overcome her. She'd gone a little starstruck. Candace was that way a bit, too. But Brady had gotten over it completely, and the sociable guy just treated me as he would anyone else. Hence, the invitation to hang out tonight.

I was grateful for the way he'd welcomed me into his life.

I had a lot of things back in California—three overpriced cars I rarely got to drive, a beach house overlooking the ocean, gadgets and expensive toys —but friends weren't really among them.

My gaze drifted around the bar in case any more Judd siblings might be joining us. I made sure the disappointment didn't show on my face when I didn't spot a tall, striking woman with short hair and a grumpy scowl.

It might be kind of nice to see Joan outside of the farm. In a place like this, so comfortable and familiar, she was probably right at home.

Surprisingly enough, she'd seemed unfazed on set this afternoon. I supposed the land was still hers, so maybe all the equipment and people hadn't thrown her off. Or maybe she was good at hiding any perceived weakness. I didn't know her well enough to answer that yet.

Witnessing her righteous indignation after receiving the NDA had been surprising and confusing. I hadn't really expected her to care about Georgie, not enough to be curious about him, and definitely not enough to confront me over a standard legal document. But she'd stood her ground and questioned my motives, cared enough to demand that I explain myself.

I'd been worried about my nephew. He'd scared me by sneaking away in a wild and unknown place. But when I'd tracked his GPS location and found him with Joan, those fears had abated, morphing into the fear of discovery. The need for secrecy and privacy.

For some reason, after our discussion on set, I'd trusted Joan. I knew instinctively that she wouldn't threaten the peace I was fighting to establish with my nephew. Nothing about her screamed potential gossip willing to sell our story to the highest bidder. She didn't seem affected at all by my fame or celebrity status. It was refreshing, to be honest.

"So what do you think of Kirby Falls?" Mac asked, drawing me out of my thoughts.

"I love it," I told her honestly. "It's beautiful here. The mountains. The town. The people. I'm happy to spend the next few months getting to know the place."

"Where are you from originally?" Candace asked.

I reached for the pitcher and poured myself a beer. "Ohio."

"Ohio has mountains, right?" Mac wondered.

I smiled. "Not where I'm from. I've been in LA for the last decade, though. I'm used to sun and surf, and nothing like this."

"Well, hopefully it'll be a nice break for you," Mac told me. "We're happy to have you here." Then her eyes drifted over my shoulder, and she grinned mischievously. "Well, most of us anyway."

Before I could turn and investigate that ominous statement, the chair next to me pulled back, the legs scraping roughly across the worn floor.

I found an aggrieved Joan Judd shrugging out of her jacket.

A flicker of nervous excitement lit in my chest. I swallowed hard against the awareness Joan's sudden appearance had caused.

"You made it!" Candace called happily.

Expression unreadable, Joan eyed me before sitting down. "Yeah, who would have thought thirteen text messages in an hour, reminding me about drinks tonight, would do the job?"

"And yet you're still late," Brady teased.

"Because I didn't want to come," Joan replied matter-of-factly.

I laughed outright. At my side, Mercer snorted in amusement and shook his head. Joan shot glares at both of us.

"Well, too bad," Mac announced as she poured beer from the pitcher into a clean glass and passed it across the table to Joan. "There's no bowling league this week, but you're still obligated to hang out with us. You know you get rusty without human interaction every now and then."

I knew better than to laugh this time, and merely smiled into my beer and took a sip.

Tilting my head, I asked, "You're in a bowling league?"

Joan met my gaze, her own narrowed in suspicion, like I was making fun of her hobby.

It was awkward sitting next to her. I wanted to turn and face her fully, watch those blue eyes spark with irritation. Instead, we craned our necks toward one another, elbows bumping on the tabletop.

But, admittedly, it was nice having her so close, feeling her warmth at my side, smelling the trees and the grass and the sun on her skin. That flicker of nervous awareness in my chest became a sputtering flame.

Before Joan could answer, her sister piped up. "Bonnie signed us up for the bowling league—that's Mac's sister. We have a sisters' team, just the four of us. Joan's a really good bowler, always has been." Candace clammed up after that, like she'd said too much, and quickly reached for her own glass before taking a hasty swig.

"Joan's good at everything," Brady said easily. "Well, except answering her texts and getting places on time."

"That's not true," Mac argued, and honestly, it seemed like second nature with these two. "Joan is very punctual when she actually wants to go somewhere."

Joan ignored this and proceeded to down a quarter of her beer.

A twinge of disappointment had me shifting uncomfortably on the wooden stool. Had her friends and family told her I was coming tonight? Was that why she didn't want to be here?

"She's also really bad at dealing with Eloise Carter," Brady said helpfully, as if another of his sister's weaknesses had just occurred to him.

"Yeah, but who can blame her?" Mac agreed. "Eloise is a hateful old bat."

"Amen," Mercer rumbled quietly.

"Oh, I know. Joan has terrible handwriting," Brady remarked. "But I guess she makes up for that by being good at everything else."

"Smart, athletic, hell of a farmer," Mac chimed in.

"A beautiful singer, plays the piano like a dream, a good artist, an amazing cook," Candace said, a small smile on her face as she listed off her sister's attributes.

Eager to see Joan's response to all this unsolicited positivity, I slid my eyes in her direction. She sat rigidly, her profile a painful outline as she stared into her glass, ears going suspiciously pink.

"Best fisherman I've ever met," Brady offered. "Good with kids. Animals love her."

Joan glanced my way so briefly I might have missed it, if I hadn't already been watching her.

She cleared her throat, interrupting the others. "Alright, that's enough listing my numerous virtues. We don't have all night," she said smoothly, no hint of the embarrassment I could see in the color climbing her cheeks.

"I want to play darts," I announced, feeling a strangely protective urge to siphon away some of the uncomfortable attention on Joan. "Any takers?"

"I'm in," Mac replied quickly.

Brady got to his feet. "Me too."

The three of us made our way to the back of the bar. Brady introduced me to the men playing pool nearby. It seemed he knew nearly everyone inside Mattie B's. Maybe that was a hazard of small-town life. Everyone knew everyone, and their business along with it.

Over the next hour, Brady and Mac taught me to play Cricket, with Mercer and Candace joining us in intervals. I spotted Joan at the bar chatting with Mattie.

I got invited to play pool and had a good time meeting other Kirby Falls residents. No one demanded selfies or autographs, but they asked about filming and my life in LA with a sense of wonder and curiosity that was refreshingly innocent, not attention hungry like I was used to.

It was nice. All of it. The laid-back atmosphere, the easy acceptance from people I didn't know.

But whenever I caught sight of Joan chatting with various locals or sipping her drink next to Mercer or her sister, I wondered if my presence here chafed a little.

At a quarter to ten, I made my way over to the jukebox. I hadn't seen one in years, and never one as old as this. I pressed the arrows to scan through the collection, the mechanical flip of the song lists a charming novelty in a time of playlists and internet radio.

"It's a lot of pressure," came a low voice from my side. I caught the hint of her scent—something subtle but fresh and verdant, like grass after it rained. "Pick the wrong song and all your new friends will turn on you."

My mouth hitched up as I gave Joan my full attention. "Is that right?"

She nodded solemnly. "I once saw some out-of-towners—the Hixson cousins, I think—pick a song that made Mattie march right out from behind the bar and unplug the whole damn thing."

"Wow."

"I know. The Hixson cousins retreated in shame."

"Did they paint a scarlet letter on their Patagonia fleece, too?"

Joan's lips twitched before she could stop them. "Nah, but they only got served Coors Light for the rest of the night."

I laughed, and Joan finally let herself smile.

Relief flooded me. I'd wondered if things would be weird between us since the NDA conversation this afternoon, and obviously, my presence here had been unwelcome. I didn't want Joan to be uncomfortable around me, so I was happy she'd sought me out and was talking to me voluntarily.

I'd thought it might be different, seeing her like this, outside of the farm. But as expected, she fit just as well here as she did in the fields. Joan still looked like a farmer—worn jeans, a baby-blue flannel, work gloves forgotten and sticking out of her back pocket. She wore her profession after hours as easily as a priest in his collar or a nurse in scrubs.

Joan looked so comfortable and casual that I envied her.

I'd stood in front of my closet tonight for an embarrassingly long time, trying to decide what to wear, what image to project. I'd hoped to impress but not intimidate. I wanted these people to like me, to know me. For the first time in a long time, I was worried about what someone might think about Ian Wells instead of Dorian Masters.

So much of my life was planned and styled and arranged. In the end, I'd grabbed my favorite hoodie that I only wore at home and a pair of jeans that were comfortable and worn.

Earlier this afternoon, when Joan had asked who knew about my nephew, she'd brought up my friends back home. I'd almost told her the truth, that I didn't have close confidants back in LA. There were acquaintances, sure. Peers and surface friendships, colleagues I grabbed drinks or dinner with on occasion. But there wasn't a single person I trusted with the knowledge that I was raising my nephew. No one I felt safe enough to confide in.

Information was leveraged in Hollywood. The last close friend I'd had—a roommate from before I'd landed a single audition—sold his story to some shitty online magazine after my big break. I'd seen other stories pop up over the years, from individuals in my hometown. It helped confirm that distancing myself had been the right decision. When I'd left Ohio behind, I'd put most of the people there in my rearview and never looked back.

So when Joan had asked about my friends, there hadn't been a good answer—not one I'd wanted to own up to, anyway. What I did have was more loneliness than I cared to admit.

At times, I thought cutting back—taking on fewer roles—might benefit more than just Georgie. Eventually stepping out of the spotlight could make having relationships easier in the future. It was something I was considering more and more every day.

"Well, what would you suggest?" I finally said, indicating the list of songs from the brightly colored machine.

"That's cheating," she replied seriously, but her pretty blue eyes were amused. "You've got to sink or swim under your own weight."

"No life preserver?"

A pause as she took a long sip of her beer—no pint glass this time. My eyes lingered on her full lips wrapped around the mouth of the bottle. As she tilted the beer higher, getting the last of it, the sleeve of her flannel slid down her forearm, revealing a friendship bracelet.

I'd seen beads like that before. There were hundreds of them currently scattered across the kitchen island back at the big house. But I didn't take Joan for a jewelry wearer, even something as simple and innocent as a friendship bracelet.

Understanding hit me all at once, and I reached over to snag her wrist without thought.

"What are you—?" She cut off abruptly as I sifted through the plastic encircling her arm.

*Apple* Lady, plus a rainbow of colors that spelled out his affection.

Georgie had made a bracelet for Joan, and she was wearing it.

"He gave you this," I said, and I could hear the wonder in my own voice.

"Yeah," she said. "He just showed up with it." The softness in her tone tugged at something in me. I could hear the gruff affection, the baffled amusement of a woman who seldom indulged in silliness or playfulness. But she had for my nephew.

Sophia had a couple of bracelets that she rotated out. Darren had one that he clipped to his keychain. Even Maggie Clark had been gifted a bracelet that read *Baker Maggie*. But Georgie hadn't given one to me.

My laughter was a quiet, aching thing. Georgie had decided that Joan was the most amazing person he'd ever met.

And, seeing this side of her—the softness, the loyalty, the secret sweetness —that hid beneath a no-nonsense exterior, I thought, I probably agreed with him.

"It's no big deal," she claimed, as my fingers danced across the beads and her pale skin.

I met her gaze. "It *is* a big deal."

My nephew had been through so much. His life wasn't normal, and never would be. I'd do whatever it took to make him happy. My eyes lingered on the source of that happiness as she squirmed uncomfortably under my gaze. I'd found that most people loved attention and praise, but really good people—the ones who deserved it—rarely liked to be acknowledged.

Suddenly, I realized I'd been rubbing my thumb back and forth over the soft skin of Joan's inner wrist and froze my movements. Goose bumps rose over her flesh, and the awareness between us intensified to a dancing blaze.

Clearing my throat, I said, "Thank you for—"

"You don't have to thank me," Joan interrupted, her voice unexpectedly soft.

She shifted after a moment, drawing her arm back to her side, and ending the conversation. She made to gather her hair in a low ponytail and then released it, focusing instead on the jukebox.

I wondered, briefly, if she was missing her hair tie. The one that was currently in my pocket.

Pointing toward the jukebox once more, Joan offered, "You wanted a hint? Well, here you go: nothing from the last two decades."

I smiled and went back to browsing, putting the topic of innocent mementos and inconvenient gratitude behind us. But that didn't stop all the feelings warming me from the inside out.

I could detect Joan's attention on the side of my face, and, as a result, I didn't register a single song title until my eyes randomly caught on something I recognized.

The buttons clicked as I selected J-85, and a moment later, the rhythmic sounds of piano keys filtered through the ancient speakers.

"Oh, now that's *really* cheating," Joan told me before giving my shoulder a playful shove.

I grinned and didn't let myself draw attention to her teasing or the comfortable way she'd just put her hands on me.

Dolly Parton launched into the opening verse of "9 to 5" as we made our way back to join the others at the table where our night had begun.

"Good choice, man," Brady called. "Everybody loves Dolly."

My gaze slid to Joan when I replied, "I know."

She rolled her eyes, taking her seat next to me.

"Now, Ian, this is kind of important," Mac said, looking serious all of a sudden. She'd loosened up pretty quickly over the course of the evening, the starstruck awe had faded into curious glances, and finally to nothing but playful camaraderie once she'd beat me at darts nearly every round.

"Oh, right. The warning," Brady echoed, and everyone turned to look at me.

I straightened, suddenly worried. "What?"

"You can't tell the other actors or the crew about Mattie B's," Mac said sternly.

"Why?"

"This is a local bar," Brady admitted. "And we've worked hard to keep it that way. We let you in on the secret because we like you."

Oddly, that made me feel really nice.

"Thanks, bro," I said, sincerely.

"No problem, bro," he replied.

I heard Joan mutter "Jesus" under her breath.

"What do you mean, you worked hard to keep it a local bar?" I wondered.

"We tanked the online reviews," Mercer offered.

A shocked laugh burst out of me. "You did what?"

"We review bombed Mattie B's. Strategically and intentionally, over months," Mac added. "Hell, years. All the leafers stay over at Magnolia now."

I looked around the table at the five very serious faces regarding me. This was crazy.

"Wait, what's a leafer?" I asked.

"Tourists," Candace explained. "The ones who come to see our fall foliage and visit the farms."

"You've seen them," Mac said, a slightly derisive edge to her words. "They don't use the crosswalks, and they don't drink the local beers on tap."

"They ask you to take their picture in front of every damn thing," Joan added. "They litter on the hiking trails."

"And they call our town 'quaint' or 'old-fashioned' or 'picturesque,'" Brady said, with air quotes. "They wear a puffy vest no matter the weather."

"You wear a puffy vest all the time," Mac accused.

Brady shot her a betrayed look. "Yes, but only when the temperature drops. I dress weather appropriate, Macchiato."

She rolled her eyes at her boyfriend and his dramatics.

"Is it just the fall people? The ones who visit in the autumn," I asked, trying to understand the term. I'd heard of leaf peepers before, but this didn't seem like the same thing.

"No," Candace replied. "It's a year-round identifier. We call them all leafers, even if they're spring tourists."

My eyes widened, and I placed a hand on my chest. "Am I a leafer?"

I got three yesses, one maybe, and one adamant no—thank you, Brady.

"But I'm here for work. Isn't that better?" I asked.

One yes, one no, and three people said, "Same difference," in unison.

"I don't want to be a leafer," I argued.

Joan snorted, and I shot her a glare. That only made her laugh outright.

"Ian, it's okay. Not all leafers are bad," Candace said calmly. "They just have a reputation for treating servers like crap and not appreciating the land they come to ooh and aah over. But there are plenty of nice leafers. Have you met Becca? She's Will Clark's fiancée and she was a leafer, too, before she moved here. And we all love her." Candace smiled like that made everything all better.

"We need the tourists," Mac said before shrugging. "So it's a weird love-hate relationship. Without them, this tiny town would dry up and blow away. And yes, some of the folks who visit the farm are real sweet. We've seen lots of families visit regularly for years, watched their kids grow up, even. They're not all bad. Don't take offense, Ian. You're one of the good ones."

Now *that* was something I could understand—the strange dichotomy, the love and hate. I had fans, and I needed those fans. My entire career was built on people across the world liking me and keeping me relevant. If Dorian Masters was no longer popular, I wouldn't be in demand for roles.

And while I appreciated the people who supported my career, I also had open case files with my local police for two stalkers and three more for restraining orders on fans who'd taken things way too far. Being a celebrity meant being in the public eye—being a commodity. People thought they knew me because they saw me on their television screen or watched me give interviews on social media. Lines got blurred often. It was why I fought so hard to keep my private life private, in order to keep Georgie safe.

So I could understand the push and pull between needing and wanting the strangers you depended on, and I didn't begrudge the people of Kirby Falls their well-meaning resentment.

"Mac's accepting you now," Brady teased. "But if you take her regular table at Apollo's or snag the last piece of Japanese cheesecake at her favorite bakery, that'll be a different story."

Everyone laughed, including Mac.

"Well, I solemnly swear to never reveal the hidden treasure that is Mattie B's. And if pressed, I'll say I got food poisoning here, and the owner tried to grope me," I told them.

"Fine by me!" Mattie called from behind the bar. "But at least describe me as the *hot* owner."

I grinned. "Yes, ma'am."

Our party broke up after that. Brady and Mac walked down the street to their apartment. Mercer had nursed one beer all night, so he was driving Candace back home.

That was how I found myself alone with Joan, walking in the direction of her car.

"Are you this way, too?" she asked, pointing north down Main Street.

"Yep," I lied.

A comfortable silence descended as our shoes scuffed along the wet sidewalk. Streetlamps glowed warm and bright, lighting up Main Street. This looked like the kind of place that went all out for holiday decorations. I was excited to see if that was the case in the coming weeks.

"Tomorrow's Thursday," Joan said suddenly. "I'm still happy to take George in the afternoon, if you want."

Guilt had me swallowing hard. Georgie wasn't Joan's responsibility. It wasn't her fault he'd taken a liking to her and was sneaking away from his nanny in order to spend more time over at the orchard. She'd gotten so irritated earlier when I'd offered to pay for what was essentially babysitting. I didn't understand why Joan would agree to something like this.

"I feel like I've maybe forced myself into your life enough already."

"What?" she mused. "By stalking me at my work—"

"Okay, we established that you were the one stalking me."

"Practically chasing after me—"

"Rude. I call that jogging."

"And stealing my favorite coffee mug at my parents' house."

I winced. "Sorry, I didn't know about that one."

Joan stopped walking, so I did too.

"I'm just giving you a hard time," she said. "Yes, you weaseled your way into my life and my farm and my parents' group chat. But George . . . he's not a bother. He's funny and sweet . . . and he wants to be a farmer."

Joan smiled then. It was barely there, a tiny whisper of amusement, but her eyes were so soft in the glow of the streetlights that I felt my throat go tight.

I didn't know Georgie wanted to be a farmer. Couldn't even imagine him initiating a conversation where we talked about what he wanted to be when he grew up. But clearly, he'd confessed his dream to someone. And she was staring at me like that was, maybe, the best thing she'd ever heard.

As much as the knowledge hollowed me out, I was grateful my nephew had a safe space to make those confessions, to share those dreams. Even if it wasn't me.

I cleared my throat. "He does?"

Joan's tender expression lingered as she nodded. "Yeah. And if he wants to learn, I'll teach him. He's a good kid. He won't be any trouble."

Georgie's nanny, Sophia, was on my payroll. She got a salary, vacation days, and time off. I paid her overtime if I was forced to travel on my own for an interview or an appearance and leave George behind. Darren protected my nephew and watched over him, too. But he was paid to do it.

Besides me, Georgie didn't have anyone in his life who wasn't compensated for their time and attention. I knew Sophia cared about him. Darren, too. But it sure was nice to stand here in the cold and hear what a good kid he was from someone who wasn't paid to think so.

I nodded because I couldn't speak.

In the last eight months, I'd been thrust into this role of guardian, afraid of not being enough, of doing everything wrong. For the first time, it felt like I might have done something right.

Joan probably couldn't understand all the feelings practically bowling me over right now, but she must have gathered some of it because she took her hand out of her pocket and squeezed my forearm.

"Besides," she said, some mischief entering her expression. "You're all the trouble I can handle."

Grateful for the reprieve, I grinned down at my shoes. My emotions loosened their grip enough for me to glance up and say, "So, you think you can handle me?"

Joan rolled her eyes and whacked me on the shoulder. "We're running three miles Saturday, and you're going to wish you hadn't just said that."

I laughed, relieved and grateful that she wanted to see me again—even if it was three days away.

Shaking her head, Joan resumed walking. I started to follow, but she called back, "I know your car is parked around the corner, you liar. I'll see you Saturday."

I made sure to raise my voice so she could hear me. "I can't wait!"

# *seven*

## JOAN

It was Saturday, and we were nearly done with our run.

Ian was breathing hard, cheeks flushed, his forehead and neck dotted with perspiration.

He'd seemed excited to get back to our workouts, or, at least, it had appeared that way the other night at Mattie B's. But looking at him now, I thought he might be regretting his decision to join me this morning.

I wasn't sure how to feel about seeing Dorian Masters at my local watering hole, playing pool with the regulars, and buying a round for the bar. He'd fit right in with my family and friends. Even grumpy Tucker Caswell had been high-fiving the movie star after a game of eight ball.

I'd expected him to turn on that celebrity charm, but nothing about him had seemed faked or rehearsed on Wednesday night. In fact, there were a couple of moments when Ian had looked a little nervous and unsure of himself. I didn't know what to think about that or the fact that I'd overheard him asking Mercer wedding questions that seemed genuine. And he'd soothed Mac's nervousness and helped put her at ease by letting her win at darts. Then the leafer discussion had caused him such distress that I'd had to laugh.

Of course, he was just a visitor here—a long-term leafer but temporary just the same. My brother may have let Ian in on our town secret, but that didn't change anything. Not really. The man was playing pretend, and he didn't need to get those lines crossed. His part in the film might be that of a Western North Carolina native, but all he was doing was getting experience for his role.

"How much farther?" Ian wheezed.

I checked my watch. "Quarter of a mile. Let's finish strong. You've got this."

He groaned but stayed in step beside me. I was almost up to my usual pace, and he was hanging in there. I was proud of him. We had some time before the Turkey Trot, and Mr. Muscles over there might just make it.

George had asked me about the 5K road race when he'd visited on Thursday afternoon. But he'd been immediately disappointed when he found out that Ian and I would not, in fact, be running alongside actual turkeys. That had made me laugh.

I'd laughed a lot during George's visit. He's stayed for a couple of hours and kept me company.

I'd also met Sophia, his very young, very pretty live-in nanny/tutor/babysitter person. She'd shown up with George in tow and passed me a Tupperware container full of Rice Krispie Treats that they'd made for me to say thank you.

Then the young woman had stayed the whole time, and that made me like her even more. It was good to be a little wary of strangers. George didn't know me very well. Neither did Ian, for that matter. The fact that she was protective when she didn't have to be provided a solid reference, in my book.

She was good with the kid, and he obviously adored her. They had an ease between them, inside jokes, and a back-and-forth that was familiar. And I noticed a few friendship bracelets under Sophia's sleeve, too. Something that had been missing from Ian's.

But that wasn't really any of my business.

Checking the distance again, I slowed our pace before saying, "Alright. Good job. Walk around for a minute to cool down before—"

"Thank God." Ian collapsed on his back and spread his arms out wide, breathing hard. "That was awful."

Frowning, I came to stand over him. "You do know how far a 5K is, right?"

"I can't do math right now," he huffed, wide chest rising and falling.

"Why didn't you ask me to slow down or take a break or something?"

He shot me a disbelieving look. "Would you have actually stopped?"

"Well, sure. If you were this miserable."

Ian croaked out a laugh. "You used to take great pleasure in making me miserable."

"That was before," I argued. "We're training now. I'm trying to get you ready. But you have to be honest with me, or you could hurt yourself. If you weren't up for the distance or the pace, I don't know unless you tell me. What's really going on here, Ian?"

"How are you not even breathing heavy right now?" he asked, exasperation evident.

"I run every day. My body is used to it."

At my pronouncement, Ian's eyes fell away from my face, as if he needed to check for himself. His bright blue gaze traced the length of my torso and took a slow and steady detour over my hips and down my legs. The running tights I wore felt very indecent all of a sudden. I shifted, ignoring the sudden awareness in my middle.

"Yeah, well, my body isn't used to it," he finally said, pushing himself into a sitting position. His breathing had evened out for the most part, but his cheeks were still flushed from exertion. "I told you I don't do cardio."

"No, you told me you're bad at cardio."

"I am. Plus, I hate it. So I don't do it." He propped his forearms on his bent knees and looked away.

It was my turn to catalog the hills and valleys of his big body. Whereas I was mostly flat, straight lines, Ian was a study in dips and arches, swells and valleys. When I couldn't take all the muscles straining his pullover and joggers, I flung a hand out and said a little shrilly, "But look at you!"

He looked sheepish. "Those are just muscles. I lift weights, and I'm on a pretty intense nutrition plan. Having a high metabolism doesn't hurt either."

"So you don't do cardio, but you wanted me to train you." It was a statement. That was exactly what had happened, but I didn't understand it.

"I wanted to spend time with you," he corrected gently.

I shifted on my feet. "You wanted to spend time with me . . . while running?"

Ian huffed a laugh. "No, not ideally. But I'll take what I can get."

I stared at him, hoping some sort of understanding would come to me, but at this point, I would need divine intervention or to phone a friend to figure out what the hell was going on right now.

"Why? I don't get—"

"Because I like you, Joan. I like you," he repeated, voice tired in a way that had nothing to do with running three miles at six in the morning.

Then what he said registered, and I took a step back.

"I wanted to get to know you," he explained. "You didn't seem very open to hanging out with me. Hell, you wouldn't even tell me your name. I thought if we worked out together, you might . . . I don't know. I don't even know what I thought."

Confusion had me frowning. I put my hands on my hips and stared down at Ian. He squinted up at me in the early-morning light.

"You're—you're a movie star," I said, voice sharp, tone clipped. It sounded like an accusation.

"You're a farmer," he replied dryly.

I gave him a flat stare.

It wasn't that I had low self-esteem or something. I knew that I was good at a lot of things. I also knew where I was lacking. Realistically, there was no reason for an A-list celebrity with his own fragrance line to want to run with me because he liked me. It just didn't make sense.

No part of me believed that any one person was better than another. Ian didn't deserve more respect or to get away with traffic violations because he was famous. But our places in the world were very different. What was normal for him—galas, movie premieres, award shows, paparazzi—was not normal for me.

So, for the life of me, I couldn't understand what this was. What his motivations were.

We were past me thinking Ian was just messing with the locals for his own entertainment. But maybe it *was* just a sex thing. I'd already signed an NDA, after all. That probably made things easier, logistically.

I considered this reasoning, and some of my vexation abated. Men did crazy things for sex.

"How old are you anyway?" I asked suddenly.

Ian eyed me skeptically. "Twenty-nine."

"Jesus, you're still in your twenties." I'd known he was younger than me, but the confirmation was brutal. "And you're what? Attracted to me." I didn't tack a question mark on the end because while I did want confirmation, I wasn't fishing for compliments.

"I am," he replied.

"And I'm old enough to be your—"

"To be my what?" he interrupted hastily.

"Your much older sister," I finished flatly.

Ian laughed and looked away. "Yeah, I don't feel particularly brotherly toward you, believe me."

Maybe he was bored, so sex with a local seemed like a nice way to pass the time. My eyes fell to his broad shoulders, mostly against my will.

Contrary to the attraction simmering in my middle, I said matter-of-factly, "Movie stars aren't really my type."

If I thought he'd be disappointed by my statement, I would have been wrong.

Amusement sparkled in his eyes. "Has that come up a lot for you?"

"No," I admitted.

Apparently recovered from his cardiovascular ordeal, Ian rose gracefully to his feet. There was no denying he was a big guy. Easily standing seven or eight inches above my height of five eight. But despite being muscular and tall, he didn't loom, and I wasn't intimidated by his size. Even when he'd been a stranger on my family's land, I'd never been afraid of Ian.

There wasn't one single aggressive thing about him, except for, maybe, how fucking attractive he was. It was visceral, his beauty. I felt it in my gut. The swift whoosh flipping my stomach over. It was there in the knot in my throat when I tried to speak. The way my eyes wanted to linger over every single one of his features and then come back for seconds.

He was a work of art. Practically untouchable. And the whole world knew it.

Maybe that was the problem.

"Well, how do you know movie stars aren't your type?" he asked.

"Because I don't have the patience for celebrities. Nor would I waste my time agreeing to whatever it is you want. You're here temporarily. Getting tangled up with you for a quick hook-up or a reliable lay while you're filming feels like a recipe for disaster."

"Dating," he insisted, taking a step closer. "The thing I want to do with you is called dating. I'm not bored or trying to amuse myself or settling for you because you're convenient."

I swallowed, my throat suddenly too dry. I liked to think of myself as fairly level-headed, but it was a lot to have all that good-looking intensity and charisma directed my way. His calm, confident tone and earnest expression had me feeling unsteady, like I'd misread the whole situation, and now I was back at step one: not understanding his motivations. It was easier when I'd assumed it was just about meaningless sex.

But then I remembered who he was and imagined the words were simply lines he'd delivered, a mark he'd hit in some production for my benefit alone.

This man was an actor, and I couldn't forget that.

When I was quiet for too long, Ian asked, "So, why don't you like celebrities?"

Before I thought better of it, my honest opinion practically leaped from my mouth. "They're helpless. They have staff that does everything for them. They're used to people kissing their ass and stroking their ego. Obviously, I'm generalizing, but do you cook your own meals?"

"Nope."

"Do you wash your own car or scrub your own toilet?"

"No and no," he replied easily, completely unashamed.

"I bet you don't even order your own takeout or know how to do laundry. Ian, if I came into a shit-ton of money, I'd still be a farmer. I'd probably just buy a nicer tractor and finally replace the conveyor belt on the apple press. Maybe go to New Zealand in the off-season. Money and fame wouldn't change who I was. I like my life. I like making my own dinner. I like taking care of myself."

"And cleaning your toilet?" he asked very seriously.

I huffed an exasperated laugh. "Maybe I don't love cleaning my toilet, but the other stuff—the things that make me a regular, normal, everyday person—I don't mind those. And, I think, that's what makes it worse. Knowing that most celebrities started out as normal people. At some point in their past, they knew how to do all the mundane shit that regular folks do every single day. Now, they just expect someone else to do it for them. And that's fine." I held up my hands in surrender before dropping them to my sides. "If you have the resources and money to live comfortably like that, good for you. But that's just not the kind of life I can understand."

Ian watched me, a thoughtful expression on his face. "Okay. So, you'd date me if I wasn't spoiled, is basically what you're saying?"

I started to roll my eyes, but he actually wasn't that far off. Not that I truly believed he wanted to date me—whatever he meant by that. Despite what he'd claimed, he probably didn't want anything more than a roll in the hay. To plant his flag, claim his conquest, and move on to the next troublesome woman who wouldn't give him the time of day—assuming he could find another one.

"Okay," he repeated, even though I hadn't answered him. He nodded to himself and then walked right past me in the direction of the highway.

I opened my mouth and then closed it.

I didn't know what to say, but Ian looked determined, and that was more worrisome than the butterflies flapping around in my belly.

That night, in the dark of my bedroom, I did something I wasn't proud of.

With a laptop screen glowing in my face, I googled Dorian Masters.

It was a mistake, I knew that. But I'd let curiosity get the better of me. It had built up over the last few weeks. The running, the conversations, a secret nephew who'd wormed his way into my life just as thoroughly as his uncle. How the man himself had fit in at Mattie B's so effortlessly, friendly with everyone and content with small-town entertainment. Or the way he'd visited our neighbors over at Lonely Mountain Winery and shared photos on his social media account that had gotten the owners, Reggie and Aurora Holmes, nearly fifty thousand new followers and a boatload of online orders.

In all the uproar of my daily life, I'd allowed myself to forget who Ian really was.

But staring at page after page of images online really put things back into perspective.

Cameras captured him at after-parties and in ballrooms. So many photos of his smiling face. Ian in a tuxedo, a suit, jeans that cost more than my monthly car payment. Ian holding up an Inferno Man action figure that wore his matching grin.

There were candids, too. Grainy, real-life photos outside of hotels and on sidewalks. Ian, with his sunglasses and Columbus Blue Jackets hat, as he sipped an iced coffee at a café table or ducked into a restaurant.

I scrolled until I saw Ian from the latest award season, posed on red carpets, with a microphone in his face, a different model or actress on his arm in each photo. Some of the most beautiful women I'd ever seen. Sleek, graceful co-stars dripping in jewelry, balancing on pencil-thin heels.

I didn't have much cause in my daily life to feel self-conscious. And as shameful as it was to admit, seeing Ian standing next to those women didn't make me jealous. It made me resigned. They looked like they fit, like they belonged. Prepackaged perfection.

It was a reminder and an example. Some girls and women looked at those pictures and felt inspired, while others felt like they'd never be enough.

I clicked away from the image search after that.

An online article touted the Dorian Masters life story with an interview from his high school drama teacher and an old girlfriend. Then there was an interview from a popular celebrity magazine dated three months ago. The accompanying image caught Ian mid-climb from a glittering swimming pool, his arms flexing, biceps and triceps bulging as he braced himself on the pool's edge. His long hair was wet, midnight black, and slicked back from his face, but his eyes were as bright and sunlit as the turquoise water surrounding him.

Even after having run side by side for weeks, I stared at that image, wondering how he could be real. It didn't matter that I'd seen Ian in real life. Hair shorter and buzzed close to his scalp. Stubble on that very same jaw. A sweaty, panting mess laid out on land that I'd worked with my own two hands. Perched uncomfortably on a wicker chair while he made my mother laugh.

There was real, and then there was fantasy. And I might have been the only person in the world who'd pick fact over fiction, every damn time.

I snapped my laptop shut and vowed to never google someone I knew ever again.

---

The following week, I got a message from the film liaison asking if I'd be willing to drive a tractor around for some B-roll, whatever that was. I forwarded it to Brady and Mercer.

Sophia was bringing George over a little early today. I'd made sandwiches for lunch and asked them to join me. Sophia was going to use the time to head into town to grocery shop, but George was content to sit in the sunshine in his winter coat and eat a peanut butter fluff sandwich.

He'd gifted me another friendship bracelet. *Tree Farmer* it read, making me smile when I caught sight of it.

Halfway through the meal, Ian pulled up to our picnic table in his borrowed side-by-side.

It was the first time I'd seen him since our run last Saturday. He'd been busy this week with work, but it looked like he'd managed to get away for now. It was . . . good to see him. *Good* wasn't the word, but I couldn't think of a better one. And I was resolved to ignore the niggling awkwardness I felt at having googled him.

"Hey," he said, smiling. He didn't look like someone who'd recently confessed his feelings and gotten rejected. "Sophia told me where you were. Mind if I join?"

"I have an extra sandwich," I offered. "But it's probably not on your approved nutrition plan."

Ian took my teasing in stride and lowered himself to the bench seat beside his nephew. "Then we'll just have to agree not to tell Maurice. Hey, Georgie. How was school today?"

"It was fine. I practiced writing sentences, and Sophia and I started reading *The Wild Robot*." Then, without missing a beat, the boy asked, "Can I drive the tractor? Joan said we had to ask you first."

Ian's gaze shot to mine. "Uhhh."

"It's the lawn tractor," I explained. "I'm mowing the last little bit of the wildflower patch before winter. I thought George might like to help me."

The conflict practically radiated off of Ian. I could tell he was worried about making the wrong decision or putting his nephew in danger.

"I'll be with him the whole time, and he'll have eye and ear protection to wear," I assured him. "My dad started bringing me along when I was about George's age." Truthfully, I'd been helping my dad mow since I was three or four.

The frown lines on Ian's forehead smoothed incrementally. "Okay, then. Be careful, though. Make sure you listen to Miss Joan."

George nodded and ripped off another piece of bread.

I passed Ian the lunch I'd prepared for Sophia, our fingers brushing unexpectedly. He took a long swallow from a water bottle, and I tried not to stare as his throat worked.

Shifting on the bench, I made myself focus on my food and not whatever weirdness was making me extra jumpy around Ian. I knew he was attractive. I wasn't an idiot. But it was harder to ignore today for some reason.

He unwrapped the sandwich and said, "What do we have here?"

"The best thing ever," George replied, sticky marshmallow dotting his upper lip.

I fought a grin. "It's just peanut butter and marshmallow fluff."

Ian took a huge bite before I'd even finished speaking. He groaned. "That *is* the best thing ever. Definitely don't tell Maurice."

George giggled. "She uses chunky peanut butter. That's why it's so good."

"Is that right?" Ian said.

"Yep," the boy replied.

I pulled out some sliced apples drizzled in a little lemon juice to keep them from turning, as well as some pretzels and cups of yogurt.

It was a simple meal. My mom used to make sandwiches like this as a special treat for my siblings and me. It had seemed like something a seven-year-old might enjoy. But it still made me feel good when George had taken a tentative first bite, and then his eyes had shot open in excitement.

We chatted while we ate. Ian told us about the deer they'd seen in the woods while filming. George recounted the first few chapters of *The Wild Robot*. The conversation was surprisingly easy and weirdly domestic. But soon enough, Ian's phone buzzed on the table, and he was needed back on set. It was nice that he'd been able to take his break and spend it with his nephew instead of going to the small set trailer where he said he normally ate. I imagined free time was hard to come by with such an irregular schedule.

So I was a little surprised when Ian managed to join us for lunch again the following day. It was a cold Thursday, and George and I were eating in the Apple House next to the space heater.

Ian approached from the orchard's main entrance this time and brought with him a travel mug. He extended the cup in my direction after greeting us.

"What's this?"

"Coffee," he replied. "Junior and Nola have a really nice espresso machine back at the big house, and I'm getting pretty good at it, if I do say so myself."

I accepted the offering and took a hesitant sip. I thought George might have hidden a giggle, but I couldn't be sure over the sound of all my taste buds screaming out in agony.

The coffee was so bitter and strong, it somehow tasted like burnt hair and pennies at the same time.

Ian watched me nervously. "How is it?"

I worked hard to school my features, thinking I should have been nominated for a fucking Academy Award. "It's great. Thank you."

Ian beamed, boyish pride and dimples on full display. I swore his ridiculous curled lashes fluttered with happiness. Christ, he was pretty. Good thing too, because he'd never be a barista.

But the thought had been nice. I took small sips and fought a wince each time.

As we were finishing up, Sophia made her way into the Apple House and greeted us all with a smile.

"Hey, bud," she called to George. "We have that video call with your grandma and grandpa this afternoon. I came to get you."

"Oh," the boy said, shoulders sagging as he stared down at the table.

Ian and Sophia shared a look, and I wondered what that was about. All Ian had said about his parents was that they'd been unable to care for George. It was good that they still wanted to be part of his life. Right?

Eventually, Ian managed a smile and said, "That's great, Georgie. You can tell them all about helping Miss Joan on the farm. I bet they'd love to hear about your mowing adventure yesterday. I know Darren really liked it when you told him last night."

That made me smother a grin. I could just imagine Ian's quiet, stoic body-guard nodding along to the kid's highly embellished story about cutting grass.

"Yeah, I guess," George reluctantly admitted.

"And if it's okay with your uncle and Sophia, you can come back over after your phone call," I offered.

"Can I?" George's hopeful little voice did something funny to my chest.

I'd never been particularly maternal. And I'd never really had someone so happy to spend time with me before.

"Sure," Ian said, gifting me a grateful smile.

George packed away his trash. "Bye, Joan. See you in a little while."

"Bye, George."

My eyes cut to Ian, who hadn't received a farewell. He was watching his nephew take Sophia's hand and walk outside. The smile on Ian's face fell away, and my heart ached watching the exchange. I wasn't sure why

George kept his uncle at a distance, but it hurt to see the disappointment on Ian's face.

When they reached the stairs leading out into the yard, Sophia leaned down and whispered something in George's ear. After a second, the little boy turned and waved, calling, "Bye, Uncle Ian."

The man across from me lit up like a Christmas tree. You would have never known that just a moment ago, he'd been crushed by George's indifference. "Bye, Georgie. I'll see you tonight."

And then they were gone.

Ian stared after them for a long time.

Eventually, he noticed my attention and cleared his throat. "We're still, uh, getting to know each other."

"It's none of my business." Didn't mean I wasn't curious, though.

Ian's gaze shifted to the remnants of our lunch, scattered on the table. He picked up a baby carrot but didn't take a bite. "I'd only seen George twice before he came to live with me. My sister and I weren't close."

I nodded, understanding how that could happen. Candace and I grew apart when she lived in New York. "And George's father?"

Ian shook his head. "Dawn was a single parent by choice. There was never a father in the picture."

"I see."

"My parents try to check in every couple of months. I emailed them a few weeks ago. I guess they set up the call with Soph."

Ian was working really hard to make all of that sound normal. But it was what he didn't say that came through the loudest. How Ian was the one working to make sure George had more family in his life.

Ian glanced at me briefly before studying the baby carrot he was still turning over in his hands. "It probably sounds strange to someone like you. You work with your siblings and parents. You're very much in each other's lives."

"All families look different. There's no right way to build one. Sometimes you do what you can with what you're given. And other times, you go out and build your own. It's as simple as that."

Blue eyes rose to meet mine. Ian studied me silently, perhaps weighing the truth of my statement. He should know by now that I wouldn't bullshit him about something important.

"You obviously care about George," I added. "He'll realize that. He's a smart kid. He'll come around."

Ian nodded, unconvinced. Changing the subject, he said, "I heard they asked you to drive a tractor for the film."

"I told Mercer he could do it."

His grin was small, tinged with lingering sadness, like he still remembered our previous conversation. "I think Della wants to show a woman on the farm."

"Why?"

"Well, she probably took to heart your passion for nontraditional roles in farming, what with the way you educated Archer."

I frowned. "Who's Archer?"

Ian burst out laughing. "Only you could lecture someone into submission and tears and then brush it aside as no big deal. Archer will probably retain that as a core memory. He'll be on his deathbed telling the story to his family, desperate to repent."

Ah, yes. The sexist moron with the clipboard.

I rolled my eyes. "Oh, *Archer*. Excuse me. I don't get the name of every youthful idiot in need of an education on feminism."

Ian chuckled and finally popped the carrot into his mouth. "But seriously, you don't think it would be fun to be in a major motion picture?"

"No? Should I?"

He stared at me in wonder. "I have literally never met someone so obviously unimpressed with all this."

"You should meet more people."

Ian's bark of laughter nearly made me smile.

"That's right," he teased, still grinning. "You don't like celebrities or anything celebrity adjacent."

I waited for resentment to creep into his expression or accusation at the very least. But his eyes sparkled with amusement alone.

"That's right," I confirmed, knowing it would make him laugh.

And he did, shaking his head with what looked a lot like affection.

Part of me was still braced and ready for Ian to bring up the feelings he'd confessed. But he was acting like nothing ever happened. Like he hadn't told me he wanted to date—or whatever—me, less than a week ago.

I was grateful that he wasn't being weird. I barely wanted to deal with my own emotions. I couldn't imagine juggling his, too.

We gathered up the rest of our trash and turned off the heater.

Making our way toward the exit of the Apple House, I told him seriously, "Be careful. That door has low clearance. You'll need to watch your big, famous head on it."

He was still grinning when he climbed into the side-by-side and drove away.

## IAN

I paused the YouTube video and poured detergent into the appropriate little trough.

"Shit," I hissed, as the liquid overflowed its borders a bit. Okay, a lot.

Hopefully, it wouldn't matter that the soap had gone over into—I squinted —the fabric softener's compartment. Damn, did I need fabric softener? I checked the cabinet and didn't see any.

I picked up my phone to google fabric softener when Sophia appeared in the doorway like a phantom. "What are you doing?"

I fumbled my phone like a rookie wide receiver. "Nothing."

She picked up my device from where it had fallen at her feet. Dark eyes took in the video paused on my screen before narrowing. "Are you trying to do laundry?"

I cleared my throat. "Maybe. Do we have any fabric softener?"

Sophia crossed her arms over her chest. "No. I don't believe in it. It creates a layer over the towels that makes them less absorptive."

"Oh, okay. That makes sense."

"Did I do something wrong? Are you unhappy with my laundry services?"

"What? No," I insisted. "I'm just . . ." Losing my mind, clearly. Fixated on a woman who thinks I'm a spoiled baby. "Trying to help out," I finished lamely.

Sophia sighed. "Ian, you pay me—very competitively, I might add—to handle all the domestic stuff. Doing laundry is part of my job."

"Right, but I can help out. I *should* help out."

She stared at me like she could see through the layers of bullshit to the truth. God, I hoped not. This was embarrassing enough. "I'm trying to decide if I should be offended. Now, if you try cooking or doing dishes, then I might start to really worry about your sanity."

My face must have given me away because her eyes widened and she gasped dramatically. "The lasagna? You were serious about trying to make that?"

My face went hot. I'd added the ingredients to Sophia's weekly grocery list after Amy Judd had shared her recipe with me. Sophia had teased me about it and given me the third degree about why I'd been so interested.

"Maybe," I confessed.

"Oh my God! That was you who loaded the dishwasher like a rabid raccoon, wasn't it? I thought it was Georgie. Ian, what is going on right now?"

Fighting a wince, I admitted, "I just realized that I should contribute more."

My employee and friend stared at me like I'd told her I wanted to learn how to pilot the space shuttle. And maybe that seemed just as likely. To her, I was equally as unqualified to wash a load of towels as I was to break through the atmosphere.

So I went a different route. "Georgie should really be exposed to men in female-dominated roles."

"Sure," she replied, flatly. "That's what we need. More men taking over."

I blew out a breath. "No, I just mean, don't you think I should set an example for him? That men can and should do laundry and dishes and clean toilets. I think his future partner or roommate someday might be very appreciative."

Sophia eyed me skeptically. "I guess. But if you start trying to teach him math, I will take great offense and go back to California."

Holding my hands up in surrender, I said, "I would never."

Scowling, she put up two fingers, indicating her eyes and then mine—the universal sign for "I'm watching you, pal." And then she swooped out of the laundry room.

I sagged against the washing machine in relief.

What the hell was I doing? It had been stupid to try to chip in with the housework. I didn't know why I'd let Joan's voice take up residence in my mind. Yes, she'd made some valid points about celebrities and "normal" people. I could see why someone so frighteningly capable wouldn't be impressed by a twenty-nine-year-old man who still let everyone else take care of him.

Of course, I'd done laundry before I was an actor. When I moved to LA at eighteen, I'd taught myself a lot of stuff that my mother had handled at home—not that that fact helped my case.

But laundromat machines weren't the same as the one I'd been trying to figure out today. Not wanting to break something in the house I was renting from the Clarks, I'd looked for an online manual first. The YouTube video had put me on the right path. Plus, it had been a long time since I'd thought about where my clean clothes came from. I'd had a housekeeper in LA for years.

Thinking back on Joan's contempt for celebrities, part of me had wanted to disagree, to force her to see my perspective. But I'd kept my mouth shut. At the time, it had seemed more important to listen to her grievances. I didn't think arguing would get me anywhere with her. In fact, it probably would have made things worse.

But maybe Joan had never considered that it was easier to hire people to handle certain aspects of my life. She'd never experienced what happened when I tried to do normal, everyday things.

Did she ever stop to think that I didn't go shopping for groceries or pick up my takeout order because I couldn't leave my house without photographers and fans cornering me on the street?

When I was home, in Los Angeles, it was easier and more efficient to hire a personal chef to come in a few days a week to stock my fridge with the meals on my nutrition plan. Realistically, I could see how that looked—spoiled, privileged—but it made sense for my life right now.

I wasn't going to drag Georgie out where people would get in his face or splash his photo across the internet.

But I hadn't brought up any of those arguments. It would have emphasized how different Joan and I were. It wasn't like I needed to draw her attention to it. The woman was well aware.

But she hadn't said no to dating me because she didn't like me as a person or because she wasn't attracted to me. She simply had a hard time with my celebrity status and fame. Those things were a part of my life, but they weren't who I was. Somehow, I needed her to see that.

The situation wasn't completely hopeless just because she thought I was.

That night, while Georgie got ready for bed, I listened to him talk about Joan. It was a running commentary of the time he spent with her and the things they talked about.

While he pulled on Spider-Man pajamas, I got to hear about the goat that lived next door, who sometimes showed up on her doorstep.

As he brushed his teeth, he told me the best kinds of apples to use for pressing.

When he climbed into bed, he considered putting together an emergency kit for Joan since she used handkerchiefs instead of bandages, and he worried that she'd get an infection.

While I was reading his bedtime story, Georgie interrupted three different times to remark on something Joan had said or thought or demonstrated.

I smiled as Georgie chattered on about his favorite person. I was grateful he had someone to look up to and admire. I even thought Joan deserved his praise and devotion. But the knowledge was bittersweet. What happened when we eventually left Kirby Falls? Would I be dragging a little boy home with a broken heart?

Closing the children's book, I placed it on the side table and turned on the night-light.

"Maybe we can make some peanut butter fluff sandwiches for dinner this week?" I offered after Georgie had asked about them again.

"Okay. Thanks, Uncle Ian."

I passed him his e-reader and set a timer on his clock. "Ten minutes, okay? Then bedtime."

"Okay," he said distractedly, already absorbed in the animal book he liked.

"I love you, bud. I'm glad you're enjoying yourself here in Kirby Falls."

He didn't respond, and I tried not to feel the sharp slice of disappointment as I closed the bedroom door behind me.

**Joan**

My father followed me out onto the front porch following Sunday dinner.

Brady, Mac, Candace, and Mercer were still inside with my mother, enjoying dessert. But I had an early start in the morning and some chores waiting for me at home.

The sky was nearly dark already. This time of year shortened the days, making me feel like every moment at rest was somehow wasted time.

"I was thinking about expanding the wildflower field after the movie people clear out," Dad said. "Might as well, since we had to clear that extra acreage for them."

I nodded. "Makes sense. The tourists like it."

In the summer, we ran hay rides out to the field so visitors could pick flowers by the bucketful to take home. We utilized succession planting, so there was always something blooming between June and September.

Dahlias, zinnias, and sunflowers turned the once-unused pasture bright and beautiful with every color in the rainbow.

U-pick flowers had been Candace's idea when she'd moved back to town and started working at the farm. I had to admit that it was a crowd-pleaser and pretty low maintenance compared to other attractions here at the orchard.

"And Margaret down at Snap, Bam, Bloom wants to contract us as a supplier if we plant some of the flowers she needs for weddings," Dad said. "We could use the extra space for that as well."

Margaret owned the florist shop downtown.

"I'll get in touch with her and see what she needs," I told him. "I've been thinking about planting some tulips out there. We could see if she'd be interested in those, too."

The orchard wasn't open to the public year-round. In March and April, without tourists to pick them, there'd be no real reason to grow tulips. But they'd always been my favorite. I wouldn't mind planting a row of bulbs in the coming weeks just to try things out. Maybe George would want to help me.

"That sounds good, Joanie."

Dad squinted into the distance. "Now who's that coming up the trail?"

I followed his gaze to see Ian jogging along the worn path between the orchard and the farmhouse. His shirt was bright in the fading twilight, a pale beacon as he ran.

But as he drew closer, I noticed his white crewneck sweatshirt was actually pale pink, with darker irregular splotches. It looked like a failed attempt to tie-dye something.

Or the result of a red sock sneaking into the wash.

My eyes narrowed as he approached. We'd had that weird conversation about laundry the other day, but surely—

"Am I doing okay, Coach?" Ian called.

I felt my lips twitch. "Stop swinging your arms so much."

Ian laughed, his smile standing out against the invading dusk. Without slowing, he hollered, "Hi, Mr. Judd."

"Hi, Ian," my dad replied. "See you for poker this week?"

"Yes, sir. Wouldn't miss it. Y'all have a good night."

And then he was gone, angling up the drive behind the house that would lead to the highway and back toward the Clarks' land.

I gave my father a long look. "Poker?"

My dad had the good grace to look a little sheepish. "He's so bad, Joanie. He has no idea what he's doing. But Reggie and I are teaching him."

Nick Judd avoided my incredulous stare. "Is this an adopt-a-celebrity situation? Is he here to make a movie or to learn life skills from the Judd family?"

"Your mother was the one who gave him her lasagna recipe. He said he wanted to try to make it himself."

"Jesus Christ," I muttered.

He pointed an accusatory finger at me, and then ruined it by sounding like a toddler. "You started it!"

"What?"

"Training him for a 5K. Pfft. Is that what the kids are calling it these days?"

"Dad," I gasped, mortified.

My father laughed before patting me on the shoulder. He turned to make his way inside, muttering, "He's a good boy. I like him, even if he can't play poker."

I stared after him until the screen door settled into place, wondering when our lives had taken such a strange turn.

<hr>

Sophia texted me Tuesday afternoon and asked if George could stop by for a bit. She said he had something important to ask me, but he wouldn't tell her what it was.

I'd already tilled a space for the tulips I'd picked up yesterday after talking to the florist, so I told Sophia to drop him off if he wanted to help me plant them.

An hour later, we were sorting through tulip bulbs. I had a new friendship bracelet dangling on my wrist, and George next to me on an overturned bucket.

His little feet dangled as he swung them back and forth. With pants too short, I could see his pink socks standing out beneath the hem.

I remembered my brother, Brady, at that age. He'd been a gangly, knobby-kneed little thing. His beanpole body would shoot up randomly, and, as a result, all his pants would be too short all of a sudden.

"How'd your socks end up pink?" I asked.

George rolled his eyes, and I thought his growth spurt must have skipped straight to adolescence. "Uncle Ian tried to do laundry and ruined all our socks and underwear. Miss Sophia said to be patient and not to be too hard on him. That he was obviously in the middle of a nervous breakdown, whatever that is."

My laughter caught in my throat. Eventually, I managed, "And this is a new thing? Your uncle doing the laundry?"

"Yep," George said. "And the dishes and cooking. We made brownies yesterday that were so gooey we had to eat them with a spoon. But I didn't mind. They tasted good. Uncle Ian even let me put ice cream on top."

There was something so sweet about his honesty. It made it even better knowing that Ian probably—definitely—would not have wanted me to know about his forays into domesticity. Obviously, our conversation had spurred him into action. I didn't know whether to be horrified or strangely impressed.

If the warm amusement in my middle meant anything, I was leaning more toward impressed . . . and attracted—well, more attracted. Ian had that face, those dimples, and that body. But now he was an A-list celebrity doing household chores in his spare time, and—yep—that was making me feel things.

I'd called him spoiled, and he'd set out to do something about it.

Oh, Jesus. Did he think I would date him now?

Before I could panic about the ramifications of Ian doing laundry very poorly, George said matter-of-factly, "My mom never let me have brownies and ice cream."

The boy rarely spoke about his mother, so I made sure my tone was casual. "Really?"

"Yep. She said it would make me too hyper or hurt my belly. But it didn't hurt my belly at all yesterday."

"Your mom probably just wanted to make sure you were healthy."

George frowned, turning that over. "So, Uncle Ian doesn't want me to be healthy?"

To myself, I thought, *Ian wants you to be happy. There's a difference.*

But to the kid, I replied, "Your uncle wants you to be healthy, too. It's okay to have a treat now and then. And maybe Ian had just as much fun cooking the brownies with you as you did eating them."

George smiled. "It was pretty fun. He let me crack the eggs all by myself."

"So, you think you want to be a chef now, or you still want to be a farmer?"

He giggled like I was silly, and the sound made me smile. "Farmer!" he shouted, earning a laugh.

"What was the big, important thing you needed to ask me about?"

"Oh, can we go fishing sometime? Uncle Ian said you were good at fishing, and I've never been. I've read about it, though."

I didn't know how I felt about George and his uncle having conversations about me. That felt a little too . . . real. I'd compartmentalized everything about the film—from the interruptions to the shooting schedule to our visitors—into temporary categories. It was important to keep those things separate. George and Ian, the movie, all of it, couldn't get mixed up with real life.

"I can take you fishing," I agreed. "I'll keep an eye on the weather for a mild day, and we'll try the pond over at Grandpappy's. You think Miss Maggie would let us fish over there?"

I already knew the answer to that, but I also knew George liked visiting the Clark matriarch at the bakery where she worked. We could swing by when I took him home in a few hours.

"I bet she would. Can we go ask her?"

"Sure thing, George."

"Maybe she'll have a treat for us."

I smiled. "Maybe she will. You ready to help plant these tulip bulbs?"

"Yep!"

I passed him a pair of kid-sized gardening gloves I'd picked up at the tractor supply store.

I tried to ignore the way it felt when he grinned up at me like I'd done something special. They were just gloves.

And this was all temporary. It wouldn't do to blur the lines between fleeting and forever . . . for any of us.

# nine

## JOAN

I stood around the corner from First Avenue in the small alley that ran behind Burke Hardware and Paperback Writer, the bookstore downtown.

Ian approached wearing his dark sunglasses and a toboggan covering his short hair.

"Did anyone see you?" I asked, looking over his shoulder to the narrow, shadowed lane beyond.

"Nah," he replied, rubbing his gloved hands together.

It was bitterly cold this morning for the 22nd Annual Kirby Falls Turkey Trot. The weather worried me a little, but not nearly as much as everyone figuring out a damn movie star was running in the race. I had a vision of people chasing Ian down the street, Beatles-style. I knew I could outrun them, but I wasn't sure if Ian's training had prepared him to flee his fans at high speed.

Eloise Carter, the festival chair and coordinator for the event, had volunteers waiting to escort us to the front of the start/finish line so that we could line up just before the gun went off. We couldn't have Dorian Masters in the midst of hundreds of people who were likely to recognize him and cause a frenzy.

I liked to think my fellow residents were neighborly enough to give a man his space—even if he was an international celebrity—but I'd seen the chatter in the town's ridiculous Facebook group. There was a daily Dorian Watch post where locals could report sightings around town.

Someone had taken a picture of Ian over at Trailview Brewing when he'd joined us for trivia night this past week. It had been blurry and poorly lit, but it had done the job. People had shown up in droves. Ian had happily signed napkins and taken selfies for an hour before I'd elbowed my way in and dragged him out to the parking lot, muttering about how people had lost their damn minds and where was Darren, anyway?

After that, I'd contacted Eloise myself to ensure Ian would be safe to participate in the 5K this morning. The grouchy old busybody had been pleased as punch to comply. She knew Ian's participation—once revealed —would be fantastic for the event.

"Hey, thanks for getting this all squared away so I won't get stuck taking selfies all morning," Ian said before attempting to breathe some warmth into his fingers.

"It was no big deal," I told him. "Now we get a premium starting position and don't have to wait in line for it. Win-win."

It was easier to say that than to admit that I was worried about his safety and annoyed with my neighbors for their behavior.

I helped him attach his race bib, making sure my touch stayed only on the stretchy black fabric of his pullover and not the muscles underneath. I could feel Ian watching me while my fingers shifted the safety pins into place over his abdomen.

"There," I told him, clearing my throat. "You're all set."

"Thanks," Ian replied with a smirk I chose to ignore.

Darren joined us a moment later from where he'd been watching the entrance to the alleyway.

"You're not running with us?" I asked, grinning.

He wore his big, puffy winter jacket again and gave me an unamused look. I knew the big man did not like to run. His bodyguard technique leaned more toward intimidation. Plus, this cold was breaking his California heart.

But we'd built a rapport in the last couple of weeks as both George and Ian had been spending so much time at the orchard. Darren was serious but with a dry sense of humor. He had a soft spot for animals, enjoyed chatting with Mercer, and loved my mother's sweet tea.

"You're mean enough to handle anyone who comes after him out on the road," Darren replied dryly.

I laughed.

"Gee, thanks, guys," Ian whined. "Glad my safety is so amusing to you two."

Darren's dark eyes sparkled, but he slapped Ian on the shoulder good-naturedly. "You're right, boss. I'll keep an eye out. Mrs. Carter assigned me someone who's going to drive me around in a golf cart. We'll follow behind, and you'll be safe. I'll make sure of it."

Just then, a volunteer turned the corner and said they were ready for us.

Darren wished us good luck as we said goodbye and followed the woman in the neon-green sweatshirt to the front of the pack. People parted and stared, whispering to one another, but no one demanded to know why we were jumping line.

"You ready?" I asked quietly.

"I'll be right beside you, Coach."

Ian held up a fist, and I bumped it with my own, feeling a flutter in my middle that meant anticipation, competition, adrenaline, and absolutely nothing else.

The countdown began, and then the starting gun signaled the beginning of the race.

Ian and I took off.

The instinct was there to pull away fast from the crowd at our backs, but it was important to maintain our pace. Or Ian might not make it up the final hill to the finish.

A few eager beavers shot by us, but I knew they wouldn't last. They were all flash, cheetahs capable of short sprints. Silently, I bet Ian and I would overtake them by the first mile.

I'd been running this race regularly for nearly twenty years. Except for that one Thanksgiving when I'd had a fever of one hundred and two, I'd almost always placed in the top five. I knew who my competition was, and I'd keep an eye out for them. But most of these people were looking for a fun holiday run with their families. And the cold would have them wheezing and walking before too much longer.

I was thirty-six. I knew there would come a day when sixteen-year-old Gretchen Rose Tate or college track star Tom Gordon would probably take the top spot. But that wouldn't be today. Despite the frigid temperature, I felt strong and fast. And maybe, just maybe, I wanted a good finish for the man at my side.

Yes, he was a spoiled movie star, and he'd started training dishonestly because of some weird, unfathomable crush on me. But he'd shown up, worked hard, and improved a lot in the last month. Ian had taken my advice to heart. Who knew it was so hot when a man actually listened to the competent women in his life?

I was proud of Ian, and I wanted us to do well today so that he could be proud of himself, too.

Running next to Ian was familiar by now. I was still aware of his body next to mine, all the defined muscles and broad expanse of masculine beauty. But there was an easiness about our movements that had grown slowly over all the miles we'd put in together. It was strange to think I was actually comfortable with the man who had fan club chapters in over thirty countries.

Yet here we were, breaths and steps in sync, the steady rhythm of my heart a soundtrack to our growing friendship.

At eighteen minutes into the race, we turned the final corner and started up the short incline that would take us across the finish line. Folks caught sight of us, and cheers went up. People were lining the road on either side, shouting out encouragement. Someone had a cowbell.

Ian puffed out a heavy breath, and I knew his lungs were burning with the effort, but I caught his gaze and said, "You've got this."

He nodded, focused, and kept going.

As we closed in on the crowd and the giant time clock, Ian slowed. I lost him in my periphery. Worried that he'd gotten a cramp or something, I looked back over my shoulder.

"What are you doing?" I asked.

He looked fine, not doubled over in pain or hobbling through a muscle spasm.

My gaze shifted briefly over Ian's shoulder to see Tom Gordon, maybe thirty yards behind us, arms and legs pumping hard up the hill.

Ian waved an impatient hand toward the finish line. "Go ahead. Take it."

Oh, this idiot. He thought he'd just hang back and *let* me win.

We'd trained together. Ian had worked hard for this, and now he wanted to diminish that with some well-meaning sweetness.

Rolling my eyes, I reached over and snagged Ian's hand, pulling him into step beside me as we crossed the finish line together.

He let out a strangled laugh and squeezed my hand. Despite the chill on my face, I could feel my pride warm and near to bursting as Ian and I grinned at one another in the face of our victory.

Neighbors and strangers clapped and cheered as we eventually slowed to a stop partway down the block. I saw Brady, Mac, Candace, and Dad standing with George and Sophia, so I steered Ian in their direction.

My brother held a sign that said, "Run like zombies are chasing you." I could tell Mac had done the artwork because a pretty impressive zombie was illustrated beneath his messy lettering.

Everyone congratulated us, and my dad thoughtfully passed over a couple of water bottles.

"Mom wanted to be here," Candace said, "but she and Mark are cooking. The turkey had to go in, and he's getting all the pies ready."

"You guys looked great out there," Sophia said.

"Thanks," I told her. Then held my hand up for a high five from George.

"I still think it would have been more fun if there had been turkeys running with you," the kid said seriously, earning some laughs from my family.

Just then, a golf cart came squealing to a halt beside us. Darren and Becca were mid-laugh as they climbed out. Of course, she was the volunteer he'd been assigned for the security detail. They were probably best friends already. I didn't think I'd ever heard Darren laugh before, but it made sense that Becca made it happen. Everybody loved that girl.

Will's fiancée came up and immediately hugged me, completely unconcerned with the fact that I was sweaty. "Congratulations, Joan!"

I smiled. "Thanks, Becca."

"And congratulations to you, Ian." She just went ahead and hugged him, too.

"Thank you?" His wide eyes met mine over her shoulder.

I mouthed, *Will's leafer*, and he nodded as recognition dawned from our conversation at Mattie B's.

"Y'all hop in," Becca said after she released Ian. "I'll drive you down to the courthouse for the award ceremony. I think they set up some outdoor heaters for the crowd."

I told my family they could leave, but they insisted on walking down to watch. Ian told Sophia that they should head back to the house. He said it was to get George out of the cold, but I was pretty sure he was worried about all the people. There was no way Eloise Carter would pass up the opportunity to announce Dorian Masters as the co-winner of the Kirby Falls Turkey Trot. Pandemonium was likely to ensue. At the very least, there would be cameras and attention focused Ian's way.

With a final farewell and another high five for us both, George and Sophia made their way toward the parking garage.

Darren climbed into the front seat of the golf cart beside Becca, and Ian and I sat down behind them, facing backward.

"You're gonna want to hold on," I warned him seconds before Becca jolted us into motion.

Ian scrambled to clutch the rail at his side. I snickered.

"Well, Coach. How'd I do?"

At his question, I swiveled to meet Ian's gaze. "It wasn't my best time, but it wasn't bad. You did . . . pretty good." Truthfully, he'd done amazing. He'd averaged below seven minutes per mile, and beginners didn't just win races their first time out—even family-fun 5Ks. It probably helped that he was in phenomenal shape. Being in his damn twenties probably didn't hurt either.

He grinned. "So, I'm a natural, is what you're saying."

I shook my head and returned my attention to watch Main Street fly by, but there was a smile tugging at my lips.

"You're a good running partner," I told him, giving him the honesty I would have comfortably withheld, but maybe he deserved a little bit of truth. "You did great out there today."

Ian stayed quiet, but I could feel his attention on the side of my face. I didn't turn—couldn't confront whatever emotion might be playing out over his features.

With my gaze on the road unfurling behind us, I noted that they'd be removing the road barriers soon and opening up downtown. The crowd would disperse, and folks would go home, most to celebrate Thanksgiving with loved ones.

I gnawed on the inside of my cheek for a moment before reaching a decision.

"You can come to Thanksgiving dinner at the farmhouse, if you want," I said in a rush, looking at Ian. "George and Sophia and Darren, too."

His head snapped back in my direction. We stared at each other for a long moment, likely equally surprised by the invitation that had come out of my mouth.

I couldn't explain it, but it felt wrong that Ian and George should spend the holiday alone. We weren't family, but it was downright unneighborly to leave them to fend for themselves while we carried on across the highway with a huge meal. It would be a tight fit for all of us in my parents' dining room, but we'd make it work. And I knew my mother would agree with me.

After some prolonged quiet in which Ian didn't graciously accept or thank me for the invitation in any way, his face did something complicated before he bit down on his very obvious amusement.

"What?" I snapped. "That wasn't a joke."

"No, I know." He nodded, eyes sparkling.

"I was trying to be nice."

"You did great."

I scowled, and he burst out laughing.

It took me a minute, but I finally caught up. "My mom already invited you, didn't she?"

His laughter continued. "Yeah, but having you blurt it in a rush, out of nowhere, really meant a lot to me."

Glaring, I whacked him on the thigh—his very firm thigh.

He clutched his leg dramatically. "Don't injure me. This is an award-winning leg."

I rolled my eyes and made to turn away.

"Wait," Ian called, tugging on my arm to get my attention. "Yes, your mother invited us, but I told her that I didn't want to impose. Maggie invited us, too. You Southerners are just desperate to feed people." I snorted a laugh because that was true. "But the Thai place downtown is open. We'll just pick up some takeout for our little group. No big deal."

Disappointment I didn't understand had me looking away, but I nodded. "What about the rest of the cast and crew? Are they doing anything?"

Filming was paused for today, but they were resuming tomorrow. I knew they were planning a weeklong break for the Christmas holidays so folks could celebrate with their families, but they were on a tight schedule this week—something about the weather and the light this time of year for outdoor shooting.

"Yeah, I think Della is having something catered at the Sterling House," he replied.

"You don't want to go there?"

He shook his head and picked at a nonexistent thread on his dark pants. "No. I wouldn't be able to take Georgie." Ian let out a deep breath. "And, well, you're supposed to spend holidays with the people that matter, right? I've missed so many things with that kid—birthdays and Christmases. It feels wrong to miss any more."

I managed another nod.

Further conversation never materialized because the golf cart stopped, and Becca led us up to the courthouse steps, where Eloise Carter waited in a pale blue winter pantsuit and matching beret.

I watched in some weird combination of fascination and horror as Ian morphed into someone else. How he wiped away the emotions he'd worn on his face during our conversation just a moment ago. The shame and regret were quickly replaced by a blinding grin.

The other top finishers arrived, and the brief award ceremony got underway. I stood, beside the podium, unable to focus.

Ian Wells had run next to me and won the 5K, but it was Dorian Masters who smiled and waved to the crowd as he accepted a medal from Eloise.

As expected, the woman took great pleasure in announcing his presence. People gasped and whipped out their phones as Darren stationed himself to the right of the podium. Eloise gave a lengthy speech about how important the visitors from Hollywood were to Kirby Falls. Then she did everything but squeeze Ian's pecs and say, "My, what big muscles you have."

The old woman should have been embarrassed. Hell, I was embarrassed for her.

Thankfully, the ceremony ended uneventfully. Darren hustled Ian over to the waiting golf cart. He looked back for me, but I waved him off and mouthed, *Go*. As soon as Ian was seated, Becca took off. They'd avoided a scene, and I was grateful for it.

I found my family and took a few pictures that Candace insisted upon, forcing smiles for my sister's sake. I felt strange and uneasy—impatient, and at the same time, disappointed. Like something was missing. Like it wasn't worth documenting today's win if Ian wasn't standing next to me. He'd been a part of it, and he should be here.

He'd become a part of more than just my running routine.

And if I closed my eyes, I could still see his face when he said he wanted to spend Thanksgiving with George.

*You're supposed to spend holidays with the people that matter, right?*

More than his pained expression so full of uncertainty, his words lingered, burrowing themselves beneath my skin and putting me on edge for the rest of the morning and all afternoon.

I couldn't focus on the football game with my dad or the cornbread my mother had me mix up. I didn't even have Brady to distract me. He and Mac were joining the Clarks for their Thanksgiving.

So when the turkey was resting, and the rolls were just coming out of the oven, I stepped into the kitchen and pulled my mother aside.

Six hours after I'd watched Ian escape in a golf cart, my family and I showed up on his porch with turkey, ham, and all the fixings.

Ian stared in confusion as we huddled near the front door.

"Happy Thanksgiving," Candace called as she breezed by him with the sweet potato casserole.

"Sorry to barge in." Mercer shrugged his big shoulders and followed his fiancée.

Ian's mouth opened, but my dad passed him a pecan pie and said, "You'll turn the game on, right?"

"Sure," Ian muttered distractedly, but my dad was already inside the house and taking off his shoes.

"What are you doing here?" Ian asked. The question was for those of us remaining on the porch—just Mom and me—but his blue eyes were focused only on mine.

"Well, you couldn't spend Thanksgiving alone in a strange place," my mother explained, as if it were obvious. "Plus, we made more than enough for everyone."

"You're a good neighbor, Amy. It's really not necessary, but thank you for this," Ian told her sincerely.

Then my mother smiled at me in such a way that I knew betrayal was imminent. Just before passing Ian in the doorway, she said, "Actually, it was Joan's idea."

Alone on the porch and holding a brown sugar–glazed spiral ham, I bravely met Ian's gaze and found it so fond and tender that I had to fight the impulse to look away.

"I—"

"Joan!" George cried suddenly as he sprang onto the threshold.

I'd never been so grateful to be interrupted by someone before in my life.

"Hi, George. Happy Thanksgiving."

"Come see my fort in the sunroom."

"I can't wait," I told him honestly.

The kid took off at top speed, socked feet slipping over hardwood flooring.

I made to follow, but Ian's free hand gently cupped my elbow, stopping me in the narrow entryway. Ian's body was close. I could feel the heat he radiated as his fingers held me frozen in place. Evergreen warmth invaded my lungs, and something flipped over in my stomach.

"Thank you," he said, voice low, tone painfully soft.

"It was nothing."

"It's *not* nothing," he insisted.

I swallowed hard, my mouth suddenly dry as a desert. Ian's face was right there. I could see the dark afternoon stubble along his jaw and all the different shades that made his blue eyes so brilliant. The curly black lashes were deeply distracting.

One careless inhale would have his chest grazing my shoulder, and then where would we be? I didn't need to know what his muscles felt like. It was bad enough seeing them beneath his clothes. But the realization was there, and attraction along with it.

Of course, Ian was handsome. I wasn't blind to his face or his body or his dimples. But he was also a commodity. America's leading man. He wasn't . . . mine. No matter what he'd insinuated. Silly, inexplicable crushes didn't matter when you came from two very different worlds.

So I remembered my place, and I kept walking, ignoring the way Ian stood completely still and how I could feel him staring after me.

In the large, open kitchen, Sophia helped unload food and chatted with my sister. Darren had joined my dad in the nearby living room as they flipped through channels, searching for the game.

I placed the ham on the counter, and a moment later, Ian entered my periphery.

I stayed quiet and forced myself to focus on preparing the meal.

Mercer produced a carving knife and platter from somewhere and took the foil off the turkey.

Thank Christ, George entered the kitchen at just that moment and distracted everyone by shouting, "Yay, turkey!"

"I thought you were a vegetarian," Ian said, grinning down at his nephew.

"That was last week," the boy informed him, making us laugh.

It was organized chaos as we set the table and uncovered dishes. All the while, I was painfully aware of Ian moving next to me or behind me. I'd feel his gaze and force myself to focus on scooping mashed potatoes into a serving dish or brushing honey butter on the rolls. But I couldn't ignore how it felt to be here in this moment or why I'd insisted upon it in the first place.

Yes, I was being hospitable. Ian had wormed his way into my life beyond the movie and the orchard and all of it. And, of course, I cared about George and wanted him to have a traditional holiday with people who knew who he was and cared about him. But it was more than that.

It was a quiet admission in the back of a golf cart. The way I could see every regret cross Ian's face as he'd spoken about missing parts of George's early life. And how he'd been forced to pack it all away at the drop of a hat to become someone else—someone brighter, someone shinier, someone perfect.

*You're supposed to spend holidays with the people that matter, right?*

Even if it was only to myself, I could admit that Ian had become that for me.

JOAN

The orchard was closed for Thanksgiving and the day after, so I didn't technically need to be at work. But George had asked if he could see me on Friday, and I'd said yes. Ian was filming, and I'd told Sophia that George was fine with me for the day if she wanted to sightsee or explore.

The weather was chilly but not too cold, and by midday, the sun was shining brightly in a cloudless sky. So I texted Maggie a quick note and then found what I was looking for in the shed behind my parents' house before making my way across the road to pick up George.

"We're going fishing? Really, Joanie?" he asked when he saw me.

The "Joanie" was new. It seemed like he'd picked up the nickname yesterday from my family.

"Yep. I have all the gear we'll need."

He pumped a little fist in the air, and I laughed, happy to see him come out of his quiet, reserved shell so much lately. He seemed like a different kid when compared to the one who'd silently watched me work and rarely smiled.

We made our way across the yard and down the hillside. Junior and Nola's house overlooked the pond at Grandpappy's, but several attractions were closed in the winter, so there were fewer tourists about. All the u-pick operations were out of season. Most visitors were up at the General Store or over by the Orchard Bake Shop.

My truck was parked on the worn tractor path right next to a cherry tree beside the water. There was a bench and a scattering of Adirondack chairs nearby as well.

I showed George the fishing rods I'd brought. There was a kid-sized one that Brady had used many years ago. It had a little case and was still in good shape.

We worked on casting for a while. It took some time, but the kid's movements evened out. He was eventually able to coordinate swinging the rod and releasing the line.

"Okay, let's go bait our hooks," I said, and moved toward the plastic container of nightcrawlers I'd left on the bench.

I was mostly going to do this part on my own. Hooks were sharp and dangerous, and he could learn just by watching.

But when I glanced over to George, he was pale, staring at the worms with a stricken expression.

"That's bait?" he asked, in a small voice.

Patting the seat next to me, I nodded. "Yeah. They're worms. Fish like to eat them."

"And you poke them on the hook like that? Alive?"

His horrified frown had me shifting in my seat. "Uh, yeah."

I guess I'd never considered the life of an earthworm. But to a sensitive kid who loved animals, I could see how this might come as a shock.

Quickly, I thought about what I had in my truck. The food pantry in town was always depleted following Thanksgiving. Using most of their stores, they put together holiday meals for families in need. They usually put a call out afterward to replenish their shelves. I was planning on dropping off a load of canned goods the next time I was in town. They were currently bagged up in the backseat of my truck.

"I have an idea," I said. "Sit tight."

George watched me carefully put the lid on the moving nightcrawlers before I hurried over to my truck.

A minute later, I returned to the bench.

Grateful for the pop top, I opened the vacuum-sealed can. "Fish like corn, too."

"Okay," the boy said, brightening a little.

He studied the way I carefully loaded each yellow kernel onto the length of the hook. When I was finished with both of our rods, I smiled at George. But he looked uneasy again.

"What's the matter?"

"How does the fish get the corn off the hook?"

I hesitated. "The fish goes after the hook. The corn is bait."

"Like a trick?"

"Well, yeah." My voice was soft when I admitted, "That's fishing, George. I'd planned on releasing whatever we caught. Right back into the water."

"After you stab it in the mouth with a hook?"

"Yes . . . I suppose so."

The kid looked so conflicted. I knew he didn't want to hurt the fish. And while it wasn't a dilemma that had ever kept me up at night, I could see how fishing might seem cruel.

"I have another idea," I said.

And that was how we found ourselves standing on the edge of the pond, feeding canned corn to the fish in Grandpappy's pond.

The murky brown water churned around the brim and catfish as they fought one another for a snack.

With sticky fingers and a big smile, I watched George laugh as he threw another handful.

I grinned too, even as the happiness in my heart was accompanied by an underlying sort of ache. George had been through so much. And despite the loss he'd endured, he was still a good-natured, big-hearted kid. He was smart and thoughtful, inquisitive and kind. He cared about animals and people. He told everyone to have a nice day. What seven-year-old did that?

George deserved goodness and light. He was owed some normalcy from the universe. Some happiness. And if I got to be a part of that—even for a little while—I wanted it.

I'd take him hiking or teach him every single thing I knew about farming. I'd let him feed the fish instead of catch them. I'd do whatever it took to make this little boy smile, to be a small part of his life.

Later, when our hands were clean and we sat side by side on the bench watching some geese float in the distance, I said, "We should invite Ian to feed the fish."

"That's okay," George said simply.

I'd noticed some friction there and was curious why the kid was standoffish with his uncle, a guy who was trying so hard. Every time Ian caught sight of my friendship bracelets, he got this look on his face. Part pride and part longing. It was painful to watch George ignore him, especially when the boy was so attached to me, someone who'd been a stranger until very recently.

George had been with Ian for nearly a year. I would have thought that, by now, their relationship would be a little less rocky.

"You don't think Ian would like feeding the fish?" I asked, making sure my tone held no judgment.

"Nah. He's a movie star. He has big, important meetings. He doesn't have time for fun stuff like that. He doesn't have time for—"

He cut himself off, but the "me" was loud in the stillness of the chilly afternoon.

With my gaze focused on the distance, I said, "Your uncle is pretty famous. I was nervous around him at first."

I felt George's attention on the side of my face. "You were?"

"Oh, sure. It's weird to see someone in real life who's been on a movie screen. Was it like that for you, too?"

"No. My mom never let me watch his movies. I didn't know about all that until I came to live with him."

I turned just enough to meet George's gaze. "I bet that was real hard, moving to California."

He nodded and looked down.

"But once I got to know your uncle," I said, "I wasn't as nervous. I realized he's pretty silly sometimes. Not like a big, serious celebrity."

George smiled a little and agreed, "He is pretty silly."

"And don't you see him every evening? Doesn't he read you a bedtime story and tuck you in?"

I knew Ian did this because he'd told me it was the best part of his day. He didn't always make it in time for dinner. And George didn't always let him watch *Wheel of Fortune*, but the bedtime story was something Ian consistently made time for.

"Yeah, I guess," George admitted. "He does the voices. He's pretty good at it."

Smiling, I told him, "The movie stuff is just your uncle's job, like farming is mine. If you really needed him, George, he'd be there for you. He'd find a way. He loves you."

"It's a weird job."

I nodded because that was true. I'd thought it enough that I'd be a hypocrite if I didn't agree. "When I was growing up, I went to school with kids whose parents were lawyers and doctors and pharmacists and businessmen. But my dad was a farmer. My classmates had a lot more money than me, and my dad was always busy, always had dirt under his nails. But he's the hardest worker I've ever known, and he'd do anything for his family. So when kids used to tease me about Dad showing up in overalls and muddy boots to my chorus concert or my piano recital, I didn't let it bother me."

Truthfully, I'd told those kids off and got in a number of fights in elementary school, but I wasn't going to mention that.

"He was my dad, and I loved him. I was proud of the work he did because it put food on our table and a roof over our heads."

I shifted on the bench to face George. He mirrored my pose.

"Doesn't Ian take care of you?" I asked. "Buys those flavor-blasted Goldfish you like and those Spider-Man pajamas that are your favorite? Made a room and a space for you?"

"Yeah," George whispered, and my heart nearly broke.

"I know your life changed when your mom—when you came to live with Ian. And none of that is fair. But Ian's life changed, too. He loves you, and he's working hard to make sure you always have a safe, stable life with him."

George was quiet. His little brows pushed together thoughtfully. Then he finally asked, "Did kids really use to make fun of you?"

"Yep."

"I went to a school in California, but kids picked on me, too. Uncle Ian said I didn't have to ever go back there."

I nodded, letting that knowledge wash over me. Of course, Ian would be protective. Maybe hiring a private tutor like Sophia seemed outlandish to some people, but not to Ian, whose nephew had been struggling.

I was sure the situation with George's arrival had been tumultuous and disorienting, but Ian had stepped up and taken control, simplified the schooling situation, and protected his nephew at the same time. I could respect that decision. Admire it, even.

Sometimes being the bigger person didn't count for anything. Especially when someone you loved was hurting. Ian had the means to make that one problem go away, and he had.

I tapped George on the knee. "That was your uncle taking care of you. And he brought you here to Kirby Falls so he could be close to you while he works."

Realization seemed to dawn across his features as he looked up at me. "Yeah, he did bring me here. Gloria wanted me to stay in California with Miss Sophia."

Gloria.

I opened my mouth to get a last name out of the kid, but before I could, he shifted gears suddenly, the way only a child can. "My mama was a lawyer. She helped people who couldn't stand up for themselves."

George rarely mentioned his mother. I didn't want to interrupt by demanding Gloria's name and address so I could pay her a visit.

"That sounds like it was important work," I said gently.

"Yeah." He chewed on his bottom lip for a moment.

"Your uncle has an important job too because it lets him take care of you and Sophia and Darren—"

"And Eddie J," the kid interrupted.

I frowned. "Who's Eddie J?"

"He's the best," George gushed. "He's Ian's assistant, but he lives in California and couldn't come with us."

"Well, it sounds like you guys are a team. You and Ian and Sophia and Darren and Eddie J."

"Yep."

I noticed George didn't feel the need to correct me and add the infamous Gloria to the list, whoever she was. I needed to ask Ian about her.

"Just like you're a team with your family," George said.

"That's right," I agreed.

"The orchard team," he said, and then looked at me very seriously. "Can I be on your team, too?"

I didn't think I could swallow around the tightness in my throat, so I didn't bother. Just croaked out, "Yeah, George. Of course you can."

He grinned wide, and I could tell he had another loose tooth. "Because I'm your assistant farmer."

"No, because you're my friend and a farmer in training."

"Thanks, Joanie. Let's go feed some more fish."

The boy bounded up happily like he hadn't just taken a wrecking ball to my heart.

That evening, I went home and dug a hole in my backyard, churning up the ground and releasing a can of worms back into the soil where they belonged.

## JOAN

Candace and Mercer were getting married in three weeks, just before Christmas, and, as the maid of honor, bachelorette party planning had fallen to me.

The other bridesmaids had given their input. Bonnie had suggested a paint and sip event up in Asheville. Becca had thought a grown-up slumber party would be right up my sister's alley. And Mac had insisted on male strippers.

I'd taken matters into my own hands.

We'd just finished up dinner at Boards and Bubbles, where we'd ordered and consumed multiple themed charcuterie boards and several bottles of sparkling wine. It was cold, but we were now walking the three blocks over to 6th Street.

Hometown Holler was the country western bar in downtown Kirby Falls, and Candace had been dying to try it out since it opened last month. This seemed like the perfect opportunity.

But before she'd even made it to the front doors of the establishment, the food truck parked outside caught her attention.

"JOANIE!" she squealed loudly, making me wince. She'd had an entire bottle of sparkling wine all on her own. "Did you seriously get Bev's Sno-Kones truck to come to my bachelorette party?"

"You're the bride," I answered by way of explanation.

My very tipsy sister launched herself at me. Laughing, I stumbled back, squeezing her tight.

She pulled back immediately. "I'm sorry. Was that too much?"

Shaking my head, I pulled her in for another hug. "Happy bachelorette."

"Thanks, Joanie. This is the best." Then my sister skipped away to order her favorite shaved ice in the middle of winter.

Bev, the owner, had been pretty agreeable to my request. She usually closed up shop after the Orchard Festival in September and only opened back up when the Spring Fling rolled around in March. I was grateful that she'd been willing to do me this favor and let me rent the truck for one early December evening to sit outside the bar, with her teenage grandson inside, taking orders and running the machine. Candace loved Bev's Sno-Kones, and I wanted her night to be perfect.

"That was very thoughtful," Bonnie told me as she walked by to join Candace, Becca, Larry, and Corie.

Larry—short for Laramie—was Mac and Bonnie's cousin. She also worked at Grandpappy's farm and was part of our book club. I'd known her for years. Corie was Larry's new girlfriend. She was going to be Candace and Mercer's wedding photographer, and she seemed like a very sweet person. We hadn't all scared her off yet, in any case.

Chloe, another book club friend and a Grandpappy's employee, was sitting out our celebration. She was newly pregnant and sick all the time. She'd called the restaurant ahead of dinner tonight and had a bottle of champagne delivered along with her well-wishes.

Mac, the final member of our party, came to stand beside me. "Now, don't be mad."

I turned to look at her. "MacKenzie Eloise, I swear, if there are half-naked dancers inside that building, I will—"

"Oh, come on. They're not *half* naked."

My eyes bulged.

She snickered. "I'm just kidding, Joan." Quickly, she added, "Calm down."

"Famous last words of many men, I'm sure."

Mac laughed. "Probably. No, I didn't hire any male exotic dancers. Even though I wanted to. But you did let me handle the invites, soooo . . ." She trailed off, attention slipping over my shoulder.

I followed her gaze to see none other than Dorian Masters, crossing the street from the parking lot, wearing cowboy boots, jeans that stretched indecently across his muscular thighs, and a plaid western long-sleeved shirt with pearl snap buttons. Completing the look, he had a pale-gray cowboy hat perched on his head. Jesus, there was even a navy-blue bandana around his neck.

"What the hell is he wearing? Is he going to rob a train?" I hissed at Mac.

She laughed giddily and clapped her hands, shouting, "This is going to be amazing," as she ran toward the others.

Ian met the ladies in front of the food truck and said, "Let's go, girls," like Shania Fucking Twain. I closed my eyes, thinking this was going to be a long night.

Squeals erupted as everyone crowded around Ian. He gave hugs to Candace and Mac and shook hands with the women he hadn't met before.

Resigned to my fate, I went and joined the others.

---

"Joanie, why have you not hit that yet?" Candace asked.

Bonnie nearly spit out her fruity-looking cocktail, and Mac cackled maniacally.

I shot my drunk-ass sister a glare. I should have made her switch to water an hour ago.

The rest of them were watching Ian and Becca two-step around the dance floor.

"What?" Candace asked dramatically as she pushed dark strands of hair away from her sweaty face.

It was nearly one in the morning, and she and the other women had been dancing and drinking nonstop.

This was the first time more than two people had been sitting in the booth at the same time.

Ian twirled Becca while she laughed, and I heard several awws from my side.

Of course, Ian was good at dancing. He'd been boot scootin' boogying across the shiny wood floor all evening. After the other patrons' initial shock, they'd pretty much given him space. Plus, Larry and Mac were good at scaring away unwanted attention from our in-house celebrity.

He'd insisted on buying the drinks tonight, his present to Candace and a contribution to her celebration.

And, honestly, the cowboy getup wasn't even a turnoff. He may have surprised me, but he owned it. The jeans alone were a work of art, accentuating the muscles in his legs and the unfairly generous curve of his backside.

I knew it was just attraction—something simple and biological, primitive even. On a fundamental level, my body recognized that Ian was big and strong and capable of providing. I knew all of this even as a modern, self-sufficient, independent woman. I was being controlled by my baser instincts.

But it didn't stop my eyes from seeking him out, from lingering and appreciating his beauty. I'd seen him on the television in my living room and at ten feet tall in the movie theater. He was handsome, striking—beautiful in a way that was undeniable, that set him apart from regular people.

And for the first time in my life, I was just like everyone else, unable to look away. It was frustrating and infuriating to realize that I was not immune to Ian's face or his body or his charm.

I watched him spin Becca again, making her laugh, and felt my own smile threaten.

"Yeah, I'm with Candace on this," Bonnie said suddenly, jolting me back to the conversation. "He is so obviously smitten with you. Why don't you go for it?"

I didn't know what the hell she meant by that. Smitten? Hardly.

Ian and I had mostly argued tonight. He'd tried to get me out on the dance floor for the "Watermelon Crawl" and "Cotton-Eye Joe," but I'd declined both attempts.

"He is not smitten with me," I insisted.

But Ian chose that moment to look our way, shooting me a grin and a wink. He may as well have called me a liar in bright neon lights.

"Uh-huh," Bonnie said, before slurping the last of her cocktail.

"He's after a challenge. Or he's bored. I still haven't figured it out," I grumbled.

But what he hadn't done was try anything. Ian hadn't brought up his crush —or whatever it was—since that day weeks ago when we'd gone running. He hadn't hit on me or asked me out. There had been no moves whatsoever.

Even with our Turkey Trot training complete, he still ran with me when his schedule permitted. And he joined George and me for lunch when he could, too. He played poker with my dad, worked out with my brother, and texted recipes back and forth with my mom.

He was everywhere, even infiltrating my limited social life. Hell, he'd probably be at our next book club meeting.

But currently, he was at my sister's bachelorette party, getting under my skin.

"So what if he's after a challenge?" Mac said. "Give him one. Make him earn it."

"Yesss," Candace slurred and tried to give Mac a high five. Spoiler alert: She missed and whacked me in the shoulder.

"Y'all need water," I murmured. "And Jesus."

"And you need to get laid," Mac offered. "Let that hot celebrity do dirty, dirty things to you, Joanie."

I looked around, but the music was too loud for anyone to hear what my friends were practically shouting.

"He's twenty-nine," I hissed.

They all stared at me.

"Twenty-nine!" I shouted, as if that might drive the point home.

"So? You're thirty-six, not dead and buried," Mac replied.

Candace nodded emphatically.

"Joan, I'm going to be real with you," Bonnie said. She was typically very soft-spoken and supportive. But her divorce this past summer had really taken a toll. I wasn't sure what advice she was about to lay on me, but I definitely didn't expect "Don't look a gift penis in the mouth."

My eyes widened as my sister choked on her laugh and her margarita.

"No!" Mac practically hollered. "PUT a gift penis in your mouth."

At this, all the women erupted into laughter. Candace was bent over, clutching her side. Bonnie had a hand over her mouth as her eyes watered.

I wondered what I'd ever done to deserve these chaos monsters.

"I've yet to meet a man that can outperform my favorite vibrator," I told them seriously. "So, no, I don't have any interest in taking the Hollywood actor for a spin."

Their cackles tapered off as they looked at me.

"God, that's bleak," Mac said, frowning in disbelief.

"That's so sad," Candace wailed, tears filling her eyes.

Bonnie winced.

Luckily, Becca chose that moment to slide into the booth and distract everyone from my depressing sex life. That was, until she said, "Whew,

Ian wore me out." She used a napkin to blot the sweat on her neck and hairline. "He's a machine. I bet he could go all night."

Mac shook her head fast, biting her lip.

Bonnie just laid her face down on the table.

Candace's tears flipped from sadness to hilarity.

I stood up abruptly and sighed.

"What?" Becca looked between all of us. "What did I say?"

The three other women burst out laughing again.

I rolled my eyes and spun away to get outside for some air—and maybe a Tiger's Blood snow cone—and smacked into a wall of muscle.

I knew it was Ian before his strong hands steadied me. The scent of his cologne permeated the air. Woodsy pine and rich amber had me leaning in before I could stop myself.

I could see damp perspiration in the vee of his neck. He'd taken off the bandana and stuffed it into his back pocket at some point in the night. And, thank the good Lord for that, because what a shame it had been to cover up the long line of his throat or any part of that sharp jawline.

"Whoa, there," Ian said.

"If you call me 'little lady,' I'll deck you."

He grinned like I was hilarious. "Actually, I wanted to see if you'd like to dance." I opened my mouth to say no, but he continued, "I know you don't line dance. I asked the deejay if he'd play something slower."

Just then, the opening of an old Tim McGraw song filtered through the dance hall.

"What do you say?" Ian wasn't smiling now. In fact, he looked very serious. The masculine throat I'd been admiring moved in a hard swallow.

There were a hundred reasons why I should say no. It was wrong to encourage this—whatever it was. He was young and temporary. We were more opposite than we could ever be alike.

But when I'd been thinking of Ian earlier, and how he hadn't made a single move since admitting that he wanted to date me, I'd been . . . well, I'd been disappointed, truth be told.

Maybe we *were* too different. His life was one I could never fit into. But I liked him. Had for a while now. He was charming and funny—which didn't impress me much—but he was also humble and kind. A good man who loved his nephew and valued the people in his life.

If most women went for charisma and sex appeal, then I wasn't ever going to be most women.

Integrity was what I valued. Loyalty was sexy as hell, in my book. Dedication was what did it for me.

So when Ian wiggled his fingers in invitation, I slipped my hand into his and nodded.

There was a moment—brief and humbling—when surprised delight flickered across Ian's features. Something subtle, there and gone in an instant, but very clearly tinged with relief.

It felt like I'd made the right decision—the honest one.

He led me onto the center of the dance floor. No wallflower hovering on the fringes. Dozens of eyes focused on us as Ian slipped one arm around my waist and brought our linked fingers to rest against his chest.

Our movements were smooth as he guided us. It seemed unfair that a body that big and masculine should be graceful, too. He was warm as we shifted together, heat radiating from his tall frame.

"I noticed you weren't partaking," Ian said lightly.

"Not tonight. Someone has to get these drunk disasters home."

Our attention strayed to the booth at the same time. And Jesus Christ, all six women were staring right at us. Immediately, they burst into a flurry of activity to appear nonchalant. Candace grabbed a bar menu the size of a postcard, and she and Bonnie both attempted to hide behind it. Larry and Corie turned toward one another and pretended to be deep in conversation. Mac, inexplicably, looked up at the ceiling as if she was expecting some rain any minute now. And Becca, God bless her. Becca grinned and gave us a little wave.

Ian chuckled even as I grumbled under my breath.

"You have good friends," Ian said.

"You're just saying that because they're all on your side."

"Whatever do you mean?" he playacted dramatically.

I snorted. "You know that if you kissed me right now, they'd stand up on that table and cheer."

His eyes, still somehow bright and tempting, even in the spinning strobe lights, sparkled as he regarded me. "Ah, but what would you do, dear Joan, if I kissed you right now?"

I read the challenge in his words, the dare. But even though my brain knew he was teasing, my body didn't. My throat went dry at the prospect. My heart rate kicked into a gallop.

He didn't give me the chance to answer. Instead, he shook his head. "No, I know you better than that. You don't have to worry."

"Oh, really?"

"I wouldn't kiss you in front of all these people. Not for the first time, at least. You'd kill me if it ended up in the Facebook group. Some blurry photo and unwanted attention instead of an intimate moment between two people."

"Thought a lot about this hypothetical first kiss, have you?" My voice was playful, but I could feel my pulse in my fingertips where they rested on his nape.

"Oh." He grinned, and both dimples appeared. "You have no idea."

Heat bloomed in my chest . . . and lower. A heavy warmth settled below my belly button.

Maybe he was right. Maybe I didn't want him to kiss me in front of all my friends. Or in any public place where we'd be exposed and judged. But maybe I *did* want him to kiss me.

And the fact that he'd thought about it, too, I didn't—I couldn't—

My face must have revealed some of my panic because his steps faltered for a beat, and his dimples disappeared.

"Hey, I'm sorry if I made you uncomfortable. That wasn't my—"

"I'm not uncomfortable," I hurried to reassure him. And it was true. He'd never once made me feel threatened or anything like that. But I did feel vulnerable, and that might have been worse.

"I'm not uncomfortable," I repeated. "I just don't understand why someone with their face on three different magazine covers in the Winn-Dixie checkout line—"

"Is it just three this week?" he wondered idly.

I glared.

"Sorry." He squeezed my hand. "Continue."

I blew out a breath and admitted, "I just don't know how to understand this. You and me."

Ian glanced down briefly as a slight smile tilted up the corners of his lips. The pressure on the small of my back eased momentarily as I felt his hand flex against me before bringing us even closer together. Our thighs brushed, and I suddenly became aware of every point of contact.

The strength in his frame. The tight muscles under my hand. His steady, reassuring grip as he continued to hold me and move us effortlessly around the dance floor.

Then, so softly that I had to lean closer to hear, he said, "You'd give me a ride to the airport, if I asked. You'd change my tire if you found me on the side of the road. You'd do everything in your power to drag me out of a burning building, but you don't trust me enough to go on a date with me. To eat food together. It's utterly fascinating."

"I don't want to be fascinating," I told him, but I wasn't sure I believed it.

"Too bad. I'm practically intrigued at this point. Next stop is enamored."

———

### Ian

Joan shook her head like she was resigned, but she smiled, clearly in spite of herself. But my words made her look away. Like I'd given her a compliment she didn't know what to do with.

To ease her suffering, I admitted, "I'm trying to not be such a spoiled celebrity baby. Was that what you called me?"

That got her attention.

"I don't think I used those words," she said primly.

I chuckled. "I think you did, but that's okay. You were right."

"Ian, you don't need to change yourself because I gave you shit about doing your own laundry."

I shrugged, painfully aware of her palm resting on my shoulder, enjoying her touch a little too much for how close we were dancing.

"I like when you give me shit about stuff. It can be our love language. Quick, give me shit about something else."

She stared at me incredulously, and I laughed outright.

"Come on. Hit me with something. I know you want to," I teased.

"This hat." She raised our clasped hands and tapped the brim with one finger. "We're in North Carolina, not Texas."

"Y'all don't wear these here?"

"No, but I appreciate you taking *y'all* for a test drive."

I grinned. "Well, if I'm wearing the hat, I guess I'll never fit in."

With that, I took off the brand-new Stetson and popped it on her head instead. "You already fit in, so you can pull it off."

She looked affronted for half a second, then shrugged. "We are in a country western bar. It probably won't hurt my reputation too much."

"That's the spirit," I forced out before clearing my throat. She looked entirely too good.

The flannel she wore, I'd seen before. The jeans, too, though they did incredible things for her ass. But her features were softer in the rainbow lights bouncing around the dance floor, pale eyes otherworldly as they reflected the spectrum of colors. Her short hair had a wave to it tonight. Like she'd taken the time to curl it, but her impatient hands had tugged all but the most stubborn coils loose. This was the first time I'd ever seen her wearing makeup. Joan's stern, expressive brows were defined and elegant. Her lips, plump and shiny with gloss. I knew the dramatic winged liner was Larry's handiwork. Mac's sassy, outspoken cousin had done up all the women tonight.

Even with the changes, I could still see the real Joan beneath. The truth was there in the fierce narrowing of her eyes, the sharpness of every expression, the way she seemed to always see through me.

And with my hat on her head, looking the way she did, I wanted to break my promise about kissing her in front of everyone.

The truth was, she'd fit in anywhere in this town, cowboy hat or not. She was welcome in every establishment, esteemed by any business owner. The Judds were staples in Kirby Falls, and everyone knew and respected Joan. It was just the way of things here.

What did it feel like to be so accepted, so embedded in a community? I knew small towns could be hell on reputations. People got labeled at young ages. I was sure there were screwups who wished they could change how they were seen, bad apples who'd long since shaped up. But did the people of Kirby Falls allow for second chances? Or did they cling to the past in favor of the future?

I wanted to know.

I'd never made sense to my parents or my sister. My hometown was just somewhere I was from. Los Angeles was simply a destination for the career I'd always wanted. A pin on a map where dreams were made.

For as much as I liked and wanted Joan, I envied her, too. She knew exactly who she was and where she belonged. And I'd never managed to fit in anywhere.

"Do you wear cowboy hats in Los Angeles?" she said, and I realized this was the first time she'd ever asked me about my life in California.

"When the mood strikes. Or if a role calls for it. I did play a rancher once."

"Is that where you learned to line dance?" she wondered. "I can't imagine that comes up often in your line of work, though."

I laughed. "No, it doesn't. But my job is basically glorified memorization."

Her fingers suddenly stopped dancing across my nape. I wondered if she'd even been aware she was doing it.

I sure was.

Very aware. And I didn't want her to stop.

But she resumed after a moment and said incredulously, "You mean you learned all those line dances here? Tonight?"

I shrugged, surprised that she seemed so taken aback. It was just dancing. "I've always been good at remembering lines and hitting my marks, blocking for scenes. This was just memorizing steps and following along."

"Huh," she replied, completely dumbfounded. "That's amazing."

It would have been nice if she was impressed by normal things, like award nominations or biceps. Still, I was pleased that she found something about me to praise, even if it wasn't my new ability to wash a load of laundry on the gentle cycle.

The slow set ended as the upbeat notes of "A Bar Song" filtered through the speakers.

Joan released me, and I reluctantly let her step out of my arms.

"Thanks for the dance," I told her.

"Guess I better herd these cats and get them home." She wouldn't meet my eyes, and I felt a sense of urgency to stretch out a hand and draw her back to me. That if she took another step away, she'd be out of my reach, and we'd be back to square one.

So, I said, "I'll help. I didn't drink either. I'll drive whoever you want."

Her eyes found mine, at last. "Thank you. That would be a big help. Even getting them into the car. They'll be way more likely to listen to you."

I glanced toward the booth to see Candace slumped against Becca, who petted her hair. "And I have the added benefit of being able to carry your sister."

Joan turned around and groaned.

"Come on, Coach. We've got this."

I held out my fist.

She smiled and bumped it softly. "Okay, then."

## JOAN

"He's going to offer you coffee," I said very quietly. "Just accept it and drink it. Don't make a face."

Brady just had time to say "What?" before Ian opened the door to me, my siblings, and Mercer standing on his front porch.

"Come on in, y'all." Ian smiled as we passed. "Thanks for making time to go over this stuff ahead of the rehearsal. I know you're very busy this week. I'm actually a little nervous and just want everything to be perfect."

And I had to admit, Ian did look nervous. It wasn't an expression I'd seen on him very often, but if you knew where to look—the overly toothy smile, the wide eyes, the stiff set of his shoulders—it was pretty obvious.

This *was* a busy week, Ian was right about that. It was Tuesday, and Candace and Mercer were getting married on Saturday evening.

But I knew for a fact that Ian was busy, too. Between the movie and George and all the time we'd been spending together, Ian had a lot on his plate.

I now saw George most days. Save for the weekends when I was busy selling Christmas trees on the farm. But during the week, George was with me for most afternoons. Sometimes Sophia was there, and sometimes she wasn't. They focused on his schoolwork in the mornings.

Ian had been finding ways to slip away. He'd been joining George and me for lunch nearly every day. And he'd been making it to most of our morning runs, too.

Despite being tugged in many directions, Dorian Masters would be officiating the upcoming wedding ceremony.

Initially, my brother had offered to marry the happy couple. He'd officiated our friends Chloe and Jordan's wedding last summer, and wouldn't shut up about it. But Brady was Mercer's best man. When Ian had found out, he'd offered up his services. Said he'd love to marry Candace and Mercer.

Ian had asked us to come over this morning to discuss the vows and make sure they were exactly right. He'd also requested the presence of the best man and the maid of honor, hence the reason Brady and I were in attendance.

Perhaps it should have been strange that an A-list celebrity was going to not just attend but officiate my sister's wedding, but for some reason, it was easy enough to accept Ian's involvement. It probably helped that he seemed genuinely happy to do it.

That was the thing about Ian. He was adaptable and easygoing. He'd charmed the locals and hadn't batted an eye during the bachelorette party. The man traveled the world and went to award shows, walked red carpets and worked sixteen-hour days on set.

The more I learned about Ian and got to know him, the more I realized that my earliest assumptions had been off base.

He loved being a performer and had been interested in acting since childhood.

And his current acting role was very important to Ian. I knew because he'd told me, and I'd been curious despite myself. We'd had plenty of conversations about the production, how it was a much smaller budget when compared to Ian's other projects. But he'd wanted to work with Della. He valued her process and vision, and respected what she did and how she did it.

Plus, he was a producer on the film, which was a big deal to him, careerwise.

One day, a few weeks ago, as we'd sat on a picnic table and watched George hop across the bounce pillow, Ian had confessed that he'd love to slow down on the acting portion of his career and hoped to write or direct someday. But he didn't know if it would ever happen. That he might never be taken seriously and always be seen as superhero material. That was another reason he'd wanted his current role so badly. So he could work with someone like Della, whose gritty, artistic films were often nominated during awards season. Ian hoped to expand his portfolio and diversify. He wanted space to pursue his interests which would allow him to cut back on acting so that he could spend more time focusing on George.

I'd learned a lot about the movie they were making in my own backyard, too. Ian's character was a blue-collar mechanic, a small-town guy who got caught up in a murder mystery plot after he and his sister discovered a body in the woods.

I knew they'd be wrapping up production in Los Angeles following the location shoot in Kirby Falls. They needed studio space to film some of the interiors they didn't have access to here. But the majority of the movie took place outdoors.

Ian had explained how they shot scenes out of order, which seemed wild to me. And that was why things like continuity were so important. Like how they trimmed his short hair weekly and kept six of the same shirt in wardrobe, just in case.

The more I'd learned about the film, the more I'd come to understand just how demanding the work was for everyone involved. Ian liked to down-play a lot, but he had dialogue and blocking to memorize, and so much going on behind the scenes that it had to be stressful.

But he never let on if he'd had a difficult day or an early start. He never seemed exhausted or frustrated with his work. George and I only ever saw cheerful, happy Ian.

The man was a professional. He'd admitted that his least favorite part of being an actor was when everything wrapped and the film was released. Promoting and dealing with the press took a toll, requiring his time and attention in a way that acting on screen did not.

Curious, I'd asked if he wasn't famous enough to get out of doing the boring interviews and jumping through all those hoops. And he'd said he didn't think anyone was famous enough to avoid that stuff.

"Let me make you guys some coffee," Ian said, drawing my thoughts back to the here and now and this wedding-prep meeting.

"Here we go," I murmured. "Game faces on, people."

Brady, Candace, and Mercer looked at me like I was insane.

"Actually," Ian called over his shoulder as he measured coffee beans and twisted knobs, "I wanted to make sure you two were still okay with me officiating. I didn't think about it when I offered—I was just happy to be involved—but I could see how I might be a distraction."

The sound of grinding interrupted us for a moment.

"Maybe I put you on the spot when I offered," Ian said sheepishly. "I wouldn't blame you if you wanted to back out and find someone else. I don't want to divert attention away. This should be your day."

With his focus on delivering the first two lattes, Ian didn't see Candace's panic.

"No, Ian. No," she hurried to assure him. "It'll be fine. The wedding isn't going to be that big. You've met most of the people who'll be there. We are thrilled to have you included in the ceremony." She smiled genuinely at this, and Mercer nodded his agreement. "I am confident our guests will be more interested in the wedding than leaking photos of you to TMZ."

I wasn't so sure about that, but it really was too late in the game to find someone else.

Still looking a little uncertain, Ian nodded. "Okay, if you're sure."

Then he shifted back to the coffee maker.

I watched as Candace reached for her mug. She took a sip and immediately spit it back into the cup. Mercer had been in the middle of lifting his mug to his lips, but after his fiancée's reaction, he set it back down.

I gave him a stern glare, and he sighed and picked it up again.

"Just drink it," I whispered over the hiss of steamed milk.

Brady stared at Candace, who looked like she was trying to scrape the taste off her tongue with her front teeth.

Fear overtook my brother's features. With his pants very much on fire, he shouted, "I'm lactose intolerant. You can skip me, bro."

*Liar*, I mouthed at him.

Brady shrugged, looking pleased with himself until Ian spun toward the refrigerator.

"That's okay, bro. I have oat milk."

"Great," Brady called with forced enthusiasm.

I didn't bother hiding my grin.

A few minutes later, we all had various mugs of caffeinated abominations in front of us. I was able to sip stoically, probably in large part to the tolerance I'd built up from all the travel mugs Ian had brought me over the last month. Today's blend was definitely an improvement over some of his other creations. But still worse than any gas station coffee I've ever had.

"Oh, something else I wanted to discuss," Ian said from where he faced us across the kitchen island. "Eloise asked me to be the grand marshal for the Christmas parade coming up. She wants me to dress up as Santa."

Candace and Mercer exchanged looks. Brady groaned in sympathy.

"You didn't agree, did you?" I asked incredulously.

Ian frowned in confusion, and it looked so unnatural on his face that I almost laughed. "Obviously, I agreed. Santa, Joan. I'm going to play *Santa*."

"A role of a lifetime. Of course. What was I thinking?"

Ian grinned, but then he went on, "Actually, I said I'd only do it if she agreed to feature Judd's Orchard on Santa's float. Since y'all have done so much for the film and—and for me. Your family has welcomed Georgie and me with open arms. I want to share the spotlight with you and highlight the farm."

Candace and I shared a commiserating glance while Mercer and Brady started laughing.

Ian looked between the four of us. "What?"

In between wheezes, Brady said, "They got into a huge food fight the last time they were in the Christmas parade together."

Ian's blue eyes widened. "What?" he repeated. "I want to hear this story."

"No!" Candace and I shouted in unison.

"It's embarrassing," my sister added. "I wasn't my best self."

"Yeah, you really weren't," I agreed.

Candace whacked me on the shoulder, and I chuckled.

"Anyway," I said, meeting Ian's amused and way-too-interested gaze. "Thanks for the offer, but we're going to pass on the float thing. It's not even a float anyway. You'll just be riding on the back of Bubba Walcott's hay trailer."

Ian looked crestfallen. "But I already told Eloise that you'd dress up as Mrs. Claus."

My siblings burst out laughing.

My mouth dropped open. "You did not."

Just then, George came running into the kitchen and hugged me around the waist. The little stinker must have been eavesdropping because he immediately launched into a sales pitch. "Joanie, I get to ride on the float too! Uncle Ian says it's okay because I'll be in a costume and no one will know me. I'm going to be an elf. I want you to be an elf, too. Sophia's going to be an elf. And Darren is going to be Rudolph."

I glanced at Ian, who was biting his lip in a futile effort to hide his smile.

"An elf sounds good," he agreed seriously, after he'd composed himself. "Or you could always be Mrs. Claus."

I shot him a glare.

"Please, Joanie," the kid begged, his blue eyes impossibly big. "Please ride the float with me."

My chest constricted at the hope on his little face.

Everyone was looking at me, waiting for an answer. I'd rather drink ten cups of Ian's coffee than ride on some stupid hay trailer for two hours in the cold this Sunday night.

"I'll take care of the costumes," Ian said. "You just have to show up."

"Pleeeeease," George pleaded.

With dread sinking like a weight in my belly, along with some truly horrific coffee, I managed a weak smile and said, "Sure, George. I'll be an elf, too."

The boy pumped a small fist in the air and let out a whoop. I could already feel the reluctant smile urging my lips into action.

My attention snagged on something clutched in George's hand as he lowered it. There was a friendship bracelet wrapped around his fingers. The beads were alternating gold and silver, but I couldn't make out the letters from here.

Before George could take off again, he ran over to Ian and said, "Here, I made this one for you."

My family was oblivious to what was happening, back to talking amongst themselves, but I straightened on my stool. I knew Ian didn't have a bracelet from George yet. I'd seen the longing on the man's face when he caught sight of mine.

But now, it looked like Ian had been hit by a truck.

George thrust the beaded bracelet toward his uncle, and Ian lowered his big body down on one knee to accept it.

"It's for me?" Ian asked quietly, so damn hopeful that I felt a catch in my throat.

"Yep," George replied easily, the way only a child could—one who was completely unaware of how he'd plowed through his uncle's emotional walls.

"Let's see what it says," Ian said softly, placing the bracelet gently across his palm. "Uncle Ian," he read.

"That's you," George told him simply. "We're teammates, so you needed one, too."

I bit the inside of my cheek hard, thinking back to my conversation with the boy during our fishing adventure.

Then I watched as Ian swallowed several times before clearing his throat. "This is the best. I'm going to put it on right now."

He stretched the elastic around his thick wrist and ruffled his nephew's hair. "Thanks, Georgie. I love it."

"You're welcome," the kid called and then skipped out of the kitchen, leaving an emotionally disheveled Ian staring after him.

After a moment, Ian's gaze drifted back to the bracelet circling his wrist. It remained there a beat before he smoothly got to his feet. When he turned, his gaze found mine, blue eyes bright.

He smiled wide, both dimples appearing. I was helpless to do anything but smile back.

Realistically, I knew that this man was an award-winning actor who had a tight grip on his expressions and could command them at will. But there had been something staggering about witnessing the raw honesty of George and Ian's exchange. A child's direct and open way, contrasted with an adult doing everything in his power to rein himself in. How deeply touched Ian had been and how he'd so obviously been dismantled by a seven-year-old who had—maybe—finally started to see how much Ian cared for him.

It felt like I'd witnessed a pivotal step in their relationship—a core memory for Ian on the terrifying journey of raising a child. I knew what receiving George's bracelet had meant to him.

And I also knew that Ian was worthy of what that token represented. Trust and love. Hope and conviction. Promise and faith.

Teammates.

Ian's smile didn't dim for a long time, and mine didn't either.

# thirteen

IAN

The wedding was in three hours, and I didn't think I'd ever been this nervous before in my life. Not even during my first stage performance in middle school or my first callback for a shampoo commercial.

It just felt like a lot of pressure. Candace and Mercer were getting married in front of all their family and friends. These vows would solidify their devotion and love. And I was the asshole reading the lines.

God, I was going to puke.

"Hey, look at this," Brady said, holding up his phone. "You're both famous. Do you know her? Lindy with the cooking videos."

"What?" I could hear the strain in my voice as Brady showed me his screen.

"Her channel is called Not Your Aunt Linda's Kitchen, and she takes regular, everyday food and puts a unique spin on it. Like mac and cheese but with Indian curry and other flavors. Or she makes alterations based on dietary restrictions."

I watched as a woman, visible only from the elbows down, kneaded bread on a floured workbench. "Oh, so like substitutions for your lactose intolerance?"

"Yeah," Brady answered, then cleared his throat. "Anyway, she's great. I love her recipes. Mercer and Wenn turned me on to her channel."

I'd known that Mercer liked to cook, as well as garden. He helped Amy Judd in the kitchen quite a bit. Georgie and I had been invited to Sunday dinner last week, and Mercer had made a salad from lettuce he'd grown himself. It was the best lettuce I'd ever had in my life. And the salad dressing I'd watched him create—honey lime cilantro—had been out of this world.

The other amateur chef in the mix was Wenn Hawthorn. He was a groomsman and Mercer's friend from Asheville. I knew the pair had met through their shared photography hobby. Actually, Wenn might be a professional photographer. I wasn't sure. The guy was quiet. He wasn't unfriendly or anything, just not a sharer.

He sat alone on the sofa in the suite we'd been given by the event coordinator. His big body took up most of the small piece of furniture. I was a tall, muscular guy, but Wenn might actually be able to take me in an arm wrestling match. He was broader, where I was lean, and carried himself like he'd been in the military.

But so far, he'd mostly kept to himself.

"I'll text you her handle." Brady clasped me on the shoulder and lowered his voice. "Watch her latest one with bacon bourbon brownies. It might help you relax and take your mind off the ceremony."

I met Brady's gaze. I'd thought I'd hidden my nervousness from the group, but apparently my acting skills weren't what I'd hoped.

"It's gonna be fine," he told me quietly. "You'll do great."

I watched as my friend ambled away to join Wenn across the room. They started talking about some contest on Lindy's page, but I tuned them out.

Closing my eyes, I took a deep breath.

Instead of the brownie video, I pulled up my text thread with Joan. We mostly used it for logistics regarding our early-morning runs and Georgie's visits. She wasn't a big texter and didn't believe in sharing memes like a normal person. But I needed a distraction, and I didn't think a cooking video was going to cut it.

Me: What's the vibe over there? How's the bride?

I was surprised when her response came through a moment later.

Joan: Well, she's not drunk, at least.

I smiled, remembering how we'd worked together to wrangle the women the night of the bachelorette party. Since I'd had to cart a sleeping Candace in my arms, Larry had insisted I carry the rest of them, too. It had taken a while, but they'd all eventually made it into the SUV.

Me: Always a plus before a wedding.

Joan: I meant, she's not drunk yet. Mac just opened another bottle of champagne. She said it's for mimosas, but she forgot the orange juice.

Me: Can you get some food in them? We ordered some pizzas from Apollo's. They should be here any minute.

Joan: That's a great idea.

The wedding was happening at the old train station in Kirby Falls. It no longer serviced train cars or passengers, but it had been renovated into a beautiful event space. The bride and all her ladies were situated in a suite very similar to ours on the opposite end of the hallway.

My thumbs hovered uncertainly. I didn't want to admit I was nervous. Mostly, because I didn't want Joan to think I was incompetent or to worry about a potential disaster at the altar today.

She was the fixer in her family. If the farm needed something, she made it happen. She was a leader, and her family looked to her as a result.

I didn't want to be one more thing Joan had to deal with. A calamity waiting in the wings.

Before I could decide what to type, I heard voices in the hallway, then a loud thump, followed by feminine giggles.

"What's that?" Brady asked, noticing the commotion as well.

"I don't know," I said. "I'll find out."

But Mercer was already on his way to the door.

I didn't realize Brady could move so quickly; he shot across the room and wedged himself in between Mercer and the door, practically shrieking, "What if Candace is out there? You can't see the bride before the wedding!"

Mercer sighed. "That is an antiquated tradition."

"I don't care. Get back. Ian and I will check it out."

"Good Lord," Mercer mumbled, but he took a step away and let Brady and me shuffle through the doorway.

We made it into the hall just in time to see Mac and Bonnie stealing our pizzas from the delivery driver.

"Hey!" Brady called. "Those are ours!"

"Not anymore!" Mac hollered at her boyfriend.

The women cackled and took off at a run, black satin robes billowing behind them.

They slammed and locked the door to their suite before we'd even made it halfway.

"They told me you'd tip," the driver said when I rushed past.

I couldn't help but laugh as I backtracked and pulled a fifty from my wallet.

Brady was yelling through the door when I caught up.

Pulling out my phone, I typed, *You know, that wasn't actually an invitation to steal our food. I was implying that you could feed your bridesmaids yourself. Maybe order your own pizza.*

Joan: Oh. See, now, I didn't take it that way at
all. Sounded like you were offering.

I grinned.

Well, I'd wanted a distraction. I wasn't thinking about standing up in front of all the Judds' friends and family and making a fool of myself now.

Negotiations over the pizza were led by Joan and me. Brady and Mac were pretty worthless in that department. They mostly yelled insults through the door before Mac had stomped out to shout in Brady's face. They'd ended up making out in the hallway while I retrieved three of the five pizzas I'd ordered.

Joan rolled her eyes at her brother and walked with me back toward the groom's suite.

Her hair, makeup, and nails were done, but she wasn't yet in her dress. Just like the rest of the women, she wore a silky robe that said "Maid of Honor" on the back. But with her long legs, it looked short as hell. I worked very hard to keep my eyes from drifting down over all the inches on display, and was proud of myself when I partially succeeded.

"You don't need to be nervous, Ian."

I glanced up in surprise. "I'm not nervous. I'm fine," I lied. "Just like memorizing a script. A walk in the park."

Joan gave me a look that clearly said, *Cut the shit.* Then she came right out and said, "Cut the shit."

"How'd you know I was nervous?" I wondered, coming to a stop and leaning against the wall opposite the door to the suite.

Joan matched my casual pose, but her gaze—intense and unwavering—focused on mine.

"Because. I know you." She said it so easily, so matter-of-factly, but there was nothing simple about it.

I didn't know what to do with that sort of faith, that sort of steadfast confidence.

*I know you.*

I wasn't sure if anyone else in this world could say the same. Somehow, this woman I'd met only a couple of months ago knew me better than anyone else.

I had employees and a team. I had people I paid to be in my life. My assistant, my agent, my manager, my trainer, Sophia, and Darren. But there weren't friends—people I trusted with who I really was, deep down. Dorian Masters had plenty of colleagues. People he grabbed drinks with, caught up with, or saw in passing. But none of that was the same.

I realized I was staring down at the lid of the pizza box when Joan wrapped a hand around my forearm and squeezed. "If Candace didn't want you officiating, you wouldn't be. My sister is a people pleaser, Ian, but I am not. If she'd truly been unhappy, she would have asked me to let you down easy."

That startled a laugh out of me. "Like her enforcer?"

Joan shrugged, but I could see amusement in her eyes. "That's how she ended up with the flowers for her bouquet that she *actually* wanted. Not the ones Margaret wanted to sell her. It was also how she got the cake frosting she preferred, even though it's a bitch to make. My sister isn't great at being honest if she thinks it's going to ruffle feathers, but I don't have a problem telling people the truth. I may not be the warmest sister. I don't sit around and gossip or do spa days like she probably wants. But I do make sure my family is happy, and that includes Candace getting the wedding of her dreams. If she couldn't work up the nerve to demand it for herself, I'd gladly do it for her."

I nodded, remembering my thoughts from earlier. Joan the fixer. Joan the trusted leader. It seemed that maybe I knew her the same way she knew me.

Smiling, I teased, "You would have broken my heart and kicked me out of the wedding if Candace had asked you to?"

"Without a second thought," she admitted, with zero remorse. "But she *does* want you here. Wants you to be a part of her and Mercer's big day. And I'm glad for it. Because I know you'll do a good job."

"How do you know?" I asked, my voice hushed.

Maybe Joan heard the quiet desperation in my tone because her face gentled, her sharp gaze going soft as she really looked at me. "Because you care. It's not just reading words off a page for them, and you know that." She paused. "Plus, you're the most charming motherfucker I've ever met, and I'll deny ever saying that."

My laughter was loud in the narrow hallway. "Thanks, Joanie."

She nodded once, still smiling. "Now go eat the pizza that you wrestled away from those maniacs. We've worked hard on your stamina, but I don't want you passing out at the altar from low blood sugar."

Shaking my head, I pushed off the wall, reaching for the doorknob, but her small fist entered my field of vision.

"You've got this," she said.

Feeling buoyed by her faith, I tapped my fist to hers. "See you out there."

---

Candace and Mercer had planned the ceremony to be short and sweet. There were no songs to be sung or readings from anyone's cousin. They weren't lighting a unity candle or pouring symbolic sand into a symbolic vase.

They'd wanted something simple to reflect their love. And I could appreciate that. But I had something I wanted to say.

"I always thought loving someone would be big and loud and chaotic," I admitted, looking between Candace and Mercer, where they held hands before me.

There were about seventy-five people seated in rows on the mezzanine of the train station. It was quiet and intimate up here, overlooking the large ballroom where the reception would take place below. The warm glow of electric candles flickered all around, painting the couple in golden hues of happiness.

"I've never been able to see a way around it," I explained. "Two people with two lives, two families, and two personalities—how could love not be a cataclysmic collision? There would be dreams to whittle down to make room. Downsizing for necessities and minimizing for efficiency. Somehow, to me, love had always meant two becoming one, but only after cutting yourself in half to balance the scales.

"But for Candace and Mercer, that's not how love works. It's opening a door and creating space—a safe space for love to grow and bloom, to change. It's seeing a need and fulfilling it without even being asked. It's not making yourself smaller to fit in the shadow of someone else, but rather, stepping into the light to join them.

"I've seen the quiet sort of love and devotion that Candace and Mercer share. I've seen the acceptance of a family, welcoming a son. I've witnessed two personalities that complement one another. Teammates, not competitors. Instead of their love being a clash of waves against the shore, it's a meeting of currents. Shifting and adjusting to create a new path together."

Tears shimmered in Candace's eyes as she and Mercer gazed at one another. I could hear a few sniffles on either side of the bride and groom, but I made myself focus solely on the couple before me, despite the urge to steal a glance at the maid of honor.

"Some of you may not know this," I said, "but I tell stories for a living."

That earned a few chuckles from the crowd.

"But I don't know a writer or a director who could dream up a love like this. One where belonging is found in the mountains, on an apple orchard, with one another. Maybe love isn't a feeling. Maybe it's discovering a home in someone else."

Smiling, I finally said, "Mark Mercer, do you take Candace Judd to be . . ."

The rest of the vows—the ones we'd discussed and practiced—went smoothly. There were some awws from the crowd when Mercer got a little choked up. And then laughter when Brady passed him a tissue before using one to blow his own nose.

I watched the happy couple. Got to see the joy and reverence on their faces as they promised to love and encourage and fight for one another. And Joan was right. It was more than words on a page. And I felt honored to be a small part of it.

After announcing Candace and Mercer partners in life, everyone clapped, and the recessional music began.

Red-eyed and smiling, Brady hugged me hard on his way to collect Joan. I laughed into his shoulder. Joan bumped my fist one more time and then walked back up the aisle with her brother.

I smiled, watching Joan march off with determined, efficient strides, practically dragging Brady between the rows of onlookers. Her floor-length gown shifted with each determined step, the satiny fabric flowing over every graceful line of her body.

I took an unsteady inhale, noting the back of the dress. It draped very low, revealing most of Joan's shoulders and back and stealing more of my breath. The deep, jewel-toned color combined with the warm candlelight on the mezzanine made her smooth skin glow golden and lovely. She looked so beautiful, and I ached to touch her.

Bonnie and Wenn came together before me, thankfully distracting me from staring after the maid of honor like a lovesick fool. Then I held out my arm and escorted a grinning Mac as we followed the others up the aisle.

When we got to the room where the wedding party would hang out until they were announced for the reception, Candace immediately threw her arms around me.

"I didn't know you were going to say all that," she cried. "Ian, thank you so much. That was the sweetest, most thoughtful speech. It was perfect."

I patted her back gently, careful not to dislodge her veil or mess up her hair. "Thank you for letting me be a part of it."

Mercer shook my hand. "Thank you, Ian."

I nodded. "Congratulations to you both."

The bride and groom stepped away as Nick and Amy arrived. The parents were obviously overjoyed, grinning ear to ear.

Joan slid next to me as we watched everyone hug and chat.

"So, how'd I do, Coach?" I asked quietly.

When she didn't answer, I grew concerned. Had I overstepped by adding my own words to the ceremony?

I knew it. I should have just stuck to the script we'd arranged. Why had I decided to—

"I think," Joan said, and her voice caught.

Dumbstruck, I glanced over, took in her shining eyes and trembling chin.

"I think you nailed it," she finally managed. Then she slipped her arms around my waist and hugged me. "Thank you for making them happy," she said.

Her breath was warm against my neck, and I relished the closeness, the honesty of her words pressed into my skin.

Strong hands held me tightly. I let myself lean into the embrace, relief and comfort and so much damn affection for this woman making me unsteady. She felt so good in my arms, like she belonged there, like we fit.

I knew now that I'd come on too strong in the beginning. I'd caused her to question and doubt.

So I'd forced myself to be patient, determined to give her time. No part of me wanted to scare Joan off. I wanted her to see that I wasn't the spoiled, incapable celebrity she thought I was. I'd let her get accustomed to having me in her life. To me, earning a spot there was more important than forcing my way in anyway.

But I didn't know how much longer I could wait. Every moment I didn't have my hands on her felt like wasted time.

"Save me a dance," I whispered, letting my lips graze the shell of her ear. Letting her see. Letting her feel.

Joan shivered against me before nodding.

The event coordinator called everyone together as guests were seated in the reception area, and music began playing.

Joan and I stepped away from one another. But with any luck, this wouldn't be the last time she was in my arms tonight.

---

**Joan**

I'd already decided that I liked Corie, the photographer. She and Larry were good together and seemed to make each other happy. Plus, every time I saw the woman, she asked me how my apples were doing. That was a good way to endear oneself to a farmer.

My opinion only warmed as we finished up the wedding photos in under twenty minutes. Corie was frighteningly efficient and knowledgeable. And she'd stolen a tray of appetizers for the wedding party while we waited for her to change cameras and set up the lighting.

For as long as the day had seemed, between manicures and hair and makeup appointments, everything sped up once Candace walked down the aisle. Much of the evening went by in a blur of hugs and camera flashes, followed by a pasta buffet and cake cutting.

The wedding had been small and intimate. The reception was loud and joyful. And my sweet sister couldn't stop smiling.

But time started to slow down again once the wine was flowing, the dance floor filling up. I'd done all the maid-of-honor tasks I could think of. I'd loaded all the wedding gifts into Mercer's truck. I'd gathered our things from the bridal suite, and I'd made sure my sister and her new husband had taken time to eat.

There was nothing left for me to do. When I saw Ian laughing with the deejay like they were best friends, I knew I'd avoided him long enough.

Ian caught my eye and grinned.

A moment later, he made his way to me, stopping three different times to take selfies with guests, plus sign a cocktail napkin for my great-aunt.

"You are a hard woman to track down," Ian said when he reached me. "And your aunt Linda would have made it to second base if your mother hadn't stepped in."

"Jesus," I muttered. "I'm sorry."

"It's okay. I'm used to it."

I stared at him before lowering my voice angrily. "You shouldn't have to get used to people touching you without your consent, Ian."

"I know. You're right. I'm sorry."

"Why are you apologizing to me? You're the one getting manhandled."

It was ridiculous that Ian felt like he had to put up with people violating his personal space. That he was content to just grin and go on with his life instead of telling everyone to fuck off—my great-aunt Linda included.

"Well, the only person I want manhandling me right now is you. You promised me a dance."

I slid him a look, but allowed the subject change. It was inevitable. I'd agreed to it earlier, and I wasn't about to backtrack. No matter how much I might want to.

Following the ceremony, Ian had caught me in a moment of weakness. I'd been so damn grateful for the way he'd moved my sister to tears. For the way he'd spoken about Candace and Mercer and their love, the things he'd said.

I probably would have agreed to just about anything in that moment.

Now, Ian calmly waited, hand outstretched, intent to collect on my promise.

As if on cue, the music changed from upbeat and celebratory to something slow and romantic that I recognized from Candace's playlist.

Resigned to my fate, I let Ian lead me out onto the dance floor. We passed other couples. Mac and Brady were fighting over who was going to lead. Becca had her head resting on Will's shoulder as they swayed gently. And Candace and Mercer were wrapped up in one another. I was glad they were taking some time for themselves.

Ian's warm hand settled against my bare back, and I fought a shiver.

He looked good in his dark suit, the tailored fabric soft beneath my palms. It struck me again how graceful Ian moved for someone his size. There was nothing oafish or lumbering about the man.

But this wasn't a country western two-step. We were barely moving, bodies close together.

Unlike the last time we'd danced, I couldn't think of a single thing to say. My mouth had gone dry, and any easy conversation about the wedding or George or the damn weather had abandoned me.

There was only the feel of Ian's palm on my naked spine. The brush of our legs as we shifted—the silky material of my dress sliding along sensitive thighs. The buzzed hair at his nape was soft and velvety beneath my fingers. I could feel Ian's heart beating. Or maybe it was mine. I couldn't tell at this point.

Time passed, and we still didn't speak.

If I could just get us back on solid ground, things might not feel so heavy. Why wasn't he cracking jokes or grinning at me?

The moment was rife with tension, charged with anticipation. I couldn't believe we weren't throwing off sparks. But I wasn't about to pull away. I didn't want to.

I'd been fighting whatever was happening between us for weeks now. Content to play pretend and ignore this unsettling attraction. Just because I didn't understand it, didn't mean I couldn't feel it.

It was always there. A slow simmer just beneath the surface. A touch that lit me up. A laugh that made me smile. A bone-deep patience that unknotted all my wary mistrust.

Then there was the way he made time for George and the people he cared about. And today, he'd added my family to that list.

I liked Ian. I did.

I never expected to, and maybe that was the hardest pill to swallow. That

I'd been so wrong about him. This felt like losing a game I was playing with myself.

The ballad ended, transitioning into "Love Shack" by The B-52s. But Ian and I stood unmoving in the middle of the floor. People whirled around us, dancing and shimmying, but we were still, staring at one another.

I exercised regularly and was in great shape, but for some reason, I couldn't catch my breath. Ian watched me, gaze intense, and I felt the weight of more than just his attention.

We were in the middle of the crowd, exposed, on display. Ian would never be able to fade into any background. And that was where I was most comfortable.

When I couldn't take it anymore, I turned, gasping and unsteady, and walked determinedly toward one of the side doors.

The December night was cold, but I didn't regret my decision. I'd rather be out here with my thin gown than inside where it was warm and I was a coward.

I leaned against the railing of the balcony that overlooked downtown and took slow, deliberate breaths.

Everything was decorated for the holidays, and warm white lights sparkled all around. A moment later, I felt Ian's suit jacket settle gently over my bare shoulders. It was still warm from his body, and something about that felt more intimate than if he'd pressed himself against me completely naked.

He braced his forearms on the railing, mirroring my pose, shoulder pressed close. "You look beautiful. I meant to tell you that earlier, a dozen different times."

I snorted a disbelieving laugh. My dress was pretty—Candace had picked it out because it didn't matter to me what I wore, as long as she was happy. The silky emerald-green material was long and clung to my body. It dipped low in the back, just this side of indecent. My hair was curled and pinned and elegant. My nails had been buffed and painted, which felt like a waste on someone who had dirt under them any other time. The dramatic evening makeup completed the look of a woman who could shine up nice on occasion but rarely made the effort on her own.

If Ian was impressed by the version of me he saw today, he'd be disappointed the rest of the time.

I'd seen the women he was usually photographed with. Curvy, youthful, objectively beautiful.

That wasn't me.

At my sound of derisive amusement, Ian turned my way. "What?" he asked, seeming genuinely confused.

"You're used to models and actresses and red carpets. I cannot imagine that me in a bridesmaid dress I'm never gonna wear again is what does it for you."

I could feel him staring at my profile, and it made me want to squirm. I'd said all that offhandedly, but maybe it revealed too much. How aware I was of his celebrity life. How unsettled he made me feel. How I'd never fit in his world.

I should have just taken the fucking compliment, but it had seemed so ridiculous in the face of what he was accustomed to. I knew my strengths. Being glamorous wasn't one of them.

"None of that is real, you know?" he said quietly.

"What isn't?"

"The red carpet. The women I'm photographed with. My manager sets me up with those people. Whoever needs media attention at the moment or to distract from whatever scandal is happening. It's all a game of you scratch my back, I scratch yours. I haven't been in a relationship—a real one—in a very long time. It's too hard to meet people. To trust them."

I met his gaze and nearly winced at the intensity there—the honesty so bold and unabashed.

"But you trust me?" I asked.

"Yeah, Joan. I do. You're loyal and dependable. You're one of the very few people who know about Georgie. For me, it doesn't get any more trustworthy than that."

Maybe it was the jittery adrenaline sparking inside me since we'd danced. Maybe it was the wedding and the fairy-tale bubble we'd been trapped in all day. Maybe it was hearing him call me loyal with such earnest reverence that I wanted to remember the moment forever.

Maybe it was every single one of those things that had me leaning in, closing the distance, and surprising him with a kiss.

Ian made a sound, something slightly dumbstruck and arousingly needy. Like I'd put my hands down his pants instead of where they lay, innocently over the railing.

But he recovered quickly, slotting his upper lip between mine and cupping my jaw. He drew me close, the heat and size and sultry scent of him only making me ache to be closer.

I felt his other hand move beneath my jacket—*his jacket*—to touch my waist. His hold was unsteady as he gripped the fabric of my dress and then smoothed it back out. I smiled against his lips, liking that he'd caught himself, been unsure. He could have torn the thing in his excitement, and I wouldn't have been nearly as affected as I was by the hand that was currently shaking against me.

I wanted him unsettled. Needed him to be just as out of sorts as I was. No one liked making bad decisions alone. And nothing about this was going to end well.

Maybe two months ago, we could have had a no-strings fling to keep the celebrity entertained while on location in the mountains. But now—

Everything was different.

He wasn't some spoiled actor I tolerated occasionally. He was my teammate. My friend. He was George's uncle. My dad's poker buddy. My brother's workout partner. He'd married my sister and my friend today. The lines were well and truly blurred.

We'd somehow tangled ourselves up in each other. And now his hands were on my body like I'd been thinking about for weeks.

My lips parted as urgency flared to life. Ian took the invitation and slid his tongue into my mouth. He tasted like the champagne I'd watched him drink—bubbly and sweet.

Suddenly, I didn't want to be out here in the cold in semipublic. I wanted to be someplace private, where I could see him and feel him and do every dirty thing I'd never let myself imagine.

My hands stroked over his pecs, the muscles flexing beneath my curious fingers. I slowed our frantic kisses, knowing that we couldn't do this here. Ian might have been seen as a commodity, but I wasn't about to treat him like one by putting him on display.

He pressed his lips gently to my upper lip, the corner of my mouth, my chin, my eyelids. I felt him sigh as he placed a final kiss against my forehead.

Reluctantly, I opened my eyes.

When he leaned back, he was already smiling. Whatever he saw on my face must have been amusing because his grin widened. "Nice to see you out of breath for once."

I huffed a laugh into the cold night air. Clouds of my amusement drifted away over our heads.

Ian's eyes danced in the glow of the Christmas lights. His happiness was so tangible, I felt like I could reach out and touch it, wrap it around me to keep me warm.

"We should go in," I told him after a moment.

"Why?"

"Because someone is going to find us out here. I can't believe they haven't already."

"So what if they do?" he said, shrugging.

I blinked. "The last thing you need is someone to post a picture of us in the town Facebook group or call into Sheila Jessup's stupid podcast tip line to report on our—our—"

"Our what?" Ian asked, clearly enjoying my sudden bashfulness. "Our canoodling? Our superhot make-out sesh? The way you couldn't keep your hands—"

"Alright. You've made your point." I rolled my eyes before taking a step away toward the train station doors.

But Ian's warm hand snagged mine before I could get too far. I turned to find his dark brows drawn low, gaze focused and intent.

The sudden seriousness of his expression had me straightening. That sparkling energy from earlier, that sense of restless unease, was back. My dress felt too tight—my skin along with it.

"Let them," Ian said. "Let them catch us or talk about us. It doesn't matter. I'm not embarrassed, and I don't regret it. You can kiss me whenever you want, Joan. Frankly, I wish we hadn't stopped."

IAN

It took longer than I anticipated for Joan to freak out about the kiss.

I blamed the timing of everything. Following the wedding, my days on set were long and grueling. Della and the first assistant director in charge of the shooting schedule tried to pack as much in as we could before the film broke for the holidays. My director was adamant about giving the cast and crew the opportunity to celebrate with their families, but the three days after the wedding only left me with time to fall into bed each night and not much else.

I hadn't seen Joan at all, and I'd barely seen Georgie.

But starting tomorrow, I would have ten days off. Sophia and Darren were flying home to California with most of the cast and crew, but Georgie and I were staying in Kirby Falls.

My parents were spending the holidays with friends. There had been no invitation to return to Ohio to celebrate together. Maybe I should have pushed it, insisted on a family gathering so that Georgie could see his grandparents. But truth be told, I felt more at home with the Judds or the Clarks than I ever had with my own family. I knew that what Georgie needed right now was consistency and stability, and he had that here, in Kirby Falls.

Regardless of our plans for the break, I was tracking Joan down and figuring out where we went from here. I wasn't going to let her shut me out and ignore what was happening between us.

The next evening, I parked my rental car beside the tidy lawn of a gorgeous two-story cabin. The house was on the far side of the Judds' property, as far away from where we were filming as you could possibly get. There was probably a metaphor in there, but I was choosing to ignore it.

The national forest pressed in on one side, and the path from the main highway was more a suggestion than an actual road. The first-floor windows glowed with warm light, and the wraparound porch looked inviting with its double hanging swings and ceiling fans. I could imagine Joan out here on hot summer evenings, a book and a beer in hand while crickets chirped and a breeze whirred lazily overhead.

Brady had told me to go to the back door and knock. He'd also been the one to text his older sister and make sure she was home tonight. He and Mac were watching Georgie for me. They had big plans for homemade pizza followed by *Wheel of Fortune*.

I gathered the stockpot from the backseat and made my way around the side of the house. In the distance, I could just make out a mobile home with a few lights on. The yard—if you could call it that—was strewn with lawnmowers, car parts, overgrown weeds, and junk piles. A white-and-brown goat sat beneath a tree, looking cold and pitiful.

I knew without having to be told that Joan must resent the run-down property next door. The neglect. The lack of care. The poor animal was tied to a tree with little freedom to speak of.

Before my boots hit the top step, the back door swung open. I froze like a cartoon escapee during a jailbreak. I couldn't raise my hands in surrender on account of the oven mitts and stockpot, but I wanted to.

"Hi," I said.

Joan stared like she wasn't quite sure what to do with me. I could see the "what are you doing here" written all over her face.

"I brought dinner," I added quickly, nerves making me question myself. "White chicken chili."

"You made it?"

"Yeah." I may have Facetimed Amy so she could walk me through the recipe, but I'd cooked it myself. Joan's mother might have also mentioned that it was her eldest daughter's favorite winter meal. I wasn't above cheating at this point.

"Come on in," Joan finally said, opening the door wide.

I unfroze from my position on the stairs and followed her inside.

The cabin was warm and surprisingly cozy. Its owner wasn't very fanciful or frivolous, so I couldn't help but stare at the placemats with ruffles that perfectly matched the eyelet lace tablecloth.

There was a drawing on the refrigerator that caught my eye. I stared, noting it was the only thing on there. No magnets or pizza delivery numbers, no pictures. Nothing, except a colorful illustration of Joan on a tractor, drawn by my nephew. "To Joan, From George" was written at the top in Georgie's messy scrawl.

Not for the first time, I marveled over Joan's softness where my nephew was concerned. There was nothing overtly affectionate or maternal about her, but somehow, she was exactly who Georgie needed. Her forthright nature, her gentle honesty, and the endless patience she had for all his questions had changed everything. Georgie was a different kid now than when we'd first arrived in Kirby Falls. And I had Joan to thank for that.

He'd been more open with me lately, too. I'd gotten a few friendship bracelets for my collection and hugs before bedtime. The progress brought a lump to my throat.

"You can reheat it here, if you want," Joan said, capturing my attention but doing nothing to ease the ache in my heart.

She indicated a burner she'd turned to low on the stovetop.

"Thanks," I told her, setting the pot down.

"I have some fresh bread I can warm in the oven," she offered, still looking and sounding unsure.

"That sounds great."

While she pressed buttons and got a cooking sheet out, I wandered around the kitchen island.

The floor plan opened right up into the living room. Joan had more throw pillows than I would have imagined on a worn leather sofa that looked very comfortable. A television was mounted over a gas fireplace that was currently on, and the built-in shelves on either side held a combination of books and picture frames that I wanted to snoop through.

There weren't many knickknacks or things just sitting around, and I liked that I'd guessed at least one thing right about Joan's personal space. Although a gallery wall of mismatched frames boasted beautiful artwork, and I couldn't really have anticipated that.

There was a blanket tossed over the arm of a big, cozy chair in the corner and a book face down on the end table next to it. I'd clearly interrupted her by showing up here this evening.

But I couldn't make myself regret it.

Not even when I turned around and found Joan watching me cautiously from the kitchen.

I smiled and admitted, "I wanted to see you. My schedule was ridiculous leading up to the break, and I know we need to talk—" My gaze snagged on something on the wall next to her. "Is that a landline?"

Walking over, I picked up the off-white receiver and held it up to my ear to hear an honest-to-God dial tone. "Wow. I've never seen one of these before. Can I use it?"

"Christ," Joan muttered, pinching the bridge of her nose.

"And an answering machine, too," I gasped. "I thought you only built this place a few years ago?"

"I like having a landline, okay?" She sounded exasperated, like she'd defended this decision many times over. "Cell reception can be unreliable in the mountains. If someone needs to get a hold of me, I want to make sure they can."

I wiped a hand across my mouth to hide my grin. That was the most Joan-like thing I'd ever heard. "Can I have a tour?" I asked.

She frowned. "You're nosy."

I shrugged, unbothered. I *was* nosy where she was concerned. My fingers itched to comb through every book on her shelf. It would be like uncovering history, a distant civilization.

Of course, I was curious about this woman. I'd been thinking about her nonstop for weeks. Daydreaming about a million different scenarios. Some were innocent and painfully domestic. Like watching a movie together just to see her reactions—what made her smile or drew a laugh. Did she eat popcorn? What candy was her favorite? I bet she required total silence and got annoyed if anyone chatted nearby.

I wanted to know what side of the bed she slept on and what kind of toothpaste she used. Was the coconut I sometimes smelled on her skin from lotion or soap or shampoo? What was her policy on opening presents on Christmas Eve? Did she sing in the shower?

And, of course, some of the fantasizing was decidedly less innocent in nature. What sounds would she make if I touched her everywhere I wanted? Would she let me go down on her? How did she feel about hot-tub sex? For or against? I envisioned those long, toned legs wrapped around my hips and propped up on my shoulders and bent over her couch cushions.

Now, at least, I knew what her couch looked like.

"Yeah, I am nosy about you," I told her honestly. "I haven't been shy about what I want."

I kept my gaze steady on hers and was rewarded a moment later when heat climbed her cheeks, and she had to clear her throat before saying, "Fine."

She led me through the house, dispassionately indicating bedrooms and bathrooms, a laundry room, and a linen closet. Her own bedroom was on the main level and was painted a beautiful and indulgent dark green.

More throw pillows decorated her bed, and that fact alone charmed me. She had artwork on her walls—photographs, if I wasn't mistaken—of the landscape, gorgeous mountains, a sunset, rows and rows of apple trees.

There were two additional bedrooms upstairs, plus an office. All with furniture, but sparsely decorated. When I stepped into the final guest bedroom to check out the walk-in closet, Joan practically lunged to stop me.

I grinned down where she clutched my arm in a panicked grip. Whispering, I asked, "Is this where you keep your sex toys?"

She rolled her eyes. "No. That would be too far from my bed and make no sense."

My brain misfired momentarily at the thought of Joan having a sex toy collection and what I'd be willing to do in order to enjoy that with her.

"It's worse," she said, pulling me out of my sex toy–induced distraction.

"Well, that just makes me want to see it even more."

Sighing, she released me.

I opened the sliding pocket door and immediately jumped back. "Ahhh!"

"I warned you."

I shot her an incredulous look. "No. No, you did not. If you had said, 'Ian, there are a thousand weird-ass, scary baby dolls in that closet,' I wouldn't have just felt my soul leave my body."

There weren't a thousand, but there were at least a hundred. The closet shelving was absolutely filled with dolls, some layered two or three deep. They were all around a foot tall, and most looked antique, like they were beloved by a Victorian child before the doll came to life and murdered the entire household.

Synthetic hair, mostly shiny and coiled, in all colors adorned their heads. Some wore bonnets, and most donned frilly dresses. Their terrifying glass eyes stared back at me as I slowly slid the door closed.

"Why do you have all these?" I asked.

Another sigh left her. "I don't really remember how it started. I think I got one as a present when I was a kid. I probably carried it around or braided its hair or something, so my family assumed I liked it. They kept getting them for me. Mom and I were at an estate sale, probably fifteen years ago, and she saw this vintage doll dressed as a farmer, in overalls with an apple basket. She showed it to me, said it reminded her of all the dolls I had growing up. I must have said something encouraging, like, 'Oh, that's cute.' Well, she went back and bought the doll and gave it to me for Christmas that year."

"Oh, no," I breathed, knowing where this was going.

Joan nodded. "I didn't want to hurt her feelings, so I thanked her and told her how much I liked it. From then on, everyone in the family started buying them for me. Birthdays, Christmases, and randomly whenever they'd find one at an antique store or a flea market. My dad pulled the ones from when I was a girl out of storage in the attic and gave them to me for my *collection*."

"Joan."

"It makes them happy to give them to me," she explained. "I can just hide them back here—"

"Where they can't get you in your sleep."

Her lips twitched. "And no one has to ever know that I don't actually like or collect dolls."

"Yeah, but what about my emotional damage as a result? I'm going to have nightmares."

She laughed, and the sound loosened something inside my chest that had been strung tight since the night of the wedding. Deep down, I'd been worried I'd never hear it again. That I might have scared her off, out of my life—and Georgie's—for good.

Three months ago, I couldn't have known how essential she'd be. How I'd wake up thinking of her and rearrange my schedule so I could run with her or have lunch together. My life was prioritized around my nephew, but I worked pretty damn hard to fit Joan and her family in where I could. Because *that* was what I wanted.

I'd missed her this week. Missed talking to her. Missed hearing about her day.

This woman who collected dolls against her will because she didn't want to hurt anyone's feelings. Joan was kind in quiet ways, thoughtful when it mattered. She had a good heart—a fierce heart—for the people she loved.

And I wanted to count myself among them.

"Let's go eat," I said. "You can tell me about your week and judge my cooking skills."

Her blue eyes sparkled. "Can't wait."

But before I could walk past her, she clutched my hand and squeezed. "Please don't say anything about the dolls to my family. I don't want to—"

"I won't tell a soul," I promised.

She nodded her thanks and released me.

Then, I added, "Because those dolls will find and destroy me."

I followed the sound of Joan's laughter down the stairs.

We ate at her kitchen table. Joan set out cloth napkins and passed me a local IPA she knew I liked. The chili turned out to be pretty tasty, and I didn't bother hiding how pleased I was when Joan requested seconds.

Our conversation stayed light during the meal. I didn't bring up the kiss or anything feelings adjacent. I wanted to catch up with her first without seeming like I was chasing her down.

Afterward, I insisted on loading the dishwasher. Joan watched me with an amused expression as she finished the rest of my beer.

I wandered into the living room once more, and Joan followed, a few steps behind.

"Did you do any of these?" I asked, indicating the gallery wall.

Joan shook her head. "No. Some of them are Mercer's photographs. The rest I picked up from local artists during festivals and events downtown."

I opened my mouth to ask to see her movie collection, but I didn't get the chance.

"What are you doing here, Ian?" she asked, not unkindly.

I had a moment of déjà vu, back to our very first encounter. How I'd been laid out on the ground, struggling to breathe after a failed attempt at exercise, while Joan leaned over me, wondering if I was dying.

I almost laughed, thinking I'd gotten a lot further this time before she'd finally come right out and asked what she'd really wanted to know.

Nervously, my hand went to the pocket of my jeans. I touched the black elastic band I kept there as a reminder and swallowed. "I wanted to talk about the other night. At the wedding."

She didn't say anything, and I felt my neck get hot.

"We kissed, Joan. Does that ring any bells?"

And then it was like I hadn't spoken. Like she was in the middle of a conversation I hadn't been a part of.

"Men do love a challenge," she murmured thoughtfully.

"What?"

"You look at me and see someone to win over with your charm. Something to conquer. A tough nut to crack. But here's the thing, Ian, there's no prize here. When you get what you think you want, you don't win anything. It's just more of the same. More of me. And no matter how much it might feel like a game, there is no winning. So you should stop wasting your time."

I stared at her, my heart beating hard. This didn't feel like rejection, though. It felt like we were speaking two different languages.

"Is that what you think? That I'm wasting my time? Is that how you really see yourself?"

I took a step toward her, and she retreated.

Frowning, I said, "I thought we were past this. I'm not messing with the locals. I'm not bored or amusing myself. Do you think I'm pretending to be attracted to you? That I'm what? Teasing you for the fun of it. Trying to get under your skin so I can embarrass you. That when you finally give in, I can laugh in your face and say, 'Oh, I'm sorry. Did you actually think I was into you?' I mean, I knew your opinion of me was low, but wow, Joan. This isn't a coming-of-age rom-com. It's not a movie. It's . . . my life."

She had the decency to look shamefaced, but then she blew out an exasperated breath. "It just doesn't make any sense."

"What doesn't?"

"I'm old."

"You're not old," I replied calmly.

"I'm just a farmer."

"And the most competent person I've ever met."

"I'm not sexy," she added, almost belligerently.

"Have you seen yourself in those little running shorts? Agree to disagree."

"You're a fucking movie star," she practically exploded. "And I'm—I'm —I'm average. Ordinary. Foul-tempered, grouchy, judgmental—" Joan cut herself off, but I knew, in her head, the list went on. "I'm just me," she finished quietly.

I took another step toward her, and this time, she let me. Her blue eyes were wary and guarded, but she stood her ground. And I thought to myself, *That's the woman I know.*

I reached out and took her hand in mine. "I like that you don't smile much," I admitted. "Because when you do, it feels like I earned it."

Truthfully, I hadn't had to earn anything in a long time. I was essentially the spoiled celebrity she'd always assumed I was. I had staff and people to manage my life and career. Auditions weren't typically required anymore. People jumped through hoops to please me, not the other way around.

Georgie was the first person in quite a while who needed more from me than just the bare minimum that I was used to.

Joan side-eyed me. "Probably a nice change of pace having someone scowl at you. You're so used to women bending over backwards."

"Hot."

She rolled her eyes. "And throwing their panties at you."

I made a face. "Gross. Why do I want strangers' panties? Also, can we not call them that? I'm not a rock star on a stage. That doesn't actually happen."

"You know what I mean," Joan insisted. "Women falling at your feet. I'm not like that. I'm never going to *be* like that."

I smiled sadly. "I know. You're not exactly impressed by me." Initially, that had seemed refreshing, a novelty in a world where all I ever got was attention. Now, though, it made my chest ache.

Joan's fingers tightened around my own. "I'm not taken in by the fame thing, no. But that doesn't mean I'm not impressed. I admire what you're doing for George. How you refuse to give up on him. You're never discouraged. You work hard, despite what you want people to think. You're good to your team. You take care of people. I like you, Ian. I do. But our worlds feel so far apart. I'm not ever going to be like the women you're used to."

"I know," I repeated. "You're not like anyone I've ever met. And I wouldn't want you to be. I like you the way you are. Grouchy and judgmental. Smart and generous. Hardworking, kind, and dependable."

"You're so good at that," she whispered. "Saying the right thing."

"You think I'm just playing a role, reciting some lines?"

"No," she replied quickly before pausing and confessing, "I don't know what to think."

It hurt to know she didn't trust me, but then I reminded myself that we'd only known each other a few months. Joan was the sort of person who didn't rush into things. Everyone in her life—everyone she cared about—had earned their place, proven their worth.

I tried to think of how to explain it.

"Acting . . . it's just a job," I told her. "It's not the only thing about me. People can be more than what they do."

"I'm not. I'm a farmer, and I'm a Judd. That's who I am."

*Oh, Joanie.*

With my other hand, I cupped her jaw. "Is that what you really believe?"

"It's the truth," she asserted.

"You are so much more than the box you've put yourself in. Even with how dedicated, competent, and passionate you are. You're also your own person outside of the farm. You're a neighbor, a sister, a daughter, a friend. You're reliable. Everyone in Kirby Falls and that unhinged Facebook group knows they can count on you. You collect dolls because you don't want to hurt anyone's feelings. You plan bachelorette parties even though you'd rather die than line dance. You donate your time, energy, and resources to help people. You're—"

I had to take a breath and let it out before admitting, "You're the only person Georgie responds to. You're safe and steady. You're exactly what he needs in a way I could never be. So, I don't accept that you've simplified yourself down. You're more than your job, and so am I. I'm not lying to you or pretending or acting when we're together. You can't explain away my feelings for you by assuming I'm falling into some pattern or habit because of who I am. I know trust doesn't come easy for you, but you *can* trust me."

I leaned down and pressed my forehead to hers. "If you want me to leave you alone, I—"

"I don't want that," she interrupted, and I was grateful. I hadn't been exactly sure how I was going to finish that sentence.

"Do you just want to be friends?" I asked softly.

She shook her head slightly, her nose brushing against mine. "I don't know what I want."

"I can understand that. But you'll let me know when you figure it out? And you won't hide from me in the meantime?"

"I don't want to hide from you, Ian."

I felt her lips press against mine, stubborn and resolute, like an oath—a vow she was making to herself—and it gave me hope.

I stroked her cheek with my thumb and kissed her back, just as reverently —an answer to a question she couldn't bring herself to ask.

Determined to give her space, I pulled back, my hand still cupping her jaw. There were so many things I needed to say, assurances I wanted to make. That, yes, our worlds were different, but we could make it work. That I had no idea what would happen when the film wrapped, but I knew I didn't want to leave. That I'd take care of her heart, if she'd give me the chance.

But before I could gather the courage to put all of that into words, we heard someone yelling outside. An engine revved, and glass crunched.

Together, we moved to the window over the kitchen sink and peered out.

"That idiot," she breathed.

We watched as a big, burly middle-aged man staggered out of his still-running vehicle in the distance. His headlights illuminated the messy yard as he hurled beer bottles out of the bed of his truck. The goat that had been huddled beside the tree bolted in fear, but only managed to get to the end of its rope, where it tugged and strained.

"Your neighbor?" I asked, wincing as a bottle shattered against the trunk of the tree.

Joan's jaw clenched angrily as she nodded. "He's a pain in the ass. A danger to himself and everyone else. Buck has been to jail, to rehab. Nothing ever sticks."

"He does this a lot?"

"Often enough," she sighed.

After a few minutes, the man managed to wear himself out. He stumbled over to turn his truck off and eventually made his way inside the mobile home, the door slamming in his wake.

I took in Joan's rigid posture, the way she clutched the edge of the sink, her attention on the goat that was picking its way across the yard, nosing at the broken glass. I could imagine how every bit of her neighbor's behavior likely wore on her. I'd be willing to bet she'd tried with him for a long time. That was just the kind of person she was.

Leaning against the counter, I crossed my arms and said casually, "So when are we rescuing that goat?"

Joan's head whipped around. "You're serious?"

"As a felony."

Her attention strayed toward the window, where it remained for several long beats. Then she looked at me, determination steady in her gaze. "Okay."

I grinned. "Yeah?"

"Yeah. Let's do it tonight before all my brain cells come back online."

I lifted my hand for a high five, and she obliged with a huff of strained laughter. "Hell yeah," I exclaimed. "This is going to be great."

JOAN

In retrospect, it was *not* great.

Right off the bat, things went sideways.

Dressed in all black and—God help me—ski masks, we entered my neighbor's backyard just after midnight. All the lights in the trailer were off, but that didn't necessarily mean Buck was asleep for the night. We stayed quiet and moved quickly.

At our stealthy approach, the goat rose from where it was sitting. Luckily, it stayed quiet.

I played lookout while Ian knelt next to the animal. He pulled out the pocket knife I'd given him, but I felt compelled to whisper, "Make it look jagged. Like he chewed through it."

Ian went to work on the rope while the goat shuffled beside him curiously. He spoke gently to the animal, just words of encouragement under his breath. The way a dog owner might speak to their pet during a walk. Despite the ridiculousness of the situation, I could feel myself going soft and warm at Ian's sweetness. His quiet reassurance to a barnyard animal sanded down some of my tense, rough edges.

The night was cold, but the full moon shone brightly enough to be misleading. The silver glow softened much of Ian, too. The hazy truth was more bearable in the moonlight. Ian was out here risking life, limb, and legal trouble . . . for me.

I was sure he'd taken one look at me while Buck had thrown his childish tantrum and seen my rage that had no outlet. Ian had offered up this reckless little adventure as a result. He didn't have to deal with my neighbor. Until tonight, he'd never even seen this goat that led a terrible, mistreated life.

But here he was, an award-winning movie star, crouched in the dirt, carefully cutting through a rope so he could ease one animal's suffering, and maybe mine, too.

It was startling to realize how well Ian knew me, how much he cared, what he was willing to risk. I didn't feel like I deserved this—this unapologetic loyalty. But clearly I had it.

I shook myself and returned to keeping watch.

Now was not the time to be caught up in all these tender, moonlit emotions. Ian needed my attention on that trailer, so we didn't get caught.

Once the goat was free, I held out a few apple slices I'd prepared ahead of time. We slowly but surely lured the animal across the field and back toward my house, where Ian's rental car was waiting with a tarp in the backseat.

The goat was pretty good-sized. I was sure Ian was strong enough to lift him, but I was equally confident that the animal would bleat in protest. The apples worked until we got to the edge of Buck's property. Ian tugged on the end of the lead, but the animal wouldn't move.

"Take your mask off," Ian whispered. "Maybe if he sees it's you, he'll follow."

"We're not exactly friends. I really don't think that will make a difference."

"Well, I don't know what else to do besides throw him over my shoulder and run."

"Don't," I warned. "He'll scream, and then Buck will wake up."

To appease the great goat herder, I lifted the edge of my mask and said, "Here, boy. Come on."

The goat stared at me like I was an idiot, and, honestly, I probably was for going along with this scheme.

Ian tossed his hands up in exasperation. "What do we do now?"

Before I could answer, the goat took a step toward Ian. When he'd raised both arms, the bottom of his flannel had come untucked from beneath his dark hoodie. The goat zeroed in on the fabric and took a bite.

"Hey!" Ian hissed.

But I took hold of Ian's arm and urged him backward. Sure enough, the goat followed, lunging toward the flannel to nibble again.

"I like this shirt," Ian complained.

"Well, if you like not being in jail, keep quiet and let him take a bite every now and then. It'll get him back to the car. I'll buy you a new shirt."

Ian shot me a glare, and I had to resist the urge to laugh.

"Hurry up," I said. "If that asshole wakes up, he's liable to shoot us."

Ian grumbled but waved the tattered tail of his shirt toward the goat, who trotted after him.

With the car in sight, Ian wondered, "Is there also a wife that we need to liberate? Anyone married to that dick?"

"No. She left him a few years ago. The town threw her a party. Besides, one theft is all I can handle tonight."

Ian made a thoughtful hum. "I really prefer 'rescue effort' or 'heist.' At the very least, a"—he stopped walking and looked at me meaningfully— "*kid*napping." Then he grinned.

"Christ," I muttered under my breath and kept walking.

"Get it?" he called as I opened the back passenger door of his SUV. "KID-napping. Because baby goats are called kids."

"Yes, I get it. Whatever it is, it's illegal, so shut up and let's go."

Still entirely too proud of himself, he hopped in the backseat and led the goat inside. I closed the door behind them and let out a huge sigh.

It was dark and quiet, save for the low hum of the hybrid engine. No movement or sound came from Buck's mobile home.

We might just make it through this without getting arrested.

With another deep breath, I climbed into the front seat and put the vehicle in drive.

"Where are we going to take him?" Ian asked. He was trying to get the goat to switch to eating the apple slices instead of his shirt.

"There's a barn at the orchard, from when my grandfather kept horses. He'll be safe there overnight until we can figure out a long-term plan in the morning. The goat is actually Buck's ex-wife's. Jolly loves that thing, so naturally, that was what Buck went after in the divorce. I figure we can eventually make sure she gets him back, but he'll have to lie low for a while at the farm. I don't want Buck to accuse Jolly of anything. Plus, Candace has been bugging me to start up a petting zoo for the tourists. She might be getting her wish for the time being."

"So, we're keeping him, then. At least for a little while." Ian sounded excited. Must have been the rush of breaking the law in the middle of the night. I knew my own heart rate had yet to slow. I ignored the part where he'd said "we" were keeping the goat. There was no "we" . . . not really.

With the felony in progress, I hadn't figured out what I wanted from Ian. I assured myself there'd be time to sort through the complications later, when we weren't committing a crime. But a little voice inside my head warned that every minute Ian and George were in Kirby Falls was counting down until they had to eventually leave.

"Well, if we're keeping it, we should name it," Ian said, breaking through my complicated thoughts.

"It probably already has a name. Whatever Jolly gave it."

"Shhh. Don't ruin my fun, Joanie. What do you think about Selena Goat-mez? Or Vincent Van Goat? Jean-Paul Goatier? Feta, or Ralph, or Cheese.

Oh, how about Gordon Ramsaaay? There's also Scape, Hornsby, or Gilbert Goatfried? Are you gonna laugh? Because you look like you want to laugh."

Ian was watching me in the rearview mirror, so fucking pleased with himself and his rapid-fire puns. He still had the ski mask on, and I thought I was going to die from trying to keep a straight face. I bit the inside of my cheek as my shoulders shook.

"Oh, I know," he went on cheerfully, "Simone Biiiiiles. 'Cause she's the greatest of all time."

My laughter burst out of me as I clutched the steering wheel. I pulled to a stop in front of the old barn and rested my forehead on my hands as I wheezed.

"Those were good, right?" he called.

"Yes, stop. Oh my God. Ralph. We'll call him Ralph."

"That's not a pun at all," Ian said indignantly. "I only threw that one in for fun."

I turned around to peer into the dim backseat. "Well, I like it. He looks like a Ralph."

The goat peered at me from its seated position, skinny legs curled under its body, floppy ears dangling adorably. He bleated as if in agreement.

"See," I said, pointing.

Ian sighed. "Ralph, it is."

***

My alarm went off the next morning at five, and for the first time in a long time, I decided to skip my run. I was exhausted from last night's events. With Mac and Brady watching George, Ian had made us sit with Ralph in the barn for two hours, in case the goat got scared, he'd said. But the animal had just settled down on a wool blanket I'd found in storage while Ian and I talked. He'd asked me about all the pets I'd had growing up and then told me about the animals he'd worked with on films.

I was surprised to learn Ian really enjoyed riding horses, and he admitted he'd love to have one someday when he didn't live in LA. That conversation had painted a pretty picture I didn't know what to do with. It got a little too close to the things we didn't talk about—like Ian leaving—and, more importantly, the things I didn't want to think about. Namely, the future and how well Ian fit in here in Kirby Falls.

Now, in bed, I sighed and sat up.

In addition to being worn out from staying up late, I was, frankly, still in disbelief over what I'd done.

I'd been a law-abiding citizen for thirty-six years. There'd been no rebellious streak when I was a teen. No youthful indiscretions that had ended in being scared straight. Hell, I'd never even gotten a parking ticket.

My brother was the reckless Judd. The one most likely to get himself into a law-adjacent situation.

And if Brady had done something as fucking stupid as steal a goat from his asshole neighbor with little to no planning, I would have lectured him until the cows came home.

Even knowing all that, I wouldn't have changed my decision last night. I didn't regret it.

Buck Adams did not deserve his ex-wife's goat. He was a terrible pet owner and neighbor, and person in general, and I refused to feel guilty about what Ian and I had done.

Despite being tired, I couldn't settle back into sleep. I was eager to check on Ralph and make sure he was okay. And the part of me that was a vindictive shit stirrer wanted to peek out my back window to see if my neighbor had noticed his goat was missing yet.

There was a text waiting for me when I got out of the shower ten minutes later.

> Ian: Good morning, Bo Peep. Your mom invited us over for lunch. I have some things for our goat child. I'll see you in a few hours.

> Me: Bo Peep is a shepherdess . . . for sheep.

> Ian: I know, but I'm still picturing you in the frilly
> dress with a staff. It's really working for me.

I snorted a laugh and shook my head. He was ridiculous. And I wasn't even touching the goat-child thing.

My amusement faded when I realized I'd need to come clean to my parents and siblings about Ralph, especially since I was keeping him on the farm. They deserved to know what I'd gotten us all into.

I wasn't at all surprised that Mom had invited Ian and George over for lunch.

Christmas was in two days, and Sophia and Darren were in California. My parents were adamant that Ian and George spend the holiday with us. I wasn't going to fight them on it or try to put distance between our temporary neighbors and us. I'd been the one to breach the divide in the first place during Thanksgiving. George deserved to make memories with his uncle. And if he wanted to make sugar cookies with my mom and watch the same holiday movies I'd grown up with, then I wasn't going to stop him.

Ian and his nephew might not have their own Christmas traditions yet, but they were welcome to borrow ours.

Just before noon, Ian knocked quietly and let himself into my parents' kitchen through the screened porch. George followed, and they both said hello to my mother, who gave the little boy a quick hug.

I was sitting at the table reading Dad's newspaper, and I immediately took in Ian's excited expression. He practically vibrated with unspent energy.

Jesus, this guy had no poker face whatsoever.

Folding the paper neatly, I stood and said, "George, would you like to help Amy finish up the pasta salad?"

"Does it have meat?" the kid asked suspiciously.

I bit my lip. He was back to being a vegetarian this week. "Just bacon."

"Oh, I like bacon," he replied happily and pulled the step stool over to the sink to wash his hands.

Grinning, my mom met my gaze.

"I need to talk to Ian for a minute," I told her. What I really needed was to get him out of the kitchen before he eagerly blurted out what happened last night. "We'll be right back."

"That's fine," Mom replied. "Georgie and I have it covered."

"Thanks, Amy," Ian said, before opening the back door for me and following me outside.

He steered me in the direction of his SUV and opened the rear hatch with a flourish.

The back of the vehicle was full of forty-pound bags of alfalfa pellets.

"Someone will be by later today to deliver the hay," Ian said, while I stared at him. "Once you figure out where you want him, Ralph can graze and forage for most of his diet."

When I continued to stare, Ian shifted uncomfortably, pink creeping into his cheeks. "I did some research this morning," he admitted.

I had too, but I suppose I hadn't really expected Ian to step up and take care of this.

"I'll reimburse you for the feed," I said. I'd never been the one in a group project accused of not pulling their weight.

With dark brows lowered, Ian gave me a disapproving look. "No, you won't. It was my idea to steal—to liberate the goat. I'm happy to keep the little guy stocked in farm food."

"I know it was your idea, but I went along with it. You barely even had to talk me into it. Besides, it was my problem in the first place."

Ian shook his head sadly. "Don't talk about little Ralph Judd-Wells that way. He's not a problem."

"What did you just call him?"

Ian tutted. "He's ours. He should have both of our names. Judd hyphen Wells. Alphabetical seems fair, but I'm open to Wells-Judd. Both have a nice ring to them."

My mouth dropped open. "You're ridiculous."

There were awful, terrible feelings swirling around my middle. Warm, fluttery emotions that had no business reacting this way to a hyphenated last name related to a barnyard animal.

Was this how normal people felt all the time? So vulnerable and helpless in the face of well-meaning, adorable behavior.

Pushing all that uncomfortableness aside, I argued, "Besides, I'm the one taking care of the goat. Hiding the goat and risking a criminal record for the goat. You just met him yesterday."

Ian shrugged. "We've bonded, Joan. It's too late. Plus, I already told Georgie about him. I promised he could meet Ralph after lunch."

I stared incredulously at the man before me. "You seriously told George about Ralph and then left him alone with my mother?"

Realization dawned, and panic took over. "Oh, shit."

And that was how my parents found out about the goat in the barn.

---

After lunch, Ian and I were standing outside Ralph's open stall while George petted and talked to the goat. We'd brought a fresh bowl of feed and replenished the animal's water. He munched happily while George chatted nearby.

From the entrance to the barn, Candace and Mercer called out a greeting, and then came to stand next to us.

Following the wedding last weekend, my sister and her new husband didn't want to miss the holidays at home. So they'd decided to wait until February to take their honeymoon. They were probably planning on helping make homemade caramels this afternoon with my mother. It was her holiday specialty.

"Mom said you guys were out here and had something to show us," Candace said as she eyed the goings-on in the barn curiously. "Are you finally taking me seriously about the petting zoo?"

"Yep," I said.

My sister's eyes widened. "Wait, really?"

"This is Ralph," Ian told her.

Candace appeared confused. "But you were so against it. Even though I said I'd take care of the animals. You just went out and got a goat without telling anyone?"

"Not exactly," I admitted, crossing my arms over my chest.

My parents hadn't cared about the goat using the old barn, but they'd been a little concerned about where he'd come from.

Candace straightened and eyed me. "Are we aiding and abetting a runaway goat, Joan?"

"No, Candace. We are not."

Then Ian helpfully added, "Definitely not a runaway. He's stolen."

Mercer's head whipped in my direction, and my sister's mouth dropped open. She stood gaping like the largemouth bass mounted on the wall of her office.

Grinning at me, Ian shrugged.

I covered my face with my hands.

It took about five minutes, but Ian happily told the story of how Ralph came to be at the orchard. Personally, I felt like he needlessly embellished his heroics, but Candace and Mercer didn't seem to mind his overacting. Plus, they seemed to appreciate all the goat-name puns he somehow recited from memory. He'd even added a few more.

"I like the name Ralph," George had said with approval as he hugged the good-natured goat around the neck.

"I understand the need to rescue the animal from that kind of situation," Mercer said evenly, once Ian had finished his tale. "But we don't know anything about caring for goats. What kind is it, anyway?"

"Ralph is a Boer goat," Ian supplied. "They're a breed from South Africa, and super popular in the US. They're known for their good temperament.

Ralph is actually pretty small for an adult male. They can get up to two hundred and thirty pounds. You'll need a sturdy fence at least four feet high for his future enclosure. They can be good at getting loose."

We all turned to stare at Ian.

"What? I *am* capable of research. I went by the library this morning, and Mrs. Crandall helped me find some books on goat husbandry. I thought y'all were farmers. Shouldn't you already know this stuff?"

"I tend to plants," Mercer argued.

"Same," I added. "Although I would like some chickens."

Ian nodded. "I bet there are some books at the library about raising those, too. I'll take Georgie this afternoon, and we'll get some."

My smile was bittersweet.

But I didn't actually want to bring up the fact that Ian wouldn't have any part in my future as a hypothetical chicken farmer. There would be no funny cut scenes or heartwarming montages of us building a chicken coop together.

I didn't want to think about how my life would change yet again, this time shifting and rearranging to make up for the hole left behind when George and Ian went back to California.

Because Ian *was* leaving Kirby Falls in a few months.

And I needed to remember that.

"What?" Ian asked quietly, his forehead creased in sudden concern.

"Nothing," I said, attempting a smile that felt flat against my teeth. "I should call the vet today and see if she can come out and look Ralph over. He probably needs his hooves trimmed."

"Let me know when she can make it," Mercer said, walking toward the goat. "We can learn how to trim them and do it ourselves."

"I read you're supposed to trim them every six to eight weeks," Ian added.

Mercer squatted beside George and smiled at both boy and goat. He reached out a big, gentle hand to pat the animal.

Ian and I both read Ralph's intent a second too late.

"Mercer, hold up," I said just as Ian called, "Watch your flannel."

But the goat had already leaned forward and gripped Mercer's collar in his strong teeth. My brother-in-law pulled away as the fabric ripped.

Mercer shuffled back and stood. "Aw, man."

"Oh, no," Candace consoled as she rubbed her husband's back. But she was definitely trying not to laugh.

Ian made a whoops face.

George was giggling and trying to tug the end of the fabric out of the goat's mouth.

"Sorry, Mercer," I told him. "The goat eats flannel."

He rolled his eyes. "Good to know."

## JOAN

"Hey. Can I come in?"

Candace glanced up from her yogurt cup, where she was digging out the last bit of fruit at the bottom. "Hi! Sure, pull up a seat."

There was only one guest chair in the small office inside the Apple House, and I lowered myself onto it, feeling awkward.

My sister watched me curiously as she finished off her breakfast. "What's up? You look weirdly nervous."

I fought the urge to shift in my seat, to cross my legs and fidget. Truthfully, I *was* a little nervous.

I wasn't typically one for gossip or sisterly bonding. Despite Candace being supportive and a good listener, it was difficult to seek her out for advice. I couldn't remember a time when I'd actively cared about anyone's opinion but my own. Plus, she was my little sister. I was supposed to be the one doling out wisdom.

But here I was, sitting in Candace's office, having a complete out-of-body experience. I did not get mixed up over men. I didn't let myself get distracted either. And yet . . .

"Ian kissed me," I blurted.

My sister's dark brows lifted in surprise. "Okay."

When I couldn't manage to say anything else, Candace encouraged, "And how are you feeling about that?"

I scrubbed an anxious hand across my forehead before snapping, "I don't know. I don't know anything."

Somehow, she appeared even more stunned. "Was it . . . bad?"

She wanted to know *if it was bad*. Was it bad to feel so affected by someone that you thought about them all the time? Was it bad to get preoccupied when they spoke just because you couldn't stop staring at their lips? Was it bad to want something so far out of reach that you couldn't even put a name to it?

Nothing about this thing with Ian was simple enough to deem it good or bad. It was complicated. It was unwise. It was baffling. It made me feel weak and confused and unsteady.

And I was painfully aware of all of it.

Even without having all the answers, I knew that kissing Ian wasn't *bad*.

The movie had been on a break for a week and a half. Ian and George had spent Christmas with my family. It had been fun to see them in the middle of our big meals and traditions. We'd made candy with my mother. Swapped ridiculous white elephant gifts. Then Ian and I had stood side by side at the kitchen sink and washed dishes together. We'd watched movies and played board games with George. The familiarity had me all mixed up.

Then Ian had helped me and Mercer and Brady build an enclosure for Ralph. Unsurprisingly, the Hollywood actor had never constructed a goat house or put up a fence, but he followed directions well. All those muscles were good for wielding tools and carrying wood.

It had been fun to work together on a project. Ian had joked around with my brother and even drawn quiet Mercer into conversation. Watching the outsider become even more embedded in my family had been equal parts joyful and troublesome. I didn't know how to feel.

It was easier to tell myself it didn't mean anything—that Ian fit in wherever he went because that's what he was good at. But even my cynical heart wasn't buying my arguments anymore.

Ian and I had also continued running together regularly. Since Darren and Sophia were still away, he brought George to stay with my parents in the mornings while we found ourselves on paths all over the farm. Then we'd make our way back to the farmhouse, and all have breakfast together. We usually separated after that. I'd go to work in the fields while Ian took George on adventures.

So far during the film's break, they'd visited the waterfalls the town was named after. They'd hit the movie theater in Asheville and the fancy Franklin Street chocolate shop there as well. There'd been the trip to the pinball museum and the toy store, and the doughnut tour they'd done of the surrounding area.

Today was the final day of the break. Ian's team would return this evening. He'd wanted to take George on a big outing before things went back to normal—well, normal for a movie star and his nephew. Early mornings on set and homeschooling with a private tutor.

But, for today, it could just be fun. At my recommendation, they were going to the old-school retro arcade over in Clemmons. And then over to the historic Bluebird Drive-in for lunch and milkshakes. George was going to love it. The diner had cheeseburgers the size of his head. Luckily, he wasn't a practicing vegetarian this week.

I was supposed to be working on breaking down the orchard's holiday displays and decorations, followed by closing up the Apple House until we reopened to the public in May. Mercer was already in the tree lot, but it was still early, so I'd taken the opportunity to talk to my sister.

"Kissing Ian was not bad," I finally replied, fighting the urge to bolt from the room. "But it makes no sense."

"Why?" Candace asked.

It wasn't the money or the fame. Okay, maybe it was the fame, a little bit.

Ian wasn't better than me, but I didn't know how to explain it. His life was loud, bright, and bold in ways that demanded attention. I was a farmer in the small town I'd grown up in. My life was quiet and contained. It went beyond compatibility.

"He's—I mean—you know—" I blew out a frustrated breath before admitting, "He's a damn movie star, Candace. Why the fuck is he going around kissing me?"

My sister smiled then, and it finally felt like someone understood where I was coming from. "You know, it is weird to get to know a celebrity the way we've gotten to know Ian. He's eaten dinner at our childhood dining table."

"Yes, exactly. I've seen his butt on a television screen, and he helped my mom change a lightbulb the other day."

Candace laughed. "The same man who was on the cover of *People* magazine has looked at our baby pictures in our parents' living room."

"He should be on a yacht somewhere."

Nodding, my sister added, "Or a red carpet."

"Or getting manscaped."

"I bet he has people for that," she said with a grin, making me recall our very first conversation about the great and spoiled Dorian Masters.

"Probably a whole team responsible for the length of his eyebrows," I mused.

She chuckled. "Even if they waxed something important off, he'd still be handsome."

"I bet he even looks good on the checkout lane security cameras."

"Probably doesn't scare himself when his cell phone camera is accidentally forward facing."

My laughter trailed off. Then I said thoughtfully, "He looks good with his hair short. I wasn't expecting that."

Candace nodded her agreement.

"And he's smarter than I thought he'd be," I continued, knowing that sounded terrible and judgy. "And he's funny. The charm was obvious from the beginning, but he doesn't wield it like a weapon, you know. I thought the arrogance thing would get on my nerves, but Ian's actually really humble. If I ask him about acting, he tells me all the technical stuff, never mentioning his awards or accolades. It's almost like he uses arrogance to deflect."

Staring off, I thought of another thing. "And he's so good with his nephew. It could not have been easy to take in a seven-year-old when he didn't know anything about kids. But Ian's unexpectedly patient and gentle with George."

"That's true," Candace agreed distantly.

"I've never seen him be demanding with people, you know, how I assumed a movie star would be. He thanks everyone and tips generously. He'd get stuck signing autographs and taking selfies all day if you let him. Did you know Darren has been with him since his very first press tour? He hired him away from the security firm his production company used. Been with him ever since. I just assumed—"

I cut myself off when I finally noticed the way my sister was watching me. "What?"

Candace looked like she had a secret, but she wasn't sure if she should spill it.

She hesitated, so I asked again, "What is it?"

"I know you're not fishing for compliments, but obviously Ian likes you. *That's* why he kissed you. You can act confused about it or disbelieving or whatever, but that's what it boils down to. He wants you. He probably has a list in his head of all the surprising, wonderful things about you, too. Like the one you said out loud just now about him."

I opened my mouth to object, but Candace held up a finger.

"You love to say he's just a person. From the very beginning, when the rest of us were all starstruck local yokels, you claimed you weren't intimidated by Ian's celebrity status. But you're all mixed up about him kissing you because . . . he's a famous actor? How is that fair? You're questioning his motives because you're the one thinking he's too good for you. You can't have it both ways, Joanie. You can't hold something against him that you refuse to acknowledge or entertain unless it suits your misgivings. If you really believe he's just like any other guy, then give him a chance. Go on a date with him. Kiss him again. Be brave about this the way you're brave about everything else."

I stared at my sister, feeling the truth of her words in the ugly twist in my stomach, in the way a ready denial shaped itself on my sharp tongue.

Candace was right. I'd been a hypocrite. I'd spent a lot of time and energy ensuring everyone knew that I wasn't affected by the great Dorian Masters. And I must have sold it pretty well, because this was the first time anyone had called me on being a liar. Lying to my friends and my family. Lying to myself.

*Of course* it mattered that Ian was a celebrity. It would be like trying to date another species. Our lives were farther apart than just North Carolina and California. There was a gulf between us. Of experience and understanding, expectations and commonality.

"Why are you pushing for me to give Ian a chance?" I asked, rather than admit the truth.

Candace placed her elbows on the desk and leaned forward. "Because I don't want you to miss out on something just because you're scared and too stubborn to admit it. Ian is so good for you, and you don't even see it. I want you to be happy. That doesn't always mean finding happiness in someone else. Instead, it can just mean sharing it with the right person."

The tiny ache that lived in my chest flared brightly. A voice whispered that I was getting too close, losing too much of myself to someone who could never stick around.

"We've been spending so much time together," I said, testing out a theory. "Maybe that's all this is. Proximity or something."

"How does anyone get to know someone? They spend a lot of time together. I don't think it matters that he's famous in that regard."

When I didn't argue or defend my theory, Candace wondered, "Are you worried things will change when filming starts back up tomorrow? That this has all been some novelty small-town vacation for him?"

A bittersweet grin twisted my lips. "Christmas with the Judds."

"A holiday special," my sister added with a small smile of her own.

Call it intuition, but something told me that the return to filming wouldn't make a difference. Ian would still prioritize George. And I worried some of that would continue to extend to me as well.

"Maybe things should change," I finally admitted. "It might be easier if we kept our distance."

"Easier for who?" Candace asked, her tone gentle, her expression even more so.

I shook my head, knowing the answer but unwilling to voice it aloud.

Ian's presence in my life—in this town—felt natural, easy in a way I never would have predicted.

I couldn't remember what my days looked like before he was running beside me. Or a time when George wasn't following along behind me in the fields. Or what it felt like to eat dinner alone in my kitchen, without a drawing from the kid on my refrigerator and a friendship bracelet on my arm.

Three months from now, I didn't want only memories keeping me company, ghosts from a fraction of my life, haunting me at every turn.

Like a damn mind reader, my sister said, "If you're worried about getting attached or Ian leaving in the spring, I think you should trust that you're both adults. Adults communicate. Adults compromise. Adults figure shit out." She made uncomfortably intense eye contact. "Be an adult."

I nodded, unable to resist my amused smile to go along with it. A year ago, I never could have imagined Candace being brave enough to disagree with me. She wouldn't have wanted to rock the boat or force an uncomfortable conversation. She wouldn't have inserted herself into my business or given me any sort of advice, and, honestly, I would never have considered asking.

It was proof that we'd come a long way since my sister had moved back home. We talked. We communicated. We compromised. We figured shit out . . . like adults.

Maybe that's what relationships were. A journey. Not a path with one single destination. Maybe you didn't cross a finish line or reach "the end" when you were dealing with people.

I recalled a little hand holding out a beaded bracelet.

I thought of terrible coffee in a travel mug just for me, a clean-shaven jaw beneath my palm, sneakers hitting the dirt next to mine.

Maybe—just maybe—there was room for the path to grow.

———

## Ian

I got a text from Joan just as I was settling into the hair and makeup chair at 5:22 a.m. on the first day back to filming.

> Joan: What do you call someone who takes care
> of chickens?

Of course, she didn't give me a chance to respond. She immediately replied with the punchline.

> Joan: A chicken tender.

"Mouth relaxed," the makeup artist called suddenly.

I worked to control my grin. "Sorry, Imogen."

> Me: Are you flirting with me, Joan Judd?

> Joan: No.

> Joan: Maybe.

> Joan: I know people your age are into texting. I
> thought I could at least try.

Hmm. I wondered what had brought this on. I tried not to read too much into it. Didn't want to get my hopes up.

The last time we'd kissed, Joan had been confused and unsure. She was the steadiest person I'd ever met. It had been strange to see her so hesitant and indecisive. Knowing I'd been the one to throw her off hadn't made me feel any better either.

When I looked at her, I felt like I'd never been more sure of anything in my life. If she wasn't there yet, I wasn't going to push her. I'd made that mistake early on, and I wouldn't be repeating it.

Did I want to kiss her again? Of course, I did. I wanted to do a hell of a lot more than that. But she needed to be on board. I didn't want to be the only thing in Joan's life that made her question herself.

Me: People my age?

Joan: Yeah. Twenty-somethings.

Me: I will be thirty in like two months.

Joan: How do you want to celebrate? Maybe by eating dinner at 4 pm, and then staying in to play Scrabble.

Me: Ha. Ha.

Joan: We could always go bird-watching. Oh, the VFW is hosting Bingo. We can do that.

Me: You're hilarious.

"Dorian, please." Imogen had her makeup brush in hand as she gave me an expectant look. "No smiling right now."

"Right. Sorry about that. Again."

My phone buzzed. I relaxed my face and glanced down.

Joan: Just want to make sure you usher in your thirties with style. What do big-deal Hollywood actors usually do to celebrate birthdays? Rent out an entire club?

*Yes, frequently*, I didn't say.

> Joan: Sink a yacht?

Oof, she'd read about that one, too.

> Joan: Orgies?

> Me: What? No. That is not my idea of fun.

> Joan: Not enough NDAs?

> Me: Too many bodily fluids.

> Joan: Gross.

> Me: You started it.

> Me: Besides, I don't actually like to share.

No follow-up came through, and I could feel my pulse in my throat. She had to know what I was implying. That I wanted her. No one else. Just her.

After maybe the longest twenty seconds of my life, her two-word reply appeared on my screen, doing nothing to calm my racing heartbeat.

> Joan: Me either.

I stared at my phone until a throat cleared pointedly.

A quick look in the mirror showed Imogen staring at me, arms crossed and waiting, while my smile grew out of control.

Hurriedly, I typed *Good* and hit send before placing my phone upside down on the table next to me.

It was a struggle, but I managed to keep my face neutral for the next forty minutes so Imogen could do her job.

After all, I was a professional. At least, that's what I kept reminding myself.

When I got a break later in the morning, I texted Sophia and had her pass along Georgie's joke of the day. We'd started doing it a while back. I borrowed Joan's chicken tender joke. Sophia replied with a photo of Georgie's giggling face.

Smiling, I quickly checked my schedule, noticing an on-set interview happening this afternoon. I sighed, refusing to let the intrusion ruin my good mood. My manager, Gloria, had arranged the interview despite my objections. The host wanted to tour my trailer on set, and that just felt like a step too far. But, at least, it wouldn't take long, and it had already been cleared with the shooting schedule.

Finally, I navigated over to an unread text from Candace. Good thing Imogen wasn't touching up the fake cut and trauma makeup along my cheekbone because I was definitely smiling now.

Switching over to my thread with Joan, I typed: *Do you have plans tonight?*

> Joan: I was thinking about staying in and
> watching a movie, actually.

A pause.

> Joan: You could come over.

> Joan: If you wanted.

I took a slow breath in through my nose and thumbed at the elastic band around my wrist.

> Me: Really?

> Joan: Sure.

> Me: That's great because your sister texted me
> earlier and offered to watch Georgie tonight,
> completely unprompted.

> Joan: Sigh.

Alone, in my trailer on set, I cracked up.

> Joan: Actually, what is the cast up to tonight? I could watch George if you wanted to hang out with them.

Frowning, I stared at my screen and tried to make sense of the message. Joan had never once asked about my co-stars. Hell, I didn't even think she knew who played opposite me in the film.

I hit a button on my phone, and a moment later Joan's confused voice came through. "Hello?"

"Why would you ask that? About me hanging out with the cast?"

"Just a thought," she said, sounding a little *too* nonchalant. "You just never mention them. You tell me about the script and filming and wide-angle lens and special effects, but you never mention your co-stars."

Suspicion had me replying tightly, "I didn't think you cared about celebrities."

"I don't. I just figured they were your friends. I feel like I'm monopolizing all your free time. You run with me. You eat lunch with me. You see me at work. You come to my house for dinner. I thought actors hung out together. Bonded over filming and shit. Like summer camp."

She was right. That was typically how it went on a set. An intense schedule and working conditions usually bonded actors on a film.

Unless someone was an asshole and kept to themselves.

Apparently, *I* was the asshole on this film.

I didn't know how to admit to Joan that those people—the cast and crew —were all fine. But being with them seemed hollow and insignificant. I knew where I wanted to be.

With her. For as long as I could manage it.

Anything else—anyone else—seemed like a waste of what little time I had here in Kirby Falls.

Finding stolen moments with Joan and Georgie felt like what it might be like to have a real life—a normal life. Family dinner on Sunday. Chores and a pet goat to take care of. Someone to make coffee for every day. A little boy to tuck in every night.

But I couldn't say any of that. She was confused about kissing me. Telling her about these weird domestic fantasies would be admitting too much— enough to make her regret letting me into her life at all.

So instead of a vulnerable confession, I gave her something else true. "My co-stars are fine. We all get along, but they don't know about Georgie. Only Della does. He's my priority whether I'm on location or not. I don't want to lie to them or pretend like I'm available when I'm not."

Joan remained quiet on the line. Then, finally, she murmured, "Right. That makes sense."

"So, am I still invited to watch a movie?"

Another pause. "Yeah."

"Want me to bring a pizza over?"

"That would be nice. Thank you. No silly toppings, though."

I chuckled. "What's a silly topping?"

"You probably eat pineapple on your pizza."

I did do that.

"No way. Only respectable toppings for this Californian. I eat kale pizza. Sometimes I go crazy and get yams with hot honey. Maybe a little crème fraiche."

"I'm hanging up now."

"No, wait." I struggled through my laughter. "Do you want to hear my acai bowl order?"

"I don't even know what that is." She sounded horribly exasperated. I loved it.

"Well, I'm making you one. I'll be over at six thirty. No backsies."

Joan sighed audibly. "You did not just say, 'No backsies.' What are you, five?"

"No, I'm twenty-nine. Which seemed like a very big deal to you. I would have thought you'd remember."

"Don't remind me."

The clock on the wall said I was due back for the next scene and three minutes late. "I'll see you tonight, Joanie."

"Bye. Go be Dorian Masters. And there better not be pineapple on that pizza."

I smiled all the way back to set.

# seventeen

## IAN

With a Mediterranean pizza in one hand, I knocked on Joan's door at 6:28 that evening.

I'd been over to her house plenty of times at this point, but Georgie was usually with me when Joan and I made dinner together.

Nerves churned in my belly as I stood there waiting, like a teenager on a first date. This wasn't technically a date, but it felt like *something*.

The door swung inward, and Joan stood there, looking frazzled and out of breath.

"Did you have to defend yourself against the creepy doll collection?" I asked.

She rolled her eyes, but she was smiling. "No, just straightening up."

I raised an eyebrow. A glance around the interior showed it just as tidy as every other time I'd been there, but I wouldn't push it and tease her. I was nervous, too.

"Are you going to let me in?" I wondered.

She was still blocking the door.

Her blue eyes drifted toward the pizza box in my hand.

It was my turn to roll my eyes. "It's an Apollo's special. Marinated Greek chicken, mushrooms, Kalamata olives, feta cheese, and banana pepper rings."

Joan nodded and stepped aside, sweeping her arm out in an invitation to enter.

"I want to see your movie collection. I'm picking," I told her.

Grabbing the remote control for her television, I attempted to find the streaming services. But Joan abandoned the plates and napkins she'd been gathering and walked over to open a cabinet beneath her bookcase.

Of course, she had an actual DVD collection.

"Wow. I didn't even know they still made these," I murmured absently, crouching down to browse the titles.

Her annoyed sigh had me chuckling as she made her way back into the kitchen.

I thumbed through the plastic cases, absorbing the titles that had caught her fancy. It made sense that she'd want to keep physical reminders of the films she found worthy of her time. Movies and television shows disappeared from streaming services left and right. Joan would appreciate the permanence of something she could keep on a shelf. The knowledge made me feel warm with affection.

My finger hovered over a DVD at the end of the top row, hardly daring to believe what I was seeing.

"You own *The Tycoon and the Aristocrat*?" I asked.

"Um, yeah," Joan replied after a long moment.

It had been the first movie I'd done in an effort to branch out and away from action-hero roles. It had won Oscars for Best Costume Design and Best Makeup and Hairstyling. The period drama had challenged me in a way I'd never anticipated. I'd worked with a voice and accent coach for three months before filming began. There had been hours of dance lessons and choreography. The sex scenes had required an intimacy coordinator and detailed directions. The sweeping romance and grandeur of the time period had been like stepping into another world. It was one of the roles I was most proud of.

Standing, I turned to face Joan and held up the DVD. "I remember Candace saying something about how much you loved this one." At the time, the knowledge had only fed my ego. Now, it meant something different, something more.

Joan placed two beers and two waters on the coffee table before joining me. "Our book club watched it together," she answered, noncommittally.

"The case looks pretty worn. Probably from too much use," I teased. "Look, there's even a little crack right here."

Frowning, Joan snatched the DVD out of my hand to examine it. "Where?"

I was already grinning when she looked up after finding nothing.

She whacked me on the shoulder with the case.

"Careful. We're watching that one."

For a moment, Joan appeared dumbfounded. "You want to watch your own movie?"

"Yep."

"Isn't that weird?"

"Nah," I insisted. "This ego you're so fond of really likes the idea."

Joan eyed me skeptically.

Truthfully, I was more nervous than I could ever remember being, but it seemed like an important opportunity to learn something else about Joan. She was the most poker-faced person I'd ever met. I never knew what she was thinking or feeling. She was locked up so tight, always protecting her emotions and guarding her heart. I didn't know exactly where I stood with her. But, in this, it felt like being handed the gift of insight. I didn't want to squander it.

Besides, if I got the chance to sit next to her for two hours, I was going to do it. She was someone I respected. Someone so good at everything that it should have been maddening, but it only made me ache to be better.

I wanted her to love the film. I wanted to catch a smile on her face, knowing I was the one who'd put it there. I wanted Joan to see me in a different light—not the careless, spoiled celebrity who didn't take things seriously. I wanted her to think I was good at something.

Finally, we settled in with our pizza on the couch. I focused on eating while the film opened. But I managed only half of a slice before nerves had me setting my plate aside.

Shifting in my seat did nothing to alleviate the restless energy and awareness coursing through me. Every brush of our shoulders or bump of our knees reminded me that Joan was right there. Her warmth and her body and her opinions . . .

Discreetly, I took in Joan's reaction to the first scene featuring my character—the tycoon—and the love interest—the aristocrat. The meet-cute was filled with banter and tension, and Joan's eyes were focused on the screen.

As inconspicuously as possible, I watched Joan as she watched me. I didn't need to stare at myself for one hundred and twenty-eight minutes. I'd rather get a glimpse into what she was thinking and feeling.

By the time the ballroom dance sequence rolled around, Joan's pizza lay forgotten on the coffee table. I witnessed the way her walls lowered as she lost herself in the story, the performance of it. Her lips moved, shaping some of my lines, and I felt my chest grow tight.

When the screen shone with bedroom candlelight, I forced myself to take a steadying breath. Realistically, I hadn't considered what it would be like to sit next to Joan while the character I was portraying made love to a woman on screen. Every gasp through the speakers, every intimate caress, every rustle of clothing seemed loud in the living room.

What was it like for Joan to watch these moments, this feigned intimacy?

For me, it was weirdly cold and technical. I could recall the equipment on set and the boom in my periphery, the intimacy coordinator having me reposition my arm to discreetly cover the actress from a certain angle.

But how did the final product come together through Joan's eyes?

She appeared rapt, gaze focused.

Was she reading desire and lust? Did she realize that none of that was true?

During the final scene of the film, emotion brightened Joan's features as my character delivered a monologue, confessing his endless, consuming love for the heroine.

The version of me sitting there on the couch with my thigh pressed to Joan's could hardly breathe.

We were quiet as the credits rolled.

Finally, I couldn't take it anymore and said, "Well?"

She turned to face me, expression serious. "It was . . . alright."

I snorted out a laugh, and she smiled.

"Shut up," she teased. "You know it was good. You know *you* were good. Every time I watch it—and there have been many—I catch something new that I missed. A subtle expression. A shift in your body language that so perfectly embodies the character that it makes me irrationally angry that I didn't notice it before. It's the best book adaptation I've ever seen."

Instinctively, I knew not to give her shit about this. I felt weirdly proud and inexplicably shy. From side characters to household names, I'd played dozens of roles in my career, but this was the one—a romance hero— who'd captured her interest and earned her appreciation. That meant something to me.

*She* meant something to me.

Joan was so insular and mysterious, unimpressed with ninety-nine percent of the world's population. It felt like a major accomplishment that she'd watched my film and enjoyed the performance.

It made me want to earn her trust, her approval in all things.

I didn't know what to do with her praise or my complicated emotions surrounding it.

So, I joked, "Oh, this is from a book?"

Joan gave me a look so disbelieving that it was like she could see straight through me. Like she could tell that I'd read the novel the film was based on six times prior to filming. How I'd taken copious notes, consulted the author, and visited fan forums online to find out what readers loved best about my character.

I'd fought for scenes in the script. I'd ad-libbed lines that had been allowed to stay, direct quotes from the text that readers still raved about.

I'd worked my ass off for the role of the tycoon in order to make sure that the pieces and parts that fans loved would translate to the big screen. Honoring the character and the novel and the author had been forefront in my mind throughout filming and for months beforehand.

Joan blinked, searching my face like she could see the truth, like I wasn't an award-winning actor who should have been able to pull off a little fib.

"You knew it was a book. There's no way you did that," she accused, sweeping a hand in the direction of the television, "without knowing. I bet you read it. More than once."

Smiling awkwardly, I looked away. "You caught me."

Fiddling with the remote, I stopped the DVD and gathered the remnants of our dinner. But I knew Joan's gaze was laser-focused on me.

I felt embarrassed, self-conscious in a way I hadn't while she'd been watching me act on screen.

Swallowing hard, I couldn't look at her as I carried our dishes into the kitchen.

After unloading the items on the counter, I turned to find Joan standing behind me, staring at me curiously.

"Why do you do that?" she asked.

"Do what?"

"Belittle yourself," she replied. "Pretend you're not one hundred percent devoted to your craft and all the work you've done to accomplish your goals."

My insides squirmed uncomfortably. "I guess . . . I guess it fits the expectation better. The brand. Gotta give the people what they want, right?"

"You don't need to minimize yourself, Ian. Not for me. There was never a time when I thought you were untalented. But after getting to know you and hearing you talk about your job, I have a better understanding of the work you put in, the dedication, the long hours, the sacrifices. You want to make it sound like you just stand in the right spot and recite a few lines, but I know better. You don't need to pretend to be a fool or play dumb."

The whole time she spoke, she moved closer. My heart rate increased with every step.

The tips of our sock-covered feet touched by the time she looked at me earnestly and said, "What I want from you doesn't involve you being clueless about anything, and I sure as hell don't want you faking it for my benefit."

I searched her face, looking for meaning, for confirmation, for a sign that Joan wanted me the way I wanted her.

"Is that so?" I asked.

She lifted a hand and placed it against my stomach, just above the waistband of my jeans. Her touch was warm through the fabric as her fingers climbed upward, over my abs to rest on my chest.

"That's right," she finally answered.

I felt myself smile, something small and hopeful, unwilling to commit to a full-blown grin just in case I was reading her signals wrong. "I don't want you to fake anything either," I confessed.

Joan's hand snaked around the back of my neck, drawing me down to her.

When we were close enough to breathe the same air, I watched her pretty blue eyes crinkle in amusement. With a teasing challenge in her voice, she said, "Then I guess you'd better give it your best effort."

I huffed a short laugh as her fingers sifted through the hair at my nape. Our mouths found one another, turning my amusement into something slower, quieter, and infinitely necessary, stealing my breath and narrowing my focus.

There was only Joan and this moment.

She relaxed against me, and I bent to scoop her up.

Her legs wrapped around my hips easily, and I could feel her everywhere. Her hands in my hair, her arms draped over my shoulders, the heat of her cradling the attraction I couldn't begin to hide.

I squeezed, holding her tight. I wanted to swallow her whole.

Because whatever this was, it wasn't reckless or hasty. There was nothing careless about the way I wanted her.

And like she'd demanded only moments ago . . . I was done pretending.

### Joan

Ian's forehead was pressed to mine, and we were still standing in my kitchen, locked together.

I knew he was strong. I had eyes, after all. The man had muscle groups on display that I'd only ever seen on professional athletes and Olympians. But the effortless way he held me made me very aware that he could stand here all day with my legs around his waist and his hands under my backside.

I used my teeth to tug on his lower lip, urging him into action. The move made him groan, and me smile. His big hands squeezed my ass as he finally moved, pressing my back against the nearest wall and kissing the hell out of me.

His tongue stroked inside my mouth, and I relished the urgency, the need, matching it with my own.

My nails scratched gently over his scalp before smoothing along the baby-fine hairs buzzed soft and short. I loved this. I'd dreamed of touching him this way—wild and affectionate at the same time, running my fingers through his hair. Throughout the movie, I'd wondered what it would be like to have Ian's head in my lap while we watched. Now, I couldn't imagine *not* touching him like this.

He was warm and hard all over. His erection settled heavily against my center, and I fought the desire to hurry him along.

For a long time, I'd controlled my own pleasure. Men hadn't really been worth the effort, and dating had been a lesson in torture. I'd been content with the vibrator in my bedside table. An orgasm had seemed like an occasional necessity, used to release tension and achieved in the manner I did everything in my life—quickly and efficiently.

So, the instinct was there to rush things. To get down to business.

But so much of my life with Ian felt like a race against the clock. His time. His attention. His very presence here. I didn't want to waste a single moment, but I didn't want to cheat either one of us out of what might happen next.

One of Ian's hands found its way beneath my sweater to my breast. He made a helpless noise when he realized I wasn't wearing a bra.

"Is this okay?" he rasped brokenly against my lips.

"Yes," I breathed, arching my back and pressing myself more fully into his hand.

Judging by his enthusiasm, I thought he'd be a little rough or demanding, but he paused, his hand hovering there. I waited, holding my breath, anticipating the moment when his palm might cup me or his fingers might pluck at my nipple.

But that didn't happen.

Ian traced a line down the center of my chest, his fingers bumping along my sternum before his thumb swept low, brushing the underside of my breast, just barely grazing the sensitive skin there.

He used soft touches to map my contours and curves, all while I panted against his lips, painfully aware that I was the eager, impatient one in this scenario.

Finally—*fucking finally*—Ian's hand closed over me, gently plumping and squeezing my small breast as he nuzzled against my neck, placing hot, wet kisses along my jaw.

The friction of his stubble was delicious torture. I knew my skin would wear the evidence of his attentions, and I wanted it—needed it.

My hips canted, eager for contact. Ian groaned softly, cursing into my collarbone as my center moved up and down the ridge of his substantial erection in little pulses. He felt good, and I'd be lying if I said I wasn't looking forward to getting the clothes off this man.

But Ian's hands came to my hips, stilling me. He brought his forehead back to rest against mine as he worked to catch his breath.

"I thought we'd worked on your stamina," I teased.

He huffed a laugh and smiled against my lips.

"I just . . ." he started. "I don't want to rush it because then it'll be over. And obviously I want there to be more of this—of you and me—but I never know with you, Joan. This could be the only chance I get, and I don't want to mess it up. Or disappoint you. Or—"

"Hey," I interrupted softly, cupping his cheeks and pressing a gentle kiss to his rambling mouth. "You're not going to mess anything up. Whatever you're worried about, you don't need to be."

But it was like he didn't hear me.

After a deep breath, he admitted, "I know I'm going to make a fool of myself. I'm going to be so fucking stupid over you. And I can't help it. Couldn't stop it even if I wanted to. I notice everything. The way you look. The way you smell like everything good and green in this world. The way you stretch your hamstrings after a run. Jesus, I can't even watch. I get hard every single time."

His words continued in a whispered rush, honesty freed from its confinement as he unraveled me, bit by bit. "The calm, competent way you drive a tractor or do anything on the farm, like you were born to work this land, like you rose up from these mountains, just as timeless and beautiful. Or the way you're so stubborn and how much you care. The way you're patient with Candace and protective of your parents, and quietly mischievous with Brady. How you give Georgie every bit of your attention and how you knew, right from the beginning, that was exactly what he needed.

I know you think I'm immature and not a serious person. But all I really want—what I need, Joan—is to be someone worthy of you."

My heart stuttered, and emotion clogged my throat. I couldn't speak, could hardly breathe in the face of his brutal, beautiful honesty.

There was a time when I would have been worried that Ian's words were practiced lines, memorized and recited for their target audience. But that time had come and gone.

He'd been a constant in my life for months now. Truthfully, he was my closest friend. I knew him, knew his heart. And now, I felt the way it beat against my chest, wild and out of control. I could detect the nervous tremble in his hands at my waist, and the nearly desperate way he held me to him.

So while the speech might have been moving and heartfelt and full of the most wonderful things anyone had ever said about me, it wasn't a performance. It was just Ian, being honest. Being forthright. Putting himself out there, being brave enough for both of us.

He was telling me what he wanted.

And what he wanted was me.

As strange and inexplicable as that might be.

I stroked a thumb over his cheekbone, marveling in his courage, his sweetness, his fruitless worry.

I couldn't remember ever being this careful with someone. Honestly, I hadn't known I had it in me. But in the face of Ian's self-doubt, I knew I needed to step up and reward his honesty with some of my own.

"You are worthy, Ian. I know I've been hard on you and judgmental, too. But that was before. Before I knew you. Before you were in my life every day, and in my thoughts the rest of the time. I let all my assumptions get the best of me in the beginning. I was wrong. I can admit that. And I'm sorry for it."

"You weren't *that* wrong," he argued, eyes still closed.

I smiled and ran my nose along the length of his, gratified by this closeness, relieved by it. "I really was."

Ian released a long breath that made me think of painful confessions and unspoken regrets. "I'm not . . . him either, the man you just watched on the screen. None of that is real. If that's what you were hoping for."

With my thumb across his lips, I stopped whatever else was about to come out of his mouth. "You think that's who I want? A character from a story that has your face? You think I can't separate the two?"

Ian finally opened his eyes. "I just don't want you to be disappointed."

I leaned back as far as I could so I could focus on him. I really wanted to drive this point home. "I've never been terribly fanciful. I don't let my imagination run away from me. You never have to worry about me confusing you with the roles you play. I'm not expecting the tycoon's dirty talk in the bedchamber or Inferno Man's superhero suit on my bedroom floor. I can separate who you are from what you do. You were right, from the beginning. You're more than an actor. Dorian Masters is great, but I want Ian Wells."

He searched my face for a long moment before the hint of a smile emerged, one lonely dimple showing itself. I pressed my lips to where the other one should be.

Shifting slightly, I urged Ian to set me down. Then I twined our fingers together and led him toward my bedroom.

The room was dark, but it didn't matter. We didn't need much light to remove each other's clothes.

Ian's touch remained gentle and reverent as he laid me out and learned the lean curves of my body, first with his hands and then his tongue.

When he settled himself between my spread thighs, his wide, muscular shoulders stretching me wide, I couldn't hide how much I wanted him there. My impatience was written in each ragged breath, in every arch of my back. But Ian was unfazed. He drew out my pleasure, teased and tortured as he nipped at the flesh of my inner thigh before using the tip of his tongue to trace every peak and valley of my pussy. When he finally managed a long, slow lick from my entrance to my clit, I groaned so loud I should have been embarrassed.

But there wasn't time for that, because he did it all over again. Ian built me up slowly with teeth and tongue before pushing one thick finger inside me at an agonizingly slow pace. My muscles squeezed, eager for the invasion as Ian focused the rest of his attention on sucking my straining clit.

I came on a rush, clinging to his head and gasping for air.

The next thing I knew, Ian was hovering above me, pressing kisses to my breasts, the column of my throat, and finally my mouth. I moaned, tasting myself on his tongue, pleasure once again ramping up, knowing I was ready for more. Desperate for what came next.

I shifted beneath him, rolling to grab a condom from the bedside table. He made no complaint as I fumbled a little, rolling it down his length with fingers long out of practice.

Ian pushed inside me slowly, taking his time. But I could hear his deliberate breaths, feel the strain in his taut muscles as he drew out the moment. All that patience made me want to be a little naughty, so I squeezed my inner muscles around those hard inches.

The way he jolted and muttered, "Fuck," had me grinning wickedly. That all went away as he rolled his hips, seating himself fully and grinding down on my sensitive clit.

I cursed and wrapped my legs around his hips, bringing him closer, deeper.

Any plans I had for seduction or delayed gratification went out the window after that. We were reduced to urgency and need. Grasping hands, desperate lips, and the absolute knowledge that Ian would do whatever it took to get me there.

"I love the sounds you make," he whispered before dragging his teeth down my throat, eliciting another broken moan from my mouth.

When he rose to his knees and stretched my feet toward his shoulders, I gripped the comforter in tight fists. He pressed a tender kiss to each of my ankles, sending a shiver through my sweat-slick body.

"Have I mentioned how obsessed I am with these legs?" he asked.

"You might have," I managed.

I was rewarded with another sweet kiss, this one on my calf.

Then Ian leaned forward, bending me in half as he started to move.

I arched, desperate to create space as his length filled me over and over again with every thrust. I could feel him everywhere, his comforting weight and his heat, the thick slide of him hitting something deep within.

When a firm touch landed on my clit, I was done for. The pressure of Ian's circling thumb sent me spiraling over the edge and into orgasm. Heat and sensation spread throughout my body, more than the simple release of tension I was used to. This was intimacy, and it wasn't the act that I'd missed but the knowledge that performing it with the right person could make all the difference.

Distantly, I was aware of Ian's thrusts slowing and deepening and finally going still as he found his release, too.

After a brief detangling of limbs and Ian disposing of the condom, I was wrapped up in two very strong arms as a muscular thigh found its way between mine. Ian's naked body was pressed so thoroughly to me that there wasn't any room for awkwardness.

I could feel his heart beating, and we were quiet long enough that I could tell when it finally slowed and settled.

"I know you didn't invite me—"

"Stay," I said without actively deciding to. But it was true. I wanted Ian here, in my home.

I thought about what it might be like to share a bed with him. He would undoubtedly be a cuddler and would probably steal the covers, too. I wondered if he snored or if he was restless in his sleep. My rusty imagination considered us waking up together. Having coffee before going on our run. Doing normal things that people did every day.

Sharing a life.

Making that choice.

His nose nuzzled my cheek. "I want to stay, but I should get back in case Georgie needs me."

"That's okay," I said. "I understand."

"You could come with me. And stay the night."

He said it with so much blatant hope that it killed me to deny him. "I don't want to confuse George. If he found me there."

"Are you kidding? He'd be thrilled, and I'd be the hero who invited his favorite person over for breakfast."

I smiled, ducking my head into his chest to press a kiss there. "I think I should stay here tonight. But . . ." I hesitated as my heart took off at a sudden gallop. "Next time."

The fingers that had been lazily stroking my shoulder paused. "Next time?"

Cupping his strong jaw, I let my lips linger on his for one breath—then another—before I said very definitively, "Next time."

## JOAN

As strange as it was to consider, my life settled down into something approaching normal in the new year.

January took shape with the return of Sophia and Darren. Mac and Brady went on a two-week vacation to Iceland and came back with treats for everyone and stories to share.

When I considered the upheaval to my life last fall, it was bizarre to think how quickly I'd adapted to a new normal.

But the farm and I were always in sync. I knew the land and what needed to be done in every season. It was comforting that way.

I found my rhythm with Ian, too. We spent as much time together as we could.

George's happiness was what mattered to Ian. The little boy was a priority for both of us. I didn't want anything about his life here in Kirby Falls to change because Ian and I were . . . doing whatever it was we were doing.

It felt inadequate to say we were just sleeping together. And inaccurate to claim we were dating. We'd fallen into a domestic routine of sorts. Running and lunches and dinners when we could manage them. Board games and movie nights with the kid.

George still visited me in the fields in the afternoons. We spent time taking care of Ralph and working with Mercer on whatever the day's tasks happened to be.

Ian found his way into my bed as scheduling permitted. Sometimes I stayed across the highway in the big house with Ian, sleeping in his bed and letting him make me protein pancakes and really terrible coffee in the morning.

My life may have taken a drastic turn somewhere in the last few weeks, but it felt more like a steady merge onto the highway, two paths becoming something new and different, all while going in the same direction.

The film was set to wrap principal photography in mid-March, less than a month from now. The cast and essential production crew would then go back to LA to film some of the interior scenes in a studio. Ian also had obligations. He had a premiere coming up for a film he'd shot last year and a press tour following that.

Real life wasn't encroaching just yet, but it was on the horizon, like a summer storm charging the air with electricity. I was trying not to let it affect my mood. I didn't want George to think I was grouchy for no reason or mad at him in some way. Similarly, I didn't want Ian to read resentment in my tone or silence.

But things were going to change, whether we wanted them to or not.

It was a chilly February morning, and I was checking over the rows of Fuji trees for any sign of disease. It was important to monitor the trees when they were dormant, and it happened to be a big part of my job in the winter.

I'd just climbed back onto the ATV when I felt my phone vibrate with a text.

Candace: You have to watch this.

This ominous message was followed by a link to a popular celebrity news site.

I hesitated with my finger over the screen. I didn't want to be bombarded with Dorian Masters gossip or something I could never unsee.

My phone buzzed again, this time in my hand.

Candace: It's good, I swear.

With a deep breath, I tapped the link.

An interviewer appeared on my phone screen after some catchy intro music. I didn't recognize him, but that didn't mean anything. He was young with dark brown skin and a brilliant smile. He leaned in to the camera like he was sharing a secret, and maybe he was.

Then he introduced an exclusive, on-set interview from rural North Carolina featuring *the* Dorian Masters.

My heart rate sped up as Ian came into view. He wore a blue tee shirt and a backward hat. He looked friendly and casual, not at all inconvenienced by this very obvious promotional event. Ian grinned widely and told the host how happy he was to invite him into his space. For the next five minutes, Ian took the viewer on a little tour of his trailer on set, showing where he ate, took phone calls with his team, and napped on occasion.

I knew where the trailer sat, but I'd never been inside. It was on Judd land, and the knowledge was strange, surreal. I squeezed my phone tighter as I focused on Ian.

The space was for Ian to use between takes. I knew he used it on long filming days. It was where he ate his lunch sometimes when he didn't have enough time to meet up with George and me on the other side of the farm. I'd already imagined him sitting at a small table inside a trailer, texting me with one hand while holding a sandwich from craft services in the other. The chicken salad croissant was his favorite, but sometimes the crew got to them before he did.

It was odd seeing the space in real life, outside of my imagination.

Shaking myself, I concentrated on my screen, bringing it closer to my face. The trailer was clean but pretty basic inside, more for convenience than any real opulence or comfort. The camera panned across a long countertop that ran half the length of the interior. A mirror hung over a portion of the area. There was a black picture frame face down on the surface, like it might have contained a photo of George and Ian hadn't wanted it to be caught on film.

As Ian spoke, I noticed the background beyond him. There was a pile of friendship bracelets—at least half a dozen—beside the mystery photo, and the sight of them made me smile. I knew things between George and Ian had been improving. The time over the Christmas holiday had really helped. There was familiarity and ease between them now that hadn't been there before.

Above the bracelets, my gaze zeroed in on a newspaper clipping tucked into the edge of the mirror. It was a black-and-white image from the *Kirby Falls Chronicle*, and it was of us—Ian and me—in costume, during the Christmas parade. We were waving from the back of Santa's float. I hadn't even realized Ian knew about the shot of him in the paper. The same one I had neatly folded and tucked away in my drawer at home.

The camera transitioned, pivoting to a different angle, and there was Ian's bib from the Turkey Trot, and mine too. I'd gone to toss it in the garbage following the race, and he'd asked if he could keep it. He'd joked, saying it was a valuable memento. I'd laughed and told him he could sell it on OnlyFans with a picture of his feet.

But there it sat, next to the friendship bracelets and beneath the grainy newspaper photo, in Ian's trailer on set. I realized my heart was beating hard enough to feel in my throat, my nose about three inches from my screen, and I hadn't heard a single word of the interview.

In the next moment, Ian exited the trailer, leading the cameraman down the stairs and back out into the North Carolina sunshine. As the image bumped along, I could now clearly see the back of Ian's shirt. It was a Judd's Orchard tee, part of the new merchandise Candace had started selling online before the holidays, baby blue and tight across Ian's muscular back. The front of his hat was now equally visible.

My eyes widened. That was *my* hat. It had the county's public library logo on it, and there was a white paint splatter on the bill from when we'd painted Ralph's shelter. Ian had stolen the cap from me that day, claiming his eyes were too delicate for the sunshine. He'd never given it back.

The camera shifted suddenly once more, and I cursed the swing of focus. Now Ian and the host were walking side by side through the apple fields—through *my* apple fields. The landscape was all around them, the light golden, the mountains blue in the distance. It was my home, and Ian looked so good—so right—in it that I felt my heart ache.

Ian was talking about the area now. How special Western North Carolina was. How he thought he needed a house here.

I couldn't swallow or blink.

The image transitioned to Ian in profile, smiling as he spoke. "We're actually filming at a local farm. The county is known for apple production—eighth in the US, actually. Judd's Family Orchard has been my home for months now, and there's no place like it. Grandpappy's is another local farm filled with amazing people. Both of these orchards are open to the public, and they'd love to have you. If you're ever visiting, tell them Dorian sent you."

He winked at the camera. "But, seriously. I love it here. The community has been welcoming, and the owners at Judd's and Grandpappy's are both wonderful people. I've made friends for life here while filming."

The sound of the interviewer's voice cut in. "That's so great, working with a tight-knit cast."

For a moment so brief I was certain no one else in the world would have caught it, Ian's face looked confused, but he recovered quickly, barely pausing as his charm kicked in. "Definitely," he replied, nodding enthusiastically. "My co-stars are so talented. I'm just the lucky guy who gets to work on one of Della Stewart's projects with them."

But I knew—I knew in my heart—that the young man conducting the interview had misunderstood Ian's meaning. He hadn't been talking about the crew or his co-stars, people he only saw when required. He'd been talking about making friends for life with my family, my friends . . . *me*.

The host's face filled the screen once more, thanking Dorian for the opportunity to see behind the scenes.

I sat in stunned silence as an ad played in preparation for the next segment on a famous actress's dietary restrictions.

After a moment, I tapped back over to my text thread with my sister. While I tried to figure out how to reply, I realized I was freaking the fuck out. I didn't know what Candace expected me to say, but it probably wasn't a collection of emojis meant to convey my brain exploding. I typed *holy shit* before backspacing. It would have been easier to send a photo of whatever my face was doing.

There had been so much of me in everything Ian had said on camera. My life and my presence in his spread out on a countertop in a twenty-foot set trailer. I'd heard my words—things I'd told him during our runs or over lunch—slip out of Ian's mouth when he'd spoken about the beauty of the land and the county's apple production.

I finally managed to type an inarticulate *wow* and hit send.

My sister's reply was immediate: *All of the orchard merch is sold out. The tee shirts, the hats, the mugs. All of it, sold out online. I've been fielding calls all morning asking when we open for the season. Mac texted, and all their stuff is sold out too, even the baking mixes and jam and stuff from the bakery.*

*Wow*, I repeated dumbly, as my mind raced, truly unable to comprehend what Ian had done, very intentionally shining a light on our family business.

> Candace: Wow is right. The Dorian Masters effect, in real time.

> Candace: Also, he's clearly in love with you, but we don't have to talk about that if you aren't ready yet.

I stared at the words on my screen as my stomach flipped over, very much not ready to think about Ian's feelings, or my own.

Later that night, I made dinner while George drew at my kitchen table. Ian had a production meeting that was running late, but he was due any minute.

Normally, we made dinner together. Usually, a recipe of my mother's that Ian was excited to try his hand at. He was great at chopping, but terrible at measuring with his heart. His heart usually put in twice the garlic and three times the salt.

Ian came rushing in just as I was slicing and plating the pork tenderloin.

George set the table while Ian washed up, and we ate together the way we had so many evenings in the last few months.

The kid dominated much of the conversation as he recounted the book he was reading on the Great Molasses Flood. Ian listened in stunned horror, occasionally asking questions between bites of mashed potatoes.

If anyone noticed how quiet I was, they didn't comment on it. I was still mulling over that interview.

When had it been filmed? Why had he said all of those wonderful things about our town and our business? Didn't he know he was supposed to be promoting his film—his own livelihood? What was that collection of stuff on his countertop, and why did it make my chest hurt just looking at it?

What did all of this mean to him? Was he really just going to leave next month and take George with him?

What the hell was I supposed to do when they left?

I stood abruptly from the table, my chair scraping loudly on the wooden floor.

"Everything okay?" Ian said quietly after a tense moment following my sudden departure.

"Yeah," I called over my shoulder, placing my dishes in the sink with forced gentleness.

But a minute later, I heard Ian stand and collect the rest of the dinnerware. "Georgie, why don't you set up Monopoly in the living room? I'll be in there in a minute."

The boy whooped and hurried out of the kitchen.

A hand touched the small of my back as I stood over the sink, forcing myself to breathe.

"What's going on?" Ian asked as he settled beside me, depositing his and George's dishes next to mine in the sink.

The warm hand on my back stayed, rubbing circles over the fabric of my flannel. I leaned into his touch, wondering how much longer it would be mine.

After clearing my throat, I replied, "Just a weird day."

"What made it weird?"

*I watched you in your element and saw how I might fit into your life. You just did more for my parents and this farm in one interview than we could have ever hoped to accomplish with any amount of advertising on our own. I wish I could be as brave as you are, as open. I think I'm in love with you, and I don't know how to lose you. I think letting you and George go might ruin me.*

But I didn't say any of that. I couldn't even look at him. "We had the final planning meeting this morning for the spring festival. Eloise was in rare form."

"That's right. The Spring Fling is next week." Ian sounded amused.

I finally managed to bring my gaze to his, curious despite my internal freak-out. "How do you know about it?"

"I'm working the kissing booth. Eloise emailed me about it, and I said I'd do it."

"Tell me you're joking."

He grinned. "It'll be great for the town."

"Ian."

"What?" He laughed the word. "You know I love this kind of stuff."

I did know it. He loved Kirby Falls. He liked playing pool with the regulars down at Mattie B's and going to trivia night at Trailview Brewing. He met my neighbors and signed autographs and took pictures with anyone who asked. He'd helped the head librarian with a fundraiser by sharing it in his Instagram stories. Her programming was funded for the next thirty years. When the barista over at Cubhouse Coffee had remembered Ian's order and asked if he wanted his usual, he'd been so thrilled, he'd mentioned it no less than a dozen times that day. Ian had been absorbed into our community, and he relished every moment of it.

Part of me worried it was the novelty of our small town that had drawn Ian's attention. My cynical side was sure it would wear off when he couldn't get delivery after 9:00 p.m. or once he realized how close-minded some folks could be. It was all fun and games when there was a pie-eating contest or a children's art show to judge. But when rural communities faced hardship or disaster, people were often left out in the cold.

Then there was the fact that I didn't much like Eloise Carter taking advantage of Ian and his generosity. He didn't owe us shit.

A kissing booth. *Jesus Christ*. There'd be a line a mile long.

"You don't have to participate in every damn thing, Ian. It's not your responsibility to help the town raise money for the new community park, or whatever she's promised you you'll be doing. Kirby Falls doesn't need to get famous at your expense."

Unbothered, Ian's hands reached for me. He clutched my hips and turned me to face him. Blue eyes twinkling, he asked, "Are you jealous, Joanie? It's only cheek kisses. No need to worry. These lips are all yours."

I tried to hold on to my anger, but my grip faltered. A resigned smile tipped up the corners of my mouth. "You are ridiculous."

"Thank you."

"And you're going to regret this whole Spring Fling nonsense."

He shrugged. "Maybe, but I doubt it."

I could hear George counting out the Monopoly money.

"Hey, before we go get our asses kicked by Mr. Moneybags in there," Ian started, "I wanted to ask you something."

"Okay."

He hesitated, licking his lips and releasing a breath through his nose.

I straightened, unsure what he could possibly want to know that would make him so visibly nervous.

"Would you—" He paused, shaking his head as if to clear it before smiling self-consciously and saying, "Fuck it. Would you like to come with me to my premiere next month? It's for the third *Inferno Man* film. I can show you around LA. We'll dress up, walk the red carpet. It'll be fun, I promise. I'll plan the whole thing. You'll just have to show up. And you'll get to meet Eddie J, finally. He won't shut up about meeting you."

I felt my jaw drop partway through Ian's nervous rambling.

"You can say no. If you want. It's okay," he added, when I'd failed to respond.

Forcing my mouth closed, I managed a swallow on the third attempt. "Ian, that's really nice of you, but I'm not sure I'd fit in—"

"I won't drag you to any parties or loud places. We could go to the beach. I know you like the ocean. The weather will be amazing. The premiere would just be a small part of it. One night."

The hopefulness in his expression hollowed my stomach. The earnest way he stood waiting filled it with butterflies.

"Can I think about it?" I heard myself saying, very distantly, like I was standing in a deep hole I'd dug for myself.

"Yes! Of course!" he replied emphatically, nodding. And I knew his reaction was because he'd been expecting a no.

Something about that made me wish I was different. Someone who could say yes easily when presented with such an opportunity. But I wasn't that person. I liked plans and didn't want to inconvenience my co-workers by taking last-minute time off. And as much as Ian might hope differently, I was never going to be a woman who could confidently walk a red carpet. I didn't understand anything about his world.

He'd found a way to fit into mine, but then again, most charming people could chart their own course. I wasn't charismatic or friendly. Dorian Masters's colleagues and friends would take one look at me and think he'd lost his damn mind.

But I didn't know how to explain all of that to a man who so clearly wanted to introduce me to the life he'd left behind. The one he'd be getting back to in a few weeks.

"Guys, I'm ready!" George called from the other room, distracting us both.

Thank fuck, because what was I going to do now?

The Spring Fling was held in downtown Kirby Falls. Just like the Orchard Festival in September and the holiday markets in December, booths lined Main Street, which had been closed to vehicular traffic.

There were artisans and food vendors set up among local farmers and craftspeople. Judd's had a booth near the corner of Main and 4th Street, and Grandpappy's was always right beside us. Eloise called it friendly competition, but since both farms were actual friends, none of us minded.

My parents were manning our table alongside Candace and Mercer as they sold treats, sweets, and Judd's Orchard merchandise. Apples weren't in season yet, so we didn't have as many offerings as the Clark bunch, whose farm was extensive and sold produce nearly year-round. They had a good spread of greens, fresh garlic, herbs, and bakery items for this early-spring event.

Will and Becca were chatting with folks visiting the Grandpappy's tent, but they both paused to give me a wave as I arrived, sliding between our neighboring tables.

"What are you doing here?" my mother asked. "I told you we were happy to work the festival."

"I know," I replied. "I just wanted to check in. See if anyone wanted a break to grab some lunch."

It wasn't that I didn't trust my family to handle things. Well, it used to be that—old habits died hard—but for the most part, I knew that Candace and Mercer had it covered. But when my parents were involved, I often worried that they were overextending themselves. I always looked for ways to ease their burdens, and sometimes that came off as bossy and overbearing.

"Thanks, honey," my dad said, squeezing my shoulder affectionately. "But we're good."

"Actually, you can do something for me," my mother piped up.

Mercer gave a look that clearly conveyed I was in for it now, and it was my own damn fault.

"What is it?" I asked hesitantly.

Mom grabbed a paper bag and started filling it with things—hand pies, coffee cake, a slice of caramel apple pie, and some . . . turkey sandwiches. "You can run this over to Ian in the kissing booth. I made him some sandwiches he likes before I left the house. He's probably too nice to ask Eloise for a lunch break. And I'm sure he's been the busiest booth on the street this morning. You go check on him for me."

My sister didn't even bother hiding her amusement.

I sighed and accepted my fate as well as the bag from my mother.

She beamed. "Thanks, sweetie."

Without a fond farewell for anyone I was related to, I trudged off down the street in the direction of the carnival games and rides set up in the bank parking lot.

This was what I got for trying to micromanage. I loved my mother, but she was not above manipulating her offspring. I knew what she saw when she looked at me and Ian and George. A ready-made little family.

Ian and I had been discreet about our relationship. I hadn't seen any sense in getting anyone's hopes up—least of all, my own. We had George to think about, after all. It had seemed simpler—smarter—to keep what was happening between Ian and me to ourselves. Plus, there was the whole celebrity aspect. If tabloids caught wind of a romance brewing between Dorian Masters and a farmer . . . I didn't even want to consider the havoc that would wreak. It made Ian's invitation to a Hollywood premiere that much more complicated.

While he might have tried to sell it as just one night and no big deal, it would mean being photographed in his world, speculated about. My life—my entire existence—would be picked apart for public consumption. That prospect was daunting.

Obviously, my sister knew what was going on with Ian, but not because I'd spelled anything out. The kiss conversation had happened after the wedding, and she'd been extra observant as a result. I'd simply told her we were taking things as they came and not to get too worked up about it.

The reality was that everyone in my inner circle probably knew that Ian and I were . . . more. I lived in a small town, and people liked to talk—even well-meaning people, like my friends. Ian wasn't shy with his affection, and sometimes I'd catch him watching me in a way that made it hard to deny what we were to one another. Other times, I'd catch myself.

We were a small-town secret . . . so basically everyone already knew.

But that wasn't the point. My mom didn't need to manufacture these reasons for us to see one another. She didn't need to get her hopes up either. I had no idea what was going to happen with Ian, but I was a realist.

My life was here, and his couldn't be.

But that didn't mean I didn't wish things could be different.

About a block from the bank, I noticed a line of people on the sidewalk. As I walked, I grew more suspicious. Dread settled in my gut as I eyed the single-file crowd of predominantly women.

When I turned the corner into the parking lot, I finally caught sight of the kissing booth. All these people were, indeed, queued up to get cozy with Dorian Masters.

As I made my way toward him, I noticed Darren stationed in front of the booth. Relief flooded my veins. Thank goodness Ian had someone looking out for him. If left to his own devices, Ian would have probably agreed to walk a bride down the aisle on her wedding day or give someone a ride to the airport.

As it was, he seemed to be Facetiming someone at the request of the lady at the front of the line. There was a lot of high-pitched squealing coming from the phone's speakers. Undeterred, Ian grinned and spoke into the device.

Darren caught my eye, looking like a man who'd seen some things over the last three hours. From his other side, Becca popped up in a neon-green volunteer shirt. She gave me a wave, and I returned it.

Becca then spoke quietly to the woman holding the phone out for Ian. Then she faced the crowd and clapped three times loudly, like a kinder-garten teacher. "Alright, y'all! Mr. Masters will be taking a quick break. He'll be back with you in fifteen minutes." Groans rose from those assem-bled. Becca made a face at the crowd like she was deeply disappointed in them. "If you don't want to wait, feel free to go ask your husbands to hold your place in line."

That got them to shut up real quick, and I let out a startled laugh. I could only imagine how annoyed the partners of these women were as they waited hours to meet a movie star.

Ian wrapped up the video call and waved to the crowd. Becca slid a red curtain closed on the front of the booth. I guess that afforded Ian a moment of privacy.

"Hi," I said to my friend.

"Hey, Joanie. He's been a champ all morning. But I'm glad you're here so he can take a little break. Here." She passed me a blue ticket.

I stared at the little paper rectangle in my palm. "I'm not taking a turn on the Ferris wheel, Becca."

She grinned. "I know. Maybe you'll need it for something else, though." Before I could argue or blush like a damn schoolgirl, Becca winked and said, "Go on around the side. There are a couple of chairs back there."

"Thanks," I muttered, still a little embarrassed by the suggestion that I'd want a ticket for the kissing booth.

I passed Darren one of the turkey sandwiches from my mother. He nodded his thanks.

I hadn't even rounded the corner before a strong hand reached out and tugged me inside the booth. The back was completely open, but the sides were covered, and now the front was as well by the red curtain.

Ian wrapped his arms around me and hugged me hard. "You are a sight for sore lips."

I grinned into his shoulder. "I think you meant eyes."

"Oh my God, these women, Joan. You wouldn't believe."

Oh, I'd believe it, alright. "I really want to tell you I told you so, but that would be rude."

He leaned back to meet my gaze, eyes wide and expression frazzled. "I feel so used. Like a piece of meat. I think my biceps are sore from all the squeezing. Will you massage them and make it all go away?"

Grinning, I shook my head at his dramatics. "Look at you being objectified. How terrible it must be to be a man in this day and age."

He'd been nodding along pitifully, but then stopped abruptly. "Oh, right. Women put up with shit all the time. You're right. I'm a jerk."

With a gentle touch, I ran my hands up the poor, abused arms in question. Smiling gently, I said, "It's okay. But you did bring this upon yourself."

He had the good grace to appear sheepish. "It's for a good cause. And it's just a few more hours. Actually, the majority of people have been great. Most only want to talk or take a selfie together. Not much kissing going on."

"Good. I brought you some lunch from Mom."

He was already digging into the paper bag with gusto. "Thanks. Will you stay and keep me company?"

"Sure. Where's George?"

Ian unwrapped the other turkey sandwich and passed me half. "He's with Sophia riding the carnival rides. I think they're going to hit the petting zoo after lunch and then head back to the house."

"I'll text Sophia and track them down, check out the petting zoo with the kid."

He smiled warmly at me. "I'm sure he'd love that."

We spent the next ten minutes eating and laughing while Ian told me about all the crying women and the crazy requests he'd received that morning. Three different people had come up to show him their Inferno Man tattoos. One was on someone's butt, so that had been unexpected, and likely the reason Darren had looked so shell-shocked when I'd arrived.

Ian had Facetimed various sisters and cousins and friends who lived out of state. He'd signed numerous autographs and agreed to record a video for someone's mother who was going through cancer treatment.

I listened to him talk about his fans and the women who wanted just a small piece of his attention, and couldn't imagine being so good-humored about it all. It was difficult to fathom sharing so much of my own life with the public, making myself available for their criticism and their love in equal measure.

But Ian seemed impervious. Maybe he was used to it by now. Either way, it felt like another big obstacle for whatever was happening between us.

Would it be this way in LA if I went? Would folks stop him on the street or interrupt his meals just to have a part of him—an autograph they could frame and hang on a wall, a selfie they could share on social media? How much was Ian's peace worth to all these people?

Finally, Ian stood and brushed off the apple pie crumbs from his dark blue jeans. "Well, I'd better get back out there. Send me pictures from the petting zoo, okay?"

"I will," I promised, saddened by the fact that Ian couldn't join us. Aside from his obligations in the booth, he'd never put his nephew at risk so publicly.

On a whim, I pulled out the ticket Becca had pressed into my hand. "I'm not usually one to skip line . . ."

Ian saw the ticket and grinned before plucking it from my grasp and sticking it in his pocket. If I visited Ian's trailer on set, would I see that little blue ticket added to his collection of mementos?

Before I had too much time to wonder, he wrapped his arms around my waist and drew me close.

"Joan Judd, I knew you were jealous," he whispered, absolutely delighted.

My hands slid up his torso, feeling the muscles beneath. I smiled against his lips, admitting, "Maybe I am."

The kiss started slow and sweet. It was all comfort and familiarity. The warm evergreen scent that slowed my racing mind. The strength in the arms holding me so securely. And I knew these lips—wide and soft and perfectly in sync with my own.

Ian's tongue licked at the seam of my mouth, and I obliged on a sigh. In this perfect little bubble, on a warm spring day, I felt safe enough to let my feelings go. To allow my hands to wander over the tops of defined shoulders, to push up onto my tiptoes to be closer, to press my body against the length of his.

It was a luxury, this privacy. It was also an illusion. Because if I listened closely, I could hear conversation from Dorian's fans in line just beyond the curtain.

In that moment, all I wanted was to be alone with Ian in the fields, lying on a blanket in the sun.

Resigned for all the things that couldn't be, I drew back and placed my feet firmly on the ground.

Ian's mouth followed mine, still eager, still caught up, his arms holding tight.

He pressed a final kiss to my jaw and groaned, "Fine. But I'll see you tonight?"

My hand stroked down his arm to twine our fingers together. I gave one final squeeze. "You'll see me tonight."

Then I told myself to let him go before I made a fool of myself.

JOAN

It wasn't until I'd finished bowling the third frame that I realized something was going on.

I'd caught Candace and Mac and Bonnie with their heads together for the fourth time, and they'd looked more excited than guilty.

The Lucky Strike Lanes bowling alley wasn't the best place for a conversation. It was loud; the sounds of pins crashing, music playing, and people talking created constant background noise. But whatever was going on clearly had my friends' attention, and I had a bad feeling it had to do with me.

"What is it?" I asked as I took the open seat beside my sister. "Just tell me."

The women exchanged tight-lipped looks.

It was Bonnie who eventually spoke up. "Well, it appears that someone in the Kirby Falls Facebook group posted pictures of you and Ian from the Spring Fling."

I winced, not expecting that.

Ian had practically announced his location here in Kirby Falls when that trailer tour interview had aired two weeks ago. His well-meaning effort to boost the local economy—and the orchards—made the location for filming easily searchable.

By some miracle, his fans and the paparazzi hadn't been knocking down any doors, mostly because the website had reported inaccurately—at Ian's manager's request—that filming had finished. Now, photos of Dorian Masters with some mystery woman in rural North Carolina might change all that.

"I see."

Bright-eyed, Mac straightened and snatched her phone off the table. "Do you want to see?"

But I held up a hand. I'd made the mistake of googling Dorian Masters early on. I'd witnessed him with models and actresses, women so beautiful they didn't look real. Whatever images a local or an amateur photographer had captured at the Spring Fling were sure to be nothing so glamorous or flattering.

"But, they're good," Mac pouted. "They got taken down by admin Becca pretty damn quick, but I'd already downloaded them."

"Becca deleted the post?" I asked.

"Yeah," Candace confirmed. "She didn't want them to circulate or make it to some entertainment site. So far, Ian has only had to deal with residents and tourists in Kirby Falls. We don't need him hounded by paparazzi or obsessed fans."

That was kind of Becca. I glanced between the gleeful faces of my sister and my friends. At least *someone* was looking out for me.

"Really, Joan," Bonnie said, "you should see them. They're . . . y'all look good together. Happy."

I was already shaking my head, but her last word stopped me.

My brows furrowed, and Bonnie smiled sweetly, nodding.

As if detecting my surrender, Mac squealed and started tapping away on her phone. She placed the device in the center of the table, and all four of us leaned in.

She swiped slowly through a collection of slightly crooked and off-center images of Ian and me in the back of the kissing booth.

The first few showed us eating and talking, knees slotted between one another as we sat on two folding chairs in the midday sun. In one shot, Ian had just taken a huge bite of caramel apple pie, and I'd been mid-laugh, shoving a napkin his direction.

The following photos caught us kissing, a stop-motion sequence of my touch running from Ian's chest to his shoulders, his arms locked around my lower back, fingers fisted in the back of my shirt.

"Damn, girl." Mac whistled.

I touched the back of her hand to stop her from scrolling for a moment.

Even with the terrible lighting and the shitty camera-phone lens, Ian and I looked like something beautiful, something timeless. The way Ian's big body curved over mine. How we were so obviously wrapped up in one another. We looked like the stars in an old movie.

Apprehension gave way to a flicker of panic. These photos could have very real consequences. The invasion of privacy, the world's reaction, the impact on Ian's career and my daily life. A story about Hollywood's leading man and a small-town farmer could explode in all our faces.

But despite the fear chilling my bloodstream, there was a warmth battling it. These images were undeniable. There was no hiding what we meant to one another, how deep that well of emotion ran.

I forced myself to take a breath, to push away the dread of discovery. Taking in the photo once more, I allowed the warmth to flood my veins and buoy my strength.

I wanted to frame it and stare at it. I wanted to send it to Ian and tell him to kiss me like that every day for the rest of our lives. I wanted to delete it from this phone and my memory forever.

There was nothing rational about my reaction, and I didn't know how to—

Mac swiped to the next photo.

Candace sighed suddenly, "Oh, this one is my favorite."

At the image suddenly on the screen, I leaned in without thought, without permission. I heard myself make a sound, part gasp, part wounded animal. Luckily, it was too loud in the bowling alley for my friends to hear me. Still, I fought the urge to cover my mouth with my hand.

The photographer—interloper, whatever you wanted to call them—had captured the moment when I'd just exited the booth.

I was looking down, my face painfully soft, and I was pressing two fingertips to my lips, like I could hold on to Ian's kiss if I just tried hard enough.

I had no memory of doing that. I just remembered feeling dazed, overwhelmed, grateful for the stolen moments behind the curtain.

But it was the rest of the image that made pressure build in my chest, behind my eyes. Ian was staring after me. He'd stuffed his hands in the pockets of his jeans, and his eyes were on my back. People talked about unguarded moments. His face was a case study in vulnerability and openness, longing so deep and endless, it was all I'd see when I thought of him.

The first night we were together, when we'd watched *The Tycoon and the Aristocrat*, he'd confessed in a whispered rush, *I know I'm going to make a fool of myself. I'm going to be so fucking stupid over you. And I can't help it. Couldn't stop it even if I wanted to.*

This image was the photographic proof.

Candace's hand gently squeezed my elbow. "He looks at you like . . ."

"Like you're the greatest thing he's ever seen," Mac said, when my sister hesitated.

"Like you're his whole world," Bonnie added.

"Like he'd do anything to keep you," Candace finally finished.

I did cover my mouth with my hand, then. And proceeded to drag it down my chin in mute despair. What the fuck were we going to do?

Part of me feared that this photograph, this split second in time, might haunt me for the rest of my life.

"Oh, honey," Mac said suddenly.

Bonnie gazed at me with sympathy.

Candace rubbed my back. "It's going to be okay."

Our attention shifted to the phone and Ian's love-drunk face until the screen put me out of my misery and went dark.

I wanted to turn it back on. I wanted to send it to myself so I could remember this moment—the damning recognition, the unrelenting fear—forever. I wanted to press my fingertips to my closed eyelids until I could only see stars.

We sat there in weighted silence as pins crashed and The Chicks played over the ancient bowling alley speakers.

Finally, Mac stood up and put her hands on her hips. "Welp, ladies. I say we call this one and go straight to the bar."

Bonnie nodded and stood. "Let's do it."

Candace looked to me. "Whatever you want, Joanie."

I glanced between my friends, my sister—these women who supported me, put up with me, who were so determined to give me exactly what I needed in my time of crisis. Even with the impending sense of doom and the agonizing realization that I'd gone and fallen in love with a man and a little boy who I'd never be able to keep, I couldn't help but smile at the determination on the faces staring back at me.

"Yeah, okay. Let's go."

Two hours later, I was in Candace's passenger seat as she drove me home from Magnolia Bar. I wasn't drunk, but I was tipsy, and my chest was warm from tequila.

We'd gone to Magnolia because I hadn't wanted to see any locals over at Mattie B's. Despite the photos being removed from the town's Facebook group, I knew people had seen them and would undoubtedly ask. We went to the leafer bar in an effort to avoid speculation and nosy neighbors.

Plus, Bonnie's boyfriend, Jack, was working behind the bar tonight.

Candace had offered to be the designated driver as soon as we'd walked in.

Bonnie didn't need a ride because Jack lived in an apartment above the bar, and the two were living there while Bonnie's house was being renovated.

Mac also did not need Candace to drive her because she and Brady lived just a few blocks away. My brother had walked over at last call to escort a very drunk Mac home.

Brady hadn't said anything or asked why our bowling team had decided to get hammered on a random Wednesday night, but he did give me a big hug and a kiss on the top of my head. And that felt like the nicest thing he could have done.

"You feeling okay?" Candace asked from the driver's seat.

I eyed my sister and ignored her question. "Are you pregnant?"

Her gaze shot to mine briefly before she focused back on the road. "What?"

I snorted. "We hadn't even gotten all the way through the front door of Magnolia before you shouted to the whole bar that you'd be DD."

Candace's face was briefly bathed in cool, pale light as a car passed by going the opposite direction. Her eyes were frantic, and she was gnawing on her bottom lip.

Laughing, I reached over and hugged her as safely as I could while she was driving. "I'm so fucking happy for you."

"Really?" she asked, and she sounded like a little girl again. The one who'd followed me into the fields every Sunday after church and begged me to put on a talent show for our parents.

"Of course, I'm happy for you," I practically yelled. Maybe I *was* a little drunk. "You and Mercer are going to be amazing parents, Candace. I can't wait to be their aunt. They'll have Brady for all the fun uncle stuff. But they'll have me too."

At that, my sister burst into loud, messy tears.

When she finally pulled over and shifted into park, she explained, "I cry at everything. I'm sorry. And I was going to tell you. It's just very early—"

"Hey, it's okay," I interrupted, pulling her into another hug, this one better because the car wasn't moving.

Still teary-eyed and emotional, my sister said, "Mark is so, so happy. He was dying to tell you. But I made him promise to let me, since, you know, you're *my* sister."

I smiled.

I was sure Mercer was thrilled. He and Candace had only been married a few months, but he loved my sister, and he had family man stamped all over him.

And considering Mercer's past, I was nothing but relieved that my friend was getting the life he deserved.

There had been a time when I'd worried that Mercer might never get over what he'd been through. Back in college, his best friend, Hannah, had gotten pregnant unexpectedly. After the baby's father had broken things off and told her he wanted no part of the baby's life, she'd shown up on Mercer's dorm-room doorstep and begged him to get married. Her reverend father would have disowned her, and Mercer knew that.

So he'd married her. They'd moved in together right away, and let everyone assume the baby was his. Mercer had dropped out of school so Hannah could finish her degree while he stayed home with a newborn.

All of that sacrifice, for Hannah to file for a divorce a year into their marriage because she'd been dating behind Mercer's back and had fallen in love with someone else. She'd told Mercer he had no rights and had taken the baby and left, moving out of state.

It had been a sad, awful chapter in Mercer's life, but that was a whole other story.

"How are you feeling? Have you been sick?" I asked my sister.

Candace told me she'd been fine so far, but there was a tremble in her voice. Her fingers tightened reflexively on the steering wheel as she gazed out the windshield.

I swallowed and asked very gently, "Are you scared?"

"So scared," she admitted in a rush. "Like, what if I don't know what I'm doing? What if I don't hold the baby right? Or what if I'm not maternal? What if I can't breastfeed or I have postpartum depression? What if the baby has sleep regression or-or-or food allergies or I end up being a terrible mother?"

"Candace, breathe," I instructed, and then reached for my sister's hand.

Her wide hazel eyes met mine, and I smiled a watery smile.

"You know," I told her, "shitty moms probably never sit around and worry about any of those things." Still smiling, I went on, "You're going to do great because you're willing to learn. You learned how to work on the farm. You learned how to be in a relationship. And now you'll learn how to be a good mother. I believe in you, Candace. And you and Mercer will figure out this baby thing together. They'll be the first Judd grandbaby. We'll all be learning together, but I promise, we'll be right there with you."

My sister nodded, some of the panic leaving her face. "Okay."

"Okay."

"Raising a kid will be a big change for all of us, but it's going to be a good one."

Candace nodded some more. I thought that might be all she was capable of currently. Sure didn't seem like she was in any shape to drive a car yet.

All of a sudden, she brightened. "You know, you've kind of been raising a kid for the last few months. I know Georgie's not a baby, but that's definitely some experience you're bringing to the table."

Whatever feelings I'd buried earlier tonight with all that tequila bubbled to the surface abruptly. Sadness battled with the happiness I'd been feeling only moments ago.

"I don't think that's the same, Candace."

"But it is. You love Georgie. He's with you nearly every day. You know his favorite foods and which stories he likes before bed. You take care of him."

"That's different," I insisted again.

"Maybe. But you've become a big part of his life."

My sister looked at me then, worry returning. I could practically hear the unspoken question. *What happens next week when the movie wraps?*

But Candace knew me well enough not to ask.

"Let's get you home," she said.

As we made our way down the dark highway, I thought about Mercer and Candace having a baby. Not all change was bad.

For so long, I'd seen any upset to my carefully constructed life as an inconvenience—something to be endured or dealt with. At thirty-six, I was already stuck in my ways. But our lives weren't static or stationary. They evolved. Families grew and matured.

That thing I'd been trying to forget elbowed its way to the forefront. Those photos of Ian and me. How we'd looked at each other. How the love was written all over our faces.

We'd been playing house for months, deviating from my perfectly crafted solitary existence. It had been effortless, and the happiest I'd ever been . . . because of Ian and George.

Not all change was bad, I thought again.

Maybe I *could* go with Ian to Los Angeles for the premiere. We'd been happy in Kirby Falls, but it wouldn't hurt to give a little, to see his life, too. To let him show me. Maybe we could figure this out if he wanted to. Be adults about it.

Yes, I was a farmer full-time, but my work was seasonal. Perhaps we could split our time, make it work.

Good things were worth hanging on to with both hands. And this—me and Ian and George—we were the best thing.

As Candace drove slowly down my bumpy drive, I pulled out my phone.

Before I lost my nerve, I typed out a short text and hit send.

> Me: If the offer still stands, yes, I'll come to LA
> for the premiere.

## IAN

The flight to Los Angeles was long and a little turbulent leaving Charlotte.

I shouldn't have enjoyed it so much, but Joan was a terrible flyer. She was nervous and jumpy, all clenched-jaw tension and white-knuckled stress.

On the ground, the woman was a fortress, bothered by very little, no problem she couldn't solve. But when the plane dipped unexpectedly due to some bumpy air, she grabbed my hand like a lifeline and squeezed the hell out of it. It probably had something to do with her passive position in the cabin. If she'd been able to fly the plane, it was likely she would have been just fine.

But I liked being the one she'd reached for. It was selfish, but there it was.

Mostly, I felt grateful that Joan had agreed to come at all. I'd been shocked to get her text last week saying she'd attend the premiere. I wouldn't waste the opportunity or the time we'd been given. Part of me worried how things might change between us outside the small-town bubble we'd been existing in. But we wouldn't know unless we tried.

Darren was accompanying us on the commercial flight. Georgie was staying in Kirby Falls with Sophia. But I imagined my nephew would be spending plenty of time with Nick and Amy Judd, Candace and Mercer, too.

Georgie had already texted me twenty-plus pictures of him and Ralph that morning before we'd even boarded the flight. Rationally, I knew that he would be fine, but I still felt uneasy that I'd be so far away.

We'd finished filming in Kirby Falls yesterday. The plan was for Georgie to stay with Sophia in North Carolina until I wrapped up my obligations for the Inferno Man franchise and could return.

First, I had a few weeks of shooting in the studio and postproduction with Della in LA. The schedule would be grueling. Then I'd have the media tour following that in early April, traveling all over to promote my final film in the *Inferno Man* series. The LA premiere this weekend was just the beginning. I wasn't dragging Georgie to New York and London just so Sophia could try to find ways to keep the kid entertained on her own while I was stuck in hotel rooms all day for interviews and meetings with the press. That wasn't fair to either of them.

Georgie had a routine in Kirby Falls. He was happy there. That was what I kept reminding myself.

I'd be back in six weeks. Then, I could figure things out regarding Georgie, Joan, and the future.

Yes, I was probably being cowardly in waiting, but fear was a great motivator. Plus, something told me that this weekend would be an important part of moving forward together.

When we arrived at my beach house on the northern edge of Malibu, we were both worn out. Multiple flights and a long layover in Dallas had us looking forward to collapsing shortly after walking in the door.

I should have known my assistant wouldn't let an opportunity like this slip through his fingers.

The kitchen was set up for a romantic dinner for two, candles and everything.

Joan looked at me in surprise.

I released our luggage and held up my hands in surrender. "Not it. Probably Eddie J's idea."

She shrugged, looking amused. "I could eat."

Joan slid off her shoes and abandoned her things in the foyer before walking through the open floor plan toward the back of the house.

My home was the first big purchase I'd ever made. The four-thousand-square-foot beach house sat on the cliffside, overlooking the Pacific Ocean. It had been decorated and furnished by a professional, and as a result, it looked like a showroom. Clean lines, monochromatic walls, and pale everything.

I thought of Joan's cabin. How warm and comfortable it was—inviting. Surrounded by a beautiful scenery.

Well, at least our homes had that last one in common.

Joan made her way around the large marble island in the kitchen, bypassing the elegantly laid table, and down two stairs into the living room. She approached the rear wall of windows slowly, as if she needed to be cautious.

The sun was setting on the water, the waves reflecting the deep orange of the sky. Joan stood silhouetted by the landscape. I considered joining her, but I let myself stand there, enjoying the moment, and her in it.

She was here. She'd said yes.

It felt like the first step in something important, something big.

We ate a delicious meal before Facetiming Georgie to tell him good night. Surprising me, Joan pulled out her own copy of the book he'd been reading before bedtime and read the next chapter over the phone. Listening to her narrate the different voices while my nephew giggled through the speaker made my throat go tight and my imagination work overtime.

I told Georgie I loved him and then excused myself while Joan finished up the chapter. I cleaned up our dinner and loaded the dishwasher—embarrassingly, for the first time in this house—so I could gain some space, if not a little perspective.

After I started the wash cycle, I moved our luggage to my bedroom. Then I found Joan once again by the back windows, gazing out, fingertips pressed to the glass. The ocean was dark, but the moon lit the waves, high-lighting each crest and peak.

"It's not the mountains," I told her.

She didn't turn. "But it sure is something."

I smiled at the approval, the undisguised awe I heard in her voice. "Our bags are down the hall. You ready for bed?"

Despite the early hour, I knew she was just as exhausted as I was from a long day of travel.

"I am," she replied, and let me slip my fingers through hers and lead her toward my bedroom.

We showered away the day, the warm water loosening tense muscles. I lathered Joan's short hair, enjoying the sounds she made as my nails scraped gently along her scalp and soap trailed down her lean body.

As the water beat against my back, my lips found her neck, her shoulders. I bit down on her earlobe, and she pressed into me, the subtle curve of her ass nestled against my rapidly hardening cock.

I couldn't get over seeing her in my space. Despite how much I'd hoped, there had been a big part of me that had never truly believed she'd accept my invitation. But now . . . she was here, and I wanted to see her in every part of this house. I wanted to memorize how she moved in my shower, how her clothes looked hung next to mine. I wanted to watch her drink coffee in the morning out on the balcony while the sun rose.

I wanted her to ruin this house for me when she left.

We fell into bed, our skin warm and still damp from the shower. Joan settled herself on my lap, her strong thighs astride my hips.

I'd never be able to lie in this bed again without closing my eyes and seeing Joan smirking down at me, tucking a strand of wet hair behind one ear. Perched on top, she looked like a goddess. Long, gorgeous lines bathed in moonlight.

Her hands smoothed up my abdomen, over my chest to the tops of my shoulders, and back again, completing a circuit. Her midnight-dark eyes followed her movements intently.

"You are so fucking beautiful," she breathed, gaze still focused on her ministrations.

I lifted my arms, crossed them behind my head. My biceps popped, and I grinned, giving her a little show. "Just muscles," I commented, but I liked her words, her attention, her approval.

"No," she argued. "It's time and dedication. It's focus. Commitment and hard work. But it's not just your body, Ian. It's your heart, your goodness, every part of you. That's what's beautiful."

From someone like Joan—who valued determination and devotion—that was quite the compliment.

I unfolded my arms and brought my hands to her thighs, ghosting up and down, scared to press too hard, to squeeze too tight. All I wanted to do was hold on, but I worried it would be too much.

Her hands found purchase on my chest, and she circled her hips. She ground down on my erection, making my hands shake from the effort to keep myself in check. She was slick, and the tip of my dick was dangerously close to sliding home.

As if she knew exactly what she was doing to me, Joan smiled and leaned down to capture my lips. The kiss was hot and intent, zero to sixty in an instant, her tongue slipping easily into my mouth. Her hips worked up and down my length in these little pulses of torture, steady and demanding.

I groaned into the kiss, my hands reaching around to cup her ass. I squeezed, urging her body against mine. She could come like this, I knew. She had before. No matter how desperately I wanted to be inside her, I didn't want to rush. I needed her to feel good, here in my bed.

But Joan broke our kiss and pushed herself up, gasping and impatient. She produced a condom from somewhere and rolled it on before I could protest, my hands fisting the sheets as she squeezed my length, pumping once, twice, a third time before guiding my cock to her entrance.

She sank down slowly, her eyes closing on a sigh.

I couldn't move. I couldn't breathe. I wanted this moment to last forever.

But Joan started to shift, a slow and steady rise and fall that made me ache to move—to thrust from underneath, to chase the pleasure gathering at the base of my spine. It was a slow simmer, this fire between us, and I had to fight the urge to pour fuel on it, to set us both ablaze.

I let her lead. Let her set the pace.

So much of our relationship had been me stoking the flames, demanding more. But in this, I could follow, give up control, and trust that Joan knew exactly what she wanted and that it included me.

Shifting one hand, I brought my thumb around to her clit. I matched her rhythm, applying pressure and circling as she moved. When her speed increased, so did mine.

In the end, it became a race. Joan's focused gaze, her panting breaths, and my dedicated touch, determined to keep pace and give her whatever she needed.

She came with a broken cry, her hips jerking, burying me deep as her pussy clenched over and over.

When I thought she might slump forward, rest a minute on my chest, she took me by surprise and urged us to roll sideways on my giant bed.

Joan's back hit the mattress, and I settled between her spread thighs, still inside her. She grabbed the globes of my ass and pulled me in tight, grinding against me, and making us both moan.

When I still hesitated, Joan's eyes searched my face.

"You don't need to be gentle with me," she said softly. "I thought you knew that."

Propped on my elbows, I used one hand to brush the damp hair away from her face. The woman who didn't need me to be gentle leaned into my touch and closed her eyes.

I smiled, pressing a kiss to her cheek, her chin, the corner of her mouth. Maybe Joan truly didn't believe she needed softness. She'd spent her life taking care of other people, being the one who sacrificed, who made concessions, who worked hard so her loved ones didn't have to.

But maybe, with me, she could let her guard down, accept the way I wanted to wrap her up in my heart and protect her from the world. Would she let me love her like that? Like a partner, a friend, someone with the best of intentions?

My lips moved down to her jaw, lingering beneath her ear when she drew in a shaky breath.

"Maybe." I breathed the words into her sensitive skin. "I just want to give you what you need."

She didn't say anything, but I felt her swallow against my mouth.

So I started to move, a steady, thorough roll of my hips that pushed her body into the plush mattress and nudged her clit over and over.

The hands on my ass loosened their impatient hold and smoothed up my back to hook around the tops of my shoulders.

She felt so good like this, close enough to sense her heartbeat, to smell my soap on her skin.

I continued moving, thrusting in shallow strokes until Joan became impatient, worked up all over again. I could detect the urgency in her touch, the quickness of her breaths, the way she met every roll of my hips with the push and pull of her own.

When her heels dug into the backs of my thighs, I grinned and placed a hot kiss on her lips. Then I lifted onto my hands and started to move.

Everything sped up. There was that edge of desperation again—to make this count, make it good for her, make it mean something.

But we'd been together for months, more than just in each other's beds. She'd been living in my heart for even longer. Just because she was here, in California, didn't change what had come before.

Suddenly, Joan groaned beneath me, her eyes going wide and glassy as she stretched her arms up and over her head, arching into the pleasure as she pulsed around me.

I wanted to keep going. I wanted this to never be over.

But with Joan's hands twisted in my pillow and her body straining and beautiful, I let myself go, finding release on a bittersweet rush a moment later.

Leaning down, I kissed Joan, who cupped my cheeks and bit my lip.

Grinning, I pulled away and stood on shaky legs to get rid of the condom.

In the bathroom, the backlit mirror created an ambient glow. My eyes caught on Joan's toothbrush on the counter.

Admittedly, this cliffside house overlooking the ocean had never felt like much of a home. It was just a place to stay in between filming, something to spend my money on. But Joan in my bed, her shoes by the front door, her toothbrush in the holder right next to mine . . . it felt more like a home than it ever had before.

I knew—*I knew*—she would never leave Kirby Falls. The farm. The mountains. The land. Her family. It was all essential—a vital part of her. But I thought it could be home for me, too.

Deep down, I worried that anywhere Joan was would be my home.

I tried to push all those thoughts away. Made sure my face was doing something normal before I stepped back into the bedroom. I didn't want to rush her or scare her. She was already in the lion's den, about to experience the spectacle that was my life.

What the hell had I been thinking, begging her to come to the premiere? I supposed, some part of me wanted her to understand, to get to know all the different pieces of me.

I'd wanted to be honest and upfront. Those things were important to Joan. And she'd only seen the Ian who existed in Kirby Falls. Not the hoops I was expected to jump through, the Ian who had trouble sleeping. Or Dorian and all the chaos that came with being him.

She deserved to know what she was getting herself into if we were really going to do this. To see if she'd ever want to take all of that on, in any capacity. To decide if I was worth it, after all.

I'd hoped this trip would lead to a discussion—a compromise. In between filming and spending time with Joan and Georgie, I'd been quietly researching. I'd thought about making Kirby Falls my home base instead of this picture-perfect beach house that looked like a showroom.

I could still make movies, but eventually I could be more involved in producing and directing, maybe even writing—my often-ignored long-term goals that suddenly seemed very real.

I wanted a cabin in the woods, a chicken coop, a place for me and Georgie with the people who cared about us. And I wanted to be able to talk to Joan about all this.

When I finished cleaning up, I paused in the doorway. Joan was naked, sitting on the edge of the bed, looking out the windows that faced the ocean.

As I watched her graceful, motionless form, it was all too easy to imagine a future. I thought about all those long-term goals and how they didn't look the same anymore. A hazy future, more defined now because there was someone next to me in it.

I must have made a sound because Joan glanced over her shoulder and smiled.

I knew how she felt about change. How immovable, how unwavering she could be. And I hoped I wasn't alone in planning for the future.

---

**Joan**

The following morning, we were both up before the sun, still running on East Coast time.

I found some coffee grounds in Ian's fancy refrigerator, the doors of which looked just like the teak cabinets and blended right in. We sat together on the balcony and sipped our coffee in the dark. I wore one of Ian's sweatshirts as the ocean breeze whipped my short hair around my head, but it was peaceful out here with the constant sound of the water and Ian smiling over at me.

I couldn't get over the ocean and the sky. Everything was so vast and wide. Yesterday, I'd ignored my window during landing, so uncomfortable with the flight and altitude changes that I hadn't even seen the beach or the water until Ian had opened his front door, and then bam. There it was. Spread out as far as the eye could see.

My home was just as big and beautiful, but the mountains made me feel surrounded, tucked in, bound to the land in a completely different way.

Here, I felt untethered, like I could fly.

As the sky gradually lightened, we walked along the beach and talked, deciding a run could wait until tomorrow when we'd caught up on sleep.

Eddie J was waiting for us inside the beach house when we returned.

Ian didn't seem startled, so this must have been part of having a personal assistant. Ian greeted Eddie J warmly, but then his assistant pushed him aside and came straight over to me.

Eddie J was probably two inches shorter than I was. He had dark hair, artfully styled, and a fashion sense that my great-nana would have called loud.

Ian had told me that Eddie J was born in LA, but his parents were Filipino immigrants. They loved their gay son, who had been obsessed with the movie industry from a very young age. He was now in his early thirties and worked for one of the biggest stars on the planet.

Eddie J had been a PA—production assistant—on one of Ian's earliest films. When Ian had needed more help managing his day-to-day life, he'd remembered the exuberant, funny, kindhearted gossip king who'd always made a point to see if Ian needed anything on set. Eddie J had been working for Ian ever since.

I could not imagine that he and I had one single thing in common. But when he grinned at me and pulled me into a bone-crushing hug, I immediately felt like he was on my team. That as long as I had either Ian or Eddie J by my side this weekend, everything would be okay.

"Oh my God. I have been *dying* to meet you," he said, finally releasing me.

He wore black horn-rimmed glasses that looked more trendy than functional, but they suited his face and his slender, dark eyes.

"It's nice to finally meet you, too," I told him, meaning it. It was good to know Ian had people like Darren and Sophia and Eddie J in his life. People he could trust.

"Sophia brags all the time, that brat." His tone was teasing and affectionate, and it made me laugh to think that she'd been holding something as insignificant as seeing me daily over this man's head.

"Well, I'm all yours this weekend," I said. "But Sophia is probably getting off way easier with George. I might be a handful to babysit. I don't know how any of this works."

Ian opened his mouth—undoubtedly to reassure me, as he'd been doing nonstop since I'd agreed to come. But Eddie J winked and spoke first. "Stick with me, kid. We'll have you red-carpet ready in no time."

I didn't know about that, but I smiled gratefully anyway.

Eddie J took the next half hour to go over Ian's schedule for the weekend. I wasn't sure if I was needed for this part, so I poured another cup of coffee and tried to sneak out of the room. But Ian snagged my hand and pulled me onto his lap as Eddie J ran through logistics and people Ian would be meeting with.

It all sounded overwhelming to me. So much to do and so many folks needing Ian's attention and input. Did he ever manage to sleep?

If George had come to California with us, would he have even been able to see Ian?

Truthfully, I was grateful that George had stayed behind with Sophia. Not that I wouldn't have loved having him with us, but I had a feeling that the kid would not have been included in many of these plans.

Back in Kirby Falls, he could spend time with my family and visit Ralph and the fields the way he liked. George could have a normal life in my hometown. He was still the nephew of a famous actor, but he didn't have to actively worry about being photographed by paparazzi or have every second of his life micromanaged . . . the way Ian's was right now.

Face alert and attentive, Ian nodded along to whatever Eddie J was saying, occasionally adding things into his notes app on his phone with one hand while the other was steady on my thigh.

"And first up, you have a quick meet-and-greet brunch this morning with some fans," the assistant noted. "The studio invited influencers in ahead of the tour. It should only take about an hour. Joan, you can come to that and hang with me."

I nodded. "Okay."

Eddie J appeared pleased, and so did Ian. It felt like I'd given the right answer to a pop quiz. However, uneasiness lingered, a tightness in my midsection that said I was nervous, unsteady, and painfully out of my element.

Maybe it was just the jet lag. Once I adjusted, everything would look brighter.

Three hours later, what really surprised me most was the amount of screaming.

I'd thought these sorts of reactions were an exaggeration, born from the Elvis Presley and Beatles era. Maybe New Kids on the Block or Harry Styles. But no, these influencers were squealing with delight, in pitch and volume, with frightening regularity.

"It's always like this," Eddie J said, as if reading my mind.

We were at a trendy restaurant in Westlake. The studio, or production company or whoever, had reserved one of the private dining rooms, and there was a spread of brunch foods and a mimosa bar for those in attendance.

Darren was posted very close to Ian while Eddie J and I watched from the wings.

Despite the chaos and clamor of twenty-five big-name social media personalities who all wanted their allotted time with the celebrity, Ian was amazing at making everyone feel seen. He carried on genuine conversations. He put people at ease. Like right now, with the young man who was so overwhelmed he was near tears.

I watched as Ian asked a passing server for a glass of water and presented it to the person who was supposed to be interviewing him, who was here specifically to make content to promote Ian's new film. The young man accepted the water gratefully and gradually composed himself.

"He's always like that, too," Eddie J added. "Probably the nicest celebrity any of these people will ever meet. Except for maybe Pedro Pascal. Nobody tops Daddy Pedro. At least *I* haven't yet."

I choked on the mimosa I'd been sipping, and Eddie J looked very pleased with himself as he patted my back and passed me a napkin.

For the next forty minutes, I watched Ian chat and take photos. He practically glowed from all the attention, so warm and animated with each person who came up to him. He told stories from his time on set, behind-the-scenes information that the influencers gobbled up in delight.

Despite being the only star there, Ian made every single attendee feel like the center of attention at one point or another. He remembered their names and really listened when they spoke. He gave little bits of himself to everyone, his energy and enthusiasm never once wavering.

I was worn out just from watching him.

The event wrapped up, and we were escorted to a back entrance with Darren in the lead. Restaurant goers lingered in the hallway to snag quick selfies and autographs. Ian was patient and kind with all of them.

By the time we made it onto the sidewalk where the driver waited, there was a crowd of thirty people or more. Men with cameras stood atop a low wall that surrounded the restaurant, poised and ready.

The sudden appearance of so many fans and the fact that we were greatly outnumbered had a thrum of fear mingling with my discomfort. There was an inexplicable urge to reach for Ian's hand, to put myself between him and all these people who wanted something from him.

Eddie J placed a guiding hand lightly beneath my elbow. "Stay with me. Darren and Ian have this whole thing down to a science. He'll say hello, let the paps snap a few photos, and then he'll be in the vehicle with us. If you draw attention to yourself, he'll be distracted and worried about you. Just follow me, okay?"

My palms were sweaty, and I swiped them awkwardly down my jeans as I nodded. My anxious gaze followed Ian, but my feet stayed the course, and soon I was in the back of the huge SUV watching everything play out just the way Eddie said it would.

Darren opened the car door a moment later, and Ian darted inside, still wearing his Dorian Masters grin. I heard the bodyguard get settled in the front passenger seat. Almost immediately, the SUV was in motion as cameras followed our progress down the busy street.

"You okay?" Ian asked, placing a comforting hand on my thigh.

"Yeah. Of course," I replied, but I had to swallow twice before the words would come.

I listened as Eddie J rattled off the plan for the rest of the day—dinner with Ian's manager and agent and various other important people. But I zoned out after that, thinking about Ian's reality here in Los Angeles.

How was he ever supposed to take George anywhere? Was he planning on keeping the kid a secret forever, only interacting with him in private? What if George had a school play or started participating in a sport? Would Ian be in the back of every crowd with his hat and sunglasses on while Darren hovered conspicuously nearby? Or did he plan on keeping George locked away with Sophia? The boy needed to socialize with kids his own age at some point. He needed a rich, full life.

The normal, everyday things I did—grocery shopping, bowling league, trivia night—Ian would never be able to manage in a place where everyone was always on the lookout for him.

But seeing him today with his fans, he'd been electric, feeding off their energy and excitement.

Ian had a big personality. How had he survived in Kirby Falls all these months with so little spotlight? Had he missed the attention? Was he suffocating in a place so small and confined?

"Joanie, you ready?"

I snapped out of my thoughts at Ian's words, the concern in his gaze.

The vehicle had stopped. We were inside the front gates of Ian's home, and he was waiting for me to get out of the car.

"Right." I let him help me down from the big SUV. "Sorry. I was distracted."

Eddie J told us goodbye and that he'd meet us at the restaurant tonight.

"We have a long time before we need to get ready for dinner," Ian said when we were back inside. "Eddie J brought some groceries over this morning. I can make us some lunch, and then we can take a nap or go back down to the beach. Whatever you want."

My thoughts were a churning mass, and I blurted, "Did you miss all of that while you were in Kirby Falls?"

Ian froze where he'd been looking through the items in the refrigerator. "Did I miss what?"

"The fans. The attention. All of it."

He closed the fridge door and turned to face me, his face wary.

"I'm not trying to imply anything," I insisted, taking two steps closer so I could place a reassuring hand on his chest. "I'm genuinely curious. Seeing you today, Ian. God. The influencers, the people in the restaurant, the fans waiting outside for just a glimpse of you. You were so good at it—so good with them. You lit up every time you spoke with someone. It was like watching you expand under their attention. You were in your element. And they adored you. I can't even begin to tell you how many people I overheard call you beautiful. Realistically, I knew you were famous, but they *really* love you."

Ian smiled, but it was wry and a little sad. "That's not love, Joan. That's infatuation at best or obsession at worst. When I was growing up, before coming to LA, where gorgeous people are a dime a dozen, I always thought that love was falling for all the parts of someone. Finding attraction in every little thing and growing to think that person—your person— is the most beautiful in the world because you love them. Maybe they have a crooked nose or big ears or whatever interesting characteristic that sets them apart, outside of traditional beauty standards. It's love that changes your perception, building your attraction and holding your attention because your mind and your heart agree on something. Maybe their nose *is* crooked, but it's *their* nose, and you love it because it's theirs."

With a weary sigh, he admitted, "I think I'd rather have one person who thought I was the most beautiful person in the world simply because they loved me than have millions of fans who only thought they did. They know the face and the body. They know Dorian Masters. None of them has any idea who I really am."

I had no clue what to say. I'd meant to compliment Ian on his success and the natural way he had with his fans. Instead, I felt like I'd insulted him. It wasn't the first time I'd offended someone without meaning to, but this was Ian. I didn't want to hurt him, not ever.

"Ian," I choked out. "I'm sorry, I didn't mean—"

But he smiled and shook his head before placing a soft kiss on my forehead. "To answer your question. No. I did not miss all the attention while I was in Kirby Falls. It was nice to be myself for once, with people who cared more about me than any character I've ever played on a screen."

<hr>

Dinner that night was held on the private terrace at some fancy restaurant. The weather was cool without the bright California sunshine, and so standing heaters had been arranged to keep all the guests at the long dining table comfortable.

"Make sure you order the steak," Ian said quietly as we were led toward our chairs. "It's so good, it'll make you forget how boring and miserable this dinner will be."

Eddie J was already seated, tapping out something on his phone, but he was the only one at the table. I waved hello and went to sit beside him, but with a subtle shake of his head, he indicated a group of people entering from a separate doorway, the bar at their backs.

An elegantly dressed woman in her mid-forties led the small crowd, drinks in all their hands. "Dorian!" she called and made a beeline toward Ian, planting kisses on both cheeks while she rested one hand on his shoulder. "It is so good to see you."

The woman was gorgeous, tall, and curvaceous, her hair, a deep auburn that complemented her pale complexion. She looked tasteful and classy in a jumpsuit and blazer.

And that was the last generous thought I had the entire night.

Ian smiled warmly and said, "You too, Gloria. I want you to meet Joan. Joan, this is my manager, Gloria Wilson."

*This* was Gloria.

The very first time I'd met George all those months ago, he'd asked if I was a farmer. I told him I was. Then I'd asked, *What are you?* He'd replied, *An inconvenience.*

When pressed, he'd admitted that someone named Gloria had called him that.

I'd wondered about it for a long time. Had even thought about bringing it up to Ian. But in the end, no one had ever mentioned anyone named Gloria in my presence, and I'd let it go, hoping she was a part of George's history.

But here she was now, not imaginary at all. Ian's manager.

This was the person who'd told a boy who'd just lost his mother that he was an inconvenience. George, who was sweet and kind and smart and thoughtful, unlike any child I'd ever met. George, whom I loved and would do anything for.

Gloria's eyes narrowed a fraction, and I had no idea what mine were doing. Probably plotting a gruesome homicide.

After a moment too long, she said, "Joan. Very nice to meet you. Maybe you can sit with Eddie J at the end of the table. I really need Dorian's full attention on our guests."

I said nothing, and I hoped she was unnerved. I hoped she had nightmares about me tonight.

"Gloria," Ian said firmly, and then waited a beat. "Joan's my guest. I want her with me. This dinner was supposed to be small, just the team."

"It is small," Gloria argued, pretending there weren't half a dozen strangers loitering behind her, waiting for an introduction. "Besides, I have them in mind for some upcoming projects for you. It will be good to entertain conversation tonight."

With that, Gloria waved the loiterers over and introduced Ian—and by extension, me—to a bunch of people whose names I'd never remember.

Before taking my place next to Ian, I grabbed Eddie J's arm and forcibly moved him to the seat beside mine. Gloria's eyes flashed, and it was the first and only time I smiled at the woman all night.

The majority of the dinner had nothing to do with me. Hell, it barely had anything to do with Ian, and he was the reason they were all here. Gloria monopolized the conversation, discussing exciting new projects and showrunners and potential leads and a whole bunch of other stuff that meant nothing to me.

Ian practically vibrated with unease. I could tell he was irritated at being ambushed by his manager, but he worked so hard to hide it. Midway through the salad course, I put a staying hand on his strong thigh, trying to convey support. His leg stopped shaking, but he still tried to include me in nearly every discussion. It was kind, but there was no need.

I had nothing to offer these people, and so I held no value to them. They didn't want to hear about my quaint life in North Carolina or get to know me. They were here to see Dorian Masters, to be in his orbit.

Obviously, I was out of place and underdressed in a basic little black dress that served me for most occasions back home, but none of that bothered me. Maybe I would have been more nervous or guarded if any of these people had mattered. But they didn't.

So I ate my steak and chatted with Eddie J and did my best to reassure Ian that all was well. I'd sat through more annoying family dinners when Brady had gone through a skater-boy phase in his early twenties. This was nothing.

When the meal had gone extremely long, and Gloria decided to order desserts for the table, Ian placed his arm along the back of my chair and leaned in to whisper in my ear. "I'm sorry."

"It's okay," I said quietly. "I'm just happy to be here with you."

He smiled softly, gifting me one lonely dimple. Then he pressed a tender kiss to my cheek.

"And, you know," I told him, when his lips lingered, "you were right. The steak really did make up for everything else."

His huff of amusement made me grin. I was happy I could make Ian laugh on a night when he was so obviously on the clock, going through the motions.

I was, once again, grateful that my own livelihood didn't rely on my ability to charm anyone else.

IAN

The movie premiere was chaotic, but that was nothing new.

Fans gathered behind barriers at the entrance, yelling and waving. Cameras flashed in intervals along the red carpet as photographers yelled out instructions. A long line of interviewers and hosts waited for their turn to speak with anyone involved with the Inferno Man franchise.

Admittedly, I didn't love this part of my job. When I cut back on accepting new roles in the future, I definitely wouldn't miss all the chaos and demands and travel that went along with promoting a film.

I was loitering near the arrival area, killing time by signing autographs and taking photos with fans while waiting for Joan's car to arrive. Darren remained by my side, always vigilant. Eddie J and Gloria were both nearby as well, on their phones.

At my request, Gloria had sent a hair, makeup, and wardrobe team to the beach house early in the day. I'd had a lunch meeting with my agent, and then I'd gone directly to an appointment with my designer. Due to these obligations and prior commitments, Joan and I had been forced to prepare for the evening's festivities and arrive separately. But now, with the cast photos and several interviews already out of the way, I was just waiting for her arrival so we could do a pass on the red carpet before heading inside for a viewing of the film.

I felt terrible about leaving her alone all day, but she'd told me over and over that she was fine—more than capable of handling a little time on her own. So, I'd trusted her.

But I knew she wasn't used to this type of spectacle or the hectic nature of these events. How she'd be pulled in different directions and overwhelmed by so many people and so much noise and attention. Uneasiness churned in my gut at the thought of her walking into all this chaos without me there to prepare her.

"The driver said they're here," Eddie J called suddenly.

My attention immediately went to the arrival area, some fifty feet away, where limos and hired cars released their passengers. My eyes searched for Joan, but I didn't see her.

"Oh my God," Eddie J muttered.

I followed where his gaze was fixed and did a double take at the woman standing there. She'd just stepped out from behind the man helping her from the car. It was Joan, but . . . it looked nothing like her.

Her hair—her hair was platinum blond and pinned up with loose curls framing her face. I was used to seeing women and men heavily made up for the camera, but even from this distance, I could see that the makeup artist had not gone for a natural look. Joan's lips and eyes were dark and dramatic, cheeks glossy with color.

But perhaps the most noticeable change to Joan's appearance was the spray tan. The dress she wore was gorgeous. I'd had a designer send over four options for Joan to choose from. They'd been altered for her body, and the elegant beaded silver gown she'd decided on suited her. The strapless column hugged her form, leaving her arms and shoulders bare. But all that skin on display looked nearly orange from the airbrush job.

The person who'd just emerged from that car looked nothing like the woman I loved. It was like they'd covered up her natural beauty, her confidence—everything that made Joan, Joan.

"I'll go get her," Eddie J said, and I realized I'd just been standing there, staring in disbelief.

Spinning to face Gloria, I lowered my voice until it was practically a growl. "What did they do to her?"

My manager pursed her lips. "I sent a trusted team over, Dorian, but they ran into some issues. Her hair, for one. The root touch-up didn't cover all that gray, so they just went blond. I, for one, think it makes her look much younger."

Anger burned beneath my skin. I knew my face was hot. "It was supposed to be simple hair and makeup, Gloria," I gritted out between clenched teeth.

"I don't see a problem." She returned her attention to her phone. "They did her hair and her makeup."

"She didn't need a dye job or-or a shitty spray tan."

My manager huffed an annoyed sigh and met my gaze. "You should be more grateful, Dorian. She had a farmer's tan, for Christ's sake. What was I supposed to do? Let you be humiliated at your own premiere? A fucking farmer's tan."

"She's a fucking farmer, Gloria. What did you expect?"

"Heeeeyyy!" Eddie J called abruptly, and I spun to face him.

He was standing there, wide-eyed with Joan. They were much closer than I'd expected, close enough to have easily heard the last part of my conversation with Gloria. I'd gotten carried away. I'd just been so angry—at the ridiculous expectations and superficial beauty standards and the way Gloria had tried to shame someone I cared about. I was used to people passing judgment on my face and my body. It was just life in this business.

But Gloria had no right to take Joan—beautiful, honest, fierce Joan—and try to change her to fit these horrible, unrealistic standards.

And now Joan stood there, silent and watchful, looking uncomfortable and rigid, shoulders tense and nearly around her ears.

"I didn't mean—"

"It's okay," she interrupted, straightening.

"No," I insisted. "I was just explaining—"

"Ian," she said firmly. "It's okay."

Gloria stepped close and lowered her voice. "You are both on camera right now, creating drama. Not the good kind. And you can't call him Ian right now," she snapped in Joan's direction. "Dorian, you need to walk the red carpet. Joan can meet you inside."

"That's fine," Joan agreed at the same time I said, "No, she's coming with me."

I held out my hand, but she didn't take it. She just stared at me, face hard, jaw set.

"I'll take you," Eddie J piped up. He slipped his arm through Joan's before I could protest. Then he gave me a meaningful look. "I've got her. You go to work."

They turned together toward the theater, and Eddie J led her behind the barricade and away from the red carpet.

Staring after them, I swallowed hard. I'd been uneasy all day. I'd known that leaving Joan alone to get ready had been a big mistake. I should have insisted. I should have demanded—

"He's right," Gloria said, her nails digging into the sleeve of my tux. "It's time to get to work."

For the next hour, I did my job. I smiled even though I was miserable. I appeared at ease even though I was an anxious mess. I spoke with the press even though all I wanted to do was hurry inside, talk to Joan, and set everything right. I needed to apologize for the makeover. She didn't *need* a fucking makeover.

When I finally made it into the theater, I wasn't even surprised that she was nowhere to be found. I pulled out my phone to call Eddie J and tried to head back outside, but Gloria planted herself directly in my path.

"You cannot leave," she demanded. "We have networking to do at the after-party."

Ignoring her, I turned away and put my phone to my ear.

"You'd better get out here," my assistant said without greeting. "She asked to go home, but I have been stalling like a goddamn courtroom attorney."

I was already moving. "Where is she?"

Eddie J gave me instructions on where to go. Joan was in the car, and the driver was waiting while Eddie J stood outside the vehicle making excuses.

"I am trying to give you the benefit of the doubt here, Ian," Eddie J said.

I sidestepped someone with a microphone. "What does that mean?"

"Gloria," he said bitterly. "Your *manager* did this on purpose."

Someone with a camera tried to wave me over. I kept my head down and finally ducked out onto the sidewalk. I had a block to go.

Sighing, I admitted, "I know you don't like Gloria." It was an old argument between us. "But she's a good manager."

"A good manager doesn't manipulate you. A good manager doesn't go out of her way to hurt your girlfriend. A good manager doesn't want to fuck you."

"Not this again."

Eddie J made an outraged squawk. "You tell Gloria you're bringing someone—not a Hollywood someone, not another actress, not a setup for publicity bullshit—but a real-life woman, a person you obviously care about. Of course, Gloria would react like this and try to fuck it all up."

I didn't take the time to respond. I didn't know what to say to any of that anyway. No part of me wanted to think about Gloria's intent tonight. Because Eddie J was right. It had been purposeful and malicious. But I didn't want to be worked up and angry when I tried to talk to Joan.

I turned the corner at the next intersection and saw the car idling and Eddie J standing nearby, phone still pressed to his ear.

Disconnecting the call, I broke into a run. Ignoring my assistant and the stern look he threw my way, I opened the door and slid into the backseat.

Joan looked up, startled. She'd been picking apart a tissue, the remains in her lap. But I couldn't see any evidence of tears on her face.

"Joan, I'm sorry. I didn't know about all this." I gestured broadly, trying to encompass the hair, the spray tan, the disrespect, all of it. "I should have stayed at the house this morning. I wish you had called me, or you could have told them no, to all of it. You didn't need some ridiculous makeover."

She looked away briefly before clearing her throat. "It's fine. But I think I'm going to head back. Let you do your thing. I know you have a party afterward."

My phone was still clutched in my hand. It started vibrating, but I ignored it. "We don't need to go to that."

"It's okay," she argued. "You go ahead. I'm sure the film will be great."

Her voice was flat and emotionless. Fear climbed up my spine, and I shifted closer, even as I felt her getting farther and farther away.

"Please don't do this," I begged, deliberately placing my buzzing phone in my pocket. "It was just a miscommunication. I'll make sure Gloria doesn't overstep again. When I said that—what you heard when you got here, I wasn't criticizing or—"

"It's okay," Joan repeated for what felt like the hundredth time.

But none of this was okay.

"No." I could hear a desperate edge in my voice, feel it reflected in my thundering pulse. I was grasping, trying to hang on to smoke.

And she was already gone.

"I know you didn't mean anything by it when you called me a farmer," she said. "It's the truth."

"Right, but—" I tried again.

"It's not a surprise to me. I've always known exactly who I am, Ian. And now you do, too."

Her face was a mask, closed off and impatient. The words, the final nail in the coffin. Joan hated wasting time. I knew this about her. And it was clear that she wouldn't be wasting any more of it tonight on me.

I could feel her writing me off—in her heart, in her mind, in her whole fucking life.

My phone would not stop buzzing. The sound was stark, offensive.

"You should go," she said. "It's your big night."

Everything about her, from the severe frown on her face to the tight set of her shoulders, screamed that she was worn thin and jagged around the edges, like a dry ink pen scratching across paper, with nothing left to give.

I stared at her, trying desperately to figure out what to say, how to fix this. But she wasn't even looking at me anymore.

The urge was there to take her hand, to hug her, kiss her. But this fucked-up disaster made it feel like the last night I might get to do any of those things, and I didn't want it to be like this.

So, with pressure building behind my sternum, I opened the door and stepped out.

Darren waited a few feet away. He must have caught up with me.

Eddie J came over immediately, shutting the door and straightening my tie. "You'd better get back over there. She's blowing me up now, too."

I could hear his phone vibrating with angry accusation.

"I don't want to leave her," I said hoarsely. "It wasn't supposed to go like this."

My assistant sighed. "I know. But you are contractually obligated to be at this event. I will make sure she gets back to the beach house safely. I promise. I'll take care of her."

Resigned, I stepped away. Darren led me down a more direct route to the theater. We didn't talk, and I was grateful. I felt hollowed out and so damn angry at myself for letting this happen.

All the inner rage found a new target when we stepped inside. Gloria waited in the lobby.

She was already talking, but I didn't hear the words.

"You're fired," I told her.

My manager abruptly stopped speaking and glanced around us. She urged me away from the crowd, and I followed.

"You cannot be serious," she hissed when we had relative privacy. "All of this over some farmer and a spray tan. Over someone who doesn't even—"

"Not another word about Joan," I said, and I thought it was a miracle that I sounded so calm. "You've done enough."

Gloria's dark eyes narrowed to slits. She opened her mouth, presumably to deliver another zinger, but instead I lowered my voice and said, "Not another word at all, or I'll tell everyone how petty and jealous and vindictive you are. How all your girls' girl empowerment is just bullshit. You were wildly unprofessional today, and this wasn't the first time. I've overlooked things because you did your job."

"My job? I made you everything you are," she insisted, vitriol leaking out of every pore.

"No, you haven't. I've gotten where I am on my own talent and hard work. I was your only client for a reason. I was the only one who'd put up with you, and you made enough money off of me to set yourself up for life. But you've always had a bad habit of ignoring what I want. You made decisions behind my back. You worked for your own best interests. You didn't support me in assuming custody of Georgie. You told me my nephew would negatively impact my career and to let someone else who didn't have eighty-eight million followers raise him. And tonight . . . you probably cost me the only other thing that's ever mattered to me."

With that, I stepped around my former manager and went back to work.

---

My stomach sank as soon as I walked into the beach house. I knew she wasn't there.

Joan's things were gone, and my sweatshirt that she'd worn was folded neatly on the end of my bed.

It had been naïve to imagine that this might have been a fun night of dress-up and playing pretend. Bringing a date to any event meant drawing attention. Even if everything *had* gone to plan—the optimistic, unrealistic one in my head—I still would have been exposing Joan to widespread judgment and media attention.

*What had I been thinking?*

Maybe I'd wanted the whole world to know she was mine. Maybe I'd wanted her to know it, too.

But that had been a cowardly and selfish way to go about it—vicious, too. Throwing Joan into shark-infested waters without a life raft.

I rubbed a hand over my jaw in mute frustration as I took in the emptiness of the beach house.

I hadn't looked out for her. Hadn't taken care of her the way I'd promised. She'd been insulted, humiliated, and angered, rightfully so. I'd ruined more than an idealistic night out, more than our public debut.

I'd ruined everything.

It was late, but I pulled out my phone.

I paced in the kitchen as I waited with my device pressed to my ear.

She answered on the fourth ring. "Hey."

"Are you okay?"

"Yeah."

I toyed nervously with the elastic around my wrist. "Can I ask where you are?"

A beat of silence. "I'm at the airport."

"I'll come there. We can talk. Please don't leave this way."

I was halfway down the stairs to my garage when she said gently, "No."

My feet slowed to a stop.

"I need some space, Ian." Her voice was soft, but unapologetic. I knew her well enough to recognize how hard she was trying. She was making an attempt to let me down easy.

The phone was clutched so tightly in my hand that I knew there'd be marks on my palm. I made myself breathe when all I wanted to do was argue, plead, and beg on my knees.

I thought of one of our earliest conversations, back in Kirby Falls, running on a dirt path. Joan had scolded me, telling me I couldn't go around doing whatever I wanted just because I was famous. She'd said that my wants and desires weren't any more important than hers. And she'd been right.

So, I lowered myself slowly to the third stair from the bottom.

"I'm listening," I said.

Finally, she sighed. "I think I just need some distance."

"Please don't let one thing ruin your time here. It was good. *We* were good. Even in LA," I reminded her.

"It's not just one thing. This is your life." A very deliberate pause. "Your *real* life. I just don't see how I fit into that. Not even with a spray tan."

Frustrated, I fought to find the right words.

This trip was supposed to show her the reality of being with me. And I guess, in the end, it had done just that.

"I love you," I told her hoarsely. "I love you, and none of this—Hollywood, my career, the fame—matters as much as you do."

Joan was quiet. I heard an airport announcement in the background as the weight of her silence settled into every crack in my heart.

"That's not true, Ian. And I wouldn't want it to be. *That* shouldn't be what love is. Carving out space, throwing things away to make room for something else. That's not love. That's making concessions. Building resentment. And even if I understood that sort of love—which I don't—I could never say that my life doesn't matter, that my family and the orchard don't matter, just because you exist."

"I know. You're right. I know that. I don't expect you to change yourself for me."

Joan huffed a humorless laugh. "There's some blond hair stuffed under a ball cap right now that would disagree with you."

I closed my eyes.

"I need some time," she explained. "I need to go home and figure some things out. Can you respect that? Please?"

"Yes, of course. If that's what you need." But my heart was in my throat, making it difficult to breathe.

"Thank you," she said, and her voice caught on the final word.

"Joan," I begged.

But her voice firmed itself. "Listen, I'm getting ready to board. Good luck with the tour. We'll talk when you get back."

And then she was gone, and I didn't have anyone to blame but myself.

JOAN

I showed up at my sister's house two days later with a box of Clairol Nice'n Easy in medium neutral brown.

Mercer opened the front door, and his eyes went wide.

I shook my head, nose stinging inexplicably with sudden emotion.

My friend stepped back and held the door wide before calling out for Candace.

My sister's reaction was slightly less controlled, but she recovered admirably and ushered me into the kitchen.

"I'm, uh, going to head out to the greenhouse," Mercer stated awkwardly. "Give you two some time."

He brushed a kiss on Candace's lips and squeezed my shoulder as he passed.

When he was out the back door and halfway across the yard, Candace turned to me, a hundred questions all queued up, I could tell.

But I held up the box and shook it a little, feeling like I might snap in half if I didn't have somewhere to divert my energy. "Can you give me a hand with this? It's safe for the baby. I looked it up. Just make sure you wear the gloves, and I'll open a window."

"Aren't you supposed to wait a couple of weeks before dyeing it again?" she asked.

"Yeah. I'm not going to do that."

I thought I might pull every hair out of my head if I had to look at it like this in the mirror every day and remember everything that went along with it. I'd risk some breakage and dryness.

Candace nodded and went to retrieve a towel.

A few minutes later, I was settled in a kitchen chair with Vaseline around my ears.

Candace, poised above me with a squeeze bottle of hair dye, said, "Are you going to tell me what happened now?"

Sighing, I closed my eyes and tilted my head forward so she could start at the back and work her way forward.

Methodically, I told her about the meet and greet with the influencers the day after we arrived. Then I described the dinner on the terrace. And after I'd given her the rundown on Eddie J and how great he was, I told her about the premiere and all the shit leading up to it. I recited the events in a disconnected sort of way. Just the facts. Candace didn't need me crying in her kitchen or anywhere else, for that matter.

Truthfully, the makeover team had been nice. I'd felt comfortable enough with them that I'd instructed them to do whatever they thought was best. The hairstylist, the makeup artist, and the sweet assistant who'd gone out and found me shoes that I could actually walk in had all been eager to help get me ready. They'd been kind, if a little gossipy. But everyone had a boss to answer to.

"And when I walked up, Ian and his manager were arguing. She was making it clear that they'd had to do so much work on me because I was an old farmer with gray hair."

Candace wore a frozen look of horror. "What did Ian say?"

"He was trying to defend me," I simplified. It was the truth. No part of me had ever assumed Ian was bashing me or insinuating I was a backwoods hillbilly.

He'd been angry and had questioned his manager's actions. Deep down, I knew that Ian hadn't asked for them to turn me blond or orange.

But my presence had caused trouble. Just by existing the way I was—the way I chose to be—with my gray-streaked hair and my calloused, sun-worn skin, I'd become someone who could negatively impact Ian's career.

Gloria had known exactly what she'd been doing by requesting updates from the makeover team and then making demands via text message throughout the day. It had been her call to drag me to a salon to bleach my hair. She'd been the one to make the hasty spray tan appointment, too. Gloria hadn't done me any favors when she'd instructed the makeup artist to use such a heavy hand and call it "glamorous." I had plenty of fine lines on my face for all that makeup to settle into.

But none of that shit mattered in the long run. Sure, Gloria was a dick. But I'd known that already, once I'd realized who she was and what she'd said to George.

The problem was me. As long as I was with Ian, he'd be forced to make excuses for me or explain my presence or hide me away. His life was smackdab in the middle of every spotlight, and that worked for him. I was never going to be that sort of person, though.

"So then what happened?" Candace asked.

"I left."

Candace moved in front of me, a frown on her face. "You left?"

"Yeah. Eddie J got me a car. Ian and I spoke briefly. I told him to go on to the premiere, that we'd talk later. And then I went back to the house, got my things, and went to the airport. Luckily, there was a red-eye."

My sister stared at me incredulously. "You left California without telling Ian?"

The chair squeaked when I shifted uncomfortably. "He called when he got home, I guess. I told him I needed time to think."

"Oh, Joan." She placed the bottle of hair dye on the counter with an impatient thunk and then ripped her gloves off. "I can't believe you just took off when his back was turned."

I blinked. "He had to work, Candace. I didn't expect him to bail on his responsibilities to come hold my hand and cheer me up. I'm not a little kid who got her feelings hurt. And I couldn't—" I swallowed hard, betraying my previous statement. "I couldn't stay there another minute. I just . . . couldn't."

Suddenly, I wished I'd held off on starting this conversation. Now, I had to sit here for twenty-five minutes while I waited for the color to take. And it looked like Candace was building up a good head of steam.

So I cut her off before she could get going. "We were never going to fit, okay? Ian and I . . . we don't make sense. We never have. His life is in Hollywood. Mine is in Kirby Falls. And you know what? I'm not ashamed of that. I like my life. You're part of that. Do you want me to quit the farm and move to LA so I can sit around waiting for Ian to take off his Dorian Masters mask?"

"No, of course not," my sister replied. She lowered herself onto the chair beside me. "But I don't think that's the only answer."

"I don't know what else there is. He can't stay here forever. It's not like Will and Becca. She made Kirby Falls her home. Ian never asked for it to be. I've known from the beginning that this was all temporary. I think, somewhere along the way . . . I let myself forget."

"I came back. Maybe Ian will, too." And she sounded so hopeful on my behalf that I felt the urge to comfort *her*.

"That's different," I said gently. "You have history. You grew up here. You stayed for all the right reasons."

"*You* could be the right reason," Candace argued.

I looked down at my lap and frowned. My nails were still painted silver to match my dress.

"Ian's never been stuck behind a tractor driving down Haywood Road. He doesn't know what fresh apple juice tastes like right off the press. He's never watched the sun set from the top of Juniper Point or swam in Lake Archer until his shoulders were sunburnt."

Releasing a shaky breath, I added, "He doesn't belong here. His life is bigger than all this. He'd just be tied down."

I watched through blurry, watery eyes as Candace took my hand in hers.

My voice was rough when it emerged again, and I hated feeling weak. "I tried, you know. I went to California with an open mind. I gave it a chance." I'd made myself vulnerable, painted a target on my back. "And it wasn't the fans or the cameras or the attention or even his shitty manager. I tried to be a part of his life there. I made an effort to understand it. And in the end, it comes down to me not being who Ian needs."

"Joanie," my sister admonished sadly.

"It's not just my age or my background. I know that. But I'm set in my ways. I'm bad at first impressions. Ian is always having dinner or drinks or taking a meeting with someone new. That's just part of his life. I don't know how to facilitate connections or network or charm. Making small talk is like pulling teeth for someone like me. I'm grouchy and judgmental. And I like things a certain way. Ian needs someone flexible. Someone who knows the industry, or at least, understands it."

The hand holding mine squeezed gently. "You think you're this rigid person, but you're not. Maybe you used to be. But you've softened for me and for George. Ian, too. You text people now, instead of ignoring their calls. You threw me a bachelorette party with line dancing. You blew off an afternoon of work just so you could take a little boy fishing for the first time."

I smiled at the memory before my chin wobbled.

"You might think you're the same hard-ass Joan you've always been, but that's just not true. And before you argue, it's not changing yourself for a man. It's growing and evolving and shifting your priorities. It's making space for people in a life that used to be all straight lines and sharp edges."

That was maybe the worst part of all. I knew I'd changed. I knew that Candace was right.

I wasn't the same person I'd been when my sister had moved home almost two years ago. I'd worked hard to be more open—more trusting and vulnerable with my family. I'd convinced myself I could afford to let in only the people who mattered—my parents, my siblings, the friends who I'd grown closer to in the last few years.

But Ian and George had slipped past my defenses. I'd been so opposed to everything about the movie until it stared me in the face. And now it was all over.

I felt lost.

There were the changes that Candace could see, but there was more.

I didn't know how to explain to my sister what it was like to love Ian. The way his sweet affection had altered my very makeup, rearranged my heart. His patience and kindness, his attention, how he'd happily hold my hand in public, in private, for the rest of our lives, and probably even buried together, six feet in the grave.

There was no flowery way to describe it. No clichés to do it justice. I'd read plenty of romance novels that made comparisons or gave helpful metaphors for falling in love. For me, it wasn't at all like wandering in a desert and having my thirst quenched. Ian's touch didn't heal something broken in me. It wasn't as simple as feeling my cold, dead heart beat to new, radiant life.

To me, it was more like our cat growing up, Dolly. It was the way my mother, before Candace was born, had coaxed an old barn cat into trusting her. The endless patience and the minimal reward. How she'd sat outside on the porch for hours, a warm presence next to a skittish creature who'd never been inclined to trust. The way Mom had hand delivered food over months of effort, and Dolly's transition from something feral to nearly tolerant and, finally, doting.

That cat went from an unbothered, self-sufficient lioness to a contented house cat. She sat on the back of my father's recliner for twelve years. There was no wild left in her, and she hadn't even been mad about it. Dolly became an exclusively indoor pet with no desire for her past life.

*That* was what it felt like inside of me.

Ian had won me over, slowly but surely. He'd charmed and coaxed me despite my snarling and spitting. He'd met my distrust with patience and good humor. He made me feel safe and warm and content, and now I was incapable of returning to the way things had been before.

I still wanted the affection and the sweetness he'd promised when he'd tamed something wild in me—something fierce and biting.

I was as predictable as an old barn cat.

Maybe that was a silly way to say you knew what love was. But more accurately, it was how I'd been changed by finding it.

The same way that damn cat no longer remembered its instinct, I didn't know how to go back to before. How to survive without Ian's affection, his heart. His smile. His hand wrapped around mine.

And when I thought about trying to say goodbye to George . . .

"I realize there are a lot of complications," Candace said. "And that's not ideal. But life isn't simple. It never is. Love and relationships take compromise and hard work. But if the love is there, that's step one. You have to let yourself be vulnerable enough to fall, and trust the other person to catch you."

"I don't know if I can do that," I admitted.

Candace looked at me in surprise. "You are the hardest-working person I know. Once you dedicate yourself to something, you fight like hell to protect it. You just need to communicate with Ian. Figure out how to work together to solve this thing. Ian is a good guy, Joanie. He's charming and fun and so good with Georgie. He welcomes everyone into his orbit. Yes, he's a movie star, but—"

"That's not the only thing he is," I finished.

My sister smiled like I was her prized student. "That's right. He fits here, and you know it. Let him decide for himself what's too much or not enough. Don't make that decision for him. Maybe he's been hoping you'd ask him to stay. Maybe he's been too scared to ask. You never know until you try."

I nodded because she was right.

"Although," she mused, "you're going to need to be honest with him."

I frowned. "About what?"

Candace grinned. "About how terrible he is at making coffee. You can't keep letting him poison you like that."

My laughter gusted out of me, even as I felt my eyes fill with tears. I thought I might put up with a lot of terrible coffee for the rest of my life if it meant Ian was the one making it.

A week and a half later, I forced myself to stop working and go to bowling league with my sister and our friends, even though there was an hour of daylight left. But with Ian gone, I knew they were all worried about me, and this was the easiest way to show everyone that I was doing okay, even if that wasn't entirely true.

I'd started a top grafting project on a few rows in the orchard. It was laborious and required my focus and energy in order to graft a new apple variety onto an existing tree. That filled my time during my workday.

In the evenings, I generally checked in with Sophia and George over at the big house. My cabin was too quiet, so I liked cooking dinner across the highway while George colored or made friendship bracelets at the kitchen island.

Sophia had been happy to see me, and a few times I'd told her I was fine to watch George so that she could take a break. I got the impression she was dating someone in town, and I knew Ian wouldn't mind if I read to his nephew and tucked him in for bed.

For months, we'd been a team, spending our evenings together—like a family. It felt natural to go through George's nighttime routine and help him brush his teeth.

Only now, Ian was the one missing.

The ancient bowling alley still smelled like fried food and cheap beer. But oddly enough, the typical cacophony of clattering pins and rowdy conversation dwindled to nothing as I made my way to my team's lane.

I was aware of eyes on me, gossip whispered into ears and behind cupped hands. But I kept my gaze forward and took my seat without acknowledging the sudden attention I'd unexpectedly garnered.

Eventually, folks went back to their own games and resumed drinking their beer.

"Do I want to know what that was all about?" I asked the group.

Candace, Bonnie, and Mac exchanged uneasy glances. A sense of déjà vu tickled the back of my mind. Last month, they'd been all aflutter over pictures of Ian and me from the Spring Fling.

Now, though, they appeared uneasy and reluctant.

"Well," Mac said, taking the lead, "it looks like some of the celebrity gossip sites are finally reporting on your presence with Ian at the premiere."

A sinking feeling pushed me lower into my seat. I had no idea what people were saying about me . . . but I could imagine. "Oh?"

"I guess photographers got a few shots of you in conversation," Candace confirmed, looking miserable. That could have just been the morning sickness, though.

"Several have been spotted around town," Bonnie said gently.

"Paparazzi?" I asked, shocked that anyone would care enough to fly all the way across the country for practically nothing. Ian wasn't even here.

My friends nodded.

I glanced around us discreetly. "Should I be worried?"

"Oh, no," Mac said. "The orchard is private property since it's seasonal and not open to the public currently. We had someone show up at Grandpappy's, and Larry talked them in circles for an hour. She loved it. Don't worry, Joan. The town has a plan."

I blinked. "The town has a plan?"

"We have a system," Bonnie confirmed. "People are signing up for time slots, leading the cameramen on wild goose chases all over the place."

"Especially the areas where the parking rates aren't clearly visible," Mac added with a wicked grin. "The meter maid sure has been busy writing all those tickets."

Leaning forward in my seat, I tried to wrap my mind around this. "You're telling me the town has, what? Banded together to fool the paparazzi and run them out of town? All for my benefit?"

"Well, yeah." Mac shrugged. "You're one of us, despite being allergic to the Kirby Falls Facebook group."

"People care about you, Joan," Bonnie said and reached out to pat my hand.

Los Angeles hadn't gone as planned, and as a result, I'd brought trouble back to my hometown. It had been naïve to think the press wouldn't figure out who I was or attribute that to where Ian had been for the last six months.

I didn't like the idea of accepting help. It made me feel all twisted up inside, a combination of guilt and self-loathing—like I should have been able to handle all this nonsense myself without bothering anyone else. But this was my town, my community. And they were standing up for me.

I swallowed an unwelcome rush of emotion and bowled the worst game of my life.

That night, I went back to my too-quiet cabin and opened up my laptop.

The photographs weren't difficult to find.

A handful of candid images from the night of the premiere. Me looking out of place and uncomfortable in a beautiful dress.

Speculation ranged far and wide. Some outlets reported that I was a family member who'd flown in from the Midwest to attend the premiere with Dorian, but I'd gotten ill upon arrival and been forced to leave. Another report hinted at a red-carpet argument. A photo of me looking wide-eyed and shocked accompanied an image of Ian, his jaw clenched, and his eyes narrowed.

It was easy to see how all of this had been twisted into fiction. I'd never look at another tabloid the same way again. Not a single one of these gossip sites had the actual story, but that hadn't stopped them from reporting it anyway.

Well, there had been one that had gotten close to real-life events. It was a website that boasted celebrity and entertainment news with all the top Hollywood headlines. They'd called me "Mrs. Robinson," and speculated over my age. A body language "specialist" had examined the photos and noted my "discomfort around wealth and celebrities," while they'd labeled Ian as "tense at the prospect of his worlds colliding."

I didn't read any more after that.

Instead, I navigated over to the Kirby Falls Facebook group to see what my friends had been up to.

True to their word, there was a post detailing my neighbors' efforts to confuse and disrupt the photographers that had come to town. They had linked to a spreadsheet where folks who looked enough like me could sign up to go running through the community.

Gretchen Rose Tate had offered up an extra blond wig to anyone who needed it since the paparazzi still thought that was my hair color. She was currently taking the 6:30–7:00 a.m. spot before school every morning, pretending to be fake Joan with a ball cap and sunglasses, waving for the cameras as she ran a four-mile loop through downtown.

Others had reported the paparazzi's interest in Ian, wondering if he was in town with me and where they might find us.

It made me curious as to whether Ian had been staying at the beach house in LA and avoiding going out in public. Well, with his upcoming press tour, things were sure to change. I figured the photographers in Kirby Falls would realize their efforts were wasted and they'd leave town once Ian popped up somewhere else.

Local residents had been doing their best to drive them out sooner, though.

Even Vera Sterling, the owner of the local bed-and-breakfast, had joined in, claiming a plumbing leak in several of the rented rooms that required her photographer guests to immediately vacate the premises.

I scrolled through comment after comment. People I'd grown up with, gone to church with, folks I'd known my whole life, all angered and frustrated by the way I'd been targeted and disrespected by the media. My neighbors were trying to protect me—to safeguard my home, my privacy, and my peace from outsiders looking to profit off my humiliation.

Pride and gratitude kept me rooted in place, reading and absorbing all their combined efforts. And woven through it all was Ian. He'd been replying to comments for the last three days, offering advice on dealing with the paparazzi and providing encouragement to my neighbors. The wild goose chase had been his idea, and the locals had run with it, literally.

His worry and concern were obvious. I couldn't get over how present he was, how grateful he seemed to everyone for looking out for me.

This whole thing seemed so wild and unlikely, like the plot of a *Scooby-Doo* episode or a *Sweet Valley High* novel. I was starring in my own Hallmark movie as my idyllic small town came together for a common goal. I guess that wasn't too far off.

Still. I didn't feel worthy of all that trouble. And I didn't know how to go about repaying that sort of debt.

Those kinds of thoughts kept me up that night. I tossed and turned, unsure how to deal with my complicated emotions—the gratitude and the discomfort, the overwhelming sense of community and awe. And buried beneath it all, a sense of loss I could no longer ignore.

---

Three days later, I cautiously made my way to the grocery store for the first time in a week.

I was picking out bell peppers in the produce section when I caught sight of someone familiar disappearing behind an endcap.

I placed the vegetables in my cart and then went to the opposite end of the aisle before emerging dramatically in front of a large, stoic-faced man.

"Darren, what are you doing here?" I asked in exasperation.

The big man sighed. "Ian was worried about the media attention."

"I don't need protection," I argued. "They're mostly gone now." And they were. Once Ian had shown up for the London premiere of *Inferno Man 3*, the world had taken notice, and any interest in Kirby Falls had waned.

"They realized he isn't here," I added.

Darren looked very uncomfortable, but he said softly, "He's giving you space."

I felt my cheeks heat. "I know."

"But he was worried about you."

Swallowing, I admitted, "I know that, too. You should be with him for the press tour."

"The studio hired security for the cast. I'm supposed to stick to you and Georgie. Keep you both safe."

Darren and I watched each other silently for a moment.

Then I sighed and nodded. "Then you'll want to come to the farmhouse for dinner. Sophia is taking the night off, and George is coming with me."

Ian's giant bodyguard smiled. "Good. I've missed your mama's cooking."

Three hours later, George was inside with my parents, while I walked over to the orchard to feed and water the goat.

Jolly Adams had been over to visit earlier. She came every few days to check on Ralph (originally Emmett), but knowing her vindictive asshole of an ex-husband, she thought it best that the goat stayed where he was for the time being. She could still claim ignorance if Buck figured out where the goat had ended up. But hopefully in the future, we could make the transition and take Ralph/Emmett back home to be with Jolly.

When I returned to the farmhouse, I walked in on George video chatting with Ian at the kitchen table. My parents were gathered on either side of the kid while he held up his phone, yapping happily about whatever he and my mother had been baking in my absence.

My heart attempted to beat out of my chest while I washed my hands in the kitchen sink, the sound of Ian's deep voice through the inadequate phone speaker so damn welcome, I had to lean against the countertop for balance.

"Oh, there's Joanie!" George called. "Say hi to Joanie, Uncle Ian."

Then the kid flipped the phone to face me. I froze, holding up a hand in an awkward approximation of a wave. But I barely got to see Ian because George immediately pivoted back and returned the phone to his own face.

The urge was there to hurry across the room and snatch the device out of George's hand, but that would be extreme and unhinged and might let on how much I was missing Ian.

Was he still in London? Was he at a hotel, or in between events? Had he been sleeping alright? Did he have my hat with him? Had that been stubble on his jaw or just a shadow?

The last time we'd spoken, he'd told me he loved me. He'd thrown it at me like a life preserver, a last-ditch effort to keep me from leaving. And I'd said nothing, too raw and vulnerable at the time to think of anything beyond simple self-preservation.

My hand tightened on the dish towel I was holding.

Then, out of nowhere, George hopped up and said he was going to set the table. He quickly told Ian bye and then thrust the phone in my hand as he ran toward the dining room. I nearly fumbled it as my heart rate spiked once more.

"Hi. Hey. Hello. How are you?" I said, when I finally managed to right the device and bring it up to my face.

I was aware of my parents sharing a look, and knew I must have sounded ridiculous.

So I cleared my throat and brought my attention back to the screen. "Hey," I tried again.

And there he was, already smiling at me, but it was soft and sweet, only one dimple shadowing his cheek. "Hey," he replied quietly.

I stared at the screen, taking in every little detail, anxious for all I'd missed in the two weeks since I'd last laid eyes on him. He wasn't in a tux or camera-ready. Ian appeared relaxed and comfortable. He was in a sweat-shirt—the same gray hoodie I'd slept in while we were in LA. That had me biting down on the inside of my cheek, hard.

There was no stubble, after all. It had been a trick of the hotel room light-ing. Ian was just as clean-shaven as always. His dark hair had grown out a little, though. He looked tired, maybe, but good.

I hadn't been totally without updates on Ian. Eddie J had been texting me regularly since I'd returned to Kirby Falls. The man was determined for us to be friends, and I couldn't say I minded. I knew that Ian had wrapped up filming in the studio very recently. And I also knew that Ian had fired Gloria after what went down at the premiere. A better person might have felt regret at that. But I was a vindictive asshole, and only wished her good riddance.

"Where are you?" I asked, curious despite myself. Then, aware of my listening parents and how awkward this might get, I walked out of the kitchen and into the living room.

"In London still. One more night, then on to New York. Are you okay? Has the media been bothering you?" Ian's face got closer like he'd leaned forward.

"No, I'm fine. Candace fielded the calls to the orchard. And I guess you heard about the town's help." My voice caught on the last word, so I switched gears. "Anyway, they're gone now. Everything's fine."

There was a moment of silence while we just looked at one another.

A hundred words crowded my throat, a dozen conversations leaping to attempted fruition.

*I'm sorry I left that way. I'm sorry I left at all. I wish I could be someone bold and glamorous and brave. I wish I could be right for you. I wish you were here, beside me. I love you, too. Fuck . . . I love you.*

But what came out was, "Are you okay?"

"Yeah," he answered roughly. "Yeah, I'm good. I wish I was there, you know."

"Me too," I told him honestly. If he were here, we could talk.

Maybe Candace was right. Maybe we could figure this out.

"I'm sorry," Ian said suddenly. "About the last time we spoke. I shouldn't have pressured you like that or told you things you weren't ready to hear."

I frowned. "No, Ian. You don't have anything to—*I'm* sorry. I reacted badly. I was hurt and—"

"All finished!" George shouted as he ran into the living room. "Now I'm going to take you to visit Ralph."

Before either one of us could react, George snatched the phone and hustled out the front door. I heard his little feet pound across the porch and down the steps.

Releasing a pained breath, I collapsed onto the sofa, wishing so many things could be different.

When George returned ten minutes later, the video call had ended, and the kid had a dozen new pictures of Ralph to show me. I didn't let my disappointment show. After all, I was grateful to have George here. I didn't want to consider how difficult this would all be if he was halfway across the world right now, too.

With Darren, it was just the five of us for dinner. Candace was having a lot of morning sickness, all hours of the day. I'd been checking on her often, bringing her different ginger food items to try. I'd been reading a lot about pregnancy and wanted to help Candace and Mercer however I could, ridiculously happy at the thought of being an aunt in the near future.

I'd never really considered having a family of my own. But it was hard to ignore how much I loved George. Spending so much time with him in the fields, witnessing his youthful exuberance and curiosity, I was grateful to be a part of his life. I thought seven-year-olds were pretty perfect. I loved how excited he got and how big his emotions were. I loved his sweetness and the simplicity of his world. But I also had the intense desire to see the kind of person he'd grow up to be.

Looking around the dinner table and watching my parents chat happily with the little boy who'd appeared in my life by chance, I had to remind myself that we weren't George's family. All of these moments, all of this time together was bittersweet. Because, in my heart, it sure felt like he was mine.

The first text from Ian came through that night.

After I'd read George a chapter from his book and tucked him in, I sat down in the dark sunroom of Junior and Nola's house to await Sophia's return. I pulled out my phone and saw the notification.

Ian: I didn't get to say goodbye when George took off with the phone, so I wanted to tell you goodnight. I hope that's okay.

I told myself to be brave and to trust my instincts. I wasn't a martyr, and there was no reason to sacrifice my happiness, especially when it was staring me in the face and texting me good night.

Me: It's okay. You can message me whenever you want. I'm not mad at you, Ian.

He replied right away.

Ian: Okay.

Ian: But you said you wanted space, and I don't want to crowd you.

Me: It would be nice to hear from you while you're away.

Ian: Then I'll text you.

Joan: Good. Have a nice time in New York.

Ian: Thanks. I miss you guys.

Me: We miss you too.

Two days later, I got a selfie of Ian in Times Square. So I sent back a photo of Ralph trying to eat Brady's shirt.

The next day, Ian sent me a link to a DIY chicken coop that looked more like a chicken mansion. But it made me smile until my cheeks hurt.

Then, the following evening, I got in late from book club and found the red light blinking on my answering machine. In the shadows of my kitchen, I listened to someone release a slow breath, and then "Hey, Joanie" came through the speakers in Ian's deep voice.

Overcome by how welcome it was to hear him in my home again, I slid slowly to the floor as Ian continued rambling nervously over the length of the recording. I laughed a watery laugh when he joked self-deprecatingly about this being his first time on an answering machine, and he hoped he was doing it right.

I wasn't sure how he'd gotten the number to my landline, but I was glad for it. Grateful to whichever family member had seen fit to hand over my happiness when I'd been too oblivious, too stubborn, too cowardly to do it myself.

With elbows pressed to the countertop, I pressed the play button again and heard the smile in Ian's voice, felt the comfort in his words. It wasn't over-the-top or demonstrative. He knew me too well for that. But it was a steady recounting of his day and things that reminded him of George or me, moments he'd been compelled to share.

It was painfully domestic and equally as romantic. A gentle reminder that he was still here in every way that mattered. A touching love letter for my ears alone.

The messages on my answering machine and the texts continued over the next few weeks, and it felt like a knot loosened somewhere in my chest. We didn't discuss our relationship or the future or what happened in LA. Instead, we talked about George and life in Kirby Falls. What Ian was missing by being gone. What could be his . . . if he wanted it. If I was brave enough to offer it.

I'd thought I needed space from Ian to get my head on straight. To come to terms with the inevitable end of us. To, maybe, fall *out* of love.

But the longer Ian was away, the more I realized I didn't want distance. Because with every message I received, it was a little reminder, an arrow to my heart, that I'd spent all my life missing a love like this. And I didn't know if I could bear to wait any longer.

# twenty-three

IAN

When I'd left Kirby Falls six weeks ago, the landscape had just been starting to come to life. There had been buds on the apple trees, tiny bits of green that hinted at what was to come. The tulips that Georgie and Joan had planted had barely been peeking out of the ground, daffodils blooming everywhere around the rental house, along with the purple lily magnolia trees.

Now, though, early May was a riot of color. So much so, it was hard to take it in all at once. I'd thought the mountains were beautiful in winter, but I had trouble remembering that in the face of all this green.

Darren had texted me where to find them.

It was early afternoon, and Joan and Georgie were next to the wildflower field in the distance. It felt like a sign. The place where I'd given up and collapsed in the dirt six months ago, dramatic and out of breath. The place where Joan had found me.

A lot could change in half a year.

"What are they doing?" I asked Darren when I came to stand beside him.

"They've been following those turkeys around for thirty minutes."

And sure enough, when Joan stepped sideways, an adult turkey and a handful of tiny turkey babies came into view.

My nephew was beside himself with excitement. He bounced on his toes, clinging to Joan's hand and tugging her closer and closer. But Joan didn't seem to mind. She grinned down at Georgie, urging him to crouch low in the grass and not get too near the wildlife.

I thought I could watch those two, like this, every day for the rest of my life.

"I'll go walk with Georgie," Darren said. "Give you and Ms. Judd time to talk."

"Thanks, Darren."

We approached quietly, but Joan still turned. I caught the surprise and the flash of happiness she couldn't hide. And for the first time in weeks, I felt myself settle.

I scooped Georgie up in a hug and spun him around, so relieved to feel his little arms clinging to me. We'd come a long way, too, me and this kid.

"Did you see the turkeys?" he asked, blue eyes bright with excitement. "Joanie said I can't have one because they're wild and their mama would miss them too much, but we've been watching them all day."

"I did see them."

"Maybe, you can show me, little man," Darren offered.

My nephew squirmed to be let down and hurried over to take Darren's big hand. "Okay!"

Joan stood next to me as we watched them creep after the meandering birds.

"You should have—"

She broke off with an oof as I pulled her into a crushing hug.

"I missed you so much," I confessed into the smooth skin of her neck.

Her arms locked tightly around my waist. "I missed you, too."

I leaned back and smoothed some of her dark hair behind her ears. Her arms stayed where they were.

"I would have picked you up from the airport," she complained.

Joan was not a person who liked surprises. She preferred making plans and showing up for people.

"I know."

I hadn't needed a ride. But I wasn't ready to mention that I'd gone to a dealership directly after touching down and bought a car, one that would stay here, in Kirby Falls.

Swallowing, I noted Georgie up ahead. I didn't want to be interrupted for this next part.

"Can we talk about what happens next?" I asked. "We've both been avoiding it, I think. But I wanted to run something by you and see how you felt about it."

Joan's gaze searched my face before she nodded slowly.

"I would really like to make Kirby Falls my home base. Ideally, I'd make one movie a year. I want to direct at some point. Eventually, I'd love to write, and I can do that from here. I want Georgie to go to school in Kirby Falls. I want him to make friends with kids his own age. I don't want him to ever wonder if he's loved or accepted or understood. It'll just be a given because he's surrounded by people who care about him. I want a life with you, Joan. Sunday dinners with your family. A chicken coop in our back-yard. I want to make you coffee every morning and go running together."

I managed a lungful of air despite my racing heart. "I should have told you all of this *before* LA. But I didn't want to scare you off. I didn't want to be too much. I was worried I'd worn out my welcome."

Joan's hands were fisted in my tee shirt, and I wanted to assure her I wasn't going anywhere.

"I thought," she began, "I thought you might get back to your real life and remember how much you missed it."

I smiled. "I got back to my *old* life and couldn't stop remembering *you*."

Joan's chin wobbled uncertainly. I pressed my thumb there to shore it up.

"I know I wasn't born in Kirby Falls," I told her. "It'll never be home for me, the way it is for you. You have so many memories here, so much history. But if I start now, we could have a good life together. If you wanted that."

"It *is* home," Joan insisted. "For you and George. There's no minimum, no requirements to make it your own. You fit here. And I'll always want you."

"You're here. That's all Georgie and I really need."

"Did you talk to him about all this?" Joan wondered. "Does he want to stay?"

"Joanie. That kid loves you so much. Nothing would make him happier than being right here with you."

"Then stay," she whispered, tugging my body flush to hers. "Leave when you need to, but come back home to me."

Her lips found mine, warm and welcoming. The hands clenched in the fabric at my sides loosened and smoothed around to my back.

After so much time and distance, I was starved for her touch, eager for her affection. So, I reached low and gripped her thighs, boosting her up. Joan's legs wrapped around my waist on instinct, and I held her close.

I'd known this place was special from the moment I arrived. But Kirby Falls wouldn't be home without the woman in my arms. Without that little boy running through the fields. Without the acceptance and joy I'd found here.

Home was what we made for ourselves, built and maintained with love. And I was never going to take that for granted.

Suddenly, Joan's mouth broke away from mine. Before I could protest or draw her bottom lip between my teeth, she said, "I love you, too. I should have told you that. I should have never made you wonder or question it. I love you so much, Ian. There are probably people out there who'd be better for you. Who'd be easy and agreeable, who'd slot themselves effortlessly into your life. But no one will love you the way I do."

I smiled, relieved and elated, overwhelmed and comforted. She was right. No one would be as dedicated, as loyal, as fiercely loving as the woman before me. It was an honor to be hers, and I'd spend the rest of my life making sure I earned all that devotion and returned it many times over.

My fingers stroked a path up and down her spine, and I nodded. "I know. And I promise, I'll never make you regret it. I love you, Joanie."

Her hands cupped my face, and I knew we were grinning at each other like idiots. But I didn't care. I was right where I belonged.

"Besides," I said seriously. "We have a goat together. I would never abandon my kid."

"Oh my God," Joan groaned, dropping her forehead to my shoulder.

"Get it? My kid. Do you get it?"

I could feel her body shaking with laughter, and I held her a little tighter. Thinking, I'd never let go.

JOAN

*Several weeks later*

"Is everyone gathered round? Can you hear us?" Brady practically shouted through the tiny speaker of my cell phone.

"Yes, we're here." I was holding up the device while over a dozen of us gathered beneath the private pavilion overlooking Lake Archer.

It was Junior and Nola Clark's annual Memorial Day celebration at their lake house, but Mac and Brady had been suspiciously absent.

I'd gotten a video call a few minutes ago from the devious pair, but they wouldn't tell us where they were until we'd assembled all relevant parties. That included parents and siblings for both of them, as well as friends and cousins.

As I held my arm out as far from my body as humanly possible, I felt the press of curious bodies. Ian was at my side. My sister leaned in behind me, her little pregnant belly pushing gently into my back. Mercer was there, along with my parents. Bonnie and Jack struggled to see the screen as Larry demanded to know what this was all about. Will looked on grumpily with a cheerful Becca under his arm. Chloe and Jordan were in my periphery with a tiny baby in theirs. Brady's best friend, Cole Abernathy, whispered something from Ian's other side, but I couldn't hear it over everyone else's yapping. Mac's parents, grandparents, aunt, and uncles rounded out our numbers.

"Y'all, be quiet," Mac called. "We have some news."

The crowd quieted, and I couldn't help but feel like this was par for the course with these two. They'd put us through all sorts of drama last Memorial Day, too.

When they had everyone's rapt attention, Mac and Brady shouted in unison, "We got married!"

And sure enough, the camera panned to show the Vegas Strip, the sun shining brightly and people everywhere. Mac was riding piggyback, her arms draped over Brady's shoulders, where she flashed a shiny diamond on her left hand.

"Bro," Ian said solemnly. "Without us?"

"Bro, I know," Brady replied, a little shamefaced. "But we're going to have a huge wedding reception this summer. We'll celebrate with all y'all."

"Okay, good," Ian decided. "I'll plan the belated bachelor party."

Conversation burst around me, everyone talking at once. The trouble-making pair accepted congratulations and fielded grumbles. And my arm grew tired from holding my phone out for so long. Larry helped me out by grabbing the device so she could scold her cousin directly. I figured my phone would eventually make its way back to me.

Ian and I drifted over to the cornhole boards, where George was playing with Darren, Sophia, and Sophia's boyfriend, Alex.

"I can't believe they did that," Ian said, but he was smiling.

I huffed out a laugh. "I can."

I imagined the wedding reception would make up for Mac and Brady getting married without us. Either way, I was happy for my brother. Mac made him a joyful idiot, and they were good for each other. It had taken some time for them to get things right, but sometimes it meant more when you had to work for it.

George laughed brightly when Darren's beanbag overshot the board by a good ten feet.

We'd spent the last few weeks figuring out what life looked like, moving forward. The orchard was open four days a week for lavender season now. We'd shift into u-pick mode for berries in the coming months before apple season began in earnest in late August.

Ian and George had moved in with me, and my quiet cabin wasn't so quiet anymore.

Sophia had decided to stay on as a nanny for George. She'd found her own place in town, and I figured her relationship with Alex had a bit to do with her decision to stay. We were happy to have her, and I knew George would adapt more easily if some aspects of his life remained consistent. The kid was actually pretty excited to start third grade in the fall after Bonnie had taken us on a tour of the elementary school and a visit to her classroom, which included a pet rabbit named Oreo.

True to his word, Ian made me coffee every morning, and I really thought he was getting the hang of it. It tasted a little better every day.

We still ran together and joined my parents for breakfast. George helped take care of Ralph, and Ian and I had plans for our chicken coop. We were in the process of putting in security around the cabin and expanding to make everything more private. Ian had made Buck Adams a generous offer for his land, and now, our closest neighbor was several miles away.

Darren would be heading back to California to find a more permanent position, but he was with us in the interim until the cabin and the surrounding area met his security specifications.

Ian was excited to spend the summer in Kirby Falls. He wouldn't need to leave for work until September, when filming was set to begin for an action film he'd been contracted for over a year ago. The schedule had him in Ireland for three months, but I wasn't worried. We'd make it work.

He was keeping the beach house in Malibu for the future. For when he would be filming in LA, and for when I needed an escape to the ocean. To all that wide-open space.

We were in the middle of weaving our lives together, making plans and promises, and allowances for mistakes.

There were challenges and revelations as newness gave way to familiarity. The sound of George galloping up and down the staircase never failed to make me smile. I didn't even mind stepping over his little shoes that never seemed to make it into the entryway closet.

Ian loaded the dishwasher like a possessed toddler. But fresh wildflowers ended up on my bedside table every few days. And I never had to wonder if he missed his old life, the one with countless luxuries and indulgences. Ian showed me every single day how grateful he was to be home.

He may have been a famous movie star with the best smile in Hollywood, but here, in Kirby Falls, he was just Ian. He did laundry and made dinner. He worked out with my brother and played poker with my dad. He cooked with my mother, and he was helping Mercer paint the nursery.

Ian had a life where people accepted him and relied on him for more than his money and his fame. That, more than anything, had shaped his wonder over this small mountain town.

"Georgie has been invited to a sleepover with your parents tonight," Ian whispered into the shell of my ear.

I felt his hand settle around my waist, fingers finding their way beneath the hem of my shirt. His skin, warm from a day spent in the spring sunshine.

I raised an interested brow. "Is that so?"

He nodded slowly, a smile twisting his lips.

We didn't even bother saying goodbye to everyone. I touched base with my parents and made sure they had everything George needed for an overnight stay. Then we hugged the kid and told him we'd see him in the morning.

The drive home was a lesson in torturous anticipation. True alone time was precious and rare these days, and I couldn't wait to get my hands on

Ian, to see his body in the waning daylight, to be as loud as I wanted when he touched me.

We left a trail of clothing from the back door, through the kitchen, down the hallway, and into the bedroom. My back hit the quilt at the same time Ian dove for my center.

"Oh God," I moaned as he licked my pussy with abandon.

His hair was longer these days, and I was grateful. Because it meant I could slide my fingers through the dark strands and hold on while he fucked me with his tongue, like he was doing now.

I'd been so worked up on the drive over, imagining his hands on me, that I was about to come, embarrassingly fast.

I must have said that last part out loud because Ian lifted his head long enough to say, "Good. I'll make you come again."

With renewed enthusiasm, he went back to work, two thick fingers filling me as he sucked mercilessly at my clit.

"Fuck," I breathed, the curse muffled from beneath the arm I'd thrown over my face.

My hips rolled, eager and a little impatient as Ian's fingers pumped in time with my thrusts.

Gasping breaths accompanied my urgent movements, and a moment later, I was rewarded. My orgasm moved through me, a slow and steady spread of heat and pleasure from my center outward.

Ian pushed inside me while I was still coming, my muscles contracting deliciously around the invasion.

"Yesss," I hissed.

He was so hard and felt so good, the thick length of him filling me just the way I liked.

Before I got too comfortable in this position, Ian pulled out and urged me to roll over.

I lifted my hips and pressed my chest into the bed as Ian drove into me from behind, groaning out his approval. He set a steady pace, but it was deeper this way, more intense. I felt his powerful thighs nestled against the backs of mine and the reverent slide of his palm smoothing up the length of my spine.

As he started to speed up, one hand found its way to my hip to hold me steady while two fingers on the opposite hand settled slippery and firm over my clit.

Surrounded by Ian's warm body, his straining muscles, his drugging scent, I couldn't ignore the way my body reacted to his touch.

Suddenly, he folded over and brought his lips to my back, my shoulder blades, my nape. Hot, wet kisses pressed me into the mattress, and still, his fingers circled.

The drag of Ian's erection inside my sensitive flesh was the best sort of torment.

I was at war with myself. I craved sweet relief. I wanted this to never end.

The touch at the apex of my thighs quickened, as did Ian's thrusts.

Ian panted brokenly, desperate words and quiet urgings tattooed across my skin. *Yes,* and *Please,* and *It's so fucking good* into the fading light.

The pleasure unspooled between us, a tether snapping taut as I came hard around him. Ian's hips jerked once, twice, a final time as he stilled and emptied himself inside me.

We lay together in a heap on the mattress, his shoulder warm against my side and a muscled arm wrapped around my thigh.

"What else do you want to do with our sudden freedom?" Ian managed once his breath evened out.

It wasn't even 8:00 p.m.

"Shower," I replied, pressing a smiling kiss into his hair. "And then I have a few ideas."

My regular alarm went off at five the next morning, and I stretched to silence it, muscles protesting after a late night of "ideas."

Ian groaned and burrowed his face into my naked back.

It was on the tip of my tongue to urge him out of bed, to go for a run like we usually did, to ignore the protest in my limbs, the sleep still clinging to me. There was a time when I would have demanded routine and stuck to a schedule just for the sake of it.

But I'd realized, it was okay to bend once in a while. It didn't mean I had to break.

I wanted a lazy morning with Ian. I wanted to lie beside him as the morning sun turned the room golden. Maybe I'd wake up in another couple of hours. Maybe I'd find my way down his beautiful body and take him in my mouth.

"Let's sleep in," I said, voice rough.

"Really?" came Ian's muffled reply.

"Yeah." As if to prove my commitment, I snuggled a little closer to him, and the arm slung over my waist tightened.

Then I felt his smile bloom against my back, and I knew both dimples were pressing deep into his cheeks.

There were worse things than being spontaneous.

JOAN

*September*

The cabin smelled like popcorn and butter, and there'd never been so many people crammed in the living room.

My family was spread out around the large sectional we'd bought a few months ago. Brady and Mac were sharing a box of Milk Duds. My parents sat opposite them with their own snacks in hand. Mercer was in the rocking chair, two-week-old Charlie asleep on his chest. Candace slouched next to me on the couch, but I knew she'd be unconscious as soon as we dimmed the lights.

Ian placed the final bowl of popcorn on my lap, and I hit play on the remote.

Della Stewart had sent over an early cut of the film. It was missing the score and a few digital effects that would be added later, but she'd wanted our family to see it first, to see the land and what she'd created. And she'd wanted us to be able to experience it with Ian.

He was leaving in two days for Ireland, and I was mostly okay about it. The orchard was busy. It was apple season, but we were also experiencing the Dorian Masters effect. Both Judd's and Grandpappy's had seen a huge uptick in visitors. The Kirby Falls Business Owners' Association had reported an increase in tourism since Ian's interview had aired all those months ago.

So, I had plenty to keep me busy while Ian filmed his next project. Plus, it was only three months. We could manage.

Sophia would be around to help with George. We'd call and video chat. And Ian would be back in time for Christmas. We could do this.

But we'd gathered tonight as a little send-off and to watch the film that had brought Ian and George into our lives.

The film opened with a man and a woman hiking in the woods. The brother-and-sister duo bantered a bit, their accents subtle and not overly done. Eventually, the pair stumbled upon a body near a creek bed. It was just shy of gruesome, but in a way that felt realistic.

At one point, Ian's character shoved his sleeves back to remove something he'd found beneath the body. When he did so, I noticed a dark circle around his wrist. It looked kind of like a bracelet, but familiar and worn. Sort of like a . . .

Ten minutes later, Ian got slapped in handcuffs on the screen, and I could no longer focus on the story or the beautiful way Della had framed the landscape. The metal cuffs circled his arm and, again, the black band came into view. I narrowed my eyes and leaned forward to see better. The item encircling Ian's wrist showed up three more times in the next half hour, and by the fourth sighting, I was already reaching for the remote.

I thought I'd seen—

"What's wrong?" Ian asked as I rewound the film.

"There," I said, pausing the image. But I'd gone a bit too far.

"Joanie, what are you doing?" Brady called.

"Trying to see something," I replied absently.

I alternately tapped play and then pause until I got the correct frame on the screen. As the image froze, I could just barely make out what I thought I'd noticed, and confusion washed over me.

"Joan, come on," Brady complained. "We want to watch."

Ignoring my brother, I hit play and reached for Ian's wrist.

I unbuttoned the cuffs of his flannel on one arm and then the other. And there, around his left wrist, was what I'd seen on the screen. A black band. A hair tie stretched to within an inch of its life, as a bit of white elastic peeked through.

*My* hair band.

I'd dropped it during one of our earliest runs, after I'd discovered Ian was actually Dorian Masters. I'd been angry and irritated, and when he'd retrieved the elastic and held it out to me, I'd ignored him.

That had been ten months ago.

"Ian," I wheezed, gripping his wrist. "Is this mine?"

He grinned at me like I was being weird.

I felt weird. I felt like my heart was turning inside out.

"Do you finally want it back?" he offered, removing the hair tie and holding it out to me.

"Have you—have you been wearing it this whole time?"

Only then did a wash of color flood his cheeks. I could see the blush on his skin even in the dim glow from the television. "I, uh, guess I have."

"Why haven't I noticed it before?" I asked, incredulous.

Ian's fingers nervously twisted the elastic as he spoke, "Sometimes I keep it in my pocket. But I always have it with me. I liked having something of yours, even if it was small and insignificant. Is that—I mean, are you upset?"

"No, I'm—I'm—"

All of a sudden, I was aware of Candace snoring softly beside me and my mother gazing at me in concern. Mac was eating popcorn and watching Ian and me, not the movie on the screen.

Overcome, I stood on shaky legs and made my way outside, dropping heavily onto the top step of the back porch. I didn't know why this was hitting me so hard. Ian's love and devotion weren't a secret. We were making a life together. I knew he was it for me.

But there was just something about seeing something of mine, from before —before we'd been anything to one another. A piece of me I didn't even know I'd lost, that he'd kept this whole time, as a memento.

Less than a minute later, the back door opened and closed quietly. I knew it was Ian. I recognized the sound of his bare feet on the wooden planks. For some reason, that knowledge made me want to cry.

"I'm not upset," I said before he'd settled fully beside me. "I just had to leave. My feelings were too big for that couch, that room, and all those people in it."

I reached for Ian's hand and laced our fingers together. "It's just . . . all this time?"

He smiled, shy and a little embarrassed, then confirmed, "All this time."

"I was so mean to you," I groaned, burying my face in our joined hands.

Ian laughed. "You weren't . . . mean. You had high expectations. And you weren't impressed by me." He tried to steal his hand back and peel the fingers away from my eyes. Laughing harder now, he said, "I had to grow on you. It's not your fault I fell in love with you right off the bat."

"Oh my God, Ian. I feel like *such* an asshole." Mortification threatened to swallow me whole. I'd given this man such a hard time. I'd questioned his motives again and again. When all along—

"Stop," he coaxed, both dimples on full display. "Remember when I told you, I'd rather have one person who really knew me than have all the fans in the world just assume they did. All I've ever wanted was a love that developed over time, something meaningful, something true. And that's what we have. You grew to love me, and I know it's real. I know I earned it."

To him, it was that simple. And I guess it was. He didn't want the easy way. He never had.

"I'm going to miss you so much when you leave," I confessed, my voice just loud enough to get the words out. Any louder and my throat would have closed up.

"I know," he said, smiling gently. "I'm going to miss you, too. But I'm coming back. I'll *keep* coming back. And, if it works out with the farm and your family, you can come with me the next time I go. And then one day, I won't leave anymore. You'll be my wife, and I'll be your husband. Georgie will still be ours, and we'll be home. For good."

I nodded. The tears that had been swimming in my eyes since I'd stepped outside finally fell. Ian leaned in, kissing them away.

"I love you," I whispered.

He grinned. "I love you, too. Now, can we go back inside and watch my movie so you can tell me how great it is and what a gifted actor I am?"

I laughed. "Okay. Okay. Sorry."

Ian stood and held out a hand to help me up.

My eyes fell briefly to the elastic hair tie on Ian's wrist. Warmth filled me up, the knowledge that I'd found something special. A love I'd almost missed, out of sheer stubbornness.

Grateful, I slipped my hand into Ian's waiting one, then yelped happily as he tugged me into his arms.

I'd spend the rest of my life working to let Ian know he'd found a family in me. I'd make sure he never questioned where he belonged. And if he ever lost his way, all he needed to do was follow the path home.

---

*Want more of Ian and Joan?*
*I have a bonus epilogue for you! Get the heartwarming series conclusion and catch up with all the characters from the Kirby Falls series HERE when you sign up for my newsletter.*

*If you have trouble with the link above, scan the QR code:*

# also by laney hatcher

**Kirby Falls Series**

Take It or Leaf It: A Grumpy Sunshine Slow Burn Romance

Leaf It To Me: A Small-Town Slow Burn Romance

Leaf and Let Die: An Enemies to Lovers Small-Town Romance

Leaf You Hanging: A Reformed Bad Boy Small-Town Romance

Leaf Well Enough Alone: A Single Guardian Small-Town Romance

**Cozy Creek Collection**

Fall Me Maybe

**Bartholomew Series**

First to Fall: A Friends to Lovers Historical Romance

Second Chance Dance: An Enemies to Lovers Historical Romance

Third Degree Yearn: A Second Chance Historical Romance

Last on the List: A Surprise Pregnancy Historical Romance

**Smartypants Romance**

**London Ladies Embroidery Series**

Neanderthal Seeks Duchess

Well Acquainted

Love Matched

**Find bonus content, reading order, and other news at my website:**

**https://laneyhatcher.com/**

# *about the author*

Laney Hatcher is a firm believer that there is a spreadsheet for every occasion and pie is always the answer. She is an author of stories both old and new where the HEAs are always guaranteed. Often too practical for her own good, Laney enjoys her life in the southern United States with her husband, children, and incredibly entitled cat.

*Newsletter sign up*